The Fall of the Sea People
Volume 5

Mars and the Sea People

BY

Henry Hallan

Leabhar Cnoc Mhuilinn

ISBN 978-0-9571585-4-2

http://www.henryhallan.me

Cover art by Linda R. James.

FBBA

Last Requests

Andánacht Scamall looked up as Lord Foscúil came into the room. "How many are in the Forest?" Foscúil asked.

"Fifty platoons strength, my lord."

"How many can you spare?"

"If we were attacked by Forest creatures? We could put another three hundred platoons out before nightfall, my lord."

"What if you wanted to patrol until nightfall tomorrow evening? What strength could you support?"

"If we put them all out into the Forest and put them on third watches, we could put two thousand platoons out there."

"And if you wanted to mount an attack on the City?"

"We have the strength, my lord, but the casualties would be massive. We do not have any defence against Words of Power or Mastery of Creation beyond outnumbering them by a thousand to one. I am not sure we would have the strength afterwards to withstand another Battle of the Blue Peaks."

"Well, Scamall, I am not about to order ye to attack the City. But the City might attack ye. So you need to deploy them to contain a City attack."

"All two thousand platoons, my lord?"

"All two thousand."

"As you wish, my lord." Andánacht Scamall placed his hand on the Hilt of his own sword and began to give the orders. Outside they heard shouts and the sounds of hurrying feet.

Cathúa was in her library reading through her catalogue of Formulae of Words when the eyes of her pendant glittered. She looked up and saw that

Gruaige had returned. "Come in," Cathúa said. "I've been meaning to ask you a favour."

She went back to reading the description and referring back to Seilidí's work on the Limits to Speed. It occurred to her that Gruaige had not answered and she looked up. Gruaige was standing with her back to the closed door. Her eyes had leaked tears over her cheeks. Cathúa thought about how she should respond. She put the books down, went over and put her arms around her servant. "What is the matter, Gruaige?" she asked. She tried to guess. "Did he hurt you?"

"He sent me away, my lady."

"He always does. He doesn't want a lover in his bed after he has finished." Except Eala, Cathúa thought.

"He never started, my lady. It turns out I have the name of an ancestor."

"He is very particular about names, Gruaige. The existence of some Gruaige from a thousand years ago could be enough to put him off. I think it is some superstition from his childhood."

"It is some superstition from our home village, my lady. I grew up in the same village as he did."

"Then why are you weeping? You know why he didn't want you."

"I do know, my lady. But I am frustrated all the same."

"Oh. I thought you were scared."

"I was, my lady, but then he was kind and it didn't seem so bad."

"I will never understand people, Gruaige."

"I will be all right," Gruaige told her. She wiped her eyes and smiled at her mistress. "What did you want me to do, my lady?" she asked.

Cathúa let go of her and went and sat down by the desk, relieved that the upset was over. "It occurred to me that it might be possible to use the Words of Folding Space to travel to the past or the future."

Gruaige sat down on the little stool, her knees carefully pressed together, and pushed the material of her tunic into her lap. She looked at Cathúa. "I don't understand, my lady. Is the past or the future like another country that someone could visit?"

"There is one way of looking at time that imagines it as like another direction, like North or East or Up."

Gruaige frowned. Cathúa noticed that by looking at her body language she could actually see what Gruaige was thinking. The little movements of her hands were as she tried to imagine what direction there could be other than North/ South, East/ West or Up/ Down. She looked up. "I don't understand, my lady."

"Well, Gruaige, an ant crawling on a table-top cannot perceive the idea of up or down. An ant is blind and walks on the surface that its feet stick to. But if you dropped the table off a Flyer and let it fall the ant could crawl around the surface of it as it fell. If it walked in a circle the path it followed in space would be a helix. The paths the ant followed through the up-and-down direction would describe its motion through time, with up in the past and down in the future."

"It would not be a good future, my lady."

"But it would be inevitable, I suppose. Anyway, I am not proposing anything as dangerous as a journey into an unknown future. I am proposing a journey into the well-known past."

"What about the motion of the Earth, my lady? You told me that the Earth moves many days' march around the Sun every day."

"It does, but the Words of Folding Space are tied to the frame-of-reference of the person uttering the Words. If I use Folding Space to go to the Great South Land, the rotation of the Earth is removed. Likewise if I return to a place I visited yesterday the Words take me to the location of that place now, not the location it occupied yesterday. The same mechanism would ensure that, if it were used to travel to the past, the past location chosen would be the same location as the present one, even though the time would be different."

"So what would you want me to do, my lady?"

"I would like to send you back into the past."

Gruaige looked frightened. "How would I get back?"

"I would think you would get back the usual way. I was thinking of sending you just one day."

"That would be all right, my lady. Where would you be doing this?"

"It probably shouldn't be the City, since I am not sure what would happen if you were to meet yourself." Cathúa winced as she remembered what that sort of meeting was like. "What about your home village, Gruaige? Where were you born?"

"Gainmheach, my lady. In Úll Oileán."

"If I were to leave you there with a few sticks of gold, would you be able to look after yourself for a day?"

"Of course. What would happen after a day?"

"You would walk out to meet me. If you saw that you were still with me then you would hide until I had sent you back. Once you knew I was alone then you could come out and tell me. Then we would go home again."

"That doesn't sound too bad, my lady."

"There is the danger that the time travel part would be inaccurate. If I sent you back three or four days you would still be able to wait it out."

"Would it be that inaccurate, my lady? Could the time be as much as three or four times the amount you were attempting?"

"I have some evidence to suggest that accurate time travel is possible but I don't know for sure. I believe that each heartbeat of time is equivalent to the distance that light travels in a heartbeat. So travelling a day would mean travelling the distance that light travels in a day. It's a long way. Light can travel to the Sun and back a little more than eighty-seven times in a day."

"So it might be that you send me quite a long way."

"It is possible. I was hoping to use the exact amount of time as a way to calibrate the process."

"That makes sense. What if you send me a hundred years, my lady?"

"Then I will notice that you have not come back and will go looking for you. If I think I am going back a day and actually go back a hundred years we will arrive at about the same time. We will ask the date and then come back." Cathúa thought. "If it makes you feel safer I will make sure you take plenty of gold."

"I don't think I will need gold, my lady. My cousins will be pleased to see me."

"What if they haven't been born yet?"

"Then you will come back and find me, my lady."

Aclaí threw sword and scabbard down together. He heard Miotal speak behind him. "What is it, my love?"

"The Mentor," replied Aclaí, knowing it was treason but long past caring. He had been past caring for decades, even before he had Retired. "He wants me to send Eala back to him – to torture her like he tortured Abhainne. It is not enough for him that her life is forfeit. He wants her to suffer, too. I won't allow it."

Miotal went over to his friend and placed a hand on his shoulder.

"He will be dead soon, Aclaí, and you will be his replacement. It really won't be long."

"You have calmed down, Miotal."

"You have agreed that she must die, my lord. We need to end this madness."

"Perhaps. Eibheara called him. I don't know why she hates Eala so much. She brought her back to light and now she's called the Mentor to get him to take her away and hurt her. What did Eala ever do to deserve this?" He turned, and Miotal felt the shoulder move under his arm, as if to shake him off. "Even if the Mentor loses his Immortality and dies I will not take his place. Eibheara is scheming to have Eala tortured to death simply because of jealousy. I am sick of intrigue, Miotal. I would not choose to live in the eye of that storm. Miotal, when the Mentor dies the City of the Sea People should die with him. I will not be a replacement for him."

"What about the Key of Creation?"

And Aclaí knew that was the weakness in his plans: the responsibility that he could not refuse. He could not let it fall into the hands of jealous or spiteful people but he certainly could not leave it for the beings of the Forest to take. Someone would need to guard it and Aclaí knew that there was nobody he trusted other than himself. He had seen the same games of power and spite in the people around him. He was surrounded by it. Eibheara might be manipulating against Eala, but he knew that Miotal was as bad. Miotal had ordered Eibheara's death – his own family. Foscúil sought to expand his band of fighting men and Liús was pursuing his obscene Words of Power and intercourse with Manifestations of the worst sort. Even the quieter, more loyal people could not be trusted to be at peace with each other: he knew that people like Damhánalla would kill Eibheara if they saw an opportunity. The only two among the Sea People that he could trust in positions of power were Éirime and Eala: and, after today, neither of them would be suitable.

He looked over. Miotal was waiting for an answer and he could see the triumph on Miotal's face as he saw his point sink home. Aclaí pulled away from the hand and left.

The Flyer skimmed over the cold ocean. It was a long way East of the Land of the Immortals and, as their journey continued, the Sun sank slowly behind them. Gruaige sat beside her mistress. She had been allowed to put a woollen dress over her tunic and pull leggings and boots on. It was far more comfortable than the last time she had been on a Flyer.

Gruaige looked at her mistress beside her, wrapped in her blue cloak and with the little cat pendant staring ahead with glittering green eyes. Cathúa pointed out various things as they went by: a bird; a whale; a formation of clouds. Gruaige admired how much Cathúa knew. Every wonder of the ocean seemed to have an explanation in Cathúa's mind.

"You love the ocean, my lady," Gruaige observed.

Cathúa was silent a moment, weighing up this unfamiliar idea. "I suppose I do," she agreed. "I love to travel too." She pointed at the Sun low in the sky and she gestured the Flyer to climb. "Now, let us see..." she said. "Oh good." She pointed out that there were three suns behind them: one bright one in the middle and two faint, blurred images, one on either side. "That is caused by ice crystals. They are part of a circle, but since the crystals are in a layer we can only see two parts.

"It's very beautiful, my lady," Gruaige agreed. Cathúa looked ahead. Beneath them they could see one island stretching away to the South and East, as big as the Land of the Immortals. Behind it they could see another and, behind that, more land behind them.

"That is the Archipelago," Cathúa said.

"I saw it when Lord Rian brought me to the City, my lady. That smaller one is the Land of the Brave. Úll Oileán is at the North-East corner of the larger one." She pointed. "I can't see it but it must be over there."

"You are a good observer, Gruaige."

"Thank you, my lady."

"It is not my doing." She leaned the Flyer towards the corner of the larger island and they descended rapidly towards it. As they approached they could see two groups of islands. "Which one?"

"Do you see where that one is split in two? Lord Rian lives on the south island and Gainmheach is just over the water on the north island. The next bay along is where I grew up, but Gainmheach is where I was born. That is where most of my family live, my lady."

With a slight lean of her body Cathúa guided the Flyer towards the twin islands and the channel that separated them. She could see smoke rising from villages on both sides and, a few breaths later, she picked out the shape of what she assumed was Rian's home. They landed in the valley above the village Gruaige had called Gainmheach. The Sun was setting as they got off the Flyer.

"Can you find your way back to the village from here? And will you be able to find this spot again?"

"I will, my lady. That rock up there that looks like a face, I can find that. I used to climb on it when I visited my cousins."

"Remember, Gruaige, it should be just one day. You are probably hiding somewhere, waiting for me." She gave Gruaige the gold sticks she had made. Then she said the Words. Gruaige disappeared. Cathúa sat back on the Flyer and waited.

After perhaps a hundred breaths she called out. "Gruaige? You can come out now." But Gruaige didn't come out. She lifted the Flyer up and looked around the landscape. She said the Words of Seeing Heat, but all she could find was a hare and a couple of stray sheep. Gruaige was nowhere to be found.

She put the Flyer down and walked into the village. By then it was full dark. She went into an inn and walked up to the end where drinks were served.

"Can I help you, my lady?" the woman serving asked.

"I am looking for a woman who came here. She probably came yesterday but she might have come a couple of days earlier. She looks like this." Cathúa shaped the Words of Illusion to produce an image of Gruaige, remembering to give her other clothing than a servant's tunic.

"That's Gruaige," said the serving woman. "She is a scribe's daughter. She lives up the coast in Tírcúpla."

"Lord Rian took her to the City," argued one of the drinkers.

"That is correct," Cathúa said, "But she was... visiting her family. I have come to collect her."

"I haven't seen her." The woman raised her voice. "Have any of ye seen Gruaige?" she shouted out. The whole place looked around but none of them had.

Cathúa returned to her Flyer and worked back and forth over the village and the countryside where they had landed. She knew with the Words of Seeing Heat that she would be able to see Gruaige even if she was asleep or dead. But she saw nothing. She turned her Flyer towards Rian's House. She landed in his courtyard.

It wasn't long before he came out to meet her. "Lady Cathúa," he said. "What brings you to my home?"

"I am looking for Gruaige."

"Who is Gruaige? Is she the servant girl I sent you?"

"She is, Rian. She came back here yesterday to visit her cousins. Nobody has seen her."

"Is it important, tonight of all nights?"

"I want to make sure she is all right." Cathúa saw Rian's agitation and wondered what he was hiding. "Why 'tonight of all nights'?"

"Wasn't Eala your friend?"

"Before she was condemned? I think she was. Why are you asking about Eala?"

"I thought you knew. Eala was captured by Lord Aclaí this afternoon. She is to be executed in the morning."

"Are you sure?"

"I saw it on the Visions. I thought that might be why you were looking for your servant."

"Why? What connection has Gruaige to Eala?"

"I'm sorry, Cathúa. I didn't say that right. I thought you might have been looking for her because of tonight. She is your scribe, is she not?"

"She is." Cathúa could see that he was still hiding something but she could not see how to find out what.

"I thought you might need a scribe tonight, Cathúa. You are the City's Archivist. Tonight may be one of the most important nights in the history of the City."

"I suppose it might. Well, if you see her tell her I went looking for her. I will meet her when I get back. Tell her I will meet her by the rock she used to climb when she was a girl."

"Aren't you going to return to the City, Cathúa? I heard you were the only Favourite left on the Hill and it will be Evening Meal when the sunset gets to the City."

"I will return soon," Cathúa assured. "I still have time."

She got back on her Flyer and took off into the night.

Aclaí's sword tingled and his Silver Cord brought it to his hand. He glanced at the hilt and saw that it was a servant. He realised who it would be.

"Report," he answered.

this is geana

"I don't think it is safe for us to meet."

safe for who

"Geana, I know the other Mind Craft Adepts went to Áthaiteorainn. Blátha, Míne, Yanti, all of them are –"

they left aclaí it is over

"I still –"

the only blue robe in the village is caora and she will give you the strength to make a stand

"It would be better for everyone if I didn't make a stand, Geana."

you are still waiting for him to die

"I am."

how long is it going to be

"I don't know. It is forty years since he chased Eala out and in that time he has not been able to breathe Immortal Breath. Éise says he his like a man in his eighties but his health is still good. Many senior Veterans live into their second century even if they don't gain Immortality. It is not a sudden thing. He might see the Fifteenth Century of the City, Geana. Or he might die tomorrow."

so this could go on for another thirty years

"It could."

what about eala

"What answer are you expecting?"

today you have my sister in your power lord aclaí

"She is not in my power, Geana. I am Sea People. I have to do what I am told."

what about our plan

"How many do you have who will stand behind you?"

less than a handful

"That is not enough. I am sorry."

one is enough

"Geana, we talked about that. We need about six hundred to carry a majority in the City."

i will bring caora to you

"I am Forbidden to speak to her."

you have said forbidden so many times lord aclaí i have heard the same excuse from my sister one day one of you must stand up to him

"You couldn't possibly understand."

she says that too

"Then what do you expect me to do?"

if you are too weak to release her you still could delay the decision

"How?"

do nothing aclaí wait and see if he forgives her

"He called this evening. He wants her dead."

There was a long pause. *caora wants her to live*

"I know."

when the mentor is dead she will grieve aclaí but afterwards you could comfort her

"What are you saying?"

if you show eala mercy today i will bring her to your bed after he has died

"You think you can just order blue-robes around like an innkeeper ordering slave girls to a guest's bed?"

you know what i am aclaí you know i can do it

"I think I do."

if you agree i will come to áthaimín and seal the bargain tonight

"What?"

i will bring caora if you wish

"I just told you, Geana. I can't agree to that."

i know you should agree to that she replied. *but even if you refuse her i will seal the bargain i won't be as good as either of them because their embraces show their immortal breath*

"Geana, I know what you are offering. But I cannot accept it. Initiation is too strong for that. Get Éirime to tell you."

lord aclaí came the cold voice, then a hesitation. Then *do you need to send the mentor a body that he will believe is eala*

"I don't understand," he replied, not having any idea what she was suggesting.

if you sent my head instead of hers would he know

"Possibly not," he answered. "Although the Words of Identification would uncover the substitution. That can be corrected. But Geana, even if I deceived him, I would not deceive myself. I would know I had disobeyed him."

you know humanity needs eala my lord the cold words reasoned.

"The world needs Eala's dream. She has taught her skills to others. They won't be lost." He realised how to escape her offer. "But even if I were to agree to your scheme, she wouldn't."

if she does agree my lord will you play your part

Aclaí reflected. Eala would never agree to it, he knew: she would not defy the Mentor even when he ordered her death and she would not permit her sister to die in her place anyway. But after Eala was gone Geana would still be there. Aclaí didn't want to make her an enemy without good reason. So he answered, "I will. But you won't get her to agree to it. She will not defy the Mentor any more than I will."

promise me lord aclaí

He wondered if she knew something he didn't. But Eala must know her and would have warned him, surely. So he replied, "I promise."

thank you she answered. Then *i will ask her*

"Do that," he vocalised. "Off you go." He released the sword hilt and looked up. Eibheara was standing in the doorway.

"Which one are you?" he asked.

"I am Elder Immortal Eibheara, Aclaí. I have to go now but I want to tell you something before I do."

"When will I see you again?"

"Not for a long time, not unless you listen to what I have to say."

"Then say."

"Aclaí, Méar is a follower, not a leader. The problem isn't to defeat him, it is to steal him from his current master."

"Is that all?"

"It is. Can you repeat it for me?"

"Of course."

"Repeat it, Aclaí."

Aclaí sighed. "Eibheara, 'the Mentor is a follower not a leader. I need to steal him from his master.'"

"It's close enough. Now I have to go."

"Will you leave me with the other one?"

"That is the idea. Be kind to her, Aclaí. We both know she is a victim of circumstance."

"I am responsible for–"

"It's all right. I forgive you. But be kind to her."

"When will I see you again?"

"Not until it is time to make him yours."

"When will that be?"

"That is up to you, Aclaí."

With that she turned and left.

Cathúa landed by the rock that Gruaige had pointed out. She knew she did not have much time but she also knew she had all the time in the world. She got out her writing set and made a little light. The light caught the eyes of her cat pendant, making them glitter. She reached back behind her own neck and untied the thong. She hung the pendant on the Flyer. "You can't come with me on this trip, my little watcher of watchers," she whispered.

Then she called on the Key of Creation to refresh her Breath. She wouldn't normally have done that as she knew the Mentor would notice it. She felt the Mentor's awareness through the Key of Creation but she also felt the darker perceptions of the other things that watched the Key of Creation. It was the skull with black fire in its eye-sockets that she hated most.

But Gruaige needed her. Breath refreshed, she found her armour and sword on her Silver Cord then said the Words of Folding Space. As she did so she still wondered if someone was watching her. But she did not have time to wait. She only had time to search.

As soon as she was gone the watchers gave the order to their pilot and the other Flyer descended through the sky. It stopped, hovering a man-height above the moorland. The door hinged down and Cathúa turned and embraced Eibheara. "Thank you, my lady," she said.

"Take care of him, Cathúa."

"I will." Cathúa walked down the ramp and climbed on her own Flyer. She looked up and Eibheara waved at her. Eibheara's Flyer folded itself closed, Metal flowing over Metal, and fell upwards into the space between the stars.

Cathúa sighed and took a firm grip on her rationality. She gestured the Flyer into the air and turned towards the City of the Sea People. She wanted to get back to her own room. She wanted to lie in Liús' arms. Then she remembered that he had left and she hoped it would not be long before he returned. For a moment she remembered what she knew but she quickly tore her mind away from that line of thought. She knew she could not think about that too much. The City needed her. The Mentor needed her. Once her duty was finished she could give way to emotion.

One part of her mind looked at the rest and noticed that she was thinking of how to give way to emotion. Cathúa saw that she had learned to feel. But she wished she had something better to feel than despair.

She reached down and took up the little cat pendant. She saw as she re-tied the thong behind her neck that the emerald eyes were still glittering.

Eala was more surprised by her sword that Aclaí had been, but she had not had a servant since Cuspa and neither of her servants had been given the Hilt. It took her a moment to recognise the pattern. "Who is this?" she asked.

it is geana sister came the reply.

"Sister," Eala replied. "I am so glad that you are sending me words."

i wish it could speak to me properly

"It is much better than nothing."

it is that

"You never told me where you got that thing."

he gave it to luchóg the day you brought him to áthaiteorainn the voice said.

She was laughing, forgetting herself for a moment. "Well, I'm glad you have it. I love you, sister. My sneaky sister. Thank-you for calling."

i didnt just call you to say goodbye sister

"Then what?" she asked.

take my name one last time

It took her a moment to realise what she was suggesting. "I can't. You know that."

eala if you let this happen you will throw away your dream her sister's words answered *the world needs you*

"The world doesn't need me, Geana. It needs the Craft we invented between us, but others know that. It will never die. Apart from that all I have done is loved a man that many others love and got my friends into trouble."

the mentor is cruel and that is not your fault

"It is my fault, sister. I was too weak to lead him. Your lovers have always obeyed you, Geana, but I can't do it."

that is not your fault sister the reply came. *his initiation is cruel*

"He can be kind too."

he can be made to be kind sister

"Perhaps."

tell aclaí to make him

"I am not strong enough for that, sister."

then what can we do

"You can do it. When he has killed me you must force Aclaí to confront Caora."

i cant he wont meet me

"How would you do it if he would?"

eala we are manipulative Geana replied. *if i get into his bed i can make space for caora too*

"I suppose you could."

"Geana, humanity needs you more. It would be better for you to take my name than for me to take yours. I have the Mind Craft, but I have failed because I am Sea People and so cannot defy the Mentor. But you are not and, when he is dead, you can do what I have failed to do."

ye have to wait for him to be dead

"You don't know what it's like to be Sea People, Geana my sister."

that is what aclaí said

"You asked him?" Then Eala realised she hadn't actually said it. "You asked him to help us swap our names? We don't tell anyone about that game, sister."

it isnt a game anymore this is about life and death the words answered *it hasnt been a game since you were selected two hundred and sixty years ago*

"You asked him?"

he agreed to it if you will

"But I won't agree, sister. He doesn't know that you know the Mind Craft. But he will keep Anleacán safe and you can make the changes. I will be an inspiring memory, not an obstacle."

how do you know he will cooperate

"I'm going to send him back to Caora. So remind her that he didn't have a choice – and that I don't either."

do you think you can do it

"As easily as you can, sister. I will have to use the same method."

that is not like you

Eala laughed to think how little her sister knew. But the words she sent were, "I'm going to be dead soon anyway. It doesn't make any difference. I will use your method."

then you are more naughty than you pretend to be

"You know I am, Geana. They should be married and, by her side, you can do anything you want. You are strong."

not that strong sister she answered *how do you bear it*

"I bear it. That is what being a blue-robe is like." She heard footsteps approaching on the other side of the door. "Geana love, my beautiful, strong sister, I have to go. I will try and send you more words if I have time. Thank you for this and, if I don't get a chance to remind you, remember: you are free to make the changes the world needs and you should take that opportunity. And also remember that I love you. I haven't told you enough how much I love you, my sneaky sister."

i will sister the voice said *i love you too*

Eala released her sword and pushed it under the bed just as the footsteps reached the door.

Eibheara landed her Flyer in the courtyard of Miotal's House. "Where is he?" she demanded of the guard.

"Lord Miotal is in the Seaview Room, my lady," he replied.

"I don't mean him. What about Lord Aclaí?"

"Lord Aclaí said that he is not to be disturbed."

"Not even by me?"

Eibheara imagined she saw the guard smirk and she resisted the temptation to strike off his head. "He mentioned your name when giving the order, my lady," the guard explained.

Eibheara realised that there was nothing else she could do. She went up into the Seaview Room. They were all there: Miotal, Foscúil, Innealta and Damhánalla. "Where is he?" she demanded.

"He is with her now," Innealta said.

"He shouldn't speak to her," Eibheara said. "Don't any of ye see the danger?"

"What danger?" asked Innealta.

"She will change his mind. He won't go through with it."

"What is that to you?" Foscúil asked.

"You don't own him," Damhánalla added.

"Well you certainly don't," Eibheara retorted.

"I never said I did," Damhánalla smiled. "But I know who does and, if I were Eala, I would be reminding him of that."

"Oh, you are well named," Eibheara told Damhánalla. "You are creepy and sneaky and filled with venom."

"Look around you," Damhánalla said. "Do you see one person here who supports your fantasy that you are his wife? Do you see one person here who even likes you?"

She looked at Miotal. "Uncle?" she asked.

"Don't draw me into this, grand-niece," Miotal replied. "You never asked me for my advice, so don't expect that I will support you in the consequences of your inadvisable behaviour."

She looked at Foscúil's blank eyes above his easy smile and at the way Innealta would not meet her gaze. Then she turned and left them alone.

"Lady Eala," came the call. This time she recognised the voice calling at the door. The bolt was drawn back and Aclaí entered. He turned to those who were with him, guarding the door. "Leave us," he commanded.

Eala looked up. The door closed. He sat by her and she made room for him.

"Eala," he said.

"You've come to say goodbye," she told him. "It's all right, I've been expecting it for some time." He still couldn't think of anything to say. "We talked about this the day you first asked me to help you. You knew that, unless the Mind Craft faction succeeded in their plan, our Art would be Forbidden and we would all be executed. That is why you would not let me teach you openly. I told you then that I thought it would be worth the risk."

"And how do you feel now?" he asked.

"I'm scared, Aclaí."

"Scared of failure?"

"Not scared of failure. I trust you, and I trust our Craft: this isn't failure, it's a delay. It may be too late for me but it is not too late for humanity." She smiled a rueful smile. "I was almost certain he would have forgiven me when he had to. We almost made it, Lord Aclaí. We must be so close. A few more years and this wouldn't have needed to happen." She looked down. "I'm scared of dying, though. The right way for someone to die for a cause is to go to their death unafraid, certain that their cause makes their death worthwhile. I am confident of my cause, but I'm still scared of being killed. I keep thinking of Abhainne. I'm afraid they will see my fear tomorrow morning."

He leaned towards her a little and suddenly she was in his arms. "They won't see your fear, Eala."

She held him tight, her face close to his chest, out of his sight. Her voice was muffled. "Like Abhainne?"

"The executioner won't be cruel, Eala. I'm going to do it myself. It will be quick and painless, I promise."

"Thank you. Will you take care of Geana and Éirime for me?"

"Geana I can take care of. Éirime is harder, because of the Mentor's orders."

Eala looked up, wet, frightened green eyes that still reminded him of the Mentor. "You are going to break free of the City, aren't you?"

"You know I am."

"Then why are you following his orders?" Aclaí did not have an answer for Eala. He couldn't use the excuse of the Initiation like he did with Geana. Eala pressed on. "Who knows about this order?"

"You do, Miotal does, Foscúil does, I do. Your sister does. Nobody else, I think."

And Éirime, thought Eala. But she didn't say that. Instead she explained, "You have defied him over Ceatha and he made you Elder Immortal. You know he would not force you to do anything. You know he wouldn't dare. You could break this order and he wouldn't say anything, because all he'd be doing is drawing attention to his lack of authority."

"You are right, but... I don't know, Eala."

"You need to choose. Do you love her more, or the Mentor?"

"I can't choose like that."

"Well, then, which one needs your love more?"

"I don't know. The Mentor only needs my loyalty and, if he understood what I was doing, he would know that he still had it anyway. And Éirime has Geana, doesn't she?"

"How do you think Geana will be tomorrow, after she sees you kill me on the Visions? She won't be able to help anyone."

"How would she feel if I turned up on her doorstep the next day?"

"Éirime would explain it to her."

"Éirime doesn't know."

She couldn't contradict him. "Éirime doesn't have to know. Éirime loves you."

"What?" he exclaimed.

"She's afraid of you, she doesn't trust you, she thinks you hate her as a rival, but she still loves you. When I told the Mentor that she wanted to be his wife, all those years ago in his chambers, it was a lie. She wants to be your wife. The Selection may have broken her heart but what pieces are left are yours. I don't know why but I've known for a long time. Geana spotted it when they were going back after our Selection and I've checked it. She loves you and, if you took care of her and told her how you felt face to face, then she would trust you. You could explain why I had to be killed. You can explain that I knew, that I agreed to it, that it was my idea. Geana knows the Mind Craft, same as I do, and she was there when I agreed to it. And you have the Words of Truthful Aura. She would believe you."

"How sure are you? Geana is manipulative."

"I know she is. But I have watched her for the last forty years, Aclaí. She needs a lot of help and nobody else can help her where she is. She wouldn't trust anyone from the City – except you, if you went to her – and Geana is the only country-person who can get close enough to help." She looked at him, pleading with her eyes. "She can only do what she does with my help, because she doesn't know the Words we take for granted doing the Mind Craft. She would be struggling in the dark. When I am gone, they will both need your help."

"Then I will do it," he said, deciding as he said it. In his mind he was reviewing his own plans and modifying them to fit this new parameter. It always amused him how he had such a reputation for plotting and manipulation and how little others knew how much was improvisation. Again he was improvising – something that always excited him. "Tomorrow I will be busy but the day after I will go to Éirime and sort this out. I should have done it eleven hundred years ago."

"You should," she said, and hugged him again, hiding her face. He felt her trembling. Then she Breathed courage and the scent of him and tried to imagine the way Geana would ask. "Would you do something else for me?"

"What?"

"If the Mentor was executing me he would have me tortured tonight, like poor Abhainne. You could do the same thing, you know: it would add to your reputation."

"That is going too far, Eala. I don't want to hurt you at all. I know he would and that is why you are not being returned to him. I have to kill you, we both know that, but I won't hurt you."

"I didn't mean that," she said. "I'm scared and I don't want to spend my last night alone. It would enhance your reputation for cruelty and prove that you are beyond his authority if you raped me the night before."

"Eala!" She saw that he looked shocked and watched as puzzlement replaced the surprise. "Is that really what you want?"

"I want to be held. I want to feel something tonight before I feel nothing tomorrow night. I don't want to sleep alone. Tomorrow I am in your power and I will be less afraid of you if tonight I was in your power too. Show them you can be cruel but show me that you can be gentle. I really don't want to be afraid."

He took her shoulders and separated her from him so he could look her in the eye. "Is that truly what you want, Eala?" he asked.

She reached up to him and put her hands either side of his face. She breathed Immortal Breath and thought of how much she loved him. And, just like the time she had shown him in the dining hall in Maoineas, they were kissing.

This time there was nobody to watch them and give them a reason to stop.

2

Swan Song

Eala knew she was dreaming but this time it was not a nightmare of the City. She stood on the familiar summer pastures of Áthaiteorainn, Yanti in her arms, and looked up at Yanti's husband standing at the door of their magnificent Flyer. And she looked up at the young sailor who stood behind Yanti with her hand on the rail. She looked into her green eyes. Her sister's eyes.

Then Yanti walked into the Flyer, hand in hand with her husband, and the Flyer closed. Eala watched as it climbed into the sky, taking her sister to safety.

She might be going to her death but Geana would live on.

Aclaí woke up. There was something fragrant tickling his face. The scent was honeysuckle and it reminded him, achingly, of Éirime. He opened his eyes. It was red-gold hair. He turned to see Geana... not Geana, he remembered, it was Eala. The Favourite, the Mentor's Favourite, sleeping in his bed. He looked at the length of her stretched out beside him, peacefully sleeping. He saw the welts where she had insisted he had beaten her and he remembered waking up all those years ago, with Éirime, the day after she had been Initiated. His one night with Éirime had been interrupted by Iolar. For an odd second he remembered Iolar as he had last seen him and, with it, he remembered what would happen to Eala.

It suddenly struck him that it didn't have to happen to Eala. Looking at her, remembering her sister, he suddenly saw why Geana's strange arithmetic added up. Iolar had been lost in the Forest, and–

Then he felt the sword-hilt and he knew it had woken him up. He moved carefully on the bed, trying not to wake her, and reached out from under the covers to find the sword on his Silver Cord. He held the hilt as the point of the scabbard rested on the stonework of the floor.

aclaí He knew that they were Sixteenth Rank but he could not remember who Rua might be.

"What is it?" he asked. Eala stirred beside him, dreaming, and as he saw the freckles on her face some memory stirred in his own mind, of Foscúil as a young man.

you should take her and run the words told him.

"How do you know?"

prophecy my lord Which was not an explanation at all. *she will refuse to go when you ask her but you must force her*

Then Aclaí remembered. "You are Foscúil's cousin," he thought at her. "You Retired a thousand years ago. Everyone thought you were dead."

i did she replied. *i swore i would have nothing more to do with any of ye until the mentors heart was as broken as mine was*

Aclaí smiled grimly to himself. "So you are coming back?"

he will die she replied. *unless you take her into the forest the city will fall*

"How do you know all this?"

come and see me and i will explain came her words. *but bring the favourite and all your companions*

"They will not come."

they will come except the favourite she contradicted. *you should bring éirime too*

"That is forbidden, Rua," he thought.

so many things have been forbidden aclaí but you are elder immortal rank and you have use of her gift

"I will –"

the gift she shares with her sister

"I will see if I can come to you."

you will come to me aclaí but if you wait too long the city will fall

"I have to –" He felt Eala stir.

you have to come here before nightfall aclaí came her answer. *do it and bring them all or the city will fall*

"I see. I –" and he felt the bed move as Eala shifted her weight. "I have to go."

you have to come here or the city will fall

He released the Hilt and put the sword down on the floor then turned to face Eala. She looked straight into his eyes and reached her hand to his face.

"Don't cry," she said, stroking his cheek. "By midday it will all be over and afterwards you will go to your love. You've waited a long time but soon it will all be over."

"We could run," he said. "The Forest is deep."

"You belong with Éirime, Lord Aclaí."

"But you want me to go to her. And your sister. We will take them, too." He looked at her face. "You don't believe they would come?"

"I am sure Éirime would come. My sister, I am not so sure..."

"To save your life she would come."

"You are probably right. But, if you run into the Forest, who will save the Mentor?"

"Why does he need saving?"

"He's dying, Aclaí. He still can't breathe Immortality, remember? If we run into the Forest, take Éirime with us, what will he think? If Foscúil, Innealta and Eibheara follow too it will only confirm his fear of the Immortals. He needs to change and fear will make him less likely to change."

"Your... I was taught that I should adjust my actions according to how much they hurt those I love... according to how much I love them. I will not lose you and I won't leave Éirime to believe that I will murder your sister. There is not any other way."

"Lord Aclaí, there is another way. Free him from the City and his fears and then everything will be all right."

"Not for you."

"Even for me. If he loves me enough he will make me alive again."

"Forbidden Art? Do you truly believe he could love someone enough to perform Forbidden Art?"

"I don't believe it, Aclaí. I know it to be true. I died on that beach at Úll Oileán, while the City was fighting the Battle of the Blue Peaks. I crashed the Flyer into the cliff and I died. I didn't even know until he told me. If he loves me enough he will do it again." Her lips tightened. "And if he doesn't I don't want to live."

"That is your plan? Force the Mentor to bring you back?"

"I don't have any other plan, Aclaí."

"That doesn't bother you?"

"I'm a bit scared, maybe. But, Aclaí my love, I would love to fall asleep and be woken up by him back in the City. I'm not choosing this because it is easiest. I am choosing this because it is his best chance to change. With the four Oldest behind you I am sure you can persuade him to change."

He looked at her, remembered that, as Rua was still alive, he would need to follow her advice to have the four Oldest behind him. Then he thought of reminding Eala that she was his prisoner. But he remembered how that had failed the night before and, anyway, he knew she was right: he wanted to take her away and she was choosing to stay. Even if Rua and her prophet thought he should take Eala by force he knew he would not do that. He sighed, slowly, with Immortal Breath. "Eala, you have much more courage than you think you have."

"And you have much more love than you think. You need to abandon the suspicions and trust your heart."

"You still think I should speak to Éirime?"

"Aclaí, I think you should marry Éirime."

"And take care of her maidservant?"

"Of course. It's the best thing for everyone. Even him. With your strength, Éirime's Breath and my sister to support and ground ye both, ye can help him. In time Geana will convince the rest of the Mind Craft Adepts to follow our plan. Then, with Foscúil, Damhánalla and Miotal backing you, there is nothing to fear. You can free him. Then he will want me back."

"Did you know that the Mentor forbade me to talk to her?"

"I know. She has been told too. Now all you have to do is make her believe it."

"Who told her?"

"She overheard someone talking about it."

He thought about that. If Éirime knew then he would not be telling her any secrets. He imagined all the possible futures they could share. But what about the girl in his arms? "Eala, are you sure you're not looking for an escape?"

"I am, but not just for me. He needs you, Aclaí." Her hands on his head drew him towards her and he kissed her. Her embrace was like nothing he had ever known.

He lay on one of her arms, taking some of his weight, stroking the skin of her breast, belly and hips. She looked up at him and remembered the promise she had made to Yanti. *All the way*, Yanti had said. What more could she do to unbalance Aclaí?

"Eala, nobody told me you would be like this. I see how your Immortal Breath expresses your Gift. I am going to miss you so much."

"My lord, Éirime will be the same if you take her in your arms when she sings. She will be stronger than me: she is three Ranks above me."

"She better be. Or I will Restore you myself, Eala."

She turned her intense green gaze on him. "Promise me you won't."

"All right, I promise. But how do you know what Éirime's embrace is like?"

"My sister compares us."

"How will I ever get Geana's forgiveness?"

"I will write her a note and you can take it to her. When you have sorted the Mentor between ye then she will see me again." She kissed him. "Would you mind the woman in your arms singing?"

"Oh Eala, you can't believe –"

She put her fingers on his lips. Then she began to sing. Her singing didn't have the Gift, of course, but he thought she had a pleasant enough voice and she had obviously learned something from living with Éirime. He could feel the tension of her singing voice inside her. Then suddenly he realised what she was singing. She was singing a song of Anleacán: one he had never heard but which had slept in his heart since he was a young man.

It was one of the oldest songs of Anleacán but it was not an accident that he had never heard it.

She was singing the Song of the Bride.

Aclaí found Foscúil with Damhánalla, Miotal and Innealta. They were gathered in the Seaview Room. They looked around as he came in.

"Where is Eibheara?" Aclaí asked.

"She is taking breakfast in her own room," Miotal replied.

"I think she prefers to avoid our company this morning," Damhánalla added.

"Have ye been fighting?" Aclaí asked.

"She demanded that you be removed from Eala's company last night," Innealta explained. "She thought that Eala would persuade you to set her free."

"I presume she didn't," Damhánalla suggested.

"She didn't even try," Aclaí told them. "She wants me to do it."

"Why?" Damhánalla asked.

"Because it's quicker than Marching?" suggested Innealta.

"It's a logical strategy," Foscúil suggested. "She doesn't fear to die so she wants to use her death to manipulate the Mentor. Either that or she wants to use it to manipulate you, Lord Aclaí."

"It is both," Aclaí agreed. "She wants me to go to Éirime."

"To protect her sister," answered Foscúil. "What does she expect from the Mentor?"

"She expects him to bring her back. She says she died at the Battle of the Blue Peaks."

"She's not the only one," Innealta admitted. "Eibheara was using Forbidden Art. She saved two of us Favourites."

"She says it was the Mentor who did it," said Aclaí. "I believe she intends to force him to do it again, but not in secret. She wants him to do it in front of everyone."

"Why?"

"Because if she is reconciled with him she can breathe his Immortal Breath for him."

"She can do that?" asked Miotal. "I never heard of it."

"How does that work?" asked Damhánalla.

"It works," said Foscúil. "But what does she do when she is doing it?"

"She hugs people."

Foscúil laughed out loud. "Well, I suppose that makes sense, my lord. Did you find that out before or after you stuck it in her?"

"Before," Aclaí admitted.

"Éirime will be able to do the same," Foscúil explained. "She will do it when she is singing."

"I will ask her."

"You are going to her, then?" Damhánalla asked.

"We need to plan this," explained Aclaí. "I will go to her and then, as soon as I have persuaded her of the necessity of it, we will go to the City."

"Then why are we killing Eala, my lord?" Foscúil asked.

"Because she wants the Mentor to raise her again. I think it is to do with Forbidden Arts. She wants them not to be Forbidden anymore, I guess." Aclaí frowned. "Your cousin Rua called, Foscúil. I didn't even know she was alive."

"She called me too, my lord. I wish I knew why she called me. She says it was a prophecy but I don't think that is reason enough. She hasn't cared about the City for a thousand years. But she said that if you kill Eala the City will fall."

"What did she expect you to do, then?" Damhánalla asked.

"She said we should take Eala, by force if necessary, and run deep into the Forest. She said that we should take Éirime and, presumably, Eala's sister too. She said we should not come back until the Mentor agreed to submit to Aclaí's rule – or until he died."

"I told Eala that. She doesn't think allowing him to die is acceptable. She thinks that if he dies we won't bring him back. She is trying to use her own death to prevent his."

"It still sounds like an alternative to Marching, my lord," Innealta observed.

"I think that is why Rua told us that we must take her by force. My lord, she named Eala. She has never met her."

"Do you know who her prophet is?"

"I do, my lord. And I trust him to have the Mentor's best interests at heart. He Retired not long after Eala left."

"So he might be under her influence," Aclaí mused.

"I don't believe it," Foscúil replied.

"Or he could be under someone else's influence."

"Geal's Breath was far stronger than he should have been, my lord. Eibheara is –"

"Are we all going to end up raving about Infiltrators, like Eibheara?" asked Miotal.

"Remember what I told ye?" Aclaí asked. "I met one of Eibheara's Infiltrators. She openly admitted that she was one of them."

"You said that she was Seventeenth Rank and that you had never met her," said Miotal.

"This is the person that warned you about Ceatha?" asked Foscúil.

"That is her."

"So we may be manipulated by Eibheara's Infiltrators right now?"

"I don't believe Eala could be manipulated by anyone." Aclaí replied. "We will proceed with the plan. But, Foscúil, you should warn your Patrols to be ready. We need to protect the City from the Forest and we also need to contain the City. We don't know what he is going to do but we ought to make sure we have control of the situation."

"The Patrols could cover our escape when we ran into the Forest, my lord. We could stay in touch with them and –"

"We will proceed with the plan, Foscúil. See that they are ready."

"I have already put them on highest vigilance. I did that last night, my lord."

"Again, Foscúil, your loyalty exceeds my capacity to call on it." He turned and left.

"I have a really bad feeling about this," Innealta said.

"You are not the only one," Foscúil laughed.

"We all have," Damhánalla agreed. "But, if he goes to marry Éirime, at least it will finally get Eibheara out of our lives."

Caora went into the commons and found the wall that she normally used. It only took her a few gestures to start the Visions. Then she turned and left again. Nobody said a word.

Geana was waiting for her in their room. Caora sat on the bed next to her. "I'm sorry," she said.

"You could stop this," Geana said.

"What can I do?"

"You could go and tell Aclaí not to do it. He would listen to you."

"Remember what Foscúil said?"

"You didn't believe him anyway."

"But Geana, if you are right he doesn't speak to me because the Mentor has Forbidden it."

"I am right, Caora. I have seen Aclaí's Motivational Chart."

"How?"

"He let me see."

"Why?"

"He wanted my help. He doesn't want to do this. He only does it because the Mentor has ordered it."

"So, Geana, let us accept that Foscúil was right and Aclaí is in love with me."

"It is true."

"The other part is that he is Forbidden from talking to me."

"I believe he is. But he is ready to defy that, for you. His motivations towards you are more strong than his motivations towards the City. Take Aclaí for your husband and you can rule the City."

"Your sister is about to be killed and all you can think of is power, Geana?"

"All I can think of is how to save her. So call him."

"I can't. If the Mentor has Forbidden him from talking to me then I must not speak to him. Don't you see?"

"Then what?" Geana demanded. "Don't you love Eala enough to save her life?"

"Perhaps there is a way." Caora found her sword on her Silver Cord and placed her hand on the Hilt.

who is this

"It is Éirime, Mentor," she thought.

nobody calls me

"I know, Mentor. But I have a favour to ask."

another one

"It is the same one, really. Aclaí sent Miotal here to Áthaiteorainn."

i know

"Will you save her for me? I will take her away, deep into the Forest, and you will never have to see her again."

i want to see her again

"If you want to forgive her then I will bring her to you."

how can i save her

"You could tell Aclaí to spare her."

i could not éirime

"Why not?"

i asked him yesterday and he refused

"Are you telling me the truth?"

why would i lie to you

Caora released the sword-hilt. She knew she should wait to be dismissed but she could not bear it. "The Mentor asked Aclaí not to do it, Geana. He refused. He refused the *Mentor,* Geana. What does your Motivational Chart say about that?"

"I..." Geana thought as she spoke. "I... then Eala must be the one driving this. Remember how she took her Flyer away when Lord Miotal came here? The person who is forcing her execution is her. Aclaí refuses to call it off because Eala refuses to call it off. She must know... she must believe the Mentor will bring her back. She intends for Aclaí to come here and –"

"Aclaí is coming here?" Caora demanded.

"Are you afraid of him, Caora?"

"Of course I am afraid of him! I thought you knew people, Geana. Aclaí is the only man in the whole of humanity that could force himself on me. I don't trust men. Remember that boy from the Westland that I sent home? Anyone much more of a man than Luchóg is too scary for me. And you expect me to want to see *Aclaí?*"

"Don't you trust me?"

"Geana, you are not asking me to trust you. You are asking me to trust someone that is about to hack the head off your twin sister!"

"This is what Eala planned, too. He loves you. We both know that."

"I don't want men to love me, Geana. That is just more motivation for them to hurt me."

"He wouldn't!"

"Are you saying that I don't attract him? If he loves me then surely he would want to put it in me."

"I am sure you attract him but I am also sure he would not force it into you."

"That doesn't make sense. That is what men are like and Aclaí more than most. He sticks it in everyone who comes near him. I have never known another man like it – other than the Mentor himself."

"That is how he controls people, Caora."

"I don't want to be controlled. I don't want to be anywhere near him."

"What about the night you slept in his bed?"

"I was stupid, Geana. I was young and I didn't know any better."

"What about him? He knew better, Caora."

"He was Forbidden. I was without Rank. Now you tell me he has been Forbidden ever since. Then you tell me that the Mentor's word is not enough to protect me from him anymore. I don't want him anywhere near me."

"I don't believe he is like that."

"I will show you what he is like," Caora replied. And, with a bitter gesture, she invoked the Visions.

"You don't have to watch, my love."

Éise and Liús were huddled together in their house in Acra. Éise had insisted that she wanted the Visions. As she watched Liús saw the tears on her face. "I want to watch," she said.

"I don't understand. You never even liked her."

Éise turned on him. "You don't understand me at all, do you? Of course I wasn't willing to risk your life – risk our lives – chasing her dreams. Look at what her dreams have gained her. But she is the bravest person to ever walk on the Hill. She made every one of us look like what we are: shallow, heartless puppets who jerk on his cords. We all of us learned her Art but in secret. Not one of us favourites is brave enough to stand by her side and –" Éise wrapped her hands over her belly and groaned. "*Cac!*"

Liús put his hand on her shoulder. She wriggled under him and turned her head towards him. Her face was lined with tension. "Get off me," she growled through a clenched jaw. Then the spasm passed and she breathed deep Immortal Breath. She reached down to where wetness was spreading on the bed. "The waters have come."

"I think I'd better get that healer woman," Liús said. He got up. "I will be right back," he said.

"You better be."

He hurried out and to the house of the healer. She wasn't there. He went on to the inn. They were all gathered around the Visions in the Commons. It wasn't every day there was an execution to see and there was a Celebration mood in the place. Liús found the healer quickly enough. She was a short woman with white hair and a few wisps of white beard. She might have been half his height but her arms were as thick as his legs. "Come quickly," he said. "My wife's baby is on the way."

"I didn't even know she had arrived in Acra," the healer said, putting down her drink and looking at him with dog-like brown eyes. "I told you it would be foolish of ye to travel. How long has the baby had to grow?"

"What do you mean?"

"When did you put it in her?"

"Oh. She has had eight months, a ten-day and three days."

"It is long enough. Have her waters come?"

"Just now."

The healer put her mug down. She looked at the Visions with disappointment.

"We have the Visions in our home," Liús said. "If you think watching a girl die is a fitting first sight for a new-born baby."

"Oh, babies don't care. And the girl is a blue-robe. One of the Mentor's favourites, they say. She probably deserves it."

"She does not."

"Oh, when you have lived as long as I have you will learn. Blue-robes do terrible things. One of them tried to destroy the world when I was your age. Perhaps that was her."

"It wasn't."

"You seem very sure of yourself, Mister Liús."

Liús showed her into the house. She went and spoke to Éise. "I am Úlla."

"I am Éise," she replied. "Does it get any worse than this?"

"How often does the labour come?"

"Less than ten breaths apart."

"Then it will be very soon." She lifted Éise's dress to her knees and put her hands underneath. Éise hardly flinched: she was used to the Mentor. "Your womb is open," she said. "The baby will be here very soon. Are you comfortable sitting like that?"

"Of course I am not comfortable," Éise replied. "I feel like she is ripping her way out."

"You might feel better if you kneel or crouch." She put her hands on Éise's belly. "Your baby is head-down and I think his back is facing forwards. That should –"

"I know her back is facing forwards, Úlla." Éise snapped.

"You think you can feel..?" Úlla stopped as she saw Éise have another contraction. "Breathe, Éise. Breathing will lessen the pain." She put her hand on Éise's head as she breathed Immortal Breath. "That's good, Éise, breathe it all out."

"Is that all you do? Tell girls how to breathe?"

"If something goes wrong –"

"Do you think something is going to go wrong?"

"You seem healthy enough to me. Your baby will be in your arms before midday."

"So what will you do if something goes wrong?"

"Don't upset yourself, Éise."

"I just want to know."

"You shouldn't ask. You are healthy and you are a fine shape for your husband's boy."

"She's a girl, Úlla."

"As you wish, Éise." She put her hand on Éise's head again as she saw another contraction start. "Breathe," she said. "Remember to breathe."

"Mentor?" Cathúa called at his door.

"What do you want, Cathúa?" he asked.

"Would you keep me company, Mentor?"

"Don't you have anyone else to keep you company?"

"I don't, Mentor."

"Very well," he grumbled. She heard him move about inside the room and then she heard him unlock the door. "Come in, if you must."

She came in. The room was dark, as it always was, except for the light that came from the Vision he had set up on his mirror. The light from the Vision glittered in the emerald eyes of her cat pendant. He was sat on the bed again, with a stick between his knees. He leaned forwards to prop himself on the stick. She sat beside him and very gently she rubbed the muscles in his back and shoulders.

"Who taught you to do that, Cathúa?" he asked.

"Liús did, Mentor," she replied.

"Well, I suppose we should be grateful that he left a few skills behind before he abandoned us." Cathúa Breathed her relaxation and rubbed a little more. He continued. "When are you going to go, Cathúa?"

"I will stay until the end, Mentor."

"But then you don't think the end is going to be long, do you?"

Cathúa just concentrated on what she was doing. She knew that if she immersed herself in a task that the emotions would just flow over her and not sink into her heart.

"Éirime called me, Cathúa. Do you know what she asked me?"

"What did she ask you, Mentor?"

"She asked me to spare Eala."

"Oh. Mentor, you could if you wanted. Surely one display of mercy would not undermine your authority?"

"I cannot. Aclaí refused to give her to me."

"Do you want me to rescue her, Mentor?"

"Cathúa, you are the most faithful of all my favourites. I believe you really would go and try and rescue her for me."

"I will, Mentor."

"You would die. You would have to take on Aclaí, Foscúil, Miotal, Damhánalla, Innealta and all of them."

"If I set out to simply fight them then I would certainly lose. But I am more clever than that, Mentor. I will not die, of that I am certain."

"You may be more clever than any of them, Cathúa, but you are not more clever than all of them. I cannot allow it."

"They won't kill me today, Mentor. That is impossible. I can fetch her back here and –"

"I will not allow it, Cathúa. You stay here with me."

"You could bring her back to life afterwards, Mentor."

He turned around and she pulled her hands away. "Cathúa! Do you dare to suggest Forbidden Art?"

"Mentor, nothing is Forbidden to you. You are the Mentor."

He sighed and the anger left his face. "Eala said the same thing. I wish it was so simple."

"I don't understand."

"I know. Cathúa, I am as much a servant as anyone who wears a blue cloak. I cannot simply break the rules."

"I don't understand."

"You don't need to understand," he told her. "You just need to not question."

"As you wish, Mentor," she said. She put her hands back on his shoulders. She wished she could hold him to her. That was what she knew she should do but she did not have any idea how to begin.

"Cathúa," he said, "I know you are trying to help."

She smiled, relieved that he had appreciated her efforts.

"But I don't need your help," he said. "I have a plan of my own."

"Can't I help with that?" she asked. "Just tell me what –"

"I will do this for myself," he told her. "Go now."

She went.

"Get your hand off my head! If you touch me again it is your own head you will be looking for!"

"That's all right, Éise," Úlla soothed. "You shout all you want. Let it out."

"Get out of my house," Éise growled. Her voice sent shivers down Liús' spine.

"I'm not leaving. I will be with you for –"

But Úlla stopped when she saw the sword in Éise's hand. "I won't ask again," she said.

She didn't need to. Úlla grabbed her bag and ran out.

Éise turned to Liús. "What possessed you to think that I needed..?" and she broke off as another contraction started. When that one subsided she got up on her knees as the midwife had suggested. It did help, she found.

He stood on the platform. Below him the crowds watched and the Vision operators multiplied the audience to include a good fraction of the human race. He was wearing every badge of his office and the most fearsome expression he could manage. He had spoken to them of treachery, of the price of treachery and of how they would see that price paid. Eibheara sat and watched from the front row with an expression on her face that Aclaí knew too well.

"Bring her," he called to his men.

Foscúil was with Eala behind the platform. He put his hand on her shoulder to lead her out. "I am pleased you have learned not to fear death, Favourite," he whispered, "But I truly hope you know what you are doing."

"I do," she whispered back as she put her foot on the steps. Foscúil watched her with frank admiration. She showed not a trace of fear.

Miotal walked behind her as she came forward. She stood before Aclaí as he unwrapped her cloak and removed it. She was naked underneath and they could all see the marks on her body from the night before. Perhaps Miotal and Eibheara would recognise that the weals were light and playful, when compared to the normal taste of Favourites, but most of the audience knew nothing of that. They saw a beautiful girl, raped and beaten, about to die. Their silence showed how shocked they were.

"On your knees," he told her, before she got cold and they mistook her shivering for fear. She knelt and looked up at her. He could not look into her eyes and do it. She reminded him too much of the Mentor. He looked away from her face as he placed his hand on her head and gently laced his fingers into her hair. He took up her sword, too short and too light in his hand but still with the perfect edge of Metal, and with one sweep it was done. The golden hair on her shoulders scattered and her blood fountained. Her head, now light in his hand, looked up at him and smiled. For one moment her lips formed the name of her sister and then the life went from her eyes.

Aclaí raised her head where the crowd could see. "So die those who betray the City," he roared at them.

"Together we are strong!" Foscúil shouted.

"The Sea People make us strong!" the crowd roared back.

Aclaí turned and left and the others followed him. He carried her head with him but the body was left on the wood. One of the servants spread her cloak over it. Eibheara stayed seated before the platform, watching the blood pool and spread out over the wood.

Many people that saw Eala die were silent but, in one stone house in the mountains, a new girl broke the silence with a cough and a cry. "Oh," exclaimed her mother. "You are the most beautiful little thing." She opened her cloak. Her skin was shiny with perspiration and her breasts were swollen. She remembered seeing how her mother handled new-born babies and she brushed her own nipple over the little baby's nose and lip. On the third attempt her daughter opened her mouth. Éise cradled the fuzzy head in her hand as the mouth sucked.

"Of course she is beautiful," Liús told her. "She takes after her mother."

"She is early but she is a good size."

"She is that." Liús glanced up at the Vision still shining on the wall. "Was it the upset that made it happen?"

"It might have been," Éise said. "But that life is part of our past."

"Then let us forget –"

Éise looked around at him. "Did you see Eibheara?" she asked. "She sat there watching. Everyone else was upset but Eibheara was concentrating on how much it moistened her –"

"We don't know what she was thinking, dear heart," Liús lied.

"We do. Eala taught us that much. People like Eibheara are the reason why the City is falling."

"Are you angry with her when she gave us this beautiful..?"

"I know she has done us good, but she didn't wish us well. And what right did she have to..?"

"Don't think of her, dear heart." Liús reached past her to touch the baby's head. "What are we going to call this little princess?"

"Oh, my brave lion. You are right. Now you are properly the leader of your pride, your family. What do you want to call her?"

"I cannot think of a name. She is too beautiful for any name I can think of. And, if she has her mother's strength and courage as well as her beauty –"

"Tintreacha," said Éise.

"That is a name for a warrior, dear heart. Our girl will never go to the City. By the time she grows up there will not be a City for her to go to."

"Would you prefer something more pretty?"

"Lightning is pretty, dear heart, but it also scares ignorant peasants."

"Lighting doesn't just scare peasants, my young lion. Lightning shatters granite."

They had tried to comfort the people of the village but, in the end, it was Geana who had led her away from them. The image that Éirime kept seeing in her mind was Eala's body as she stood then knelt before him – and the marks on it. She remembered sharing a bed with Aclaí but, in those terrible first days, he had been the only company she had wanted at night because he was the only one who had not forced himself on her. She knew he must have been sexually active but they had never been lovers. He had been a brother to her, someone she could trust, when she needed a brother.

Then she had seen Eala, bruised, battered, soiled, but still so like her sister, standing before him like that, watched by the world. He had done that to her then he had killed her before them all. She knew the Mentor had ordered it but the Mentor had told her that he had asked Aclaí to spare her life. How could he have done that when the Mentor had told him not to? In her mind she had always wanted to believe that, behind the games that the City played with them all, Aclaí was still that brother to her. But now she knew that this was nothing more than a dream. Aclaí did not have any secret goodness in him. He was just what he seemed: a killer.

Geana found wine and they went back to their room, to hold one another and to try and drink enough to stop the hurt.

Aclaí walked back into Miotal's House, Eala; s head still in one hand, her sword in the other. He found her Flyer still in the courtyard and climbed up into the seat.

"Do you want company, my lord?" Innealta asked.

"I am not sure I will be safe as company," Aclaí replied. He placed Eala's head gently in his lap. "I am afraid she has affected me more than I expected."

"I am your friend, Aclaí. You will not hurt me. But I have also spoken to Geana about you and Éirime. If I come with you I might be able to help."

"I spoke to her myself, Innealta. I have been friends with Eala's sister for a very long time."

"I still think you might have problems with her. Will you let me try and speak to her first?"

"If you think it would help. I have given her a Hilt. You can use it to communicate with her."

"I will try it. Shall we go to the Midsummer Palace first, my lord?"

"At least let us set off that way. If you would try and call her then maybe we can change direction on the way."

"I think we should go straight to the Midsummer Palace, my lord. I don't think that is the best thing to take with you when you first meet her sister."

Aclaí looked down into his lap. "I think you are right."

Innealta gestured the Flyer into the air and turned it westwards. Once she had given it orders she found her sword on her Silver Cord and placed her hand on the Hilt. She thought of Geana, knowing she had a Hilt. As she concentrated she thought what she would say. Theirs was a strange relationship: Geana was a peasant but she was also Innealta's teacher.

But Geana would not answer. Innealta tried again and again until they got to the Midsummer Palace and the others caught them up. Innealta even tried Éirime but she would not answer either. So she took Aclaí to bed with a promise that they would visit first thing in the morning.

Rúnda looked up as the old man came into the commons. It was late and her patrons had gone home early: the place was almost deserted. "Do you want a room?" she asked.

The man shuffled over to her and placed his hand on her wrist. She looked into his green eyes and saw something there: some shadow of malevolence. "I am looking for Éirime," he said.

"*Sionnach*," she called.

"What is it?" he called back as he entered the room.

"This gentleman is looking for someone called Éirime."

Sionnach looked into the old man's face for a moment then he flinched away. "She is in one of the back rooms, my lord."

"Show me," Ceann said.

"At once, my lord. Follow me."

As the old man followed Sionnach out of the commons Rúnda saw him touch the stone knife at his belt. As the fear knotted in her belly the old man turned back and glanced at her. His mouth twisted into a semblance of a smile.

By the time Sionnach returned she had dropped a pot. She was gathering up the pieces as he crouched beside her to help. "Who is Éirime?" she asked. "I didn't think we had many guests tonight."

"Éirime is the name that Caora's mother gave her."

Rúnda relaxed. "Lady Caora will take care of him, then?" She put the pieces of pot down. "I've just been so worried. He seemed like a horrible old man and... I suppose I'm upset about what they did to Lady Eala. I don't like having someone like that staying in my inn tonight of all nights. But she'll keep us safe, won't she?"

From the other end of the building they heard voices raised.

"I don't believe she will, Rúnda my love," Sionnach whispered. "We just need to keep ourselves to ourselves. This is City business."

"Who is he, then, that he can be a threat to her? He's not Lord Aclaí. He's not big enough."

"He is the Mentor."

They heard more voices and a sound that might have been a very muffled explosion.

"Mistress Geana is in there with her," Rúnda said.

"We cannot help her," Sionnach answered. "If she cannot help herself, if Lady Caora cannot protect her, then there is nothing that ordinary people like us can do." Rúnda saw the expression on her husband's face that meant that he had made up his mind. "We will go and see which of our children can offer us a bed for the night."

Rúnda allowed him to lead her out of the commons and into the night. As they left they heard a short scream but Rúnda could not tell if it was from Caora or Geana. Her husband's hand guided her away, though. He was right. It was not any business of theirs.

They would find out in the morning.

3

Another Funeral

Innealta woke with a start. She was in Aclaí's big bed but he was not beside her. She got up and wandered around the room looking for him.

He was on the balcony watching the Sun rise. She heard him humming.

"My lord," she asked. "What is that tune?"

"It's an Anleacán folk-song."

"Does it have words?"

"Come here." He reached out and she went close to him. He scooped her up and lifted her onto his lap.

She let him kiss her and she put her hands on his back. When he released her a little she spoke. "We ought to call Éirime."

He smiled. "Do you think we should? Or should we just go there and speak to her?"

"Let me call Eala's sister, at least."

"I dreamed she called me last night. But, when I woke up, my sword-hilt was dead."

"Our thoughts and experiences find their way into our dreams, my lord," Innealta shrugged. "But dreams can't be relied on. They might be frightened of you. We don't know how much they know of Eala's last thoughts."

"I have a letter."

"They might not ever read it. I don't think this is a time for surprises, my lord."

He hugged her again. "You are probably right. At least we should keep the surprises to the essential ones."

She found her sword on her Silver Cord and thought of Geana. But she looked up straight away. "There is nobody there," she said. "Are you sure she still has the Hilt?"

"She had it last night. She used it the night before last. I didn't un-dedicate it but I suppose Éirime might have done so."

"This is not good, Lord Aclaí."

39

"We don't know what it means. I think there is only one way to find out."

"Do you want me to go?"

"We will all go."

Liús left Éise and little Tintreacha to sleep. Their daughter had kept them busy all night and, although Éise could feed her while half-asleep, one of them needed to be fully awake to say Words of Freshness. He resolved to spend some time making a belt or something with a Codicil on it that was triggered automatically by wetness. But first he was going to the inn to find them something for breakfast.

There were a few of them in the inn when he arrived. People had to get up early for milking and there was a shift that had worked the mines in the night. He could tell which were which: the miners were dirty and the farmers comparatively clean. They all went quiet when he came in. He and the innkeeper were the only humans among them. The rest were Delving People, short and powerfully built.

The silence remained as he went over to the innkeeper. "Aren't you going to congratulate me?"

"Úlla said that your wife was birthing," the innkeeper replied. "She also said that your wife is a blue-robe."

"She is Retired," Liús said.

"Why didn't ye tell us?"

"Did ye see the Visions yesterday?"

"I saw. So is Lord Aclaí going to come to Acra looking for your wife?"

"I don't see why he would. We had nothing to do with Eala's Art. Éise is in good standing with the Mentor. But the City is not a place for a baby."

"Does he know she is here?"

"He doesn't even know that she is with child."

"Is that the only thing ye are hiding from him?"

"It is."

"The Sea People do not marry, young Liús. Do you realise the danger you are in?"

"I am fully aware of the danger," he replied. "I have lived in the City since I was a boy."

"Which is not so long, is it? Lady Éise is Sixteenth Rank. She is Immortal."

"She is. But Immortal Ranks can look any age they please."

"I see she is beautiful in her foreign way, Liús, but for a mortal man to be married to someone like that –"

"I have my wife and now I have my daughter. We came here to escape the politics of the City." He gathered the food and then he left them to their whispering. He went back to his family.

When he got back to the cottage Éise was awake. She was sitting up with their daughter in her arms, latched onto her breast. "That smells good, my lion," she said. "Is it all for me?"

"If you can manage it, dear heart." He sat beside her. "You are still eating for two people."

They ate in silence for a while, enjoying each others' company and the miracle of their little girl. It was Éise who broke the silence.

"What are we are going to do?" she asked.

"About what?"

"Are we ever going to return to the City?"

"Yesterday you were talking about leaving that behind us."

"I know, my lion, but I can't help thinking of him. There is only Cathúa left with him now. He will need people by his side."

"What about Aclaí?" Liús looked down at Tintreacha. "It is not just our own lives we are risking. This little monster needs parents, dear heart. If Aclaí murders one or both of us then who will look after her?"

"You have the Words of the Gateway, my dear. We can come and go to the City as we please."

"We can." Liús frowned. "So, do you want me to open a Gateway to our bedroom in the City?"

"I think it would be best. But we should make sure that this little one is not seen."

"I think they will notice you have changed too, dear heart. If you squirt milk at the Mentor he is bound to ask questions."

"At least you should be there."

"I probably should."

"We could find a nursemaid for her."

"She needs her mother, Éise."

"Customs vary. In your village babies are strapped to their mothers until they are ready to walk. In mine the women share the care of babies. I have cared for many babies before I went to Selection." She looked into his face. "You are not happy, my lion." She sighed. "Very well, I will keep her attached to me."

"You will find yourself a girl from the village to help you, I am sure. Although I have an idea for attaching the Words of Freshness and the Words of Contingency to a sash and using it to keep her clean and dry."

"That is a good idea. In fact, that is such a good idea that I can't believe nobody has ever thought of it before."

"There has never been a parent among the Sea People before."

"I suppose not. Anyway, open the Gateway and see if you can find me some more breakfast. They will be putting food out in the Court of the Favourites now."

"And now your motivation becomes clear, my love."

"Wasn't it always clear?"

Liús stood up and marked out a space on the wall. Then he said the Words of the Gateway. A section of the wall became hazy and then disappeared. Light shone in: the first rays of the Sun shining on the Land of the Immortals.

"Hurry back," Éise ordered.

Liús stepped through the Gateway. She heard him open the outer door and close it behind him.

Eibheara woke up. She had been dreaming of Eala and of Aclaí cutting her head off. Eibheara lay in bed a while, remembering it, savouring the victory.

Finally she said Words of Freshness and turned aside the covers. She put on a striking blue silk dress and boots and went to find where the others were having their breakfast. After she had tried a few rooms she called to a servant. "Where are they?" she asked.

"Who, my lady?" she servant girl squeaked.

"Miotal. Lord Aclaí."

"They went last night, my lady. They took Flyers."

"Did nobody think to tell me?"

"I don't know, my lady. If there had been orders left by Lord Aclaí and his friends I am sure the housekeeper would know. Would you like me to ask if a message is waiting?"

"I am sure there is none. Do ye know where they went?"

"I don't, my lady. Should I ask the housekeeper..?"

"Never mind," she said. Then she thought of the main hall in the Midsummer Palace and said the Words of Folding Space.

"Good morning, grand-niece," Miotal greeted her.

"Ye all left without telling me," she grumbled.

Miotal put down the fruit he was eating. "Eibheara," he said, "I don't think this is the right time for you to intrude on Aclaí."

"Why am I an intrusion when the rest of ye are not?"

"I don't know, Eibheara. Why is it that, when the rest of us are supporting him, you insist on trying to advance your own position?"

"That is not fair, uncle."

"Do you even understand how he feels?"

"I don't have any clue, but that is because he talks to the rest of ye when he doesn't talk to me."

"Eibheara, he knew where Eala was for the last forty years. He didn't do anything about her until you forced him into it."

"The Mentor said that she should be found."

"The Mentor also said that Aclaí should not search Áthaiteorainn."

"Nobody told me."

"Nobody needed to tell you. If you had spoken privately to either of them about what you had found then they could have made a decision about how much needed to be revealed. But you didn't consider talking to either of them privately. That is why they don't trust you. You are not trustworthy."

"I am higher Rank than you, Uncle."

"So you are. Threatening people is hardly a way to win their..." Miotal looked over her shoulder and his frown was replaced with a smile. "Innealta," he said. "Lord Aclaí. I trust ye slept well."

Aclaí swept into the room. "I want Flyers in a hundred breaths. We are going to Áthaiteorainn."

"I will find them for you," Eibheara replied, standing up.

Aclaí, Innealta and Miotal watched her go. "What is she thinking?" asked Innealta.

"She is trying to take charge of the situation," Aclaí replied. "She is feeling left out."

"Well," said Miotal, "If she wants to take charge of the situation who is going to stand in her way? You are the only one who out-ranks her, Lord Aclaí."

"I will stand in her way when it is necessary," said Aclaí. "We have bigger problems. Geana is not reachable anymore. She had a Hilt and it is not responding. I suspect that she didn't like us trying to reach her last night and she asked Éirime to un-dedicate it."

"Well, that is one alternative," replied Miotal. "The other alternative is that she is dead. Are you sure you got the right twin?"

"Eala's Hilt does not respond either," replied Aclaí. "If I got the wrong one then Eala has un-dedicated her sword and is hiding somewhere. I'll know when I have talked to Éirime."

"When will that be?" asked Miotal.

"When I have time," growled Aclaí. "If today goes to plan I may be ruling the Mentor by Evening Meal."

It was a short flight from the Midsummer Palace to Áthaiteorainn: the village was in sight almost as soon as they took off. As they got closer they could see men out building a heap of wood. "Is it a Celebration Day in Anleacán?" Innealta whispered.

"It is not," Miotal replied. "It looks like a funeral pyre."

"Do they burn their dead?"

"They do," replied Miotal, "But I don't see that they have anyone to burn. Eala's body is still in Port Teorainn and Aclaí still has her head in the Midsummer Palace."

Innealta was about to reply but she felt the Flyer drop. They landed. Aclaí turned to the first peasant he saw. "Where is Éirime's home?" he asked.

Perhaps Miotal had expected resistance or a pretence of incomprehension but there was neither. Instead the man replied, "You are too late, my lords."

"Take me there," warned Aclaí.

He led the way to a room in the inn. It was bigger than Éirime had been born in but tiny for a someone of the Twentieth Rank. He stooped to go in. He saw her lying on the bed. Her skin was pale and her eyes stared up. The flies had already started to notice. He heard movement behind him and he turned around. Miotal had entered behind him, followed by Eibheara. Innealta stood in the doorway and behind her Aclaí could see peasants.

"Leave me," he commanded. The peasants hastened to obey. Miotal looked incredulous. He had never seen Aclaí so angry. He did not fully understand it but he knew that Aclaí could be very dangerous even without being this angry. He beat a retreat, He was trying to be dignified for the peasants outside but he did not want to stay in danger any longer.

Eibheara stayed. She touched Aclaí's arm. "What is it, beloved?" she asked.

"*Leave me!*" he shouted. His sword was in his hand. She backed out, quickly.

* * *

Foscúil looked up as the servant placed the bowl on the table before him. "Thank you," he said.

"It is nothing, my lord," the servant replied.

"Off you go, then."

The servant departed and Foscúil put aside the document he was reading and took up the spoon. It turned out that a band of warriors as large as his required a lot of boring organisation. He carried on reading as he ate.

There was a soft pop and he put the spoon down and looked up. Aclaí stood before him. "Please sit down, my lord," he asked. "Sit down and... and tell me your news."

Aclaí sat. He seemed to remember himself on hearing the voice and calmed a little. Then he took a slow breath and calmed much more. Two more breaths and he was ready to speak.

"Foscúil, you remember that, years ago, when you became my Favourite, I told you that some day you might need to choose your loyalties?"

"That day is today, Aclaí?"

"That day is today. Do you remember your answer then?"

"I remember, lord. You taught me the value of loyalty that day. My answer is still the same. I am yours to command." He reached his hand to Aclaí's. Aclaí was trembling: the feel of it gave him another thrill, to think that something was so important to affect cold Aclaí. It made it real. "Who are we to fight?" he asked.

"We will march on the City. We will destroy the City of the Sea People and end the Mentor's rule."

"Well, my lord, I have been waiting for you to give that order for many years." Foscúil laughed, from deep in his chest, the laugh of a man relieved to be told his future, even if it was a dark one. "All my life I've wanted a fight and this will be the fight of my life."

"Don't you want to know why?"

"My lord, you taught me the value of loyalty to hold together a force. I've built you a band of fighting men based on loyalty and on obeying orders without questioning them. You have given me my orders and I will not question them." He laughed some more. "But when the Mentor first spoke to me at Selection, he accused me of being a pirate, just because I was one of the Sea Hounds. I will show him how we do things in the Land of the Brave: what a pirate can be."

"You're a good man, Foscúil. I saw that on that day in the fighting hall. But don't you want to know why?"

"Of course I want to know, my lord. Do you want to tell me?"

"I want to tell you."

"Then tell me."

"It is not as easy as that. Eala did something to my heart before she died and I am afraid I will lose control of it. She has surprised me with my own rage."

"I am a better swordsman than you, lord. And you need me for this. I will trust your pragmatism and I will trust my own Gift." Foscúil gently tugged his Silver Cord. The hilt of his sword was familiar and comforting. "I will also trust that you know that I am too useful to strike down in the sort of tantrum the old Mentor has," he said. "So, tell me your news."

Aclaí thought it through, looking for the summary, the fewest words, to allow him to control his feelings. He tried some words. "The Mentor has destroyed everything I care about, so I will destroy everything he cares about." It was too many words. As he spoke them he lost control of his own voice and it came out in sobs. "Promise me that we will destroy him, Foscúil. This has gone on too long."

Foscúil reached out his other hand, gripped his old friend's arm. "We will do it, lord. Even if it costs my life, even if it costs all our lives, we will do it."

They had built the pyre to the north of the village. They dressed her in a simple linen dress like the one she had worn the first day Aclaí had seen her. Then over it they put her cloak: a pretence of warmth over the cold skin. He carried her in his arms up onto the piled wood, tiny light thing she was, and laid her down as gently as he could. He brushed the hair from her cheek, touched the cold skin of her forehead with his lips and drew the blue cloak over her face. Then he turned from her and stepped down. His Breath was in his chest, imprisoned, all the power of an Elder Immortal ready to scream out his anger and grief – scream words that could destroy the world.

Aclaí looked up. He saw fear on their faces. But he could see that many of them were looking not at him but behind him. As he saw how they stood together and the similarity of features between them he realised that they must be her family. He remembered talking to her parents, more than a thousand years before.

He raised his voice. "The lady who called herself Caora was someone I first met in the City on the day of her Selection. The Mentor had told me that he did not intend to Select anyone that year because the standards had become so poor. His heart was set: but Éirime's sweet voice melted it and she was the only one Selected that day.

"She hadn't come to be Selected that day. She had come to sing for the Mentor and for the Sea People. She didn't want to be Selected. She never grew to want it. In her heart she remained what ye are and what I am not. The City is full of people like me: cold ambitious people, who rise through the ranks to become cold powerful people and make ye fear them because it is easier to rule people by fear. She hated fear and she never wanted to rule anybody. She wanted only to be an ordinary person like ye. Ye gave her that, something that someone like me could not give, even though her age made her a stranger to ye.

"When I first saw her here, lost to us all forever, I wanted her to be mourned by every one of the Sea People. Now I see ye here, her real kin, I am glad that the City is not here. She belonged to ye. She did not belong to us and so it is fitting that she is here with ye.

"Some of ye have realised that this is something that will be seen in the Visions. Some of ye are conscious that, the last time ye saw me in the Visions, I was executioner for another of yer kinswomen, condemned by the Mentor. Well, Eala belonged to the City and so it was just that the City should choose her end. But Éirime did not and it was not for us to choose her end.

"Blood unjustly shed calls for revenge. I hear that call of unjustly shed blood. Éirime would not have wanted her blood avenged. But justice is often not about what we want.

"I am Aclaí, the Oldest, Elder Immortal, and this is my vow. The City that maimed and then that ended Éirime's life does not deserve to stand. It will not stand. I will cast it down and ye will see it fall."

As Aclaí was speaking Miotal saw Eibheara put her hand on the hand on the hilt of her sword. She glanced up at him and he laid his hand on the hilt of his sword too.

miotal what is he doing her words began. *the visions will take this speech all the way to the mentor what is the plan*

"There isn't a plan, grandniece. This is how he feels. This is the real Aclaí."

are you saying that he loved her

"He never loved anyone else," Miotal replied, watching the humiliation on Eibheara's face.

then he has made a fool of me

"He has made fools of us all. But surely you knew it before you came to him?"

he was always my friend since i was a little girl i didnt think he would do anything to hurt me

"And he won't. He is a good friend, grandniece: the best friend anyone can have. His heart has belonged to Éirime since before I was born. He may get free now but I think that, before he gets free, there is going to be a lot of destruction."

does he mean it when he says he will throw down the city

"I have never heard him say he is going to do something unless he intends to do it."

then what are we going to do

"I am going to do what I always did. Éirime may have owned his heart but he still owns mine. I will follow him on his angry journey and – who knows? Maybe he will do what he says he will. Or maybe we will all die the way Eala died yesterday. Immortality doesn't mean living forever, grandniece."

and the sea people do not marry she answered. *why do we let these sayings rule our lives*

"Who knows what will happen after the City is gone?" And with that Miotal let go of the hilt of his sword, breaking the connection, and stepped forward to Aclaí. Standing before the flames he placed his hand on his master's shoulder. "I am behind you, Lord Aclaí," he said quietly.

"I know. And because of that I may have just condemned you to death."

"Immortality doesn't mean living forever, love."

He was about to say something else but an old man from the village was coming over. "My lords," he addressed them.

Aclaí felt another flash of anger that a peasant might get close enough to see his tears – to see his weakness. But then he remembered what Geana would have said. He had renounced his position by what he had just told them anyway. He blinked hard and looked around to see the man clearly.

"What is it?"

The man had white hair and was stooped but Aclaí could see the same upturned nose that Eala had. "I am Sionnach, Lord Aclaí. Lady Eala and Mistress Geana were my kinswomen. Now that they are gone, my lord, I am the oldest of our family. I understand what you say about Eala's life belonging to the City. They gave their lives in service to Lady Caora as payment for her saving their brother, my ancestor, and Lady Caora took Eala to the City just as you said. But Geana never joined the City. She is gone and we don't know where. The Mentor was here last night. We think he may have something to do with it."

"She is dead, Sionnach," answered Aclaí.

"Are you sure, my lord?" he asked. Then he saw the look in Aclaí's face and added, "I am not questioning your word, my lord."

"I am sure, Sionnach," Aclaí replied. "I am sorry. It wasn't well known, but Geana Áthaiteorainn was my servant. I give my servants a way to communicate with me and it will call them even if they cannot or will not answer. It will not call her anymore. She is dead." He sighed. "She was a good friend to me. I have many reasons why I was in her debt."

If Sionnach was thinking that he had executed Geana's sister only the day before he did not mention it. Instead he said, "We cannot avenge our dead against the City, Lord Aclaí. Avenge her for us."

He reached out his hand to grasp the old man's hand. "I will."

"Thank you."

"Sionnach, Eala told me that she was descended from the older brother of Éirime."

"It is correct, Lord Aclaí."

"Today I came to ask Éirime to marry me. There was a time, back when we were both young, that I should have asked her. I even came to her family and spoke to them here in Áthaiteorainn. I have spent eleven centuries regretting that I did not ask her then and I do not think the regretting is over."

Sionnach glanced over to the flames. He knew who Caora was. "Geana used to tell me that what Lady Caora needed was someone who could be her equal but who cared about her. She said the Sea People don't love in that way. 'The Sea People do not marry,' she used to say."

"I have heard 'The Sea People do not marry' since I was a boy. But my parents left the City and married. These are the lies that bind us, Sionnach."

"I think you would have made her a good husband, my lord. It is true that I am the descendant of her older brother and that, if you had married her, you would be kin to me. You would also be kin to Geana, my lord."

"I have not forgotten that."

"Would you eat in my house, my lord?"

"Only a mouthful, Sionnach. One way the Mentor may react to my challenge is a quick attack. I will have to go soon to make sure that warriors loyal to me are ready for that attack if it comes. But I will accept your hospitality on this dark day, if only for a short time."

* * *

Sionnach led Aclaí and Innealta away. Miotal turned back to Eibheara. "He needs loyalty from those who love him, grandniece. If that loyalty comes at a price then you should go. Today he will not be paying prices. And, if you wish to show the Mentor your loyalty to him, you had best do it quickly. So now you have to choose."

"How can you choose, uncle?"

"It is easy for me, grandniece. I love him: that is all the choice I need."

"Don't you love the Mentor?"

"We all do, grandniece. But the Mentor obtains our love with Words of Power. Aclaí obtained my love with gentleness and with care when I needed care. He does his kindnesses in secret, for fear that he will be thought weak, but those of us who have received his kindnesses know better. I couldn't kill the Mentor for Aclaí but I could look away while Aclaí does it. He means to, you know? The Mentor's Words of Power at the initiation are meant to prevent us from ever being able to harm him. I think that Aclaí's anger is the thing that is strong enough to break through that."

Eibheara wondered about another puzzle she had seen a long time ago. "Uncle, the day after Éirime left the City you two met me and talked about her. He said that he was following her Tradition, looking for something in each years' novices. Was he looking for someone to break the bonds the Mentor places on our hearts?"

"I don't know what he was looking for, grandniece. He told Eala, I think. But he thought Eala might be what he was looking for when he first heard that Éirime had sent her. Then he told me that Éirime had not wanted to send her at all." He shook his head. "It is all very confusing. I think Eala may have broken the chains of Initiation on Aclaí. And yet he killed her yesterday. If it wasn't for the Mind Craft I would be sure that Eala had failed. But the Mind Craft turns everything upside down. I don't know if Eala gave up her life to break his chains but I think she did. She knew she would be killed: she insisted on it, it seems. What do you think happened on their last night together?"

"I could see that someone had raped her. That was to be expected. She was a traitor and she deserved it." As she said it Eibheara realised that Miotal had already decided to be a traitor himself and had asked her to join them.

"How do you know it was rape, grandniece?"

Her mind recoiled from the implications of that. "The Mentor made Mind Craft a Forbidden Art because it corrupts everything, he said. I think I see what he means."

"Maybe it is a Forbidden Art because it is the only thing that can possibly free our hearts."

"Do you know it, uncle?"

"I don't. I wouldn't learn such a thing. But they came here, and –" he looked up. Aclaí was coming out of the hut of the old peasant he had been talking to. Miotal could see that walk and knew it meant it was time to go. Aclaí took Eibheara's hand and led her towards his Flyer.

Liús looked around the Court of the Favourites. There were only a couple of servants around. He could not see a single Adept.

"Lord Liús," one of the servants said, "Would you like breakfast?"

"Am I the only Favourite here?"

"Lady Cathúa is in the Library, my lord."

"Thank you. I want you to tell the servants they are to stay out of our room. I also want you to find me a curtain that is big enough to cover a door. Leave it outside my room along with the rail to fix it to the wall."

"As you wish, my lord."

He went over to the Library and looked in. Cathúa was asleep with her head on her desk. He went up to her and looked. Her face was on a book and her tears had caused the ink to run. The little cat she wore around her neck lay on the desk, among her dark curls, looking up at him with glittering green eyes. He whispered Words of Strength and then he gently picked her up.

She turned her head towards him. Blue eyes opened. "Liús?" she mumbled. He saw that she really was beautiful but her grief made his heart ache. He turned towards the door.

"Where are we going?" she asked.

"I think that you need a better bed than your desk and a book for a pillow, Cathúa."

"You are taking me to bed?"

"You were asleep."

"I must have fallen asleep after dawn. I don't think I will be able to get back to sleep, though."

He carried her across the courtyard. The two servants ignored him and there was nobody else to comment. He took her into her room and sidled carefully past the tables of equipment before placing her gently on her bed.

He was about to go but she said, "Stay."

He sat beside her. "What is the matter?" he asked.

"I cannot explain."

"Is it about Eala?"

"That is a small part of it. Did you hear Lord Aclaí promise to cast down the City?"

"I did."

"I'm afraid."

"It doesn't make sense, Cathúa. Aclaí is a cautious man. The Mentor is not going to last much longer: all Aclaí needs to do is wait for him to die and he can have the City for himself." Liús could see that Cathúa didn't believe a word of his reassurances. "It is only logical."

"Liús, I don't need logic this morning. I have enough logic to last me for the rest of my life. I need you to help me forget logic." She reached up to touch his cheek. "Can you do that for me, my friend? Please?"

Then Liús didn't need Eala's Forbidden Art to tell him what she wanted. But, although he did what she wanted and did the best he could to distract her, he couldn't stop her crying. And, listening to her, it scared him to wonder what Cathúa's cold logic had seen.

As the Flyer curved up from the village Miotal laid his hand on his sword. Aclaí responded. *what is it* his cold words asked.

"It is my grandniece. I think she is going to betray you."

thank you for the warning Aclaí let go the sword, then said, "Flyer, take us to the Midsummer Palace." It continued the curve around to the north. Then they were descending into the Midsummer Palace. As the little toy building below them became a courtyard enfolding them, Aclaí seemed to relax.

He turned to Eibheara. "Would you come with me?" he asked.

He saw Damhánalla scowl and Eibheara smile back. He tried to conceal his own revulsion at the petty games they were playing.

Aclaí led her up to the south wing and into his chambers. The bedroom connected to the balcony and, looking out, she could see the column of smoke, still. She hadn't realised that his bedroom faced Áthaiteorainn but, now that she knew, it seemed obvious.

"Leave us," he said to the servants. Then, when the servants had left them, he added, "All of you."

As Eibheara wondered why a warrior of the Midsummer People appeared, standing by the bed, armed with a spear tipped with Metal. "As you wish, Father," he said to Aclaí, "But I would talk with you later, if I may." Then he added, "Come on, Feochadána."

As he departed a Midsummer girl appeared with him. She smiled her admiration at Aclaí. Aclaí said, "Everyone wants to talk to me today, Carraig. I will find you when I have time."

"As you wish, Father," he replied, as they went.

When the door had closed, Eibheara said, "Do you mind them just coming and going like that?"

"Why shouldn't I?"

"Do you trust them?"

"They are my kin, Eibheara."

"They make me feel uncomfortable. I'm always wondering if they are spying on me."

"You would have to take that up with the person responsible for their creation," he reminded her.

"I created them to stay in the garden. I never expected you to bring them into the house."

"They are people, Eibheara. They needed a role and the role you had in mind is not enough."

"They are monsters from the laboratory. They are toys. I never expected you to take them so seriously. I certainly never expected you to breed with them!" And then her anger came to the fore. "You take them seriously and then you treat me like the little girls that they resemble. Would you take me more seriously if I had wings too?"

"I have done my best to treat you as an adult since the day you were Selected, Eibheara. It has been hard for me. Your parents were my friends and I saw you grow up. I've not seen many people grow up, you know. I'm sorry if I've not treated you properly because of it."

Eibheara's anger abated but she still hurt inside. "You've never loved me, though, have you?" She waited a moment to see how he reacted but she did not even get an instant denial out of him. "I've tried to be a good woman for you, in bed and out, but you've never let me into your heart. Today I saw why: your heart has always belonged to another. But then you've always looked over my shoulder at the thing that interests you, haven't you?" She turned, looked over her shoulder to see the column of smoke rising.

"I don't know what to say, other than that I am sorry for how I've treated you. Do you remember when you first came to the Midsummer Palace and I told you that I didn't think I could give you what you needed? You said I would grow to give it. You said that you loved me and that would be enough. I did, and I do. I admitted it then but I also told you that it wouldn't be enough."

"You didn't tell me why."

"How could I? The Mentor Forbade me telling Éirime how I felt about her or a whole load of other secrets about her and me. I was Forbidden to communicate with her – even indirectly through gossip."

"I would have kept your secrets."

"You didn't keep the secret of Eala in Áthaiteorainn, did you?"

Eibheara was embarrassed. "I didn't understand what was going on. I still don't. I think she has some kind of hold over you with her Mind Craft."

"She doesn't have any Mind Craft hold over me."

"Since the night before last you changed completely. Since then you've been doing crazy things. Now you've raised your sword against the Mentor and the City. How could you do that, Aclaí?"

"That is because the Mentor killed Éirime. It has nothing to do with Eala." He realised as he said it that this was untrue. Eala had broken through his emotional protection and so could be considered to be responsible for the intensity of how he felt. But Eala could not know that Éirime might have been killed. Or had she? If Éirime had been killed trying to defend Geana, Eala's sister – well, Eala might have predicted that. More likely she was trying to get Aclaí back to her sister before the Mentor got there, and using Éirime as the obvious incentive. But, if Eala was right, and she would have welcomed him, then Éirime was a good reason: Eala was doing it for Aclaí and Éirime too. That fitted his mental picture of Eala. She manipulated people but only to help them. She had manipulated people, he reminded himself, and remembered that he had struck the blow, even if it was the Mentor that had given the orders. *Cac us fuil*, he thought, what have I become? Where is this all going to end? For the second time in his life, he realised he had lost control. The last time had been in the month after Éirime's Selection. It had been a wild, passionate business then, and it was again: infatuation and outrage, joy and fear, all mixed together to make an intoxicating brew that left him feeling like he could die before nightfall or live forever.

"Aclaí, look at yourself!" Eibheara insisted. She had been talking to him while he thought. "Your mind is far away. She has got to you. This is the Mind Craft. The Mentor said it corrupts and drives people mad. Eala has sent you mad."

"It is not the Mind Craft, Eibheara. Trust me on that."

"That is what you always say: trust me. But you never tell me what you are thinking. How do you trust that it is not the Mind Craft? What do you know about Mind Craft?"

"I know the Mind Craft, Eibheara. They taught me. Eala and her sister were my friends and, in the end, she was my lover. If my heart was not full to overflowing with grief I'd miss her."

"*Cac us fuil,* Aclaí!" Eibheara looked at him, trying to understand and failing. "Is there any end to your secrets?"

"It feels like there isn't. When I was young the Mentor taught me to keep secrets and to hide how I really feel. He taught me well and it is all I have done for the eleven hundred or more years since I was Selected. I can't break that habit, not overnight."

"I've been with you for forty-two years, Aclaí. Isn't that enough?"

"Eala was helping me with it, for longer than that. It wasn't. I'm sorry. But now, you know, the secrets are not going to be secret for much longer. Soon you will know everything."

"Why do you trust others and not me?"

"I don't trust anyone, not properly. Eala came closest."

"You trust my uncle." She realised that actually he didn't trust Miotal with everything. "What was Éirime's Tradition? You kept going back to meet the newly Selected, even when you had Retired. What were you looking for?"

"I have never told Miotal that."

"I know."

"All right. I cannot explain myself, Eibheara. I have a bad habit of secrecy and I will have for a while yet. But I will answer your question: take it as a sign that I am trying, will you?"

Perhaps he was trying. "All right then," she agreed.

"Do you remember the Legend of the Wife?"

"That?" Eibheara could not believe it was something so trivial. "Who believes that?"

"The prophecies suggest that it might be true: it is one of the most consistent things they say. Éirime thought it might be true and, every year, she looked at the newly Selected to see if one of them could replace the Wife. When I saw Eala, the first Candidate of Éirime's to be Selected, I thought she might be the Wife. But I don't think it was her even if she was Favourite within a ten-day. I think the Wife should have been her sister. Geana was the stronger of the two. Unfortunately her sister had a forbidden name."

"Her sister was a peasant."

"Her sister was a peasant yet she had Éirime at her beck and call. She won the loyalty of many of us. What could she have done with the Mentor?"

"Why would it matter if she had been The Wife?"

"Don't you see, Eibheara? If Geana was The Wife she could have unravelled this tangled mess that is the City of the Sea People. She could have changed the City to something closer to the heart. Look how close her sister came."

"And I ruined that at Áthaiteorainn? Is that why you hate me?"

"I don't hate you, Eibheara. I'm just too good at keeping my secrets. You didn't ruin anything. Eala always hoped that they could work something out but the people around her knew the truth. The clearest-thinking was Yanti, although her passion for secrets makes me look like a Novice. She was the only one we never traced. We don't know where she came from or where she went. It was like Yanti just fell off the face of the planet. But Yanti knew it, you could see. Eala's chance was over the day that the Mentor made Mind Craft a Forbidden Art."

Aclaí saw the expressions cross Eibheara's face when he mentioned Yanti. But all she asked was, "Do you mean that?"

"I mean it. Now, there are two ways to unravel a tangled mess. Eala wanted to do it with intelligence and patience, teasing the knots of each of our relationships apart rather than pulling them tighter. She wanted to take lots of time. The other way to untangle knots is with a blade." He seemed to realise how he was speaking and looked back at her. "I don't hate you. I never have. I'm just too distracted by my secrets to give you the attention you need. Will you be patient with me until this is over?"

She still didn't know what she had decided but she came closer to try and decide. She still cared about him even if he was changing before her eyes. "I will be patient," she said. "I want you to learn to trust me."

"Maybe I can learn," he told her. "Is that what you want?"

"More than anything," she told him.

"Very well." He reached out to her.

As she came over he guided her to sit on his knees. She felt then that maybe it could be all right. He kissed her neck, like he often did, and she felt the familiar feelings in her body. His hand slid up, under her dress and inside her clothes, and she opened her legs to allow his hand to reach her. His other hand was around her arms, holding her and wrapping her in his strength. His mouth left her neck and he began to speak Words of Power. His hand was on her just as the Mentor's had been on the night of her Initiation. That was a Forbidden Art, too, but she just had time to realise he was going to do it before the shock of sensation and emotion burst through her. He held her, her struggles useless against his strength, while the Power-driven love feelings coursed through her, overwhelming her mind, her emotions, greying her vision and threatening to blot out her consciousness. He held it for so long, held her for so long, longer than the Mentor had ever done. She could not breathe, she thought she would die, but by then she didn't care if she did. All she could feel was what he was doing to her.

Afterwards he carried her to the bed. She was soaked with sweat, quivering, and clinging to him. Then it was like it had been when she had first come to him – sweet and passionate and gentle. But she knew that he had used Forbidden Art on her and she knew that her feelings were confused by what he had done. Now there were two sets of chains on her heart and she didn't know if she wanted either.

— 4 —

Two Heads

The messenger rode out of the gate and along the road to the City. He was not under any illusion: he had been given this errand because Lord Miotal disliked him. So he breathed away his reluctance and let the horse carry him over the bridge that crossed the river and through the gate that led up to the Hill.

He rode up to the stable, handed the beast over to a Novice, then strode up through the Court of the Veterans, hoping that he could persuade an Immortal to take his errand from him.

There were Novices guarding the Court of the Immortals. They looked at him as he walked up. The girl spoke. "Lord Broc," she said, "What is your business in the Court of the Immortals?"

"Lord Miotal has sent something to the Mentor," he replied, hoping they would volunteer to take it.

But his luck was not in. The boy looked at the bundle he had and noticed he was carrying two swords. His eyes went to the sword of the Seventeenth Rank and he breathed, "Lady Eala?"

The girl looked at him and followed his gaze. As she realised Broc's errand he saw her discipline fail. He saw her eyes overflow. The boy must have seen it too for he stood aside. "Pass, Lord Broc," he said, holding his voice calm. Why would a girl be shedding tears for Lady Eala, he wondered, when she went into exile since before the girl had been born. But he realised the girl's tears were not the first signs of grief he had seen in the City. He realised that it had been what had spurred his own Retirement, thirty years before.

From the Gate of the Court of the Immortals to the Gate of the Court of the Favourites was only a short distance but Broc looked at the houses there as he went. Most were shut up, for there were so few Immortals on the Hill these days and those were favourites: Lord Liús and Lady Cathúa were the only ones he could remember. Lady Abhainne had died in the Court of the Novices and Lady Míne had followed Lady Eala into exile.

59

Lord Rónmór had Retired and then Ladies Blátha and Féileacána had left too. He realised that the empty mansions of the Court of the Immortals were the most visible sign of a wastage that he had seen ever since he had set foot on the Hill. The exile of Eala's followers had ripped the heart out of their Order.

The Novice guard waited for him there: two boys. They must have known, for they stepped aside before he even had a chance to state his business. Lord Liús was waiting for him.

Míne closed the door behind her and looked around. The daylight was gone and the space was lit by the glow of Words of Power. The *Ocean and Star* was an ordinary inn but it was in the City of the Sea People. She looked around at how the place had changed in forty years. There was less change than she had expected. She felt the challenge of someone directing Immortal Breath at her and she looked towards the back of the room. She saw Blátha wave at her.

As she sat down in the booth they made room for her. Cabairí was on one side of her and beyond was Luaith. On the other side was Blátha, with Féileacána on the other side. Opposite, sat between Féileacána and Luaith, was one more. She recognised her after a moment: Innealta the favourite.

"There are so few of us left," Míne sighed. "I remember when –"

"We used to fill the place," Cabairí agreed.

"What happened to Eala's sister?" Míne asked.

"She is gone too," Blátha said. "I suspect she died when Éirime was murdered."

"Who murdered Éirime?" asked Míne.

"It was the Mentor," Innealta answered. "That is why Lord Aclaí promised revenge."

"Is he sure?"

Míne heard the catch in Innealta's voice. "He is sure that the Mentor murdered Éirime. Geana was Éirime's maidservant. Most likely she died trying to save her mistress."

"It's the sort of thing she might have done," Blátha agreed.

"It is certainly the sort of thing she would have done," said Innealta. "She was never Selected yet she would look any of us in the eye. She had more courage than anyone who put on a blue robe, including her sister. She put us all to shame."

"But how can he consider avenging himself against the Mentor?" Luaith asked. "Surely Initiation..?"

"Elder Immortals can defy Initiation," Blátha smiled.

"Don't be so sure," Cabairí cautioned. "He's not defying anybody."

Innealta leaned closer. "It's true, Blátha. He hasn't done anything for days. We all expected he would instantly take the war to the City but he has done nothing."

"He's taking his time," said Blátha. "He's over a thousand years old. He has the patience to take his time and make his preparations."

"If he is making preparations he hasn't shared them with me," Innealta answered. She pulled a face. "I think he is going through a grief process. He will come through it in a ten-day or so and then he will come out the other side."

"Grief processes can take a lot longer than a ten-day," replied Luaith.

"We don't recover from grief," added Míne, glancing at Innealta. "We learn to live with it in our lives. Or we March."

Innealta looked her in the eye and she knew that she had understood.

"Why March, Míne?" asked Blátha.

Féileacána spoke. "Míne, we were hoping for more than that. Ever since Eala first started teaching us you have been her second. When she hasn't been there to lead us you have taken her place."

"It's true," Blátha agreed. "Eala is gone again. We need your leadership, Míne."

"Is that what this is about?" Míne demanded. "Is this why ye called me here tonight?"

"It is," Blátha agreed.

"I can't," Míne replied. "I am grieving." Her voice choked in her throat. "I can't even breathe Immortal Breath anymore," she whispered.

Blátha put her arm on Míne's shoulder. "We all feel it."

"Lord Aclaí is the same," Innealta said. "It will take a while but we need to prepare for what we do afterwards. Eala didn't want us to abandon her vision."

Míne held Blátha. The part of her mind that did the thinking watched helplessly, like a shipwrecked sailor on a heaving ocean, clinging to the last log of a raft in the middle of the emotional storms, waiting to see if she would survive. Random thoughts flitted through her mind: meetings and conversations. She remembered kissing Rónmór the Chamberlain. What had he told her?

She sat back up again and turned to them. They watched as she wiped her eyes with one hand. "Then prepare," she said. "A friend once told me that our hearts always heal." She sighed. "I cannot say how long I will take, though."

"There are some things we can plan now," said Luaith. "We have to decide if we will take a side."

"Or even if we can take a side as a group," Innealta cautioned. "I already have loyalty."

"I have loyalty too," agreed Blátha.

"We know," agreed Féileacána.

"It is not what you think. The Elder Immortal Eibheara never told me what she planned but I know Yanti was her servant. We have a pretty good idea what Yanti planned."

"It wasn't this," Féileacána suggested.

"I never met this mysterious Yanti," Cabairí interrupted. "Why do ye trust her?"

"She was a prophetess, working for the Elder Immortal Eibheara," Blátha answered. "Eala talked to me because I didn't trust Yanti, not until right at the end. Yanti sent Eala to Aclaí to change him somehow."

"How?" asked Cabairí.

"I don't know. Eala never told me. But Yanti had asked her to do it right from the start, forty years ago when we first met her."

Innealta smiled relief. "So the reason Aclaí is behaving so oddly is because that is what Eala..?"

"Only if we can trust Yanti," Cabairí suggested.

"Only if we can trust Eibheara," Luaith added.

"We can trust *that* Eibheara," Blátha replied. "The Elder Immortal Eibheara is acting for the good of the City. Her unique perspective enables her to see through this muddle."

"Because she is Elder Immortal?" asked Luaith.

"Something like that," Blátha said. "That is it. Elder Immortal." She looked at Innealta.

"The Elder Immortal Eibheara has always been good to me," said Innealta. "The younger one picked fights with Damhánalla and caused trouble but the older one was wise. She tried to take care of us all."

"One of them betrayed Eala," replied Míne.

"That was the younger one," Blátha said. "The older one tried to stop her."

"How?" asked Cabairí.

"I think they fought," Blátha answered. "But the Elder Immortal one couldn't get the younger one to obey her."

"Couldn't she just have killed her?" Féileacána asked.

"That wasn't possible," replied Blátha. "But we can trust the Elder Immortal Eibheara and so we can trust the instructions Yanti gave to Eala."

"Now we just need to figure out what those instructions are," said Innealta.

"How long will that take?" Míne asked.

"We need to ask Aclaí," Cabairí said.

"He's grieving," Innealta said.

"Or he's trying to make sense of Eala's subconscious instructions," suggested Cabairí.

"How long?" Míne asked.

"I will tell you when there is any change," Cabairí told her. "But, meanwhile, will you lead us?"

"I... I am grieving too. I think I can try but only if I know what I am trying to achieve. You, Innealta and Blátha will only follow Aclaí. Your reasons may be completely different but that is what you will do."

"I will follow Blátha's lead," suggested Féileacána. "Unless you are willing to lead us, Míne."

"And I," agreed Luaith.

"We cannot follow Aclaí," Blátha answered. "We are condemned by the Mentor's decree."

"That might not matter," said Innealta.

"If he will honour Eala's work then we can work with him," said Míne. "But first we need to keep hidden until we can see what he does."

"Or at least we can see what Eala has set him up to do," suggested Cabairí.

"Well, tell me as soon as you know," Míne answered.

"I will," agreed Cabairí.

Míne left. The others looked at one another.

"She really is hurting, isn't she?" suggested Blátha.

"We're all hurting," answered Innealta.

Méar heard someone at his door. The whole City had been subdued for the last ten-day and he knew what news they were reacting to. But he would have expected the mood to have lightened now this threat to their existence had been eliminated. Ceann had told him so. But nobody else in the City seemed to share Ceann's insight. He got up to answer.

There was a Veteran standing outside. Méar could not remember – his memory was so unreliable these days – but the Words of Memory found the Veteran's name. "Welcome, Broc," he said. "Did Liús send you?"

"The Chamberlain?"

"Liús acts as Chamberlain, Broc."

"It was Aclaí that sent me, Mentor."

Méar found his sword and armour on his Silver Cord. He raised the sword-point before him to guard himself against this Adept, feeling a pang of complaint from his shoulders. His body was too old for this kind of thing, he thought. "Cathúa!" he yelled, "I'm being attacked!"

Cathúa came running out of the library but Liús was faster: he had used the Words that Stop Time. In a heartbeat he was standing between Méar and Broc, with his armour on and his sword in his hand. But Broc had not raised the point of either sword he had. If he was an assassin then he was a reluctant one.

As Cathúa ran up behind him Broc found his voice. "Mentor," he said, "I did not come here to hurt you. I couldn't hurt you even if I wanted to. I came here to bring things from Lord Aclaí. Neither of them are harmful, Mentor. Lord Liús knew my errand and let me into the Court of the Favourites." Broc turned his face to Liús. "I swear, my lord. I never touched him."

Méar let his sword-point fall. "Very well, Broc," he said. "What has Aclaí sent me?"

Liús moved aside. Broc had two swords. The one at his hip had the bulb end of his Veteran Rank, but the one in his hand had the jewel of Immortality and, beneath it, two thin gold bands. He offered it and Méar took it. He knew that Words of Identification would tell him who this sword had last killed, but he had also seen it on the Visions. It was Aclaí's proof.

"What is the other thing, Broc?" Méar asked.

He saw the hesitation in Broc's face. Then he reached behind him and opened a bag. For a moment Méar saw a gleam of white and then he realised what Broc held in his hand. He felt weakness in his belly. "Who told you to bring me this, Broc? Who dared?"

"Lord Aclaí gave me my orders, Mentor. He is an Elder Immortal." Broc continued to offer the skull in the bag.

Méar took it. "Leave me," he said. With his other hand he reached for the door. They got out of his way as he closed and secured it.

Get rid of it, Ceann said, even before he had opened Ceann's bag. *You have to get rid of it. It is a trap.*

"Explain the nature of this trap," Méar replied. But Ceann did not explain.

He turned Ceann's bag out. Ceann rolled a little but he set the skull upright. The snake stone that Ceann had acquired when he had first started to talk to Méar sat on the desk. Méar tenderly placed the other skull beside him. Then he went to the door and opened it. Liús was standing by the door of the Watch Room.

"Liús," he called, "Will you run an errand for me?"

Liús ran over. "As you wish, Mentor," he replied.

"Will you take this and Replicate it for me?" He handed over the bag.

"At once, Mentor." Liús ran off and Méar closed and bolted the door again.

You must get rid of it, Méar.

"Explain this trap to me, Ceann. Are there Words of Power written on it?"

If you keep it then you will die.

"Don't you realise I am dying anyway?"

"You will lose your last chance. Méar, don't you trust me?"

"I don't, Ceann. You are demanding this because you are jealous of her. Well, now she has come back to me and she is not going to leave again. She is going to stay with me for the rest of my life."

Again, there was someone at the door. Liús was there with two identical bags. He offered them. "Do you want to know which one is the original, Mentor?" he asked.

"I don't care," he said. He took the bags. "You may go now."

Méar put the new skull carefully into its bag then gently placed it in his chest.

Your life will be longer if you listen to me.

Méar picked up the skull of his brother. "Ceann, if this is a trap then explain it to me. Or be quiet." He shoved Ceann's skull into the other bag. "I have made up my mind," he said.

When they had left the inn the serving-woman went over to the innkeeper. "What is the matter with you?" he demanded. "You have ignored guests all evening. You have just been sitting around."

"I think I'm going to be sick," the serving-woman replied.

"You'd better not be about to have another baby," the innkeeper grumbled. He looked at her. "Go on, then, go home. We will manage without you tonight."

"Thank you," the woman groaned. She staggered out into the night. Once she was out of sight of the Ocean and Star, she stood up more straight. She turned down an alley and into a small house. She bent over a sleeping form on a bed. The sleeping form was a woman identical to herself.

She sat down beside the sleeping woman and whispered Words of Power. Then she remembered the evening and used Eala's words to fill in a version of the night's events: including headaches and sickness but removing the conversations she had overheard. Then, when she was finished, she slipped back out into the alley.

By the time she had returned to the City she had returned to her true appearance. She whispered Words of Concealment then crept up the Hill into the Court of the Favourites and, from there, on to her own room.

Eibheara used the Words of Folding Space. The actual transition took less than a heartbeat even though it had taken the best part of a ten-day for her to decide that she ought to do it. She looked around her old room, half-expecting to see evidence that the other her was living in it, but everything was put away neatly and covered in a thin film of dust. She looked over at her shelf but her Wild Woman was still missing.

She opened the door. Liús and Cathúa were sitting by the fountain, eating breakfast. They were in blue cloaks but beneath she could see that he was naked and she wore nothing more than a white silk dress as short as a servant's tunic. Eibheara could see the emeralds in Cathúa's pendant glitter through the material. Seeing them together like that Eibheara realised that they were lovers.

Nobody else was in sight except servants. Neither Liús or Cathúa looked around. For a moment Eibheara wondered how they would react when they saw her. She considered closing the door again but Liús gathered his tray and stood up. There was a lot of food on his tray. He saw Eibheara as Eibheara saw that his cloak was open.

"Good morning," he said, without the slightest trace of guilt. He set the tray down by the edge of the fountain, gathered the cloak around him, and came over. "What are you doing back?"

"I'm a favourite, Liús. I was a favourite before your grandmother was born. I am Seventh Oldest."

"Sixth Oldest," answered Cathúa. "Éirime died, remember?"

"It turns out that Foscúil's cousin Rua is still alive somewhere deep in the Forest. So she is Third Oldest now and Foscúil is Second Oldest."

"Foscúil has a cousin?" Liús asked.

"She was in the 307th Year of the Sea People," Cathúa explained. "Foscúil Sponsored her when he was a five-year Veteran."

"Veteran in five years?" Eibheara asked.

"He was Immortal in nineteen," replied Cathúa. "Just as you'd expect."

"Expect?" asked Liús.

"There are two well-known paths to Immortality. One is to train Words of Power and the other is to train sword. Guess which one Foscúil followed."

"Eala was Veteran in her second year," Liús pointed out.

"Only just," Eibheara replied.

"If Eala had stayed with us we could have learned another path to Immortality through her," Cathúa said.

"What is that?" Eibheara retorted. "The 'steal the Mentor's Breath' path?"

"I think that, if she were still alive, she might have been able to help him. Remember what Foscúil did for Rian?"

"That is pointless speculation," Eibheara snapped. "I saw Aclaí cut her head off. I was close enough to see the fear in her eyes as she died. And good riddance to her." Eibheara turned and strode back into her room, being sure to slam the door behind her.

Cabairí had tried to call at the door but nobody had answered. The door was locked but in the end he used Words of Concealment and waited for the servants to come and go. Of course he didn't take much notice of the servants, so when he followed someone into Aclaí's room he was surprised to notice that it wasn't a servant he had followed.

"I brought you food," said Lá. Her baby was almost ready to be born and she was almost unable to take flight at all. Instead she waddled with a heavy tread.

"I'm not hungry," Aclaí replied.

Lá sat beside him on the bed and put her hand on his. "Please, my lord," she said. "Try to eat."

"I'm not hungry," Aclaí insisted. He rolled over and turned away from her. Lá sighed and walked back out of the room. By the time she had got to the door her natural Concealment had taken her out of Cabairí's awareness again.

"You should eat, my lord," said Cabairí.

Aclaí sat up. "What do you want?" he demanded.

"I'm more concerned about what you want, my lord," Cabairí replied.

"I just want to be left alone."

"It's funny, my lord, but that is not what I remember from the Visions a ten-day ago."

"I was angry."

"And what are you now?"

"I am less angry."

"Does that mean you have decided to forgive the Mentor, my lord?"

"I... it is not about forgiving the Mentor."

"You promised to cast the City down."

"And I will. But first I need some time."

"Your time is running out, my lord. Eala assembled a powerful group of Adepts who could make the difference for you: not just casting down the City but building the replacement for it. But they are leaderless."

"What do you expect me to do about that?"

"In that last night before her execution, what did Eala ask you to do?"

"How is that your business?"

"I am an Adept and one of Eala's mind-craft faction, my lord. I was in it right from the start: Eala was a purple Novice with us in the dormitories. So was Abhainne. We are the ones that first followed her. Now she is gone, we need to find someone else to follow – or we will be gone too."

"Why do you have to be gone?"

"They are grieving. If they don't have anything to keep them working, half of them will March on Chaos."

"I cannot see how that is my responsibility."

"It is your responsibility if Eala made you promise to do something. There are two beliefs about you and Eala and that last night. One is that you chose to make an example of her because you are a loyal follower of the City and the Mentor. The other is that, somehow, she passed her mission over to you. Given your appearance on the Visions at Éirime's funeral, most people are inclined to the second theory. But we don't know. So, my lord: did Eala ask you to promise to do anything after she was gone?"

"She did," Aclaí replied, bitterly. "She asked me to marry Éirime."

Cabairí was watching Aclaí's face enough to see that there was more. But he also saw the rest of Aclaí's body language. He stood up and walked to the door. Aclaí didn't see him close it behind him: he had already turned away again.

Eibheara didn't sit in her room for long before she heard someone at her door. She got up to answer.

Cathúa and the Mentor were waiting for her. "Can we come in?" Cathúa asked.

Eibheara stood back and they came in. Eibheara noticed that Cathúa positioned herself between them. After a few breaths of silent dance they ended up with the Mentor sat on Eibheara's chair, with Cathúa close by him on Eibheara's bed and Eibheara sat at the other end of the bed. Eibheara noticed that Cathúa was watching her, not him. The glittering emerald eyes of Cathúa's pendant also watched her accusingly through the thin silk of Cathúa's tunic.

"Why did you come back?" the Mentor asked.

"Don't ye want to start with the Words of Truthful Aura?" Eibheara sneered.

She saw the wrinkles around his forehead and mouth deepen a moment but she didn't see the green glare she expected. For a moment she felt his pain in her chest before it was consumed by anger. How did the whole City tolerate Initiation? Then she saw Cathúa's fingers move as she thought of her Silver Cord.

But the Mentor spoke again. "Eibheara, I want to understand. Aclaí has sworn to overthrow the City. We need to prepare for that."

"We also need to know what brought you back to the City," added Cathúa.

Eibheara looked at Cathúa, "Tell him about the Infiltrators," she said.

"Not that again," the Mentor sighed.

"Mentor," Cathúa answered, turning her back on Eibheara a moment, "I have met two at least. Lord Geal was an Infiltrator. So was Yanti."

The Mentor gestured and Cathúa looked back at Eibheara. "I still don't know what happened with Geal." He frowned. "Why *Lord* Geal, Cathúa?"

"He is Elder Immortal Rank, Mentor. I saw him fight Lord Aclaí and I am sure of it."

Eibheara shook her head. "Geal died in the Forest. In the far future dead Adepts will be resurrected and trained, then returned back to the moment of their death and –"

"Forbidden Art, Eibheara?"

"In the future Forbidden Art will not be so Forbidden. Elder Immortals are not bound by Initiation: they can perform Forbidden Art. That is why I left Aclaí, Mentor. I couldn't tolerate what he was doing with Forbidden Art."

"How do you claim to know about the future?"

"Mentor, you must have noticed that there are two of me?"

"She told me that you didn't know."

"Well, now she has told me herself. She is me but from the future. That is why she is Elder Immortal. She has come here to –"

Eibheara saw understanding cross the Mentor's face. And, a moment later, she saw the frown and the green flash of anger she had been waiting for. "So it is you who is responsible for all this?"

"It is not," Eibheara snapped back. "She is the leader of the Infiltrators but I am not. She has opposed me for my whole life and –"

"*What did you do with my wife?*" he yelled.

"Mentor, she doesn't know," Cathúa interjected. "She hasn't done it yet."

"How can she not know? We've both seen her in her Flyer, stealing Geanúile away from me."

"She doesn't remember because she hasn't done it yet. It is in her future even though it is in our past."

"It is in her past too. Why wouldn't she remember?"

"She hasn't done it yet. This is what time travel is like, Mentor. All she knows is what she has been told by her future self, or has inferred from her actions. It has happened in the past but she doesn't know it yet. Her future is entangled with our past."

"How do you know so much about it, Cathúa?"

"I did some experiments, Mentor. Remember Gruaige?"

"The servant-girl with my great grandmother's name?"

"She was your great grandmother, Mentor. I experimented sending someone back in time with the Words of Folding Space. She went too far. By the time I found her, ninety-two years before the City was founded, she had a husband. They had their first baby on the way."

"Yet you dared to make my great grandmother a servant girl? You dared to let me take her to my bed?"

"I didn't know then, Mentor. I knew that it was possible to travel through time, but why would I believe that a servant girl might do it?"

"Why believe that anyone could do it, Cathúa?"

"Eibheara used the Words of Identification on Yanti. As soon as we knew she was born in the future, we knew it must be possible to travel through time. That is why prophecy works: the thoughts of prophets overhear the thoughts of time travellers."

"I never Selected Yanti."

"You haven't Selected Yanti yet, Mentor. She will be born in the 7628th Year of the Sea People. So I would guess you will Select her sometime before 7650."

"If it is you doing Selections by then," Eibheara broke in. "Yanti tells us that there will be a City in the future. But she told us nothing about who the Mentor is."

"So Aclaí will be Mentor in the future?"

"We don't know who," said Cathúa. "It might be you. If someone wanted to replace you they would have to Initiate all of us."

"One Initiation doesn't cancel out another one," said Eibheara. "Both of them leave their brand on the heart."

There was a silence as Cathúa watched Eibheara. Finally she spoke. "Aclaí has been experimenting with Initiation?"

"I told ye," Eibheara responded. "I left because I was sick of his Forbidden Arts."

"So," said Cathúa, glancing back at the Mentor a moment, "When someone has the Words of Initiation used on them by two people, she can't choose one over another?"

"Of course not," said Eibheara.

"So both of them could trust her not to harm him?"

Eibheara's face became a little pink. "That is what I was saying. Are ye sure ye don't want the Words of Truthful Aura?"

"I don't need a Truthful Aura," Cathúa replied. She turned to the Mentor. "We can trust her."

"Good."

"She will not be able to help us oppose Lord Aclaí, though."

"Of course not." The Mentor turned to Eibheara. "You can stay," he said.

"Why?"

"Look around you, Eibheara. Only Liús and Cathúa remain. Éise is gone. Liús was gone for a long time. We need you. The Immortals are the strength of the City."

Eibheara's mouth tightened in anger as she felt her eyes prickle. "I cannot oppose him, Mentor."

"But we need to survive at least until he comes."

"Then I will stay."

He got up and shuffled to the door. "Eibheara," he said.

"Mentor."

"Thank you for coming back."

"It is nothing, Mentor."

"And, Eibheara?"

"What is it, Mentor?"

"I am sorry we didn't believe you about the Infiltrators."

After the door had closed, Cathúa spoke to Eibheara. "I am sorry too," she said.

"I understand. It is hard to trust me with her interfering."

"It is much easier now we understand," Cathúa replied. "But that wasn't what I meant. I am sorry for all the things that have happened to you."

"And all the things that will happen to me, I suppose," Eibheara shrugged. "It is my destiny, I suppose."

"And all the things that will happen to all of us," Cathúa replied. "Time travel is a horrible thing."

"I see that Aclaí is not the only one who has been messing about with Forbidden Arts, Cathúa."

"Things are breaking down in the City, Eibheara."

"What about you? You have been reading Eala's book."

"We all have. The Mentor's happiness is the only thing that can keep him alive, now. We break his rules because we love him."

They both heard someone at the door and looked around with the same hope. "Come in," Cabairí called. The door to his room opened and Míne looked down at him and Innealta sitting beside him. "Did he talk to you, then?" Míne demanded.

"He did," Cabairí replied.

"And?"

"I was right. Eala did get him to promise something."

"What was it? Did she appoint him the new leader?"

"I still think she did, but that wasn't the thing he told me. He told me something else but I could see he didn't tell me everything."

"What did he tell you?"

"He told me that she asked him to marry Éirime."

"*Cac*, Cabairí!" Míne exclaimed. "*Cac us fuil!*"

"What is it?" Cabairí asked.

"Don't you see what has happened?"

"I'm afraid I don't. What is the problem?"

Innealta spoke. "Eala was trying to protect her sister. Geana was Éirime's maidservant."

"So Eala got a promise out of Aclaí," added Míne. "But it wasn't for us."

"Oh," Cabairí said.

"That is what has happened to him," Míne explained. "That is why he has lost his mind. If Eala was trying to protect her sister she will have done everything she could. They were closer than any family I have seen."

"Because they were twins?" Cabairí asked.

"Because they were both immortal," Luaith explained. "Because they were twins but also their last links to their own childhoods. All of our families are dead but they had each other. Eala will have done everything in her power to make sure Aclaí got to marry Éirime and protect her maidservant – Eala's sister."

"We've always acknowledged that the Mind Craft could be used for ill as well as good," added Míne.

"Are you calling Geana and Eala evil?" Innealta demanded. "They were –"

"Of course she wasn't evil," Míne replied, "but the outcome is the same: Eala's craft, Eala's Gift, concentrated on one goal. And then he arrives to discover Éirime's body and Geana gone. His mind has fractured under the strain. He is not of any use to any of us."

She turned and closed the door behind her.

"Have we lost her?" asked Innealta.

Cabairí smiled a sad smile. "I think we have."

"I guess it's about loyalty. She loved Eala."

"What about you?"

"I was... I will stay and look after Aclaí."

"What if Aclaí never comes out of his room?"

"Well, I will wait for him. And, while I wait for him, help to conserve his power here."

"Against the City?"

"Who else?"

The Patrol was on its assigned route when one of the scouts appeared. She was sitting in a high tree, breathing hard, with her wingtips still trembling. "There are blue-robes," she said. "They're riding up to the Cloud Forest Path."

"Are they headed to the Table Clearing?" The Patrol leader knew that the Table Clearing was somewhere that attracted Lady Eala's followers. He wondered what they would call themselves now that Lady Eala was dead.

"They're certainly on the right path," the scout agreed.

"Let's go," said their leader, turning off the path and into the deep woods. The rest of the Patrol fell in behind him.

The Forest paths to the Table Clearing were mostly uphill and the Patrol leader took his time. The archers were on foot and, although they were out of sight, he still did not want to leave them behind.

By the time they reached their destination the blue-robes had already got there. The Patrol leader saw that there were only three of them but they were led by an Immortal. He put his hand on his own sword-hilt.

"This is Patrol Forty-Two," he thought. "We are at the Table Clearing and there are three Adepts here. They are led by a Seventeenth Rank."

i will find lord foscúil came the reply. *monitor their movements but do not engage* There was a brief pause. *patrol twenty-three reports two more are coming up the trail*

In the clearing the three Adepts spoke as they waited. "I feel we are being watched," Míne said.

"I doubt it," Iasc said. "We're just nervous. Foscúil's Patrols don't bother sneaking and stalking. If there were any of them around us we'd know by now. They would have challenged us, like they did on the Blue Peaks trail."

Míne shuddered as she remembered what had happened there, but that was what they were doing in the Forest after all.

"Why are we worrying?" asked Imir. "Foscúil says that, once you accept death, there is nothing to fear."

"Perhaps if you are Foscúil," said Míne.

"I don't know about fear," Iasc said. "But these last days I have felt more alive than I have since she died."

"I understand that, cousin," agreed Imir. "I still miss her but it used to be like carrying a weight."

"That is the fear of death," said Míne. "It is something to shift the sadness."

"When Lady Eala invited us out of Retirement," Iasc began, "She said that –"

Two more riders came out from under the trees. The Seventeenth Rank drew her sword and raised it high in salute. The other two rode up.

Luaith and Broc saluted back. Míne looked beyond them and whispered Words. Then she found her armour on her Silver Cord and kicked her heels. Her sword remained high but she swept it forward to indicate the space behind the new arrivals. "You were followed!" she shouted. "It's a trap!"

Luaith and Broc had to turn their horses but Imir and Iasc rode straight past. Míne's horse balked at passing and she could only watch as they slammed into riders coming up the trail. Suddenly the air was filled with the swish of arrows as they passed and the clatter as they bounced off armour. Míne pulled her faceplate down. The arrows were coming from every direction: they were surrounded. She spoke Words of Summoning to call a Manifestation of Fire to surround them. She swept the sword around and the bushes around the clearing exploded into flame. She felt her horse panic beneath her and she Breathed forward, placing her other hand on the horse's neck.

Ahead of them Iasc and Imir were using all the Words they knew. Words of Ice to freeze them; Words of Fear to drive them away; Words of Shaping to make them harmless. But their minds lost concentration and their Breath faded, even if they were Immortals. They found themselves side-by-side, surrounded by three Patrols. Then they found themselves back to back. Then Imir felt Iasc stumble.

He turned around. Iasc was lying at his feet, struggling to remove an arrow that had gone in under the helm. It must have been tipped with Metal. "Sister!" he shouted, as he fell to his knees to help. But the enemies behind him ran up and struck with spears as he bent over. Imir felt the blow and fell forward onto Iasc. He just had time to notice that Iasc was limp before it was over.

The Patrols that survived did not stop to gather their dead. They ran up the trail to catch the rest of the Adepts. As they ran most of them became naturally concealed. It did not stop them working together. They were Mountain People: they knew how to work together with concealment.

Cabairí was saying his Words of Freshness when he felt his sword-hilt. He found the sword on his Silver Cord and put his hand on the hilt. It was Foscúil.

"What do you want?" Cabairí thought.

i wanted some advice came the reply. *are you in your room*

"I am."

i will come to you

Cabairí finished getting dressed, opened the shutters and tidied the bed a little. He heard Foscúil at the door. "Come in," he called. "It's not bolted."

Foscúil opened the door cautiously. "Good morning," he smiled. "You are very trusting for one of us."

"Because I don't lock my door?"

"How do you know someone won't come into your room while you are asleep?"

"What if they do?"

"They might kill you, Cabairí."

"Immortality doesn't mean living forever, Foscúil. My sword teacher encourages me not to fear death."

"He certainly doesn't encourage you to welcome it into your bedchamber."

"Perhaps not. But, if death comes calling in the night, who am I to care?"

Foscúil's smile had gone. "What is with this place? Does her loss make so much difference?"

"Have you seen much of Lord Aclaí recently?"

"Well, some of us still have ambitions to motivate us."

"Good. What are your motivations, Foscúil?"

"I want to help Aclaí cast down the City."

"Why?"

"What happened to Abhainne. And what happened to so many others. Do you know I have a cousin, Cabairí? She ran away into the Forest as soon as she got Sixteenth Rank. Nobody knew where she went, but she swore she would have nothing more to do with any of us until the Mentor's heart was as broken as hers."

"When did she Retire?"

"Autumn of 386. I assumed she would be dead."

"How do you know she isn't if she has nothing to do with us?"

"She used the sword-hilt. She told me that we shouldn't execute Eala. She said that Aclaí should take Eala and Éirime and run deep into the Forest."

"Why didn't ye?"

"Aclaí said that Eala refused to go." Foscúil smiled a wry smile. "Rua knew she would refuse. Her prophet told her to tell me that Eala would have to be taken by force."

"Because she refused to go?"

"Rua knew. She told me to force Eala before I passed the message on to Aclaí."

"Is she like Yanti?"

"She had never heard of Yanti. She had never heard of Eibheara, even. She Retired two centuries before Eibheara was born. She cannot have anything to do with Eibheara's Infiltrators. Her prophet knew Eala. He Retired when Eala fled the City. Many Retired at that time. If they knew Eala's Art there were three choices: Retire; join with Eala; or let the Mentor kill them."

"Or March," added Cabairí.

"Or March," conceded Foscúil.

"What advice did you want to ask?"

"Did you know we are using Eala's Art to make the warriors more effective?"

"I did."

"I want to strengthen the effect. I want them to be more effective with less leadership. You studied Eala's Art, Cabairí. How would you weaken the link to their leaders without weakening their effectiveness?"

"Why are you asking this, Foscúil?" Cabairí frowned. "Are you considering leading them without Aclaí?"

"We don't know if he will ever come out of his room."

"We don't. So you want to be able to strengthen their ability to follow without linking it to one person? You are looking for an alternative to what Initiation does in the City, but one that can be transferred from one leader to another?"

"I wasn't interested in the City," Foscúil replied. "But I suppose that, if the City wasn't doomed to fall, it could have been applied."

Cabairí shrugged. "What you need is a way to build loyalty into their identities but attached to a group rather than a leader. Eibheara did something similar with her Orphans."

"But Eibheara's Orphans were started as children. We don't have time."

"Then we need to destroy the identities from their childhoods before replacing it with the identities we want them to have."

Foscúil laughed. "What would Eala have thought of that?"

"I would think she would have thought it was the most despicable evil imaginable."

"Yet you think you can do it?"

"It is normal in the City. Initiation damages our identities every bit as much. I have lived with it most of my life."

"Can you do it even if you believe it is wrong?"

"I can. The rest of Eala's followers have surrendered and are going to March. But I have too much anger at the way of the City to surrender to anything."

"Are you sure?"

"I am sure, Foscúil," replied Cabairí. "I have lost too many friends to the City's evil ways. Abhainne was my friend too."

But Foscúil wasn't listening. His sword-hilt was demanding his attention.

Mountain people have long legs but they are not good at running. The three of them, the remains of their Patrol, were in trouble. The three could not evade their blue-robe hunters even using their natural concealment, so they ran into the mountains, climbing and hiding. The three archers had sniped at their pursuers until their arrows were exhausted but now there was not any choice. All they could do now was run up into the high Forest and hope the Maoineas could find a big enough force to rescue them.

The Adepts that pursued them had realised that horses were slowing them down in the high country and they had abandoned them. Instead they used Words of Shaping and Words of Extension. Míne had taken the form of a dragon and rode the winds four thousand man-heights above the hills, finding the waves of air that broke over the mountains to keep her bulk aloft. With Words of Far Seeing, her keen draconic eyesight and Words of True Sight she followed the movement of their quarry while she used the sword-hilt clutched in one fore-claw to communicate with the rest of her group.

Luaith looked up at her, shading his eyes with his hand.

"Is she safe up there?" Broc asked.

"We're Marching," Luaith replied. "Does it matter?"

"I remember when Marching meant attacking creatures of the Forest," Broc observed. "These are one of Aclaí's Patrols, aren't they?"

"I believe they are," agreed Luaith. "But, if they insist on getting between us and the creatures of the Forest, what mercy can they expect? They have not shown mercy to the City's patrols."

Broc grunted his agreement. They carried on climbing, picking their way from tree to tree. The archers had stopped firing at them, but they could not be certain that a last arrow wasn't held for a perfect shot. A shadow among the trees above them moved and they both looked up. The dragon that was Míne stooped down from the sky and landed heavily among the broken rocks. The wind of her landing made the branches above them thrash around and scattered dirt and pine-needles over Luaith and Broc. By the time they looked back she was back in human form, with her armour and her blue cloak on.

"This way," she said. "There is some kind of pass above us and they have gone through that."

"Why did you land, then?" Luaith demanded.

"I think they Forest-walked," Míne replied.

"Patrols don't come this way," said Luaith.

"How can we follow them safely?" asked Broc.

"The path is easy to follow," said Luaith. "We won't lose them."

The puffed and blew their way up into the notch, scrambling among the tree-roots and rocks. Their lungs struggled for breath. The trees that grew there only survived because of the equatorial Sun overhead and the wild magic of the Forest. Finally they came over the last rise and started to descend. They saw light shining between the trees, ahead and below.

It was a cliff. The three friends stood at the edge, expecting to look down a valley. But instead they saw a whole land beneath them. The lofty mountain they stood on was part of a whole range of mountains. Behind the mountain peaks they saw a sheer wall of green Metal, rising up until its brightness was lost in the sky and stretching away right and left. Before them was lower-lying land. They looked down on the blue of atmosphere with cloud-icebergs floating in it and a bottom of fields and moors, trees, rivers and oceans. There was not any horizon. The land stretched out before them, flat, but either side it gently curved up to a vanishing point at left and right. From the vanishing point a thin ribbon of blue rose up, alternating between sky-blue and a dark indigo, thinning as it soared to a bright thread until it seemed to touch the Sun's disc.

"What is this place?" asked Broc.

"I don't know," said Luaith.

Míne shaded her eyes as she looked at the arch above them using her Words of Far Seeing. "It is too far away," she said. "It is nearly as far away as the Red World. It goes right behind the Sun."

"How can it?" demanded Broc.

"I don't know," she said. She pointed ahead of them, to the sharp line where the blue of the sky below them became the darker blue of the sky above them. "I still have the Words of Far Seeing and, when I look out that way, I am looking four times further away than the Moon."

"That's impossible," said Broc. "If that were true, that valley below us would be more than a hundred years' march to the other side."

"We should tell the Leader of Patrols," said Luaith.

"Tell them quick," said Broc, looking up. "Use the Words of Vision."

Luaith looked around as he kept his hand on his sword-hilt. Foscúil, Innealta and Miotal stood under the trees. What shall I tell them, he thought, as he concentrated on the City's Patrol Leader.

"Míne," said Innealta. "It is Míne, isn't it?"

"What do ye want?" Míne asked.

"Will ye surrender?" she asked. "Ye could turn and go back to the City."

Míne looked at Foscúil. "Is that the orders ye have been given?"

"We have been ordered to find Eala's followers," Foscúil told her. "But Innealta tells me that ye are nothing to do with her."

"We are Marching," said Broc.

Foscúil laughed. "I am hardly a creature of chaos," he said.

"This land is free of creatures of chaos," said Miotal. "In fact it is something of a credit to your ability to walk the Forest that you have even got here."

"Because this is an artificial land?" Míne asked.

"Wrong answer," said Foscúil. He drew his sword.

"It is the right answer," Broc said. "It is called a *March on Chaos*, Foscúil, but that is not the original point of the Tradition. The *March on Chaos* is actually a march on the enemies of the City."

"That's right," said Luaith. "It is a march on the enemies of humanity."

"I think it is time to dispute with your swords, not your tongues," said Foscúil.

"I don't care for any dispute," Míne replied. "Your master killed the best friend I ever had."

Foscúil shrugged. *"Immortality does not mean living forever."* He raised his sword in salute.

The three of them saluted back. Foscúil lowered the point of his sword and walked towards them. He did not run but, as he walked, he Breathed ahead of himself. Míne shifted her weight. She didn't quite see what happened next but it seemed to her that Luaith stepped forwards straight on to Foscúil's sword-point. A hands-width of the blade protruded from the back of his neck-hole.

Broc swung his sword at Foscúil's head as Luaith's falling body trapped Foscúil's blade. Míne jumped around and lunged at him.

Somehow he wiggled out of the way and, as he twisted in mid-air, he pulled Broc's wrist. Míne's sword slid across Broc's breastplate and narrowly avoided entering under his arm. Broc whirled around, sword stretched, to follow Foscúil's movement. He knew that Foscúil had left his sword in Luaith's body and rushed forward to take that advantage.

Foscúil batted Broc's blade aside and then grabbed the visor of his helm. Broc's whole movement shifted as Foscúil twisted his head. Then Foscúil's sword was in his hand, drawn by his Silver Cord. Broc's body fell and Foscúil turned to Míne. He dropped the head at his feet.

Míne raised her own visor so Foscúil could see her face. Knowing that she could not defeat him with the sword she whispered Words. She smiled her best body language at him and saw how he reacted. His sword-point lowered. She reached out her arms, inviting him to stand down.

She felt the blow to the back of her neck and, as she fell forward, everything went disorientatingly wrong. The dirt bounced against her cheek and she rolled over.

Foscúil shook his head to clear his thoughts. *"Cac,"* he swore. "She almost had me there."

"She did have you there," said Innealta, shaking the blood droplets off her sword. "These mind-craft types are sneaky."

* * *

Liús closed the shutters then drew aside the curtain in front of the Gateway he had made. He lifted the basket and stepped into another world. The curtain fell back behind him. In the darkness he found his family's bed. He whispered Words of Seeing Heat then put the basket down. He could see his wife's warmth in the darkness and the bright little shape of his daughter.

"My lion?" Éise whispered.

"I'm here."

"Did you bring food?"

Liús picked up his wife's hand and placed it on the basket. She sat up carefully then unpacked things by touch. She began to eat. Her other hand found his leg. "Thank you, my brave lion," she whispered. "What is happening in the City?"

"Míne Marched, dear heart," he replied. "She took over a hundred of them with her."

"A hundred of who?"

"Eala's followers."

"There were a hundred of them left?"

"According to Cathúa there are over five hundred unaccounted for."

"I bet she gave you an exact number."

"She didn't, dear heart. She gave me a maximum and minimum number, then discussed the reliability of the accounts of their ends."

"So how did they end? Or are they still out there?"

"They met their end. We don't know where or how. Their accounts are consistent but nobody understands them. They transferred Visions back."

"Blátha went with them?"

"She didn't. She is one of the ones that are not accounted for. Cathúa looked at the Visions and... well, I've never seen someone so clearly despair."

"Didn't you say that Cathúa is full of despair anyway?"

"Not exactly despair. She still organises Patrols and the City's defence, which isn't despair. But she believes, all the way to the bottom of her heart, that the City will fall and that she will die defending it."

"How long does she expect it to take?"

"I am not sure because I can't flat-out ask her a date. She probably knows that we studied Eala's Art, but we still cannot offer her definite proof. We don't know what she would do. You know how literal she can be about things. But from what I have heard her say and how I have heard her say it, the way she reacts when I talk about dates or about plans, I doubt she expects the City to last five years."

"As long as that, then?" Liús thought Éise might be laughing.

"She talks of plans for Celebration Days and the Selection without too much concern. But she is not interested in plans to teach Novices to become Immortals, for example. She is willing to lecture but not to change the curriculum. She doesn't expect it to matter."

"Why is she despairing?"

"Because... Éise, dear heart, she claims that she has used Words of Folding Space to travel through time."

"How does that work?"

"She says that the past and future are just another direction, like up and down or east and west. She also says it is very hard to do it accurately."

"So she travelled into the future."

"She told me that she travelled back. But she talked about the future. She says the Eibheara with the strong Immortal Breath is from the future. Her Immortal Breath is strong because she is seven thousand years old."

"Which is why she came to the Battle of the Blue Peaks?"

"Of course it is."

"What does that mean about Cathúa's fears for the City? Why is...?" then Éise stopped as she realised. "Oh," she said. "Oh *cac us fuil*, Liús. She is despairing because she knows the future."

"She is not only despairing because she knows the future. She told me how she interpreted Míne's Visions. She said that the simplest explanation of Míne's observations was a flat world."

"Like Anleacán?"

"Anleacán is a slab: a tiny chip of Metal drifting around a star. Cathúa suggested that Míne might have met her end on a world that is a ribbon ten thousand times wider than Anleacán, and stretched out the other way to encircle the whole star. She said that ten thousand million Anleacáns could be cut out of that ribbon."

"Didn't Aclaí make Anleacán?"

"He did. And Cathúa presumes he made this thing too."

"Why? Is it just ego?"

"Anleacán has a population of about a thousand people. Ten thousand million Anleacáns might have a population of ten million million people. Take one person from each village and recruit them into a warrior band –"

"How can we possibly hope to resist that?"

"I don't think we can. And neither can Cathúa. Which is why she is despairing."

* * *

"Lá, are you sure you want to do this?" Bánúa asked again.

"I am sure. Diase will look after the family if he kills me."

"What about your baby?"

"Diase has milk from her own baby. She will share with her little brother or sister."

"What if he kills both of ye?"

"I don't care anymore, Bánúa. The only place we have as a people is the place he gives us. He is obsessed with death and thinks life is without meaning. Maybe I can show him the true meaning of life."

"But it would be better if it was someone else. You know why he is grieving. It could put you in danger."

"Or it could keep me out of danger. Bánúa, do you think he will put another baby in me this summer?"

"Not the way he has been this last month. But, Lá, you know how much you remind him of her."

"Maybe that is what he needs now."

"It's too big a risk," said Bánúa. "Look, the things he will see will not help. He will see more pain and more blood. I don't think that is what he needs now."

"We have to do something."

"Wait, Lá. When we have our children we will bring them to him. It is good to remind him that he is a father. But after the children are born is the best time."

"All right then," she agreed. "But it had better work."

"It will," assured Bánúa.

"How can you be sure? You might look like her but you don't have her talent any more than I have Lady Éirime's."

"It will."

The four of them sat together and shared a meal even if their master was not there to share it with them. They ate without talking for a little while: they knew each other well enough.

It was Damhánalla who broke the silence. "Ye three were in the Forest today," she said.

"A group of Adepts Marched," said Miotal. "They found their way to the Rim."

"How did that happen?" Damhánalla asked.

"I think they may have been avoiding our own Patrols," Foscúil answered.

"Well, perhaps we are dealing with Adepts who March in the wrong way," said Innealta. "Perhaps we should order our own Patrols to fall back and let them through."

"It might have been a good idea in this case," agreed Foscúil. "We lost twelve platoons of warriors."

"Isn't that a threat to us?" asked Damhánalla. "You have tried to prepare for a counter-attack."

"It wasn't the counter-attack," said Foscúil. "There were a lot of Immortals, though. The Patrols brought back five swords, including an Seventeenth Rank."

"Is the City testing our defences?" asked Miotal.

"They didn't come from the City," said Innealta. "The Seventeenth Rank was Míne. They were Eala's followers."

"Why would they do that?" Damhánalla asked.

"Despair," said Innealta. "Míne was always Eala's organiser."

"She could have led them," objected Damhánalla.

"She did lead them," said Foscúil. "They got as far as the Rim. The City Patrols never got that far."

"I mean that she could have done something useful with her life."

"It's hard when people despair," said Innealta. "I know you are strong, Damhánalla, but not everybody has your strength."

"Then they should. What is the point of having Immortal Rank and behaving like that? Doesn't anyone have any control over their emotions?"

"Like Lord Aclaí?" asked Miotal.

Damhánalla looked away.

"What do you think we should do about him?" asked Foscúil.

"Give him time," said Innealta. "He is hurting and he won't let anyone close enough to help."

"What if the City attacks?" asked Damhánalla. "We might not have time."

"Don't worry about that," said Foscúil. "Míne's Patrol was more Immortals than the City can find. There is only Eibheara, Éise, Liús and Cathúa."

"That is three Eighteenth-Ranks," said Miotal. "If Eibheara is in her other mind then she is much higher Rank. I don't know we could resist an Elder Immortal without Lord Aclaí."

"I don't worry about them," said Foscúil. "Éise and Liús don't really have the motivation to defend the City. They will run. Besides, Aclaí has her loyalty – and Eibheara's. I don't think they could fight him. So Cathúa would be the only enemy we would have to face. And she got to be Eighteenth Rank only by default: she spent centuries on the top of the Hill hiding in her library. I'm not scared of Cathúa."

"What about the Key of Creation?" asked Damhánalla. "If the Mentor was to lay his hand on that and wish for us –"

"There is nothing we can do to meet that threat," said Foscúil. "He could wish us all out of existence tomorrow."

"So you don't care?" asked Innealta.

"What point is there in caring if we can't change it? Immortality doesn't mean living forever." Foscúil laughed. "There are things we can change and preparations we can make. We should focus on those changes."

"What about him?" asked Miotal.

"Well, we could just contain the City until the Mentor dies," said Foscúil.

"Is that your plan?" asked Damhánalla.

"My plan is to wait and see for a while. But eventually I will intervene."

"How long?"

"I'll give him until the end of this month – until the end of Winter. But, if he's still shut in there when the Lost Days come, I'm going to go up there and get him out."

"Mentor?" Cathúa called.

He opened the door and looked around before he let her in. She was wearing a dress that gathered around an elaborate knot between her breasts. Her little cat pendant sat on the knot, watching him with glittering emerald eyes. He looked down at her empty hands. "Did you bring the books?" he asked.

She looked around. "I have them," she said. "I don't let anyone take the Forbidden Arts out of my library, Mentor, but I think we should keep them. If we destroy the last copy we will never be able to get it back. And, Mentor, we never know what the enemies of the City might one day use –"

"Cathúa," he said, "that is exactly the point. I need to be aware of what the Forbidden Arts can do, even if I don't practice them."

"Only one of them is Forbidden Art, Mentor."

"I assumed it was three copies of the one book," he answered. "Let me see."

She took them with her Silver Cord and gave them to him. He turned them over in his hands. *Human Motivation* he read. He swapped them over before he could spend too long looking at her name. *On the Culture of Úll Oileán* was the title of the next one. He pointed at it.

"This is the third one?" he asked.

"It is, Mentor."

"How did you come by it?"

"Um... Lord Aclaí sent me a copy. It doesn't describe the Mind Craft, Mentor. It assumes you already know the Mind Craft to make sense of it. The discussion in it is full of those Motivational Charts she used to use."

"Why did she study Úll Oileán, Cathúa?"

"I don't know, Mentor. But my servant met her there."

"Grandmother Gruaige?"

"That was her, Mentor. Of course I didn't know she was your ancestor. She met the Favourite and her sister. They were disguised as peasants but the description of them is very clear. Gruaige had the Gift of Anleacán and somehow they recognised one another."

"Cathúa," he asked, "Can I ever trust Eibheara again?"

"Why couldn't you, Mentor?"

"Because Aclaí has used Words of Initiation on her."

"So have you, Mentor. As I understand it we cannot enlist her help to protect the City... yet."

"Yet?"

"Mentor, one day she will be Elder Immortal. Then she would be able to defy Aclaí. But then you will not be able to trust the Initiation."

"Perhaps the Elder Immortal Eibheara will come back to save us."

"I don't think so, Mentor."

"You said she saved us at the Battle of the Blue Peaks, Cathúa."

"I did."

"Then why can't she do it again?"

"I... she didn't, Mentor. She won't."

She saw disbelief on his face battle with disappointment. She wasn't sure which one had won. "Go now," he told her.

As she closed the door behind her he opened Eala's last book.

Don't do that, said Ceann from inside his bag.

"I will," he whispered. "I want to know what she said about me."

It will only hasten your end.

"Ceann, what secrets are you trying to keep from me?"

I am trying to protect you, Méar. That is all I have ever tried to do – to protect you.

But he didn't believe it anymore. He began to read.

Lost Days

Aclaí was sitting on his balcony and staring out at the horizon. In front of him he could see the tower that Damhánalla had built for him and, beyond it, he could see smoke rising from the celebration fire of Áthaiteorainn. He listened to the distant music from Áthaimínn and remembered watching the smoke rise on that horizon from the funeral pyre. It was the First Lost Day of Spring but to him every day was lost.

He heard someone at the door again. Idly he noticed that he ought to reply but he could not find any way to care enough. He wondered if they would dare to come in uninvited. How would he react if they did? Did he care enough even to –

"Lord Aclaí?"

He carried on looking out, seeing the smoke rise with the slow, silent precision of a snail. He heard the seat beside him creak then felt a hand take his fingers.

"Lord Aclaí," Miotal's voice came again, nearer. "Please, Lord Aclaí."

He knew he should move his head. For a heartbeat he rehearsed the muscles he would have to move and thought reluctantly of how his body would feel. Then he looked down. His left hand was held in thin brown fingers. He looked up into Miotal's eyes.

Disinterestedly he noted what Miotal was doing with his hands. Aclaí was surprised his body still responded to the old tricks Miotal used. But it was as if it was happening to someone else – to someone who cared.

"Stop there!" the Mountain Warrior called out. He stepped into the Forest path in front of the old woman. Behind him his band were there: two archers like himself; four Forest Warrior and, somewhere, a Midsummer Person.

The old woman lurched towards him until she was close enough that he could smell her. She looked up and her breath hit him: stale wine and decay. "What you want?" she demanded. "What you want with me?"

"Nothing," he said, recoiling. "Go your way."

He watched her stagger away along the Forest path and wondered if he should order them to follow or if he should leave her for the Forest monsters to eat. The way she was going had few Forest monsters anyway, he told himself. She was walking away from the perimeter.

And so he lived to see another day.

The old woman staggered up to the tree and squinted up and down the path. She found an earthenware jar from somewhere and removed the stopper to take a deep draught. Refreshed, she hid the jar under a bush. Then she climbed into the bush herself.

A short way further along she found one of the tributaries that led to the great river. A fisherman standing like a statue with spear upraised turned his eyeballs to see her as she tottered from tree to tree, hoping she wouldn't come too near the water and scare the fish. She found the jar again, unstoppered it and raised it to show him. Then she drank deep again before she disappeared back into the trees.

At the bank of the river near the village women were washing clothes. They saw her come up to the riverbank and attempt to cross the fallen tree that provided the bridge into the village.

"Hey," one of them called, "Where are you going?"

"See Blátha," the old woman slurred.

"Is *Lady* Blátha expecting you?"

"Leave her alone," one of the other women called out to her companion. "If she makes it across the bridge then Lady Blátha can deal with her. But I think she will fall in."

"Falling in might improve her appearance," suggested another.

"And her smell," a third one laughed.

They went back to their washing but, as the stranger took her first unsteady step onto the bridge, they all watched. They were disappointed to see that, even if her step was so erratic, somehow the drunken stranger found enough balance to cross the bridge without getting wet.

"Is this wise?" Innealta asked again.

"He knows what he is doing," Damhánalla replied. "Miotal has served Aclaí for nine hundred years."

"Better that Miotal tries to stir him with love than that I go up there and try to stir him with a sword," Foscúil laughed.

The three of them were sitting around a table. The doors were open to the gardens. The breeze brought scents of blossom on the trees and the distant music of the village, where they celebrated the First Lost Day of Spring. Two places at the table were unoccupied but the servants were still bringing in food. Although the smell of the food made them all hungry none of them made any attempt to begin.

"Is that the backup plan?" Innealta asked. "To go up there and challenge him with a sword?"

"It's all I know how to do," replied Foscúil. "It's up to the rest of ye to deal with matters of the heart."

"You studied Eala's Art, didn't you?" Damhánalla said.

"I was taught a lot by her sister," Innealta answered.

"Her peasant sister?"

"How can a peasant teach Forbidden Art?" laughed Innealta. "Peasants are harmless, everyone knows that."

Foscúil just smiled. If Damhánalla was going to offer a reply she never got a chance. The door opened and Miotal led Aclaí in. All three of them looked around with concern on their faces. Innealta got up and went over to him. She led him to a seat and found a bowl for him.

"I'm not hungry," he said.

"They've made the spiced pork you like, my lord," she said, as she took the lid off the pot.

"I'm not hungry."

Foscúil looked a question at Miotal and Miotal nodded agreement.

Damhánalla spoke. "When did you last eat, my lord?"

"The servants brought me a bowl of pottage yesterday evening."

"And they took it back to the kitchen still full. You have to eat, my lord."

Aclaí looked at Damhánalla. "Have you been spying on me?" he demanded.

"We care about you," Innealta interrupted, taking his fingers.

He froze. Then he looked down at her hands. "Innealta," he asked, "Do you remember where you learned to do that?"

"Geana taught me," she replied.

"You know that Eala used to do that?"

"I hardly knew Eala, my lord. I was never taught anything by her." Innealta looked at his face and tried to read the signs. "I know you miss Caora, my lord, but –"

"Eala taught me."

"I know."

"I was taught the Mind Craft by the best, Innealta. Do not presume that you can replace Eala."

"I never thought that I could, my lord. But can't I help my friend?"

"By treating me like some difficult toddler that won't eat his supper?"

"My lord, I –"

"That's enough," interrupted Foscúil. "Innealta is trying to help you, my lord. If she is treating you like a difficult toddler it is only because you are acting like one."

Aclaí stood up suddenly, upending the table and spilling everything on the floor. Innealta stepped back off her stool and Damhánalla spun away on her knees to avoid the tide of food and crockery. Aclaí turned towards Foscúil with his sword in his hand. "You are still the same insolent lad that you were when I first met you," he growled.

Foscúil stood his ground. When he spoke, his voice was still calm. "Of course I am, my lord," he answered. "Maturity doesn't make us into different people. At best it gives us the experience to be what we truly are more effectively."

"I should have killed you then."

"Perhaps," Foscúil smiled. "Perhaps you can correct that mistake, my lord. But there are very few of us Adepts who have the Gift of Anleacán left and if you don't know why our Order needs us you need to pay more attention." Aclaí made to move towards Foscúil. Foscúil reached his fingers and his own sword was in his hand. "Even if you don't know why the Gift is important to the City you ought to remember the nature of my Gift."

"Do you dare to challenge me?" Aclaí demanded.

"Challenge you to what? Actually do the thing you promised the world that you would do? Or maybe just get out of bed in the morning?"

Aclaí's swing was wild, over his head and through the space Foscúil had occupied an instant before. Foscúil stepped close and pinched Aclaí's nose. "Look at you," he said. "Twenty-Fourth Rank and can't control his temper."

Aclaí swung again and Foscúil danced backwards out of the doorway and into the garden. The sword-blade smashed into the upright supporting the door lintel. The blade sliced into the stone and, with a roar of falling masonry, the whole lot gave way. Behind him Aclaí heard Innealta make a noise that might have been a stifled scream. He saw the lintel fall, so slowly but too fast for him to move the sword-point out of the way. His weight was on his front foot and there wasn't time to shift. He felt the impact as the lintel swept the sword-hilt out of his hand, then as it hit his shin and foot.

Damhánalla ran forwards as the roof stones landed around him. Aclaí tried to pull his leg back. His foot was trapped and he felt the flexibility in his lower leg. The shinbone must be shattered. "*Cac!*" he swore to himself.

Beyond the dust he heard Foscúil's laughter. "Nicely done, my lord!"

He found his sword on his Silver Cord again. One good blow separated his own leg a hands-width below the knee, and the Words of Restoration provided him with a new foot. His Silver Cord provided armoured boots and gauntlets as he clambered over the fallen stone. When he saw Foscúil the Words that Stop Time provided the opportunity to lay hands on that sly fox.

But Damhánalla sat back down on her seat and looked around her. This was not the first celebration since he had retired to his room. What was it that triggered him off, today of all days, she wondered.

"Éirime!" Blátha had seen the woman fall as she tried to jump between the houses and she ran over to help. As she ran she felt foolish. Of course Éirime was dead. The old woman just reminded her of her lost lover. She knelt beside the woman lying on the porch. The woman had straight blonde hair shot through with white, accented by her yellowish skin. She rolled over onto one side. Her feet were covered in mud up to her knees and she had only one sandal. Her hair and dress was crusted with vomit. The smell of it burned in Blátha's nostrils. But it was Éirime. "*Cac,*" she swore. "What has happened to you?"

Blue eyes opened. The whites were yellow at the corners. "Hide," she slurred. "Got to hide."

Blátha whispered Words of Freshness then Words of Strength. She picked her up and carried her lightly into the house. She sat her down, propped up in a deep chair, and knelt beside her. "What is the matter with you, love?"

"Got to hide," Éirime whispered. Then she started to laugh. The laughter somehow became sobbing.

Blátha lifted her chin. "You are in a bad way, beloved. Look at me."

Éirime looked at her. "Used to know you," she said. "Got to hide from you."

"Sing with me."

"Mustn't sing. Give it away."

Blátha drew breath and began to sing, looking into Éirime's eyes. And then Éirime sang back. At first her voice was tuneless and cracked but, in just a couple of Breaths, the strength of her voice returned. Blátha led her and they finished the song together.

"I have to hide," Éirime insisted. "Aclaí is trying to kill me."

"I find that hard to believe."

"The Mentor told me. He told me to hide."

"Éirime, everyone thinks you are dead. They had your funeral in Áthaiteorainn. We all saw it."

"Who led it?"

"Aclaí did. He swore a terrible revenge on the City."

"He swore what now?"

"He swore to cast the City down."

"You see why I must hide? Hide me, Blátha."

"Very well, then." She began to gather together the few things she didn't have on her Silver Cord, bundling them into a chest.

"Where are we going?"

"I know a place. I was one of the Orphans before Eala got rid of us. We can go there."

"How?"

"Words of Folding Space." Blátha leaned over her. "Take my hand."

With Éirime's hand in her own and her other hand on the handle of her chest, Blátha sang the Words of Folding Space. They fell through the emptiness.

Damhánalla watched as the dust swirled into the space Aclaí had occupied a moment before. Miotal clambered over the fallen stonework. "I should find out if he's killed Foscúil," he said.

"Will he really?" Innealta asked.

"I would guess so," Miotal replied. "But I don't know. I have never seen him like this. The Aclaí I know has control over his emotions."

"What will we do if he kills Foscúil?" Innealta asked. "He was right: when the Mentor is gone we need Foscúil's teaching to preserve our Order."

"If Aclaí needs him he will Restore him," Miotal replied. "He has done it before, as you well know." He jumped down the other side of the rubble and ran off out of sight.

"Everyone knows, don't they?" Innealta sighed.

"We know," Damhánalla replied. "But we are Lord Aclaí's closest friends. He has confided in us for centuries. That doesn't mean he's told everyone."

"I said this might be a bad idea," Innealta said.

"He's out of his room, at least."

"With Miotal's love and Foscúil's sword."

"Perhaps both were needed."

"I think the music from the village might have helped, too. When Éirime Retired and Blátha Fell the Mentor banned music from the top of the Hill. Something like that is happening with Aclaí, I suspect."

"Oh. Shall I go and stop the Celebration?"

"I don't think so." Innealta picked up one of the chairs and set it upright, moving some of the rubble to clear a space. She sat down. "I'm scared," she admitted.

Damhánalla picked through the chaos until she found an unopened jar and a couple of mugs. She sat beside Innealta and poured the wine. She raised her own mug. "Courage!" she said.

Innealta sighed. "Courage, then," she agreed. She drank deep. "When I came here I promised to comfort him. I never knew he could be so... dangerous."

"Then you were not paying attention," replied Damhánalla. "He has always been dangerous. He has always been a killer."

"But Miotal said that he had control of his emotions."

"If he had control of his emotions then why did he need your comfort, Innealta?"

"I don't know."

"You are the one who studied Eala's Art."

"I'm not Eala."

"Evidently not. Why did he need your comfort if he had control of his emotions? And why did you want to give it?"

"I... I wanted him to have emotions."

"But now he does you are afraid?"

"I am."

"You thought his emotions would be like yours?" Damhánalla poured more wine. "And now he has shown you his emotions you discover that he is actually a violent man?"

Innealta thought. "He has every excuse to be violent."

"He does."

"Doesn't he scare you?"

"He scares me so much. But he is the one I serve. If he kills me then I will die. But I will never turn my back on him. Perhaps I will die soon or perhaps I will not die for many centuries. But I don't care where or when as long as I die by his side. Even if it is by his hand."

"I don't know I can give that much."

"Didn't you March because you couldn't get him to care about you, Innealta?"

"I... I am confused, Damhánalla. I don't know what to do."

"Well, you need to decide. Examine your heart and see how much you can give. Then make your choice: run away or come and stand beside him."

Innealta drained the mug and stood up. She walked away into the building, away from the rubble and the ruin of their meal.

They landed on the ice between the houses, near the House of Heat. Éirime shivered until Blátha reminded her to find her cloak. Blátha walked over to the House of Heat and banged on the door. "What is it, mistress?" came the little-girl voice from behind the door.

"Make it warm," Blátha ordered.

"As you wish, my lady."

By the time Blátha had led Éirime into the dining house and sat her by one of the warm-walls the oil in the pipes was starting to knock and click and the warm-wall was, if not actually warm to the touch, warm enough that it could be touched.

"What is this place?" Éirime asked.

"This is the Orphanage," Blátha replied. "This is where I grew up."

"We spent years together in my childhood home," Éirime said. "Now we end up in your childhood home."

"I think yours was better," Blátha replied.

"Why did Eibheara bring ye here?"

"I think she wanted to keep us secret."

"Then maybe this is a good place to hide."

"I hope so." She sat beside Éirime and reached out her hand to touch her face. "I can see an improvement in your skin as quickly as that. You haven't lost your Immortal Breath, have you?"

"I have not been singing. I was afraid it would give me away. If I don't sing I age quickly. I drink too much to stay young for long."

"Of course you do. Well, you can sing here. There is nobody to hear you. We two are the only people on this continent." She leaned close and kissed Éirime's mouth. "Happy Nativity," she whispered.

* * *

With Words of Strength and the Words that Stop Time Aclaí quickly caught his dangerous prey. Then as he lifted Foscúil off his feet, Aclaí said the reverse of the Words of Strength and then the Words of Silence. His Breath was strong enough to overwhelm Foscúil's. Then he picked up the slowly struggling body and ran back into the house.

He dumped Foscúil face-down on the bed. The struggles were feeble but then he noticed they had a purpose. Foscúil was not fighting. He was touching his arm with the finger of the other hand, as if he was making dots on his skin.

Aclaí jumped to his feet in rage and punched the wall hard. The Words of Strength added to his own fury and he felt the stones loosen before his fist. Outside he heard rock fall from the outside of the wall and clatter into the garden.

He sat down on the edge of the bed again. He spoke the Words that Heal Bone over his hand and then the Words that End.

"So you do still have some willpower, my lord?" Foscúil said from behind him.

"Willpower probably saved your life, Foscúil."

"I was willing to take that risk."

"You play a dangerous game."

"Of course I do. I only want one thing and I cannot obtain it without you. You promised to cast down the City. I want to collect on that promise."

"Is that all you care about?"

"My lord, don't you want to cast down the City anymore?"

"I do. I am not sure I am strong enough. I am afraid my reason may have failed."

"I don't think it has. You are grieving but you are still doing your best."

"Eala's voice is in my head even now. She told me that I treat you all like stones in my own Flanking Game."

"You needed Eala to tell you that?" Foscúil laughed.

"I needed Eala to tell me to stop doing that."

"So what now? You up-end the board and scatter the stones in rage?"

Aclaí turned suddenly and put his hand on Foscúil's neck. "I should scatter your stones."

"You threatened me with that when I was a purple Novice, remember? You said that if I didn't learn some self-control you would cut me like a servant."

"And after that you learned quickly." Aclaí let the hand on Foscúil's neck soften a little, a caress but still with the promise of death.

"Freckles, my lord," Foscúil smiled.

"You say that word far too often," Aclaí grumbled.

"And you respect it when I say it. Or even when I can't say it." He took Aclaí's hand gently away from his throat. "Thank you for that, my lord. Thank you for trying to be a good person."

Outside the wind howled but the *siocarracht* servants had started the village's great furnace and they were warm. They were on the benches in the learning room watching the Visions: two women arm-in-arm surrounded by a hundred empty seats.

"*Cac us fuil,*" said Blátha as Aclaí's face faded away. "You said that the Mentor wants to rid himself of Aclaí, Éirime, but now it seems that Aclaí wants to rid himself of the Mentor."

"I have been telling ye all that Aclaí is dangerous," Éirime whispered. "Now ye can see I was right."

"I see it," agreed Blátha. "What has Geana said?"

"I have not heard from her," Éirime replied.

"Did you leave her behind?"

"The Mentor insisted."

"Have you any way to contact her?"

"She has a Hilt that Aclaí gave her but it is not responding. Either Aclaí has taken it back or she is dead."

Blátha hugged her. "Oh my love," she said. "Don't give up hope."

"If Aclaí has taken the Hilt from her then it is unlikely that he has let her live. Not after what he did to her sister."

"I'm so sorry," Blátha whispered back.

Méar woke up. It was dark and he had been dreaming. He whispered Words of Light and went over to sit at his desk. His reflection in the mirror stared back at him: an old, old man dying before his eyes. He looked at the two bags on the wood. He reached for the one on the right hand side.

Of course you are dying, came the voice from the left-hand bag. *You spend all your time talking to that thing.*

"Would you prefer that I talked to you?"

I have always taken care of you, Méar. She betrayed you.

"What do you think will happen? She doesn't speak to me. She hasn't spoken to me in forty years: not since you told me to kill her. You said that killing her would save me."

If you keep that thing then it will take away your last chance.

"What chance, Ceann? I don't have any chance. I am dying. Everything I care about is being taken away from me. I won't give another thing up, not before it is forced away from me."

Throw it away. You must throw it away.

"I will throw you away before I throw her away. I'll do it tonight if you don't leave me alone."

The heavy feeling that Méar associated with Ceann's voice dissipated. He opened the other bag and weighed the bone in his hand. He felt the shape of her cheekbones and saw the gleam of her teeth. "Won't you talk to me?" he begged her.

But she did not reply.

He carried the bone back to the bed. He climbed in and lay back into the pillows. He laid the bone beside him and remembered what it had been like when her hair had been on his pillow. He curled up under the covers and squeezed his eyes shut.

It was a day and a night and nobody had seen Blátha. Féileacána told her family that she wanted to go fishing and her son took her out into the river on his boat. As soon as they was out of sight of the village she reached for her sword on her Silver Cord and took the jewel in her hand. She smiled reassurance at Dóchas as she did so.

this is blátha

"Hello Blátha," she thought. "What news?"

éirime is with me

"She is dead."

she is in hiding from aclaí or from the mentor

"We all saw her funeral."

i think that was another body made to look like hers with words of shaping

Féileacána thought about that. She would not expect to be able to fool Aclaí like that: her Breath would not be strong enough to fool Words of Identification, if Aclaí had thought to use them. But she was not the Mentor. She remembered that Blátha was still trying to use the sword-hilt.

"Where did ye go?" she thought.

somewhere far away from everyone

"And it is Éirime that has convinced you that there will be war between Aclaí and the City?"

she says that the mentor wanted to pardon eala and aclaí refused to allow it

Féileacána wanted to scream shock but she kept it off her face and out of her breathing. "Is that true?" she thought. "Did Aclaí really choose to kill Eala?"

i dont know but if it is true then the mentor might be right to try and dispose of aclaí

"He might. But unless he pardons us at the Evening Meal, Blátha, we cannot get involved. We only thought we could get involved by taking Aclaí's side."

that is true

"So, are ye well hidden?"

i think so

"Then that is how we should remain. When all this is over we can see where we stand."

A glimmer of light caught Cathúa's eye and she looked down. "So you've remembered me again, mythical creator?" she whispered, looking at the glittering eyes of her cat pendant. "Well, what do you want with me?" She felt the tingle of her sword-hilt. "Oh," she said. The illusion of light on the hilt said that the caller was Eighteenth Rank. Liús, she wondered.

But it was Blátha. "What do you want?" she thought.

i want to ask questions about city history

"I am City librarian," Cathúa replied. "Ask your questions."

i wanted to ask about aclaí

"There is a lot about Aclaí in the chronicles. It will take a long time to tell you everything."

i have some questions about aclaí

Cathúa remembered that, when Blátha had been a favourite, people still asked favours of one another on the Hill. She tried to remember how she stood with Blátha. Then she remembered why Blátha had left the Hill and then she remembered that Eala was dead. "Ask your questions."

did aclaí ever rape anyone

"I am sure he did. That sort of thing was quite common for most of the City's life. It was too common to be noted in the chronicles."

do you have any record of it

"Let me see." Cathúa reached for her golden tablet on her Silver Cord. It only took a moment to frame the question and pass it to the House of Power. "I have quite a few cases," she explained. "The Mentor has ordered Aclaí to punish many people. Those punishments often included rape."

what about without the mentors orders

Cathúa removed the cases where the Mentor ordered it from her list. "I have three," she said.

is that all

"I have eliminated cases where Eala's followers appeared to have been raped before execution since they are easily justified as punishments under the Mentor's orders. With one exception – Eala herself."

why is eala an exception

"The Mentor ordered Aclaí to return her to the City. Aclaí refused."

Of course Cathúa could not sense any reaction from Blátha – there were limits to Eala's Art. *what about the other two*

"The Mentor showed me evidence that Aclaí put it in Eala before she Fell. It would have been in the summer of 1188. But I believe the evidence may be suspect."

why

"Because Eala had a twin. I cannot tell them apart in Visions because the maker of the Visions might not be able to tell them apart."

oh There was a pause. *what is the other case*

"When Éirime was newly Selected, before she had been given Rank or had her Initiation acknowledged, she was caught in Aclaí's bed. It was the morning of the Second of Autumn."

did he force her there

"I don't know. Something happened that led them to fall out."

it did agreed Blátha's words. *but none of these cases involve coercion*

"I don't have any evidence of coercion except by the Mentor's orders. Except Eala's execution."

what evidence do you have that she was coerced

Cathúa realised she was being too emotional. "I am sorry, Blátha. My emotions are clouding my logic. I don't have any evidence of coercion except under the Mentor's orders."

thank you cathúa

Aclaí was sitting by the fountain in the garden of the Midsummer Palace. Bánúa sat on his knee and looked up at him. On the grass in front of them three of Bánúa's children played a chasing game.

"Lord Aclaí!"

Aclaí looked around. He could see the blue of the cloak through the trees. Bánúa slipped off his knee as he stood up. By the time he had his sword in his hand they were all gone. The blue-robe stepped out.

"Éise," he said. "Why are you here? And... what is that thing you're wearing?"

"Liús insists I wear it," she laughed. She came over to the fountain and sat down. Aclaí heard a little mewling noise like a cat waking up. Éise opened the bag strapped to her front and Aclaí looked down to see what kind of animal was in the bag.

"Oh," he said as he saw the little face. "Why do you have..?"

Éise looked up at him and, below her chin, her daughter also stared. "Eibheara did it. Don't you remember?"

"I remember. So you went through with it."

"And I'm glad I did. Look at her."

"She is a cute thing." Aclaí sat down beside Éise. "So why did you come here? Don't you know I am the enemy?"

"I wanted to talk to you about what you are doing. I wondered if there was another way."

"I can't see another way, Éise. He killed..." Aclaí turned away and Éise looked at his shoulders and the way he held his head as he breathed Immortal Breath.

She put her hand on his shoulder. When he continued, his voice was barely audible. "It turns out that is too much for me."

"Aclaí, I've known you for more than two hundred years. You don't do this sort of thing." She stroked his back and shoulder. "Did she really mean that much to you?"

"She did."

"Then why not bring her back?"

He turned around. "What?"

"Lord Aclaí, we refrain from Forbidden Arts because the Mentor commands us to. But you have sworn to throw him down. Why are you still avoiding Forbidden Art?"

"I... I don't know."

Éise reached up and touched his cheek. "Aclaí, what is the matter with you?"

"I don't know. Since she died I find... I am not doing what is sensible anymore. I spent the whole of the Month of Planting in my room. It's like it is not me at all. All that matters is how I feel. I am simply doing what my heart tells me to do."

"It is what Eala wanted us all to do, Aclaí. But I don't think she wanted you to kill him."

"You might be surprised to hear the things that she wanted, in the end."

Éise frowned. Little Tintreacha began to fuss and she casually opened the front of her dress and latched her daughter on. She looked back at her friend. "Who raped Eala?" she asked.

"It wasn't rape, Éise."

"How do you know?" Éise looked at his face and tried to understand. "Lord Aclaí, was it you?"

"It was."

"How long were you with her?"

"All night." She saw the tears in his eyes and it gave her a thrill of fear in her spine. Her daughter sensed the change and fussed a little. "I would miss her if I didn't miss Éirime so much."

Blátha stood beside Éirime, holding her hand and looking out over the wilderness of snow. It was one of the rare windless days in the winter. Light behind them streamed out into the darkness and over their heads the cold stars shone down through the nearer light of the current of fire that came from the Sun's Wind.

Éirime looked up and her cloak fell back off her hair. "I never realised it would be so beautiful," she said.

"It is beautiful," Blátha agreed. "The winter storms blow for days on end but, just occasionally, the wind drops. Then we could go out and see this. I stood and watched this as a little girl. I didn't see a tree before I went to the City but I saw this so many times."

"It seems strange to me that it is so cold and dark. This is supposed to be the Month of Life."

"We are standing on a ball, love," Blátha replied. "When it is Summer in the North it is Winter in the South."

"I learned that at the City, my flower. But it still seems strange to me."

"Will you ever go back to the City, do you think?"

Éirime looked up at the plasma shifting and twisting in colours above the atmosphere. Blátha heard her softly singing to herself. "Aclaí will destroy the City," she said at last.

"Do you think he really will?"

"He does what he says he will do."

"But, even if he destroys the City, he will still end up with the Key of Creation. Someone will need to take it. Whoever they are they will be Mentor."

"Geana used to ask me that, Blátha. She thought I should marry him." Blátha knew enough to keep quiet and wait for the rest. "My flower," Éirime continued, "I don't want him anywhere near me. The Mentor told me to hide because Aclaí wants to kill me."

"Lord Aclaí thinks you are dead."

"That is good."

"Is it good, Éirime? How do you think he would be if he knew you were alive?"

"Why would he be different?" Éirime looked around at her in the starlight. "My flower, have you been listening to Geana?"

"Not recently. I am sure Geana is dead. I think the Mentor killed her."

"Why?"

"I don't know. Maybe he needed a body to shape into looking like you."

"He killed my Geana to save me? Oh *cac*..."

When Blátha saw her start to weep she put her arms around her. "We don't know that."

"It sounds like him," she said. "Geana would have been nothing but a peasant to him. I hate him."

"A lot of us hate him, love."

"But even if he killed Geana, Aclaí killed Eala. He killed her even though she was one of us. He raped her even though she was Mentor's Favourite."

"How do you know it was rape?"

"What else do you think it was? You studied under Eala, Blátha. You know what she was like. She would never betray the Mentor like that."

"I spoke to Cathúa. She was far from sure it was rape."

"That is what Cathúa is like. She collects doubts."

"She didn't think that Lord Aclaí has ever raped anyone, other than on the Mentor's orders."

"Possibly not even then, my flower. I think sometimes when he was told to kill someone he comforted them by..." she stopped. "We mustn't be taken in by him. He is manipulative."

"He is human. Éirime my love, I think you could save the City."

"How? By going to Aclaí? He would kill me for sure."

"It is not sure at all."

"The Mentor told me."

"How do you know he was telling the truth?"

"Well, I..." Éirime looked away. "I don't care. I could choose to believe that the Mentor is telling the truth and that Aclaí is lying. I could choose to believe that the Mentor is lying and that Aclaí is trustworthy. Or I could just stay well away from both of them."

"The City will fall."

Éirime pulled herself out of Blátha's arms. She turned and glared up at her. "Did it ever occur to you that maybe the City should fall? That maybe, deep down in my broken heart, I want it to fall?"

Liús closed the door behind him, said the Words that Hold the Portal and then walked through the Gateway to Acra and his family. "What is wrong, dear heart?" he asked.

"I visited Aclaí," Éise replied.

"Why?"

"I hoped to broker some sort of peace. We need Aclaí to forgive him. We need... I don't know who we need but we need someone's help. The Mentor is dying and Aclaí's army is like a hand on the throat of the City."

"And how was Aclaí?"

"He is as crazy and lost as the Mentor."

"Aclaí is the person that Eala's faction relied on to bring stability to the City. Could she have made such a profound mistake?"

"She sent him crazy, my lion."

"He killed her."

"He spent the night with her before he killed her. She manipulated him. The commands she gave his heart control him to this day."

"Revenge, dear heart?" Liús frowned his denial. "That is not how Eala was. I don't know what she intended him to do but I don't believe it was revenge." He thought a moment. "Did he explain why he wanted to do it?"

"He said that he missed Éirime."

"That is what he said at her funeral." Liús smiled a joyless smile. "She programmed him to return to Éirime and, when he got there, he found her murdered."

"She wanted to protect her sister."

"And instead she has doomed the City."

Éise stroked her daughter's hair. Liús sat down beside her. "What do we do?" she asked.

"We have to broker the deal with his heart without him knowing."

"That will need Forbidden Art, my lion. The only way to stop him will be with Éirime."

"I think Eala intended them to come back to the City as conquerors."

"The Mentor wouldn't be able to resist them in his state."

"Then we need to get her back."

"We can't, my lion. You saw the funeral pyre. There is nothing left for the Words of Restoration to work on."

"There is always the Key of Creation."

"The Mentor will know you have done it. He will kill you."

"He can't kill me, dear heart."

"You think you are so important to him that..?"

"I can't be killed, dear heart. I just can't."

Liús could see that she didn't believe him. But then Tintreacha started to cry and Éise got up.

"Now the important thing for this exercise," Foscúil explained, "Is to get the feeling of your Breath from low down in your belly to the point of the sword. Use the overhand cut to the head. Partners, you will need to step in to divert the flow, to merge your Breath with the attacker, like two rivers becoming one."

Most of the students in Foscúil's lesson were green-clad Forest warriors, but in one corner at the front were the blue-robes, practising together. Damhánalla was the first to receive the attack. She saluted to them and Innealta stepped forward. She raised her blade and tried to think of the exercise, extending her feeling out until the sword-blade was like a part of her arm. She hardly felt Damhánalla's Breath meet her own, but somehow she missed. She stepped aside and watched as the others attacked. Foscúil was also watching. It was Aclaí who attacked next and Innealta saw that she could not divert his Breath. The sword-point touched her helm and skidded down her shoulder.

Foscúil said nothing as the others attacked her. It took her a moment to recover but Miotal was successfully diverted and, a moment later, so was Cabairí. Aclaí stood at the front of the queue as she saluted them. Then he attacked and she cringed. She couldn't help herself. The cowering motion might have been nothing more than the width of her little finger, but Aclaí followed her.

"Attack again," said Foscúil.

"As you wish, teacher," Aclaí growled. Then suddenly, like lightning, he turned. Before Innealta had a chance to move his sword was on her shoulder.

"Attack again," said Foscúil.

Aclaí said nothing this time. He just raised the sword. Innealta waited for him to attack, but he didn't. How long is he going to take, she wondered. Will Foscúil say any... And, as quickly as that, the sword point struck her head again.

"Attack again," said Foscúil.

By the time the lesson was over she was crying. She did not know what Foscúil was trying to teach her but she had not wept at sword-practice since she had been a purple novice. She was furious with herself for letting it get to her. When it came time to leave the sword-hall she walked away as quickly as dignity would permit.

She hadn't even said Words of Freshness. She had simply hidden herself away, taken off her helm and sat with her head in her hands. She didn't even notice Foscúil come up to her until he sat beside her on the bench.

"What do you want?" she demanded.

"What do you want?" he smiled.

"Did you think you were trying to teach me with that?"

"Innealta, you are going to die. If you stay around Lord Aclaí you will die soon. I doubt many of us will live five years. Are you afraid to die?"

"You tell us not to fear death but what does that actually mean? Everybody fears death."

"Did you see how Eala died? Not everybody fears death."

"I'm not Eala, right?"

"Of course you're not. You're Innealta. But – why do you follow Lord Aclaí if you don't want to die?"

"Where else would I go?"

"Would you want to live without him?"

The tears stung her eyes again. "You know I don't."

"We're going to lose him. He will take the Key of Creation and we will lose him."

"He will be Mentor."

"He won't. He will go into isolation somewhere and try and un-bind it. But he won't succeed. The day we march on the City is the day we will all lose him. If you don't want to live without him then the alternative is to die on that day."

"How can you think like that?"

"You Marched, Innealta." He put his hand on hers. "You died. Why are you still afraid of something you have already done?"

"I don't know. What about you? Aren't you afraid of what you will lose?"

"Not anymore. I am going to avenge Abhainne."

"You loved her, didn't you?"

"She was my friend. But she didn't deserve to die like that."

"Many people die a slave's death, Foscúil. That is what happens in the City."

"He doesn't kill like that, Innealta. He chose to kill her as a slave because he knew what it meant to her. It was a special punishment for her."

"Why?"

"She was a slave before she got her blue robe. She was a runaway slave who stole into the City and stood in line."

"How could she dare...?"

"Because she had courage, Innealta. She started as a slave-girl and became an Immortal. She was the reason I ever believed Eala could do what she tried to do. I saw Abhainne and I saw what a peasant could become. I see peasants and I remember her."

"I never knew."

"Most of us didn't. So you see what he did when he ordered her to die as a slave? He chose to do that because it didn't just kill her. It made her whole life meaningless."

Innealta looked up and saw his eyes. Then she reached out her hand to him. "I never knew. Do you really hate him?"

"He took from her everything she had won for herself. I will help Lord Aclaí to take everything from him."

"Everything?"

"He built the City. And we are going to cast it down again. Will you help?"

"I don't want revenge, not like that. But Foscúil, I don't want to live without him. I will help or I will die trying."

He put his hand up and covered her hand on his shoulder. "Thank you," he said. "Now remember that and it will give you courage."

"I will, teacher," she replied.

Cabairí was walking out in the gardens. The wall had been repaired with Words of Power but the servants were clearing the flowerbeds and removing a shrub that had been broken by the falling masonry. He might not been there when Aclaí had come out of his room but he had certainly heard about it.

Then Aclaí was by his side. Cabairí jumped around with his hand ready to find his sword on his Silver Cord. "My lord?" he asked.

"You tried to talk to me a ten-day ago," Aclaí said.

"You told me what I needed to know," Cabairí replied.

"I didn't tell you everything."

"You told me enough, my lord. I am sorry for your loss." As his calm returned Cabairí realised that it was true.

"I needed time to grieve. Eala had to work hard to persuade me. To marry Éirime would have meant defying the Mentor. She had to get me to a state of mind where I could defy him."

"Did she plan it to work out like this?"

"I cannot believe she did. None of us could predict it. Nobody believed the Mentor could kill Éirime."

"How did we make that mistake, my lord? How did *Eala* make that mistake?"

"It is not the Mentor that gives the orders. He believes there is an ancestor that gives him orders. It turns out that, even if we can predict the behaviour of the Mentor, we cannot predict the behaviour of this ancestor that he believes in."

"That is why Eala researched her last book, then?"

"It is. But there are people who seem to have two personalities and we don't understand how that works."

"Like Eibheara?"

"Maybe. As I said, we don't understand how that works."

Cabairí turned away.

"Cabairí," Aclaí called. "You asked me my plans, didn't you?"

"I tried to remind you of the plans you had already shared, my lord."

"I didn't share... I see. I told everyone that I plan to cast the City down."

"You did, my lord."

"I cannot do it straight away. If the City falls and there is nobody to protect humanity from the Forest then humanity will fall along with the City. I will not destroy the City at the cost of destroying humanity. Cabairí, Eala dreamed of a life for ordinary people where there was more justice. I cannot make her dream come true if everyone dies."

"I never thought of that, my lord." Cabairí frowned. "We would need something to defend the Forest for thousands of years after the City has fallen. The Forest houses would not be enough. There are not enough of them and they would not have the skills of an Adept. Without Words of

Power or Mastery of Creation they would not be able to defend humanity from Wild Mages."

"I can defend the Key of Creation, Cabairí, if I have somewhere to defend it."

"But you promised to cast down the City, my lord, not to be Mentor."

"I won't be Mentor. If people are loyal to me it will not be because of Initiation."

"I can promise loyalty, but Eala was convinced that Initiation was the only reason that the City lasted as long as it did, my lord. Without Initiation... loyalties change. And the Key of Creation is a very tempting prize."

"I am the only Elder Immortal. Without the City the Mentor won't grant Rank anymore."

"One of the Eibhearas is Elder Immortal, my lord. Geal was Elder Immortal Rank too, wasn't he? And that Yanti was never granted Rank."

Aclaí thought. Then Cabairí saw his face set. "I won't be the Mentor," he said. "The City needs to fall. It is time humanity learned to live without the City of the Sea People." He looked around. "Foscúil tells me that, with enough ordinary warriors, even Adepts can be defeated."

"So how many peasants with field implements would it take to kill you, my lord? One thousand?"

"I don't know. What if I said I could find a million Forest warriors for every Adept that was ever Initiated?"

"I don't..." Cabairí remembered who he was talking to. "That is, my lord, I would like to see that."

"Then come with me. Let me show you something."

It was hard Forest Walking, as hard as walking to Anleacán, but Cabairí watched the route Aclaí followed and tried to remember. Aclaí helped him with some of it to make sure that Cabairí would be able to find it again.

There was one instruction that Aclaí kept making that did not make sense. "Keep the Sun high in the sky."

Then they came out of the trees beside a lake. An island on the lake was the foundation for a fortress that reached to the sky. The Sun beat straight down. Cabairí looked up.

Instead of the horizon he saw a sort of blue shape, like a deep-rooted tree with a slender trunk that became a line, soaring up into the zenith behind the blue of the atmosphere. It was light and dark in bands all the way up to the Sun. He turned around. Behind him the same apparition showed itself. The blue shape was speckled with the white of clouds, the greens and browns of continents and the deeper blue of oceans.

"I don't understand, my lord," Cabairí breathed.

"This is where I breed my warriors," Aclaí answered.

"I know that, my lord. But I don't understand what I am seeing. What is that thing on the horizon?"

"You understand that Anleacán is a flat world?"

"I do. It is obviously an artificial creation."

"I made it, Cabairí," Aclaí smiled. "I also made this." He pointed his arm at the horizon. "This world is a ribbon of Metal looped around its Sun. What you can see is the rest of the loop."

"But, my lord, light takes a thousand heartbeats to get to the Sun and back. Is that... is the light we are seeing a thousand heartbeats old?"

"I suppose it must be."

"But light travels seven thousand days' march in a heartbeat, my lord."

"So to walk there would take seven million days, Cabairí." Aclaí shrugged. "Fortunately we don't have to walk."

"But, why?"

"Why is it so big?"

"Why build it at all?"

"An Adept proposed in theory that it was possible long before I came to the City. I wanted to know if it could be done in practice. It can."

"And you use this to raise your warriors?"

"Of course. It is big and it is hard to find in the Forest."

"It is not just big, my lord. There is more land here for people than on every world in the whole galaxy. And people can live here, my lord, and they can live on fewer than a dozen of the galaxy's worlds."

"That makes it a good place to breed warriors, Cabairí. With this place to raise them I can win the war against the Forest without a single Adept."

"I understand, my lord. And... I am a little intimidated. But why are you showing me this?"

"Because this needs to be used to defend humanity from the Forest. I need someone to look after it so I can cast down the City."

"I... are you asking me to be Steward of all this?"

"Someone has to do it, Cabairí. And you did offer to help."

"Very well, my lord. I will do it."

— 6 —

The Last Selection

Cathúa knew she should be getting herself ready for the last Autumn Celebration but she did not feel ready. She had worked all through the Lost Days but she still had not finished. She had promised herself that she would be finished before the start of the final year, so she could devote her energies to the City's defence, but this was the Autumn Day of 1370 and there was a whole shelf left to go.

She saw the glitter of the emeralds in her cat pendant and she remembered the experiment they represented. Three years it was since she had lost Gruaige in another experiment and she still did not know how she was supposed to feel about that. Was she supposed to celebrate Gruaige's life – her happiness with her husband and her family? Was she supposed to remember that gentle Gruaige was ancestor to the first man she ever loved? Or was she supposed to grieve because Gruaige was long dead?

Or was she supposed to blame herself for losing her servant when there was such a big task in front of her?

Cathúa frowned. Perhaps, she thought, I am supposed to stop daydreaming and finish the job. There is only one shelf left. Maybe I can get it finished before they call us down. Or some of it, anyway.

She said Words of Freshness and she put on the turquoise blue tunic that she had chosen for herself. It was the same cut as a servant's tunic but the colour was one that a servant could never wear. She looked at the gold cord that was supposed to tie it but then she changed her mind. Instead of the gold cord she put her sword-belt on. She turned and stretched but the sword-belt was enough to keep it covering her. She said Words of Many Images instead of finding a mirror. The other Cathúas in the room moved and turned. The tunic was long enough, she saw, and the colour did suit her skin and eyes. She knew that it would be seen on the Visions and she wondered if Aclaí would see it. Here she was dressed as a servant but wearing a sword. I am his sword-servant, Aclaí, she thought, and my sword is waiting for you.

111

When she was dressed ready for when they called her Cathúa returned to the shelf. She saw the faint tracks in the dust and she remembered how Eala had nearly died when Eibheara had poisoned her. She took the first and second of the books down and brought it over to the table. The shelf was not properly ordered. The first two she took down were the last two that had been read: Eibheara and Eala's Arts.

She said the Words that Shape Metal and she reached down. Beneath the table was a raw chunk of Metal as big as her two feet together. It glowed with green light as her hand approached it. She plucked two little pieces off it as if it were clay and put them on the table. She touched one of them and one of the scrolls. The Metal, still glowing, spread itself out and flattened itself into a smooth sheet. Then she touched the second scroll and the second piece of Metal. Then she said Words that End.

Once the Words had expired and the green glow subsided she picked up the first sheet. She turned it to the light and saw the tiny, tiny writing that covered it. By holding it close to her eye she could just read it. "Human Motivation," she read. "Eala's Art."

She put the sheet down. Even if the City was to fall that sheet would remain legible, hidden on the Coral Mountain. It would remain legible until the stars had gone cold.

But I won't be there to see it, she thought. I won't live to see another Autumn Day.

The girl held her nose and squeezed her eyelids as tight as she could. She felt the warmth of the water sluicing over her face and the irritation where strands of hair had washed over her skin. But she waited patiently until the servants spoke.

"We're done, mistress," the boy-servant said.

Réalta opened her eyes. She was standing in the courtyard so they could pour warm water on her to rinse the soap out of her hair. The girl enfolded her body with the towel and began to rub. Réalta knew that if she stood too long in the Sun her skin would burn, but she was enjoying the attention. She glanced down at the boy servant. It secretly pleased her to see that her body stirred him even though he was a slave boy.

Wrapped in her towel and with her hair gathered behind she let the servants lead her into her chamber. Her mother was waiting. "I thought the red dress," Mammy said.

Réalta looked at the garment on the bed. It had been dyed with one of the bright colours that came from the City. It was not a dark wine red but instead was a shocking colour like fresh blood. "It's not subtle, Mammy," Réalta observed.

"Today is not a day for subtlety, dear heart," Mammy replied. "You won't catch the Mentor's eye with the force of your personality. You have courage, daughter, but you are too shy for that. So this dress will do it for you." She picked it up and offered it to her daughter. "Try it on. You will see."

Réalta allowed the servants to unwrap her towel and put the dress on her. She always felt more shy and awkward around her mother. Réalta's mother was a storyteller and entertainer who could keep crowds of hundreds in thrall with her wild tales of ancient heroes and imaginary worlds. Her stories were justly famous not only in their home town but up and down the river all the way up through the desert and down across the Inland Sea.

"You're dreaming again, Réalta," her mother said.

"I'm sorry, Mammy."

"It's all right," Mammy replied, "But you mustn't daydream in the Hall of Selection. Look the Mentor in the eye, smile, and answer him in a clear voice if he speaks to you." She led her daughter to the mirror. "Look at yourself."

Réalta looked. The stranger in the reflection looked like a slave-girl ready for auction. The lacing at the sides of the dress stretched over the softness on her hips and around her chest and the hem hardly reached more than a hands-width down her thighs. "I'm too fat to wear this," Réalta said.

"Nonsense, daughter. You have beautiful curves and any red-blooded male will desire them."

Réalta grunted a reply that disagreed but not strongly enough to compel her mother to respond. "Come on," Mother said. "Time to get you to the Flyer."

The Flyer met them out in the courtyard. They followed the river down to the gate. Réalta looked in wonder at the whole of the delta laid out beneath them. She saw shiny water, black soil and virulent green everywhere. Beyond it they could see the glittering sea ahead and, on the horizon around and behind, the dull reddish colours of the desert.

Réalta kept what she hoped was a respectful silence, but her mother behind her prattled on about everything and nothing. Their pilot, a blue-robed old man with white hair and a grey beard, refused to be engaged in conversation. With movements and gestures he guided the Flyer down until it plunged through the Gate and into the grey space beyond. When they burst out again into sunlight Réalta's ears popped loud and painfully.

Her eyes were forced shut by the brilliance of the Sun on the snow beneath them. They were high among jagged mountains.

They climbed up above the mountains and the Earth beneath them quickly marched past. As the land rolled by she thought she could see the outline of the Inland Sea again – but she was not sure. Then they flew over ocean and descended towards an island. A bay in the island revealed a city and a fortified hill resolved into a courtyard and a hall larger than any building at home.

"We're here," their blue-robe announced as soon as they were landed. He got up. "Follow me," he said to Réalta. Her mother trailed along behind.

Réalta looked around the hall as she was led in. About half of the hall was taken up with musicians and entertainers. Some of them waved to her mother. On one side there were Adepts in their blue robes, each the centre of a small crowd of ordinary people. Each little crowd included a young person dressed up in their best. She quickly took in the appearances of the other girls like her, but it seemed to her she was the only one who looked ready to be auctioned as a slave. She counted them: twenty-six girls and seventeen boys.

On the Day of Autumn, any town's streets should be thronged with people celebrating. But these streets were silent. Here and there things were abandoned: a pot smashed on the stones of the path; a sheep's skeleton picked clean where it had fallen; a door that had rotted beneath its shroud of ivy and now sagged off its hinges. It was forty years since the night Ceatha had died but still it belonged to the weeds and the wild animals.

Damhánalla had arrived prepared. She had done this many times before. She got down the baskets from her Flyer then unfolded a cloth which had embroidered on it the Circle of Warding. A smaller basket contained a collection of Crystals. She unfolded the cloth and laid it on the ground then found a Crystal and placed in the centre of the Circle of Warding.

Although what she said then was Words of Power it was hardly a Formula. It was more like a lullaby: nonsense words that would lull the lesser intelligence of a Manifestation. As she chanted the repetitive sounds she tried hard not to fall asleep. To fall asleep in Ceatha, to drowse while night fell, would be fatal even for an Immortal.

In due course her patience was rewarded. She saw the shadow move out of the corner of her eye. When she turned, of course, it seemed like just another shadow in among the ruined buildings. She let her voice drone on, encouraging, hypnotising. She deliberately looked away from the circle in the cloth.

She saw it move. Damhánalla sprang to her feet with her sword in her hand. The dark form flitted around inside the circle, trying to find an escape. Now she saw the red sparks occasionally flashing out of the darkness. She stopped chanting. Then she carefully uttered the Words of Forgetfulness, pushing all the force of her Breath, her will, onto the Manifestation trapped in the circle. Then, when she was sure it had forgotten everything, she forced it into the Crystal.

Only then did she lean into the circle herself. She picked up the Crystal. Inside it there was a little black twist of shadow just like the one in the Crystal on her sword-hilt. She put the Crystal carefully in the basket and set out the next one.

As the day ended and the shadows grew longer she found it easier to persuade them into the Circle but of course she was in more and more danger. By the time she had the last Crystal loaded she could see how the shadows around her were alive with barely-visible motion and she could see the sparks of red among them. She hurriedly folded the cloth and lifted the two baskets onto her Flyer. Then she gestured the Flyer into the air and turned North and East, towards the Midsummer Palace.

Liús was in the room on the Hill that he shared with his wife, but he was alone. He set out the small table that he reserved for talking with his Manifestation – for practising Rónmór's Art. At first he had used a Circle of Warding to summon the Manifestation but he now had it bound to a roughly carved stone. The pebble was crudely carved into the shape of a snake's head. There was nothing about the stone's function that required it to be shaped like that but Liús felt it was appropriate somehow.

He placed the snake-head pebble before him on the table. It was there, he knew, as soon as he touched it. It was there as soon as he thought of it. The hard thing was to keep it from intruding in his whole life.

"What will today be like?" he whispered. "What do I need to do to make his Autumn Day a good one?"

Find him pretty girls and boys, the Manifestation replied. *It doesn't matter anymore.*

Liús returned the carved stone to its box and slammed the lid shut.

The City is doomed anyway, the Manifestation continued. *Don't you want to save yourself?*

He tried to think of Éise. It was thinking of her that was the only thing that could drive the Manifestation from his thoughts. He thought of her smile and her bright eyes. He thought of the way her clothes followed the shape of her body, of her perfect brown skin. He thought of her voice, of how her tones could range from a deep animal growl to the laughter of a little girl.

You could save her if you abandoned him, it said. *Or if you took his place –*

"Shut your mouth," he hissed, thinking as he said it that the Manifestation did not have a mouth to close. *Cac us fuil,* he thought, what have I become? He thought of Éise again, of her soft strong arms and her welcoming embrace. He thought of little Tintreacha, a bright girl of only two winters, sitting on his wife's knee. His girl. His daughter.

Take it from him, the Manifestation added. *You could save her, too.*

"Now then, dear heart, we will be back this evening. Will you be good for Úlla?"

"Will, Mammy," little Tintreacha replied.

Éise kissed the top of her head and stood up. "We might get called into the evening celebrations," Éise told Úlla. "But even then we should be back by midnight."

"As you wish, my lady," Úlla replied.

Éise went through the door into the bedroom and bolted it behind her. Then she glanced in the mirror, said Words of Freshness and walked through the Gate. Liús looked up as she came through and she noticed the unpleasant feeling about the place that she had come to associate with his working of Rónmór's Art. "How is it?" she asked.

"It's another small Selection," he answered. "There are forty-four of them."

"Any good?"

"There's a cute boy in a wolf skin and a rather wanton girl in a red dress. But none that I would bother Selecting if I was Mentor."

"They know, don't they?"

"The Candidates?"

"The world, my foolish lion. They are keeping their sons and daughters home until Aclaí comes."

"Of course they are. They want to see how it ends. You are a mother. Would you bring our girl to the City in the current situation if she was of marriageable age? Or would you wait a couple of years to see who the Mentor was?"

"I would bring her, but only because we could keep her safe. Lord Aclaí is my friend too."

"There are very few parents who are both Immortals and Favourites, dear heart."

"Well, there are two." She peeped out of the door. "Are we ready to go?"

"I'll find out." He hugged his wife a moment and left. Éise glanced at the mirror and straightened her dress. Then she followed her husband out.

The Mentor was sat by the fountain with Cathúa on one side of him and Eibheara on the other. Liús had just finished talking to them. The Mentor leaned on Eibheara's arm as he stood up. Liús rang the bell and Éise lined up behind them. Then the Mentor began to shuffle towards the gate that led down to the Court of the Immortals.

Damhánalla leaned out over the edge of the Flyer and looked through the darkness. The Words of Seeing Heat allowed her to see the difference between the rivers, trees and fields, but the only details that showed clearly were animals and houses. Still she hardly needed much to navigate: this had been her home for nine hundred years.

She guided the Flyer down through the autumn winds and landed in front of the Midsummer Palace. As the Flyer touched down she pulled the hood of her cloak over her head. The power of the Flyer dissipated and the autumn wind threw rain on her. She picked up the two baskets and ran inside.

Aclaí was already in the basement as she came down. She put the baskets on the bench and he looked up. "You are quite late," he said. "It is risky to stay too late."

"It might be risky to stay too long but they are much easier to catch when the Sun is not full. Tonight was dark and raining and it was good hunting."

"How many did you get?" he asked.

"Thirteen," she smiled. "Including a big one. Do we have enough now?"

"It depends how big they are. Not all of them are big enough for our purposes."

"We could combine several, couldn't we? That is what is done in a normal House of Power."

"And a normal House of Power can come unravelled again. A single Manifestation will not come unravelled. Someone would have to use Words of Power to fracture the Manifestation. Of course the Manifestation would resist. It would hardly be a suitable Formula of Words to use in the heat of battle."

Damhánalla frowned. "But an attacker could force a larger one to unravel during the battle? That would be... messy."

"It would. We are giving these things to warriors to make them stronger in battle – to enable them to face Adepts. We must assume that the Adepts will try and find a way to take that advantage away."

"If they did it could be used against us, too. The Crystal on our sword-hilts contains a Manifestation of Creation."

"These are bigger," Aclaí commented.

"But they are vulnerable in the same way."

"I suppose they must be." Aclaí opened the smaller basket and began to take out the Crystals. He picked each one up in turn and measured it, sorting them into groups. Damhánalla sat at the bench and re-packed her basket.

As he took them out he sorted them. He divided them into three sizes. The smallest ones he put away in a chest that was full of others they had trapped. The biggest one he put aside too before gathering the rest. There were five. He took the first of the five Crystals and raised it until it was in front of his nose, three hands-width from his face. He stared at it, breathed his Will, and spoke Words.

The little patch of darkness in the Crystal began to shift until it seemed to gather into a drop of black oil inside the facet. Aclaí could see that the drop had two tiny red-spark eyes glowering back at him. Aclaí repeated the Words. This was a tough, stubborn one, though, and moisture appeared on his brow as he repeated the Words again.

Then the Manifestation yielded to his Will. The blob of darkness came out of the Crystal, like a single curl of smoke, and wrapped itself around his finger. He put the empty Crystal back in the basket and then he removed the Manifestation. It had taken the shape and solidity of a ring, apparently made of jet or ebony, with two tiny red jewels. He opened a box and put his new ring among many others.

Four more times he picked up the crystals and repeated the operation, placing three more rings in the box. He kept the fourth one on his finger ready to strengthen him for the next exercise.

"Is that to help you handle the big one?" Damhánalla asked.

"It is," Aclaí agreed. He reached down into his chest and took out a larger bag that was as big as his two hands clenched together. He opened the bag.

"Oh," said Damhánalla.

Aclaí lifted out a carved piece of Crystal. It was round with cracks in the surface on the long side. But when he turned it the shape of the face carved on the front was clear. As he placed it down she could see the underside where the jawline went back towards the base of the skull.

"It's beautiful," she said. "Who carved it?"

"I got an artist to make me one out of quartz. This is duplicated and transmuted."

"How do you transmute something to Crystal?"

"A small amount of Metal must be used."

"I didn't know that. What are you doing with it?"

"The same as the rings. I wanted a House of Power that was small enough for a household. Something that could be left on a high shelf somewhere in the home to provide Breath for the household magic."

"That sounds practical," she agreed. Then, as she saw him reach for the Crystal that contained the big one, she added, "I'll be quiet now."

As she sat she looked over at Aclaí. She saw him focus on what he was doing and she saw how, when he forgot himself, his face relaxed into boyish concentration and the grief was erased.

As she watched he took the Crystal that she had brought and put it on the Crystal skull. Then he said Words again and raised his hand. She saw the red-spark eyes on the ring glitter, then the shadow in the Crystal flicked into the skull. It was there lending darkness to the eye-sockets.

She spent a few breaths watching him, then she got up.

"Good night, Damhánalla my friend," he called after her.

"Good night, my lord," she called back.

Réalta was doing exactly what her mother had warned her not to do: she was daydreaming. She heard the metallic sound of the bell in the distance and returned to her surroundings. The bell stopped and they stood in silence for a couple of breaths. Then the music began. It was a song they had heard many times on the Visions: one that her mother had sung to Réalta in the night when she had been a little girl.

As the song reached its end the great doors began to open and the musicians segued into a fanfare. Five Adepts entered. Réalta saw that they were four young people leading an old man. The tallest was a girl with curly blonde hair who offered her arm for him to lean on. Beside her was someone Réalta thought of as old Sea People: a slender girl with black curly hair and pale skin. Behind them were another couple: a handsome girl from upriver and, on her arm, a youthful-looking north-man. Seeing the man who led them shuffle she wondered how old he was. Then she suddenly realised. He must be the Mentor. What she was looking at was the effect of thirteen centuries.

It took the old man a long time to work down the line of them but, at last, he was in front of her. She shifted her weight onto one leg the way her mother had taught her. When he looked her in the face she was surprised that his eyes were green. She stood still while he examined her body, feeling ridiculous. He put a hand on her hip and she felt his touch between the lacing. His skin felt cold and dry like the skin of a lizard. Then he reached up a little and his hand brushed over her breast. She was aware that her mother was right behind her and she felt embarrassment colour her cheeks. His thumb found her nipple through the cloth and he pinched it, taking her by surprise. She knew she had made a noise.

"What is your name, child?" he asked. His voice was stronger than she had expected in such an old man.

"I am Réalta, my lord," she replied.

"And you are a bright young thing. Would you shine in my darkness, Réalta?"

"I will do my best, my lord," she answered. Then, without thinking, she added, "But stars do not give much light."

Innealta sat in her own room in the Midsummer Palace, ignoring the sound of the rain battering on the shutters. Words of Light illuminated the room and she had used the Words of the Vision to turn one wall into a window that looked into the City. She was not paying attention so she hadn't noticed the voice outside her door.

Aclaí put his head around the door but Innealta still didn't notice. He saw beyond her to the Visions and the Candidates lining up. He closed the door behind him and sat on the bed beside her. "Innealta?" he asked, "Are you all right?"

"I'm remembering," she said. "Hold me."

He put his arm around her shoulder and she leaned closer to him.

From the Vision on the wall they heard the bell in the Court of the Favourites. Aclaí noticed that he still reacted to the sound of it even though he had not been to the City for forty years. They watched through the eyes of someone on a Flyer as they looked down at the Hill. Five blue-cloaked figures walked down from the Court of the Favourites: an old man flanked on each side by young-looking women with a man and woman bringing up the rear. As they entered the hall the viewpoint changed. Aclaí and Innealta looked along the line.

"There's less than fifty," Innealta said.

"The City is dying," Aclaí replied.

"You won't have anything left to lead."

"I told you many times, Innealta. I won't be Mentor. Let it die."

They sat in silence while the Mentor picked his way along the line. Aclaí felt Innealta's body beside his and noticed the little tensions in her shoulders and neck increased and decreased. As he felt her muscles go rigid, he spoke.

"She looks like she is ready to be sold." The girl the Mentor was speaking to in the Visions was dressed in a short red tunic laced at the sides. The Mentor placed his hand on her body. "Look at him. I would think he will Select her. It wouldn't surprise me if he Initiated her tonight."

"It's cruel," Innealta replied.

"Look at the way she has dressed herself. What do you think she came for?"

"She was brought," Innealta growled. "Look at her mother behind her. She is the one who is selling her daughter to the Mentor. The daughter is consumed with embarrassment."

"Her cheeks are nearly as red as her dress, but that might be excitement." But Aclaí could see the way the girl was uncomfortable from the little motion she made to pull the hem of her dress down.

"She has never even been kissed and there he is handling her like some piece of over-ripe fruit. If he takes her tonight it will be simply because he is an evil old man satisfying his lusts on a girl who won't know what he is doing to her."

Aclaí turned to look Innealta in the face. "What is the matter with you?" he asked. "You know nothing about that poor girl."

"Aclaí, I remember my own Selection. He brought me up the Hill and he... I had never been kissed by a boy either. They dressed me up like a slave-girl but that wasn't how I felt. I was scared and humiliated and I knew every one of ye was watching me and knowing what he was going to do to me."

"You are really angry about this, aren't you?"

"Of course I am angry!"

"Innealta, you know how it turns you on to be watched. It –"

"Is that all that matters? It doesn't matter what is happening in my brain as long as the other end of me is aroused enough? My arousal is rooted in shame and embarrassment. That makes it easy to arouse me but that doesn't mean I want to be aroused like that. I want it to strengthen the friendships I feel. I don't want to be made to feel like a slave just because that gives me the strongest orgasm. I need to live my life after those feelings have passed."

"I want to strengthen my friendships too," Aclaí replied.

"Do you remember when you first discovered how much it made my body react? Do you remember how you made me do it sitting on the edge of the fountain?"

"I didn't force..." Aclaí stopped and drew breath. "I'm sorry, Innealta. It is taking me a long time to learn to put aside the ways of the City. I am sorry I hurt you."

They sat beside each other a while, him watching the muscles in her face as they slowly relaxed. "Hold me," she whispered.

He held her. "I am sorry," he whispered back.

"I have forgiven you, my lord. It's just that watching the City's rituals reminds me."

"Then why watch?"

"My lord, you have sworn to destroy the City. None of us know for sure if you will do it or merely re-mould it to your will. But we need to follow you and your anger terrifies all of us."

"I am sorry I frighten you, Innealta. As I become stronger I need to become more controlled. But I find I can't do it anymore."

"I understand, my lord. I know why your are angry. But it is easier for me to follow you if I remember how much the City hurt me."

"So you watch the Visions to make yourself more angry?"

"I do, my lord. I don't know if I can follow you against the City without being angry."

"That sounds strange. I'm trying to control my anger and you are trying to kindle yours."

"It makes sense, my lord."

"I see that now. But it still sounds strange."

He turned to the next Candidate in the row and she silently let her breath out. Her nipple was sensitive where he had pinched it and she could feel it against the texture of her dress. She felt like a slave-girl in the market waiting while the rich man considered buying her and looked at a couple of others. At least he did not haggle for her in front of her mother. She knew the old man would sooner or later want sex with her and she wondered what that would be like. Would he be gentle with her? She glanced down the row at him talking to a boy with hair braided in spiral patterns. She felt she wanted to help look after him, like the girls that had accompanied him into the hall, but she did not feel any attraction towards him at all. This was why her mother had dressed her as a slave-girl, then. She was offering her daughter's body in exchange for her chance to win Immortality.

Then she heard her own name and looked up in surprise. She was daydreaming. The Mentor was calling names but she did not know why. She hoped he would repeat his instructions at the end of the list. There were five more names after hers, then he added, "Ye are the one thousand three hundred and seventieth cohort of the Sea People. Come and learn."

Some of the others came forward and lined up behind the Mentor and his four pretty companions. Réalta went up and stood behind them. She glanced back and saw her mother's smile and a pride that she had never felt before. She wanted to run back and hug her mother goodbye but she knew it was too late. She would have to wait until Midwinter now. She squeezed her lips together as the musicians began to play again and they walked out.

They had hardly left the Hall of the Novices when a couple more blue-robes came out and called as they walked. "New Candidates," one said, "come this way."

She started to follow them but the pretty north-man who accompanied the Mentor came back to her. "Not you, child," he said. "You carry on with us."

She wondered why he had singled her out as they climbed the stairs. As they went through each gate the buildings became more grand but she could see that more and more of them were deserted. She suddenly realised that these were the Courts of the Hill she had read about in one of her father's books: the Court of the Veterans then the Court of the Immortals. She also saw that all the grand palaces of the Court of the Immortals were empty. Was the Mentor really the only Immortal left in the City? She knew Immortals were rare enough, but could there really be none left?

But they carried on climbing, into the Court of the Favourites. Twelve identical cottages stood in a circle around a fountain, with a larger thirteenth at the end overlooking the sea. Again, only three of the cottages seemed to be inhabited. Behind the cottages, nearer the wall there were other buildings. The pretty north-man took her into one of them. Two servants were there, and the one who was shaped like a woman looked Réalta up and down. "What do you think she needs, Lord Liús?" the servant girl asked.

"Not much," Liús replied. "I will say Words of Freshness so she ought to have more perfume." He turned to Réalta. "What perfume are you wearing, child?"

"It is jasmine, my lord," she replied. "And I am not a child," she added, looking at his beardless chin. "I have nineteen winters. I think that is a few more than you, my lord."

Liús laughed. "I am well into my third century," he replied. "Immortal Breath allows us to choose what age we seem. Appearances can be very deceptive on the Hill."

"So the Mentor chooses to look like an old man?"

"He does not. Immortality does not mean living forever. Now, child, I think you need to ask fewer questions. It would be wise for you to learn to be careful, at least until you understand more. Offending higher Ranks is one of the biggest dangers for purple Novices like you. Do you understand?"

Réalta resisted the urge to ask why Novices might be purple. Instead she answered, "I do, my lord. I will try not to ask too many questions."

"Good. Now take off that dress. What is your name?" he added, as an afterthought.

"I am Réalta, my lord."

"Of course you are," he answered, remembering. "Now, Réalta, your job tonight is to shine for him. Smile and listen, like you would to your favourite grandparent."

"My favourite grandfather never pinched my breast, my lord."

"That doesn't surprise me. For that part you should treat him like the boyfriend you were most in love with, when you first felt it. Don't ask questions, don't nag, don't tell him you love him. Just give him what he wants with all your heart. Can you do that?"

"I... I think I can, my lord."

"Good. Now, Réalta, why is that dress still on?"

"I... I have servants to undress me at home, my lord."

"If you obtain higher Rank you will be able to get servants to undress you here, too. I suppose you could in the dormitories, but I never saw it or heard of it." He watched Réalta struggle with the dress and then he looked at the servants. "Help her," he said.

Réalta relaxed a little as the younger, less obviously female servant lifted the dress off her. Liús said strange, unnatural Words and then put his hand on her body. She cringed and tried not to giggle. "Are you all right, Réalta?" he asked.

"It's... ticklish, my lord." she answered. She glanced down and saw that his hands seemed to brushing hair off her body, falling to the floor around his fingers. "Will it grow back?" she asked, just before she remembered that she shouldn't ask questions.

"This is the way the Mentor wants us," he answered. "We are all like this."

His fingers under her arms were the worst and she tried not to curl up completely. But then he seemed satisfied. He placed a hand low on her belly and she wondered for a moment if he would make her have sex with her there in the dressing room. But instead he whispered Words and she felt a sudden cramp under his hand. She tried not to cry out for a heartbeat and then the pain was gone.

"What was that?" she gasped.

"Words of Sealing," he told her. "You wouldn't want to get pregnant, would you?"

"I..." Réalta felt the heat on her face. "The Sea People do not marry, my lord," she said.

He smiled at her. "Dress her," he said to the servant. The servant girl found undergarments of silk while the other one helped her put her dress back on. She saw as they reached and bent that the servants were naked beneath their tunics and that the tunics opened easily as they moved.

Liús spoke more strange Words and touched her and she felt a crawling sensation on her skin like the feeling of dried-on sand flaking off. Then the more ambiguous servant dabbled oil of jasmine here and there. The girl-servant hung a necklace around her neck and bangles around her wrists and ankles. A hair-grip like a butterfly in enamelled gold grasped her hair at the back. The gold made her feel like the king's best courtesan: still a slave but property of someone powerful and important at least.

Which, of course, she was. Who in the world – in any world – was more powerful or important than the Mentor?

As soon as Liús left the dressing room with the new Candidate the female servant went over to the other. "Do you think she will cry?" she whispered to him.

"I don't know, Fionna," he snapped. "Did you?"

"Don't be like that, Donn," she whispered.

"I'm sorry," he answered. "She looks like a girl from my home country, the Riverbank."

"She's pretty," Fionna said. She knelt down at Donn's feet and looked up at him. She brushed her cheek on his thigh. "So are you," she added.

"I wasn't pretty enough," he answered. "She was Selected. I ended up as a servant."

"Oh, Donn," she whispered back. "That doesn't matter to me." She reached up under his tunic. "I don't think you were rejected for not being pretty enough. I am sure you were plenty pretty enough. You just weren't cruel enough."

"I am not cruel enough to enjoy what the Mentor is about to do to that poor girl."

Fionna stroked him under the tunic. "It seems that some part of you is enjoying it."

He put his hand down on her head. "What do you want from me?"

"Don't you know?" she asked.

"Don't you get enough of that from blue-robes? Or there are other servants who will indulge you. Cnámh is always willing to –"

"He only does that after a punishment," she sighed. "I want to share love, Donn. I don't want to be a receptacle for someone who doesn't care about me. I want it to be a friend for once."

"Fionna, I am just a boy. Not even that. I have nothing to offer you."

"I don't need anything. Just your love and your friendship."

"I never have," he whispered. "I don't even know if I can. I don't know if –"

She planted a kiss on him and felt the way his skin shivered. "I think you will be fine."

"Let's go down to our dormitory, then," he whispered. "If that is really what you want."

"I want it here. I want it when I hear her cry."

"What if we're caught?"

"Then she won't be the only one crying." Fionna looked up at Donn. "Come on, Donn," she said. "Just take a risk once."

"All right then," he sighed. He reached down for her and helped her to her feet. They crept into the back of the dressing room, among the clothes.

When they heard the purple novice girl cry out Fionna bit her own lip to keep silent.

Réalta knocked gently on the door. She did not hear a reply. She looked back. Lord Liús motioned to her to knock again and she did so – a little harder this time. Then, on the third time, she heard a voice.

"Who is it?" he called.

"I am Réalta, my lord. I am a purple Novice."

"Come in," he said.

It was dark in the room after she closed the door behind her. He was sitting on the bed waiting for her. She saw the blue cloak around his shoulders and realised he was not wearing anything else. His skin around his face, neck, arms and feet were more wrinkled than the rest of him. His face and hands showed his age far more than his actual body.

"Come and sit beside me," he said.

She sat on his bed. "Here, my lord?"

"You are Selected now, Réalta," he answered. "Adepts call me 'Mentor'."

"I am sorry, Mentor."

He reached to the table beside the bed and touched the goad there. "Once I would have beaten a purple Novice for that mistake. But *she* doesn't like me to be cruel."

Réalta remembered Liús' instructions not to ask questions. She turned to him and tried to imagine that he was a handsome young man. Looking at the shape of his face beneath the wrinkled and marked skin and the shrunken flesh she could not see that he had ever had the same beauty as, say, Liús. She smiled at him. He put his hand into the side of her dress, below the lacing, and she felt his fingers between her thighs. She parted her legs as she knew she should.

"Lie back," he told her. As she complied she felt the fingers inside the undergarment that Liús had given her. His thumb brushed against her secret spot and his fingers touched her lower, deeper, where–

He whispered Words and she cried out as the feeling hit her. It was centred between his thumb and finger but it forced itself up through her whole body and down her legs, knocking the breath out of her and curling her toes. The sounds that came from her throat were animal noises: a low growl that she could neither modulate or control as it grew inside her to a scream. He held her like that for maybe five breaths before releasing the feeling. She lay there and shuddered as the muscles of her legs quivered and threatened her with cramp.

"Relax a moment," he said. Then she felt his fingers slip into her body. "Have you never had a boyfriend?" he asked.

"Never, Mentor," she whispered. She looked at his face and saw his disappointment. "Is that all right?"

He took his hand away from her body. "Do you have any idea what to do?"

"I have seen animals do it, my... Mentor," she replied. She opened her knees wider. "I know what you want."

"I doubt you do," he answered.

"I am sorry, Mentor."

"Don't be sorry. *She* wouldn't want me to make you sorry. Just go and... just go."

Réalta got to her feet and staggered to the door.

"Go on," he said.

She went.

Aclaí closed the door to Innealta's room as softly as he could. He crept quietly to his own room and shut the door behind him. For all his care not to make a noise he did not notice Damhánalla watching him.

After he closed the door to his room she tiptoed up to stand behind the door. She reached for the latch to let herself in but then she stopped. She bit her lip and Breathed a couple of breaths. Then she reached again, but again she stopped before she touched it.

Then she turned and ran on the tips of her toes back along the corridor to her own room.

7

Cheating Death

"Hey lads, look at this!" He lifted the branch a little further, revealing more of the space beneath it where the tree was hollow. In the space there was a red-haired girl curled up, asleep.

"It's a vat-creature," one of his companions whispered. "Look at the shape of the ears."

"And the wings," the other added. What he had taken for some sort of a cloak was shaped like the wings of a moth, freckled in pink and brown.

The little Forest-creature stirred and big green eyes looked up at them.

"Don't be scared," the leader said. "We won't hurt you, will we, lads?"

The other two laughed and the creature looked from one to the other.

"You are a cute little thing," the leader said. "You look very like –"

The creature launched herself out of the hollow space in the tree and the three of them, taken by surprise, were buffeted by her wings as she took flight. Their leader was knocked back into the other two. All three found themselves lying in the mud. The wind of her passage raised a storm of leaves that settled back down on them.

Their leader sat up and drew his sword. He wiped his nose with the back of his hand, carefully avoiding the wobbly feel of it, and his hand came away covered in blood. One of his companions did not stir: they had been knocked out. The other one looked at him from the one eye that had not been swollen shut by the blow.

"Evil little monster!" the leader said. "We're not going to let her get away with that!"

"Don't you ever shut up?" Liús laughed.

"You know I don't," Cathúa replied. "You say you admire my brain? Well, my brain never stops. This is what the real me is like."

"I know." He leaned a little more weight on her, making her gasp with pleasure. He looked down at her and noticed the way the blue glint in her eyes was matched by the green glint in the eyes of the little cat pendant that lay on one of her breasts. But even as he saw the pink growing on her cheeks he knew the mind behind her eyes was still racing ahead.

And as soon as she had her breath back she spoke again. "So how did you learn your Immortal Breath?"

"You left me behind," he grumbled.

"Oh, I know how to fix that," she smiled. "Just relax and I'll do this _"

He grunted and half rolled off her. She wriggled out from under him and lay beside him, resting her head on his arm. He turned his head so he could see her as he lay on his belly. "That's good," he told her.

"I know what you like," she said. "But I want you to tell me where you got your Immortal Breath."

"Can't it wait?"

"Can you wait?"

"You know I can." He smiled at her. "I think it was to do with..." she felt the tension inside him. "I first got the feeling of Immortal Rank when Eala was teaching me empathy." He relaxed a little and then suddenly her stimulation overwhelmed him. "You know I could be killed for that, don't you?" he gasped.

"You could be executed at Evening Meal," she agreed. As she watched him she saw his arousal show on his face.

Then, at last, she whispered Words of Freshness then caressed his neck, bringing another fresh shudder from his body. "What about Éise?" she asked.

He took a moment to get his breath back. "Éise was working on Words of Power. The Mentor started to teach her Words that require Immortal Breath: Words that Heal Bone; Transmutation; that sort of thing. Then one day he told her she had Sixteenth Rank." He turned over onto his side. "Why do you keep asking?"

"I have a theory about the process that leads to Immortal Breath."

"Can you share it?"

"I'd rather not."

"All right then," he agreed. "Tell me when you are ready."

"I will," she promised.

* * *

Eibheara sat and watched in the lazy sunshine of the late afternoon. She was sitting by the fountain but she had used Words of Concealment to prevent her from being noticed. She knew that Éise must be in the house she shared with Liús but she never heard Éise anymore. She wondered why that might be.

Of course Liús was not there to make Éise cry out. Eibheara knew he had gone into Cathúa's room and that the two of them were playing in there. If she had been Éise she would have been consumed with jealous rage. It occurred to her that perhaps Éise was also consumed with jealous rage but concealing it behind a smiling mask. Eibheara knew that Éise was much better at concealing her true feelings than Eibheara was. Éise was a sneaky sort of person.

It wasn't that sort of sneakiness she was looking for, though. She knew that Cathúa's Patrol was rostered at midnight. They were supposed to be going out to Linn Dubh to deliver an ultimatum to the Forest house but, if Cathúa did not emerge, it would mean that a low-Rank Patrol would be sent instead. Given the strategic nature of the ultimatum it was just the sort of thing that Aclaí's agent in the City would interfere with.

Eibheara knew that Aclaí had an agent on the top of the Hill. She was simply waiting for proof before she acted.

Eventually, only a few hundred breaths before midnight, Cathúa emerged with Liús. Liús had nothing on but the blue cloak on his shoulders and Cathúa wore nothing but a few golden bangles and the glittering pendant around her neck. Eibheara could see from the way they held hands that they had been intimate. She saw them having a whispered conversation as they held each other before they parted and Cathúa went down to the Patrol house. As she walked she found a blue silk dress and leather boots on her Silver Cord.

Once they were out of sight Eibheara walked back to her own bed. She sat down and she found her sword on her Silver Cord. She thought of the Patrol leader.

what is it my lady the Patrol leader's words asked.

"Is Cathúa going on Patrol?"

she has taken a flyer my lady but she is not with her patrol tonight

"Will you report to me if anything happens to the patrol assigned to Linn Dubh?"

i will my lady

"Thank you," Eibheara replied before she let go of her sword.

* * *

Éise heard him coming and she threw her sword under the bed, out of sight. She looked up just as Liús was about to kiss her forehead. So he kissed her mouth instead. Her hands stroked his nakedness.

After a few moments she spoke. "So, how was it, my lion?"

"She is learning."

"Has she learned everything you can teach?"

"Probably."

"Then why?" Éise looked at his face. "Are you getting attached to her?"

"I feel sorry for her. Do you mind?"

"A lion should have more than one lioness. Enjoy her." Éise frowned a little. "You are still enjoying her, are you?"

"When she turns her mind to something she does it well. She is capable enough and she is pretty, even if people rarely notice."

"People notice," Éise smiled. "She is far better at getting others to notice when she remembers to try. Cathúa is the same as us. She has learned it in secret."

"Does she know what we are trying to do?"

"Probably not. Do you think she would approve if she did?"

"I don't think so – but I am not sure. She seems very keen to defend the City from Aclaí but it is obvious that she believes the battle to already be lost."

"Perhaps we could persuade her that it would be better to work for a good defeat than for an unattainable victory."

"I doubt it, my love. Cathúa is very literal-minded."

"She is. Where is she now?"

"She has gone on Patrol."

"To Linn Dubh?"

"She had some idea she wanted to pursue. I think it might be something to do with Immortal Breath. Anyway, she has gone somewhere else."

"Did she suddenly have her idea in bed?"

"She did," Liús laughed.

"Do you want me to finish what she started, my lion?"

"I'm fine, love. I should probably return to the watch room. I should try and be Chamberlain."

"Do that, then." Éise reached up to stroke his shoulder as he left. Then, when the curtain was closed and the door sealed with Words that Hold the Portal, Éise found her sword. She thought of Aclaí.

éise

"There's a change of plan. Cathúa is not going to Linn Dubh. It will be some Novice patrol."

good

"Will you be nice?"

of course Aclaí replied. *i will honour our agreement*

"They will be a Novice patrol, Aclaí," she reminded him.

if they turn back then they will be unharmed

Coinín led his Patrol through the Forest. This was the price he paid for being a hero back in the City: to lead a little band of Novice girls into the Forest. He knew that, when he got them back to the dormitories, he could pick any one, any handful that appealed to him. He had worked his way through the most forward girls. Tonight he was planning to try out the dreamy girl and her shy little friend with her strong tribal accent. He had learned that still waters often ran deep.

Osna rode her horse close to Réalta's horse at the back of the group. She put her hand on her sword-hilt and glanced over at her friend. As she did so Réalta felt her own sword-hilt tingle. She smiled at Osna and put her hand on her own Hilt.

"What is it?" Réalta whispered.

She saw Osna's lips move slightly as she formed the words. *think will try kiss us tonight*

"He's worked his way through the rest of the Patrol," Réalta whispered back. "It is bound to be our turn one night."

well taken much time

"Did you have a boyfriend before you came to the City?"

not one boyfriend Osna smiled back. *many boyfriends*

"You didn't."

did her friend replied. *quiet in city language not quiet at home*

"I suppose you might not be," Réalta agreed.

you

"I never did."

mentor first

"The Mentor didn't either. He Initiated me with his fingertips but he never stuck his thing in me."

second rank virgin

"Not for long, I guess." Réalta sighed. "I wish it could be someone more... more than Coinín. He has a big mouth but he is not..." Réalta realised the Patrol had stopped ahead of them.

They heard voices.

"Turn back," the voice called through the trees.

Foscúil was walking through the darkness of the Forest. When he travelled with Aclaí and Miotal he rode but sometimes he preferred to walk and get a better understanding of the territory. That day he was looking at his own defences and hoping to set up an exercise that would take them by surprise. None of them knew he was out.

He had identified that there was a patrol ahead of him which was not on any of his scheduled routes for the evening. Either one of his own patrols was not following their schedule or one of the City's patrols had come out far further than they normally did. Either was a crime for which he would exact a punishment. The patrol was riding and he was on foot, but he knew this part of the Forest very well. Aclaí had shown him shortcuts.

A few breaths later and he was standing behind a tree-trunk listening for them. He heard hooves ahead. There didn't seem enough for a whole patrol. He watched a single blue-cloaked figure ride into the clearing and he stepped out. The moonlight glittered green on a pendant at her breast.

"Cathúa," he called. "What are you doing here?"

"Patrolling," she replied. She breathed the horse still.

"Didn't the Mentor tell you all to stop?"

"He told us to turn back as soon as we encountered one of ye," she agreed. "But sometimes it is better to do what is best for him than what he instructs us to do."

"That is the sort of thing Eala taught, Cathúa," Foscúil warned.

"Did she?" Cathúa smiled. "How would I know? I quickly realised that I was too socially awkward to benefit from her lectures."

Foscúil stepped out from behind his tree and smiled back. "Do you know that Aclaí's forces have standing orders to kill any City patrol that will not turn back?"

"I do."

"So, will you turn back?"

"I know that the House of Maoineas follows a discipline of obeying orders or dying in the attempt. It makes reasoning with them difficult, since they will not reason until their discipline is already broken. That leaves killing them the only alternative."

"Do you think you can kill me, Cathúa?"

"I think there is a good chance that, should we duel, I would be able to kill you. But I spoke of –"

Foscúil laughed. "Do you think that the extra two Ranks the Mentor has awarded you enable you to beat me at sword, Cathúa?"

"I don't," she replied mildly.

"And yet you boast that you would be able to kill me in a duel?"

"It is not my habit to boast. Boasting is grounded in emotions and I am not very good with emotions. I prefer truth. You asked me a question and I replied truthfully."

"I should give you an opportunity to put your 'truth' to the test," he laughed.

"I would prefer that you listen to what I say instead. I spoke of the discipline of the Maoineas patrols and how it made them deaf to reason. The logic I used only applies if they have been given orders. If instead they are the givers of the orders, perhaps reason could prevail."

"What are you talking about?"

Cathúa sighed. "Did you give the order to turn back or kill the City patrols, Foscúil?"

"I did. What of it?"

"If you felt there was a reason to countermand or limit that order, or to make an exception, you would?"

"Of course I would."

"So it is worth talking to you, isn't it?"

"Perhaps," he smiled, understanding at last. "Why didn't you just say that at the start?"

"I was trying to," she replied. "You mistook it for a duelling boast."

"I..." Foscúil stopped. "All right, Cathúa, talk to me."

Cathúa got down off her horse and came over. She was not wearing armour and he saw the way her body moved inside her dress. Part of his mind was surprised to see the rest of his mind respond to someone he had long ago dismissed. She walked over to him. "I wanted to ask you about the Mentor," she said.

"What about him?"

"Do you want to see him die?"

"I work for Lord Aclaí, Cathúa."

"That is not what I asked."

"You asked if I give the orders, rather than obey them. Well, sometimes it is one and sometimes it is the other. Lord Aclaí gives me orders and many of the orders I give are ways to follow his."

"Has he ordered you to kill the Mentor?"

"Not yet," Foscúil grinned. "But he will. You have not seen what Aclaí has become."

"Do you think you could do it if he ordered you to?"

"I think I could."

"Would you repeat that with the Truthful Aura?"

"All right, I am not sure I could. Initiation is confusing as I am sure you know. But if he ordered it – when he orders it – I will do my best. Elder Immortal Rank seems to undermine the effects of Initiation."

"I know."

"How?"

"Eibheara. She is able to ignore the Mentor's orders, able to perform Forbidden Art. What she is not able to do is to set out to hurt him."

"Well, perhaps Aclaí will be able to do what she cannot."

"He has only been Elder Immortal for four decades. She is Twenty-Sixth Rank."

"Well then, time will tell. I will follow Aclaí as far as he leads." Foscúil shrugged. "Anyway, the point will be moot soon enough."

"Because he will be dead?"

"Because he will be dead."

"Have you told Aclaí that you could breathe Immortal Breath into him?"

Foscúil's smile vanished. "How do you know..?"

"I am not stupid, Foscúil. It is not hard for –"

"Has anyone else realised? Have you told anyone?"

"Not yet. Anyone who made a study of the subject of where Immortal Breath comes from ought to be able to figure it out. Both of ye have a Path to Immortality and Eala's Path, although not recognised, is clear enough in the City's statistics. Presumably if Éirime had taught singing in the City then her Path would have been recognised too."

"That is how Blátha gained her Immortal Breath," admitted Foscúil.

"How do you know?"

"The Mentor tells me to teach the Favourites Immortality. I recognise when the job is done by someone else instead. Éirime taught Blátha to sing and she also taught her Immortality."

"My study was statistical: I started with the large number of Immortals to appear when Eala was teaching and worked backwards from there. Since Blátha was also being taught by you I wasn't going to spot her."

"How do you know I can do it when someone has lost their own Breath?"

"Cabairí is my grand-nephew, Foscúil. He told me about Rian."

"I see. Now I think it is time for that duel."

"What?" asked Cathúa. "Why?"

"Because although you are clever you are also stupid. You didn't tell anyone. If I kill you then the secret will die with you."

"Don't you want to save him?"

"Only if Lord Aclaí wants to save him."

"Someone else will figure it out, Foscúil."

"But they won't. Nobody else is boring enough to sift through the archives looking for patterns in the numbers. I doubt anyone will keep the archives after you are gone."

Cathúa shifted her weight and breathed deeply. She reached her hand up and touched his cheek. "Boring, am I?" she asked.

He reached his hand up to put on hers. "Did you learn that from a book?" he breathed.

She whispered Words and he jumped back as he felt her Breath through her touch. "You sneaky little –" he cursed as he pulled out his sword.

Now this was the dangerous bit, she thought. But Immortality doesn't mean living forever even if she was sure she would survive this encounter. She found her armour and sword on her Silver Cord and danced out of his way. She knew she could not last long but she just needed to manipulate him into one of his hand-changes. She feinted to the right then danced around to the left. He changed grip with his Silver Cord as he stepped in to deliver the killing blow. She snatched his sword up off the ground and stepped back.

"Now do you think I could kill you?" she asked.

"Go on, then," he replied, refusing to show fear.

"You know that I won't unless you force me. I won't throw away the opportunity for you to save his life."

"I will do it if Lord Aclaí orders it. Not otherwise."

"Aclaí has sworn to throw down the City. He hasn't sworn to kill the Mentor. You might preserve his life if you manage not to lose your own."

"Well, I won't make this mistake again. I don't know what Words you used but it went wrong at the hand-change."

"It went wrong when you underestimated me, Foscúil. This time I used the Tangling of the Silver Cord, one of Ulchabhán's Formulae, but next time I will use another Formula of Words that you don't even know exists. You see, you may have the Gift of Anleacán in sword craft but I am the City's librarian."

Cathúa turned and walked away into the Forest, carrying his sword. He watched her as she went out of view and wondered at how much he had underestimated her.

But he had survived and it was not a mistake he was going to make again.

* * *

Réalta muttered Words of Seeing Heat and looked ahead. Four Forest warriors were blocking the way: Réalta could see their ears poking up through their hats and hair. "Coinín," she called, "Lady Cathúa said we should disengage immediately we saw Aclaí's forces."

"I am not a coward," replied Coinín, "And I don't take orders from a purple Novice girl."

"Be ready to ride back," Réalta whispered, her hand on her sword. "They are only on foot but if we stay and fight they will slaughter us. They have a Mountain Warrior among them and a Night Warrior too. One of them is an archer and the other one has hand on sword. Even if we defeat them they will have reinforcements."

see so much

"I am using the Words of Seeing Heat. We will –"

Réalta saw Coinín draw his sword and spur his horse. The Mountain Warrior stepped forward in front of the others in the enemy party as the Novice girls halfheartedly followed their Veteran leader. The Mountain Warrior must have seen him coming but he just stood with his sword before him. As the horse was about to run him down he stepped aside and swung.

The blow caught Coinín just below the jaw. The armour held but he was knocked backwards over the horse's tail. He landed hard on his back and, before he had a chance to move, the Mountain Warrior put his foot on Coinín's breastplate.

From behind the Mountain Warrior came the sound of a bowstring, and Réalta heard an arrow swish by. "Let's go," she whispered, as with her Breath she turned the horse. She kicked her heels hard and tried to stay on.

Osna was ahead of her as they galloped down the Forest trail. Then she realised that Osna had a small figure sitting on the saddle behind her, just as that figure stabbed a knife into Osna's neck, under her helm. She saw the blood spurt out and Osna fell off sideways, like a full sack tumbling to the ground. The little winged boy waved the knife at Réalta as she rode by, and plunged it down through the neck-hole and under Osna's breastplate.

Réalta knew it was too late. There was nothing she could do but keep riding and hope she didn't fall off.

* * *

As Cathúa rode back to Lorgcoiseaigéan she noticed Foscúil's sword vanish. Well, she knew the Tangling of the Silver Cord would not last long. But she climbed in her Flyer before he had a chance to catch her up – assuming he was stupid enough to have followed her.

The Flyer took off and she leaned forward to make it accelerate. The waves beneath her blurred. She thought back to their conversation. He had called her clever but also stupid and, as she considered it, she realised he was right. She was taking her survival for granted, even though it was not proved, and it was making her careless. She needed someone to confide in: someone she could rely on to take care of things if her plans went wrong.

The first person she considered was Liús. She enjoyed his company more than she had ever expected to enjoy the company of a boy. She noticed how her emotions encouraged her to trust him but she was too good at observing the effect of her own feelings to trust them to be the judge of him. What reason do I have to trust him, she asked herself, other than the way my feelings respond to his talents in bed? Absolutely none, she concluded. He was a blue-robe, an Immortal as highly Ranked as her, and his first loyalty was to Éise.

That was, if his first loyalty was not to the Mentor. Cathúa knew she was trying to do the best for the Mentor in what little time was left but she also had to accept that Liús did not have any reason to believe that. To explain her actions in terms of her motives required that someone understood the things she had experienced. But firstly she had to recognise that nobody would believe her; and secondly she had to accept that these were the very things that the Mentor had forbidden her from revealing. Even Eibheara had recognised that. She would not be able to recruit Liús as an ally.

Then she needed a servant. Her hand strayed to her cat pendant as she remembered Gruaige as she had last seen her – happy with her family at last. The emerald eyes glinted as she moved it. Gruaige would have been perfect but of course she had not even considered trying to get Gruaige to return to the City. She could not imagine what the consequences of such an attempt might be but every possible consequence she could deduce would be disastrous for Cathúa and everything she cared about. Gruaige was not an option. Gruaige was never an option, she reminded herself. She told herself every time she thought of what had happened to Gruaige was determined by fate and that any free will she thought she had was just an illusion, but the the thought of the opportunities that had been lost when she chose to experiment on Gruaige made her want to vomit.

Ahead she saw the white peak of the Coral Mountain appear through the haze: a bright flat top, shining in the moonlight, disturbing the flow of the clouds. As she steered the Flyer towards the summit the sea beneath her gave way to the regular fields and ordered woodland plantations of the Land of the Immortals.

The little creature was not easy to track. Although the trail she left was clear enough at first they kept losing sight of it after a few hundred paces. Their leader was aware that she was following the Paths. She was not following Paths they had been assigned to patrol but instead Paths that led deeper into the wild Forest. But the memory of her green eyes and of the tears in his own eyes when his companions had straightened his broken nose spurred him on. They could go back and finish their patrol when they had settled this matter.

He could see in the grim determination of the others that they shared his intentions. They were blue-robes: a Veteran patrol. None of them would let a pretty little creature like that humiliate them.

"I think we lost her," one of them announced.

"Well, look around," the leader insisted.

Then they heard her voice calling. He looked up. She was sitting high in a conifer two or three times the height of a man above them. He pointed his sword but, before he could think of Words, she leaped off the tree and, with a flutter of those wings, she vanished ahead of them. They picked up the trail where she had landed and ran on after her.

They saw her again several times. It was as if she was flirting with them and each new appearance simply swelled their determination to catch her. They had gone deep off their assigned Path when they saw her sitting on the opposite bank of a stream. She was threading purple irises, plaiting the stems together, and had her back to them.

Their leader motioned to the other two and they carefully stepped into the stream. They were experienced in the woods and the sound of their movement was quieter than the water over the stones. The leader thought he saw one of her ears move, like a cat, when –

There was a blow to his neck and he couldn't breathe. He reached up and found an arrow protruding. Behind their quarry were three more of the little creatures carrying bows. Unable to say Words he caught a glimpse of one of his companions, falling, with one of the creatures riding his shoulders and wielding a heavy hand axe. Then he fell forward into the water as he fell into the greyness of unconsciousness.

* * *

The Words of Light reflected off the limestone of the cave and below the water splashed blue and green even in that darkened space. The glittering light was reflected in the eyes of her pendant. Cathúa was standing on a ledge and reaching through a door of Metal. Inside the door was a space just large enough for her to fit if she curled up. She was just putting the last of the Metal sheets into it. By her feet, on the ledge, was the chest she kept in her library in the City.

She glanced at the last Metal sheet as she slotted it into the wooden rack behind the door. She could feel the roughness of the engraving on the box: tiny letters covered it. Each sheet was one of the books from the Library, the letters miniaturised almost to illegibility to make the print fit on the available space. Being Metal they would last forever. She had wanted to make the lettering even smaller but she wanted the books to be readable without needing Words of Power. She knew not to rely on Words of Power in the future.

As she slid the sheet into place her sword-hilt tingled. She moved her hands in reaction and caught her finger on the edge of the sheet. The slight drag warned her that her skin was caught. She stepped back and put her other hand on the sword-hilt. The cut finger went in her mouth and she tasted blood.

"What is it?" she vocalised.

this is the patrol leader in lorgcoiseaigéan came the reply. *a patrol has been lost*

"Again? How this time?"

they ran into forces of maoineas

"Nobody survived?"

one survived my lady she is in lorgcoiseaigéan do you want to speak to her

"I will come and visit. I have a fast Flyer. Keep her there until I am ready."

as you wish my lady

Cathúa released the sword-hilt and took her finger out of her mouth. Redness spread from a cut as wide as her nail. She quickly whispered the Words that Heal Skin and then slammed the door shut. Then she whispered The Words that Hold the Portal. Finally she turned from the cavern and climbed and wriggled her way back out of the cave. A Word of Misdirection and the cave entrance was hidden in the bushes. She climbed on her Flyer and gestured it into the air, turned eastwards towards Lorgcoiseaigéan, and leaned forward to get all the speed it would muster.

Réalta did not remember how she had got back. It seemed that maybe the horse was smart enough to know the trails but of course it was impossible that a dumb beast should walk the Forest. She had ridden into the Watchtower's camp in Lorgcoiseaigéan and tried to tell everything. But the words were so hard to find. All she could see was Osna's blood splashing out and that murderous little creature brandishing the knife at her. The watch leader got her something to drink and left her to try and recover, huddled in her cloak.

They had told her that she should wait for some high Rank to come and talk to her but Réalta found that the silence was filled with screaming in her head. Normally she would have daydreamed but all her mind's eye could see was blood and violence. To quiet it she found a book on her Silver Cord. It was an account of Great Principles related to the Language of Power, rather than the sort of story-book that she would have preferred, but she was waiting for some high-Rank. Anyway, it was still things to fill her head.

She had just started on the chapter about the Abstract Principles when she realised someone was talking to her. It was a woman, an Adept like herself, but as slender as she was fat, with skin as pale as her own was dark. The woman was wearing a blue silk dress that exposed her neck. Black curls brushed her skin and a little golden cat stared out from between her breasts, emerald eyes glittering. Réalta looked up and tried to remember who it was. "Lady Cathúa," she guessed, hoping it was right.

"What is your name?" the high-Rank asked.

"I am Réalta," she replied.

The high-Rank woman sat beside her. Réalta noticed that, beneath her cloak, the high-Rank woman's boots had mud, dust and water on them. The high-Rank woman looked down, following Réalta's gaze, and whispered Words of Freshness. Then she looked up again from her now-clean boots. "Tell me what happened," she said.

"I am... I was in Coinín's Patrol, my lady. He took us out with a message for the House of Linn Dubh. Before we could get there they blocked our way."

"Who is 'they,' Réalta?"

"It was Aclaí's forces, my lady."

"How do you know? Was Lord Aclaí among them?"

"He wasn't, my lady. But you described them in your Forest lecture a month ago. I saw a Night Warrior and a Mountain Warrior among them. I saw four Forest People and... Osna was murdered by a Midsummer boy." With the last admission Réalta lost control of her breath. She tried not to but she couldn't stop crying. "We never saw him until he stabbed her. We were running, my lady."

The high-Ranked woman looked awkward a moment then put her hand on Réalta's hands. "I am sorry for your loss," she said. She waited while Réalta calmed down then she spoke again. "You turned back and they followed you and attacked you?"

"Coinín wouldn't turn back, my lady. Most of the Patrol were already killed when we turned back."

"Who turned back?"

"Just Osna and me, my lady."

"I see." Réalta watched the presumed Lady Cathúa think a moment. "I think you need to be a little careful about your story, Réalta. It sounds like you two ran away when the rest of your Patrol needed you."

"I'm sorry, my lady."

"I don't think you should apologise for taking an action that saved your life. I am not stupid. But others will view things differently."

"What... what do you think I should say?"

"I think you should tell people that you became separated from the rest of your Patrol." Cathúa smiled a crooked smile. "It is certainly true that you became separated from them."

"I... I suppose it is, my lady," Réalta sniffed.

"Now I have another question for you," Cathúa asked, looking down at the book. "Why do you take a book on Patrol?"

"I didn't, my lady. It is on my Silver Cord."

"Do you have many books on your Silver Cord?"

"I have a few, my lady. I am trying to learn the subjects we are taught. I can learn Novice subjects from reading books."

"Good. Are the Novice subjects the only books you have on your Silver Cord?"

"I... There are others, my lady," she admitted.

"What else?"

"There is a book of stories that a scribe made for my mother. My mother is a storyteller and a scribe worked with her to write some of them down."

"That's good," Cathúa replied. "Would you show me?"

Réalta found her mother's book on her Silver Cord and passed it to Cathúa. Cathúa opened it and looked at a few pages. "It's simple script," she replied. "Is it from the River on the Inland Sea? In the shadow-world with the River Gate, beyond the Sky Gate?"

"It is, my lady. How do you know?"

"Each scribe school has its own distinct style of forming the letters. Here the pig-snout of the broad M is a circle with the nostrils linked, see?"

"I see. How is it supposed to be?"

"If it's recognisable, however the scribe wants it to be."

"What is the official way?"

"Define 'official'."

"I don't know, my lady. What about when writing was invented?"

"The inventor of writing always said that, if the symbols are recognisable, it is up to the scribe." She looked down at the book again. "How long have you had it?"

"My mother gave it to me for my Thirteenth Nativity, my lady, Six winters ago."

"Was it new when she gave it to you?"

"It was, my lady."

"Then you have read it many times?"

"Many times, my lady. I know it is only stories, but I –"

"You love to read."

"I do, my lady." Réalta glanced at Cathúa's face expecting to see disapproval or scorn but that was not what she saw at all.

"I love to read too," said Cathúa. She looked down at the book and back up at Réalta. "What will you do now you don't have a Patrol?"

"I don't know, my lady." Remembering what had happened to Osna prickled at her eyelids. "I will have to find another Patrol."

"Would you help me with my library instead?"

"Of course, my lady!"

"Come on, then. Let us go back to the City and get you acquainted with the books."

"My lady?"

"What is it, Réalta?"

"Did you ever meet the inventor of writing?"

"Just once. The meeting will... was... awkward. Nobody would believe how awkward that kind of meeting can be unless they had seen it for themselves."

"So how do you know what she thought, my lady?"

"I am the inventor of writing, Réalta. That is how I know."

* * *

Liús came out of the watch-room and went over to ring the bell. The Mentor was there and Cathúa and Eibheara stood either side of him. As soon as the bell was rung, Liús went over to join them.

It was Cathúa that led them down with the Mentor leaning on her arm. Liús looked down at her black curls on the perfect skin of her shoulders and the way her hips swayed as she –

"What do you see in her?" Eibheara whispered.

"She is pretty and she is intelligent," Liús whispered back. "She is a good friend, too."

"You were training her, weren't you?"

"It is my duty to make sure that Adepts please the Mentor."

"Do you know many tricks?"

"I've been learning as well as teaching."

She leaned a little closer. "Will you teach me?" she whispered.

"I am sure you have plenty of experience," he replied.

"Like she does? She is eighty-odd years older than me, Liús."

Liús wondered how she would react if he suggested that Eibheara had taken many more partners than Cathúa. He could not think of any way to put it with tact. He sighed. "All right, then," he said. "When?"

"Tonight?" she whispered.

He never got a chance to reply. They entered the hall and walked over to the raised table. They sat. The Mentor looked over the crowd at the Evening Meal, counting them silently. He leaned to Cathúa sitting beside him. She noticed and leaned towards him a little, letting him see down the front of her dress. Her pendant glittered green from the shadows. He knew Cathúa was doing it deliberately but he found it so hard to feel the reaction she was trying to provoke. He remembered Eala waiting silently in his room and he tried to breathe the tightness out of his chest.

"Did we lose some?" he whispered.

"All but one of a Patrol was killed today, Mentor. And another one is still missing."

The mug shook in his hand. "Cathúa, why do we keep sending them?"

"Do you want them to forget what the City is for? Or to be unready when we are attacked?"

"How many have we lost this year?"

"Seventy-six, not counting the three unaccounted for today. But it is fewer since I cut back the Patrols."

"How many did I Select this year?"

"Nineteen, Mentor."

"We need to stop the Patrols, Cathúa."

"What about the monsters of the Forest..?"

"It's not the monsters of the Forest that are killing my Adepts, Cathúa. It is Aclaí. Until I can deal with Aclaí we must stop the Patrols."

"As you wish, Mentor," conceded Cathúa.

He looked at her face a moment then he put the cup down and got up. The four of them hastened to their feet to follow him as he marched out but he did not wait for them to catch up. He walked quickly up the stairs. By the time he got to the Court of the Favourites he was running, ignoring the ache in his knees and hips. He went into his room and closed the door.

"Is he all right?" Eibheara whispered to Liús.

Liús thought to his Manifestation. Does he need anybody?

He should be left alone, the Manifestation replied. *He wants his solitude.*

"He is best left," Liús told Eibheara.

"Then you can teach me," she replied.

"I still don't think there will be that much to learn," he said.

"Well, we should still practice my skills. You did promise."

"Very well," he agreed.

"Let's go off the Hill," she said. "I want to be out of the City."

He looked around. Cathúa had already gone into the library. Nobody was needed. He let her lead him by the hand, through the gate, down the steps and into the Low City. She led him around the outer walls and into the dunes. He remembered being with Éise. Looking back at the wall on the seaward side, from the rocks in the surf all the way up to the Mentor's balcony, he smiled as he remembered. Eibheara led him between the dunes. The sand was still warm from the sunshine. He looked at her looking back at him. He was curious, since he had never put it in her, but he felt nothing for her. Still, he had Words to help him rise to the occasion.

She found a blanket on her Silver Cord and spread it out. "Don't worry," she said. "I know what you like." Suddenly there was a rope in her hands. "Sit down," she said.

He sat. "Is that what you are planning to do with the Mentor?" he asked.

"Of course not," she said. "But I know what you like." She looped the rope around his head and the cord pulled into his mouth. Her hands were strong and, in a moment, she had roped his wrists and pushed him over. She spoke Words of Power and he saw her body flow in the moonlight. Her clothes were too tight and she removed them. He felt a hollow place in his stomach as he saw the exaggerated masculinity of the form she had chosen.

She tore his tunic in one movement and looked down at his naked body. "You do like this, don't you?" she breathed. "Toirneach was right about you." She wadded up the rags of his tunic and shoved it beneath his hips. He tried to relax as she bore her weight down on him but it still hurt. Then she looped the rope around his neck.

"Let me tell you a bedtime story," she smiled. "Would you like that? Oh, of course, you can't answer. But you can listen." Eibheara tightened the rope and Liús felt the familiar sensation as his face swelled and his vision greyed.

"Once upon a time there was a girl who lived in the last days of the City. She noticed that every time the Patrols went out they were intercepted by the City's enemies and killed. She knew that the lady in charge of the City's defence would never betray the City: Lady Cathúa was her friend. But somehow the enemies knew the Patrols that she sent.

"So she realised that someone close to Lady Cathúa must be telling Lord Aclaí which Patrols were going out. She watched very carefully to see who knew. And she found that Lady Cathúa had placed her trust in someone that she shouldn't have trusted."

Eibheara was moving with a good rhythm now, enjoying what she was doing, and Liús was really frightened. He realised that she really meant to kill him. He had dreamed and wondered about being executed before but he had always imagined that he would be guilty. But he felt the rope tighten and she leaned down over him, forcing his legs further apart. "Is this what Aclaí did to make you a traitor, Liús?" She pulled hard on the rope and he was drowning in noise and greyness. He saw the glint of the blade that would make sure he was dead.

"Die, you traitor," she gasped in his ear.

Méar barred his door and found the bags. His hands were shaking as he opened them.

"What is happening?" he demanded.

Aclaí is shutting you in, Ceann replied. *He wants to take everything away from you.*

"What can... how can I stop this?"

You must defeat him.

"I can't defeat him, Ceann. You know that. What would... how could I make peace with him?"

You could give him everything he wants. That would make peace with him.

"Would it?"

It would. He would take everything away from you and then he would make you an example.

"An example?" Méar whispered.

Do you want to kneel before his sword? Do you want everyone to see your body after he has used it, before he strikes off your head? Do you want to die the way she died?

Méar looked beyond Ceann at the other skull on his desk. "Eala, you know about love. You know Aclaí's heart. I don't want to hear his advice. I already know it. I need yours." He went over to the desk and picked up the bone. "If he is willing to talk to me why won't you?"

But she did not answer. He laid the bone down on his pillow, beside him and he remembered waking up to the scent of her hair.

He kissed the bone. "Then sleep," he whispered. "Perhaps you will talk in the morning. Eala, I so need your wisdom."

Eibheara was lying in her bed, remembering, when she heard voices outside in the Court of the Favourites.

"Good morning, Mentor," Cathúa's voice called out.

"Where is Liús?" the Mentor asked.

"Do you need him?" Cathúa replied. "I could see if I can find him."

"Do," the Mentor replied.

Eibheara remembered him on the blanket in the moonlight, his body bound and bleeding, and she silently breathed out her gasps. She was just relaxing when she heard more voices.

"Good morning, Mentor," Éise said.

"Oh, ye decided to visit us?"

There was a moment's pause and then a slight cry from Éise. "Mentor," she breathed.

"Have breakfast with me, ye two," he said.

"We will, Mentor," Éise said. "Liús my cowardly lion, find us something nice."

"I will, my lady. Mentor, do you want anything?"

"Will you find me some of that fruit?"

"Of course, Mentor. They have those dark little oranges."

"That would be perfect."

Eibheara shrugged on her dress as quickly as she could and whispered her Words of Freshness as she ran her fingers through her curls. She opened the door. Cathúa turned to look at her and, as she moved, the pendant glittered. Liús was serving Éise and the Mentor and had his back to her. But he was relaxed and he was enjoying himself. And he was clearly alive.

"Are you all right?" Cathúa asked her.

"I am fine," she said. Éise smiled at her from the Mentor's table. But Eibheara could read the accusation in the eyes that went with that smile.

"So what are ye doing today?" the Mentor asked.

"Whatever my lady tells me to do," said Liús.

"What do you wish?" asked Éise.

"Do you want me to take the Veteran's Words of Power lecture again, Mentor?" Cathúa asked.

"I know you think I should do it," he answered.

"I don't mind, Mentor," she said. "I have a novice I want to train as an assistant in the library, but –"

"Is she pretty?" the Mentor asked.

"She is very pretty," Cathúa said. "She has beautiful curves. She likes books, too."

He looked up at Cathúa's face, looking for approval. She looked down at him and frowned for a moment as she decoded his expression. "It's fine, Mentor," she said. "This novice girl can wait. I will teach them the Purification of the Blood, I think."

"I will come and help teach," he said, "As long as I don't have to do it on my own." He smiled up at her. "I didn't sleep well last night," he explained. "I... I dreamed that one of you had been killed."

"Who?" asked Éise.

"It doesn't matter," he answered. But both Éise and Cathúa saw his eyes turn towards Liús.

It was evening and Réalta found her way to the Hall of the Novices. Her feet found their way to the place where she had always sat: the spot at the end of the bench beside Osna. But of course Osna was not going to sit beside her. She remembered how Coinín had bounced around as he told his anecdotes to the rest of the Patrol and how she felt the bench shift as he moved. And she remembered how Osna would whisper in her ear, puncturing all Coinín's self-importance with awkwardly translated but brilliantly observed earthiness.

Now she had the table to herself and she knew she should break out of her daydreams and make new friends. But she didn't have the energy. She would sit alone for another evening, then. Perhaps it would be different tomorrow. She looked up at the high table where the Mentor sat between

Lord Liús and Lady Cathúa. Réalta remembered the Mentor's touch and wondered if he would ever notice her again.

It had been Lady Cathúa who had spoken to her after the... after they had all died. Then she realised Lady Cathúa was looking back at her and she looked down at her food. It's the silence, she thought. I am daydreaming because nobody has talked to me all day. Then she felt the tingle of her sword-hilt. She found her sword on her Silver Cord and lay it on the bench beside her. The hilt showed Eighteenth Rank.

It was Lady Cathúa. *réalta*

"What is it, my lady?" she whispered.

will you come to the top of the hill after the meal

"As you wish, my lady. What should I wear?"

whatever you want to wear Réalta looked up and saw Cathúa looking puzzled. *it is not for the mentor réalta* came more words, as Réalta saw her realise. *i wanted to show you the library*

Réalta smiled. "Of course I will come, my lady," she whispered. "Thank you."

it is nothing réalta Cathúa replied. She glanced down, distracted, and the light on Réalta's sword-hilt died as she released the hilt.

"I want to talk to you!"

Éise let go of the door and turned back to Eibheara. "What do you want?" she sighed.

"Forbidden Art!"

"What are you talking about, Eibheara?" Éise demanded.

"I know what you did last night."

"Well, that is great for you," Éise sneered. "Because I have do not know what you are talking about."

"Necromancy was the first Art to be Forbidden," Eibheara accused.

"Well, thank you for the history lesson, Eibheara. Now can I get on?"

"I know what you did, Éise. Why shouldn't I tell him?"

"Sure, and then I'll find out what you are talking about. Or perhaps you could tell me first."

"You raised the dead. I know you did."

Éise shook her head. Then she spoke Words of Truthful Aura. "I have never raised anyone from the dead, Eibheara. And I truthfully do not know what you think you are talking about. Why don't you go and bother someone who cares?"

Eibheara glanced up at the bright aura around Éise's head. Then she stared. "If you didn't do it, who did?"

"How should I know? You have not even attempted to explain what you are talking about."

"Liús... died last night, Éise. I assumed –"

"How did he die?"

"I –"

"You killed him?" Now Éise was looking at the silvery aura around Eibheara's head.

"Why... why would I kill him?"

"You were after him for sex last night. Cathúa told me. Did you accidentally kill him?"

"I can't carry on with this conversation, Éise," Eibheara said. She turned and ran back to her own house. The door banged shut behind her.

Éise looked around the courtyard. A Novice girl in a revealing red dress stood in the gateway, looking as confused as Éise felt. Let someone else deal with her, she thought. She closed her door and slipped through the portal behind the curtain, back to Acra and little Tintreacha. But she was going to speak to Liús and find out what Eibheara was talking about.

Foscúil swept into the room, with Damhánalla and Innealta behind him and Miotal and Aclaí bringing up the rear. Before him a hundred swordsmen stood in rows, wearing green cloaks. He saw how they stiffened as he entered the room. He stood before them, with his hand on his sword-hilt and waited for them to react to the power of his Breath. Then with one fluid movement he raised his sword in salute. A hundred and four swords were raised before him.

He led them through warm-up exercises and watched the ones who were learning to move with Breath. Then he made them all sit down. He called Aclaí out.

"Now," he said, "Today we are going to practice sixth attack with an underhand fourth reversal. Lord Aclaí, will you help me demonstrate?"

"As you wish, Teacher," Aclaí smiled, getting to his feet.

Foscúil reached up and closed Aclaí's breastplate. He drew his own sword. "The sixth attack begins like this," he explained. "The partner will step aside and make an open defence." Aclaí moved his sword-point up, projecting his own Breath to keep Foscúil away. "Then the reversal..." he said, releasing the sword-hilt and instantly snatching it back with his Silver Cord. He swung the blade up between Aclaí's knees. Aclaí leaped in the air, dived over the rising sword-blade and landed on one hand. He rolled over one shoulder and up onto his feet.

Foscúil turned to the students. "Now ye all have practised reversals using the Silver Cord. But this is different. Try it like this instead." He turned back to Aclaí. He moved back to the stance for the Sixth Attack and swung in again. Again Aclaí made the defence but this time Foscúil didn't release the sword-blade. He lifted his hand quickly, pulling it back to set the sword-blade turning out towards Aclaí. He Breathed out as he did so, keeping Aclaí back as the hilt pivoted in his hand. At the top of the motion he grasped it again, reversed. Then he swung it up again towards Aclaí's body.

Already stumbling back, Aclaí overbalanced and crouched sideways into a roll. Foscúil stepped forward with one movement and stood on Aclaí's wrist. His own sword-blade pointed at Aclaí's chin as he lay there on his back. Foscúil heard the students behind him gasp.

He turned to them. "Get yerselves in partners and try it. Keep all your armour on and, above all, *be aware*. We're going to have swords flying all over the place!"

"What do you want?" Eibheara demanded.

The Novice girl looked suitably terrified. "Lady Cathúa told me to come up and visit her," she said. Her voice sounded much more confident than her eyes suggested. Perhaps she was learning.

Eibheara pointed in the direction of the library. "Over there," she said. "Go on. Don't spend your time gawping at your betters."

"As you wish, my lady," she answered. Eibheara watched the way the dress moved over her hips as she walked around the fountain. If Aclaí was still here the poor girl would have been in danger, but nowadays nobody really noticed pretty girls on the top of the Hill. She wondered who the girl was dressing up for.

Cathúa looked up. "Come in," she said. "Is that what you normally wear?"

Réalta saw that Cathúa was dressed much more plainly than she was. It appeared that Cathúa had simply wrapped a piece of cloth around her middle to make a dress and tied an elaborate knot between her breasts. The only jewellery she wore was a gold pendant in the shape of a cat, with glittering emerald eyes, and a sort of plain wire hairgrip that sat on her head like a tiara, keeping her black curls from falling forward over her face. Seeing Cathúa she wondered if she was over-dressed. "Lord Liús wants me to... I mean, I thought that the Mentor wanted the girls around him to be pretty."

"Liús thinks we should try to be attractive for him. But attracting him is about a lot more than the clothes we wear. He doesn't look at clothes the same way that we do."

"What do you mean, my lady?"

"It's hard to explain with words. There is a notation for expressing motivations mathematically but it is Forbidden Art. So we are left with the imprecisions and ambiguities of natural language."

"Men are motivated by different things than women?"

"They are not so different: it is more that they respond to stimuli in different ways. I wrapped this thing around me because it is easy to put on – and because I have been experimenting with knots. The mathematics of knots is deep and can be used to model some quite surprising things." Cathúa reached her hands up to the point where the cloth fastened, a complex knot two hands-widths below her chin. "What I have here is two loops linked through each other. It's a puzzle."

"For the Mentor, my lady?"

Cathúa looked down. "He wouldn't be interested," she said. "But... if he calls for me I will undo it for him. He will see the wrapping and think of the present inside it. That is the way men see clothes. He won't see puzzles or anything about me."

"So who do you want to solve your puzzle, my lady?"

"I like puzzles. I like people who can think. I... I just wanted a dress that says I am for intelligent lovers."

"I don't think in that way, my lady. I dress how I do because I've been told that's what men want: bright colours, lots of skin and shiny things. I want... I imagine how they might respond. I'm a daydreamer not a thinker, my lady."

"I can see. The books you enjoy tell stories, don't they? For you, books are entertainment."

"Chronicles tell stories. They are information and entertainment, my lady. And I can't really separate the two. Since I came to the City I have learned from books but I still enjoy reading."

"That's good. This is the library and you could get a lot of entertainment here." She dragged a stool into one corner then stood on it to reach up to a high shelf. She spread the book out on the desk. Réalta looked.

"That's beautiful, my lady," she breathed. "It's like the pictures in the writing are telling stories of their own." She looked at the script and at Cathúa's expression. "Which scribe school is this?" she asked. "Did you write this?"

"It wasn't me," replied Cathúa. "This was... this is going to be a very strange explanation. I'd rather you didn't share it with everyone, Réalta."

"You don't have to tell me, my lady."

"I have to tell someone. There is a... have you studied inheritance?"

"I read a book about how life works, my lady. It talks about how living things are made of little living bricks and how there is a sort of library of forty-something secret scrolls in each brick of our bodies."

"There's forty-six of them and each one is divided into a few thousand chapters. So there is a chapter that controls how dark our eyes are. I have two light-eye chapters and you have at least one dark-eye chapter."

Réalta remembered that the books of life were paired. "One? Or two?"

"We can't tell from looking at you. You have brown eyes because you have a brown-eye chapter. One paints your eyes brown but if the other one doesn't it doesn't make any difference."

"I see."

"Good. That saves a lot of explanation. It is possible to write Words of Power into those books. Mountain People have Words of Concealment written into their books of life."

"So have those Midsummer People, my lady." Réalta felt the memory of Osna's death sting her eyes. "Horrible things."

"Not all of the Words of Power written into our books of life are carefully crafted like that. There is a chapter that was created accidentally as a result of an Art, now forbidden, that creates worlds. It is called the Gift of Anleacán."

"I've heard of that, my lady. Some people have suggested that my mother might have it."

"Is she from Anleacán?"

"Her parents were slaves taken from the City," replied Réalta.

"The Gift is prevalent throughout the Sea People," said Cathúa. "In the early days of the City there was... one man who had the Gift and fathered a lot of children. Before Lord Aclaí devised the Words of Sealing the Gift was scattered throughout the Sea People."

"But, my lady, I thought Anleacán was discovered by Lord Aclaí."

"Anleacán was created by Lord Aclaí, Réalta. The Mentor asked him to create a world containing someone who was greatest at something. The Gift of Anleacán makes someone the greatest at something."

"So my mother is greatest storyteller?"

"Maybe. The girl who drew this page is... was the greatest scribe. Foscúil is the greatest swordsman. Éirime was the greatest singer. Eala was the greatest at... well, at her Forbidden Art. Either that or it was her sister. She was one of twins."

"Does the Gift get people Selected?"

"Sometimes. Eala was Selected but her sister wasn't. I know of four who put on blue robes. But Gruaige, the girl who drew this, was never Selected. To be Selected you need to be able to kill. Gruaige wasn't able to kill."

"Was she a servant girl, then?"

"She was my servant. She was also the Mentor's great grandmother."

"How can she be? If the Gift of Anleacán was created in Aclaí's life, how could she be the Mentor's great grandmother?"

"It is possible to use the Words of Folding Space to travel to another time."

"Another time? Like... she was sent back before the Mentor was born?"

"That is it. It was an accident. But she was the Mentor's ancestor. It was a small village and –"

"The Mentor has the Gift of Anleacán, my lady? He was the one who spread it through the Sea People?"

"He was, Réalta. You need the Gift of Anleacán to teach Immortal Breath."

"How... so that is why the two paths are swordsmanship and Words of Power? Does the Mentor have the Gift for Words of Power?"

"He has."

"So Lord Foscúil teaches swordsmanship and Immortal Breath while the Mentor teaches Words of Power and Immortal Breath?"

"That is exactly right, Réalta."

"But Lord Foscúil has left the City and the Mentor's Breath has failed."

"There is another thing, Réalta. Immortals who have the Gift can breathe Immortal Breath into someone else. Eala's sister was kept alive for nearly a quarter-millenium by Éirime after she Retired. The Mentor's Breath failed suddenly after Eala left because she was breathing Immortality for him."

"So who is teaching the City how to breathe Immortal Breath now, Lady Cathúa?"

"Only the Mentor. And I don't know if it still works."

"Then the City is doomed?"

"It is, unless we can change things."

"What can we change? Which Immortals that have the Gift are left?"

"Only Foscúil. Éirime was murdered by... someone, Aclaí executed Eala, and the Mentor's Breath has failed."

"My mother has... but nobody can train her in Immortal Breath."

"I don't know, Réalta. It might be that learning from her might teach Immortal Breath without her knowing it. The Mentor kept himself young with Words of Power until Iolar learned Immortal Breath from him. Perhaps your mother could teach Immortal Breath to someone who knows that Breath is the key. But she cannot breathe Immortal Breath into anyone because she is not Immortal herself."

"How would she do it?"

"She would have to teach her talent along with... well, I don't know what the path would be like. There is a path of singing: one of the favourites learned her Immortal Breath from Éirime. They were lovers but she also taught her to sing. Eala's students ended up Immortal very quickly so she was probably teaching Immortality along with her now-forbidden Art."

"Can they teach themselves?"

"They can if they understand Breath. All of them progress to Immortality quickly. Éirime was Immortal in seven years – but her talent lent itself to breath."

"I see," said Réalta. "Should I bring my mother to Selection?"

"She would be too old."

"I know, my lady, but what else can we do? Why else would you be telling me this?"

"Because Foscúil knows that I know. Unless I tell someone else my life is in danger. The City is under siege and I have to find hope somewhere. Perhaps when this is over Foscúil will breathe Immortal Breath back into the Mentor."

"But Lord Foscúil is leading the siege, my lady."

"The siege of the City has been going on for much longer than that, Réalta. It has been going on for thirteen centuries."

"What do you mean?"

"I'll show you," Cathúa said. "Come with me on Patrol tomorrow and I will show you."

8

Memory and Imagination

The Lady of the Midsummer Palace walked in the grounds, enjoying the cool air and the mist, the scents and sounds of the dawn. She passed the roses and the trellis where the honeysuckle grew, intending to sit beside the fountain and plan her day. But Damhánalla was not alone.

Someone had been there before her. Three sharpened stakes had been driven into the ground. Rough cross-pieces were lashed to them like crude scarecrows. The cross-pieces supported blue cloaks and each stake was topped with a severed head. She looked at the swords stuck in the earth beside them: three Veterans.

There was writing on the ground roughly daubed in blood. "A gift from the Redcaps," the writing said.

She reached her hand to her hip and thought of Aclaí.

what is it his words asked.

"Your pets have brought home trophies again," she began.

"Lord Foscúil," the old woman said. She shuffled over. "Is this an inspection?"

"It isn't," he replied, taking off his gauntlets and dumping them on the writing desk. "This is a library. I was looking for books."

"Books, my lord?"

"Books. Collections of words arranged to convey meaning, each organised into a complete work. Books."

"Very well, my lord," she replied. "Is there any type of book you wish to see? Lady Abhainne wrote an interesting treatise on the structure of command in a band of warriors, and how it may be used to command large bands as easily as small ones."

"*The Tree of Command*? I read it with her and offered my own thoughts. We used her techniques to build up the warrior band that defends this House."

"Of course, my lord. So what sort of book do you want?"

"I am looking for Forbidden Art."

"We keep Forbidden Art shut away in that room over there, my lord."

"Show me."

The librarian opened the door and a collection of bones hanging from the ceiling clattered together as the door knocked past them. Foscúil looked up at the bones jerking on their thongs. Looking around the room he could see that all the others working in the library were watching to see who had opened the forbidden door. They saw his blue cloak and went back to what they were doing.

The librarian made a gesture and a lamp illuminated. In the cold phosphorescence of the lamp Foscúil saw a row of dusty shelves. Spiders had draped cobwebs over the books. She shuffled over to the shelf and looked back at him. "Which Art, my lord?" she asked.

"I want the Mind Craft," he said.

"That is a difficult one to categorise," she began to explain. "We have many books that were written by Adepts who learned Lady Eala's Art. If we take the Mentor's words to include everything written by one of those, the Mind Craft books would fill this room and many others."

"Why?"

"Because, my lord, the Mentor said that Mind Craft taints everything else."

"It is true," Foscúil agreed. "Abhainne's *Tree of Command* is certainly tainted by Mind Craft."

"I haven't read it, my lord."

"But I have. Do you have Eala's books?"

"We have all three of Lady Eala's books, my lord."

"She only wrote two books while she was in the City."

"She wrote two books at the City: one on the Mind Craft and one on rules to govern people. Then she wrote another book just a few years ago."

"How did you get that one?"

"Lord Aclaí deposited it in the library, my lord."

"What is that one about?"

"It is about the traditions and customs of Úll Oileán, my lord. I don't know why she wrote about that particular island, my lord, but the book describes –"

"I know why she wrote it. Make me a copy."

"As you wish, my lord."

* * *

"My lady!"

Damhánalla looked around to see who was at the doorway. It was one of those Midsummer People, biting her lip and looking around. She could see the wingtips tremble as the little creature wondered if she should run. Damhánalla knew they infested her gardens and often the house too but she hadn't seen one since she had chased that insult out of her home.

"What do you want?" Damhánalla demanded.

As she rose to her feet the creature rocked back and she almost lost sight of it. But it spoke. "It's... it's Lord Aclaí, my lady. He is in the tower."

"So what?" But Damhánalla could see the creature's concern. They were, after all, his children.

"He's near the edge, my lady, and –"

"And what?" Then she realised. She ran out into the garden then up the stairs to the top of the tower.

He was seated on the rail, his back against one of the roof supports, looking out at the southern horizon. She gasped out whispered Words of Strength as she walked up to him, carefully: afraid of surprising him but wanting to be near enough to catch his hand if he decided to –

"Damhánalla," he said.

"What are you doing, my lord?"

"I am sitting in the tower you built for my Nativity."

"I am sorry, my lord," she said, coming close enough that she could grab him. Her nose picked up the faintest scent of him in the wind. "I never meant it to hurt you."

"I know you didn't."

"It was supposed to give you hope, my lord."

"I know. But I miss her. I know I never spoke to her but I always knew that I could. I went for years never seeing her face, except on the Visions, but I could come up here and look at the next village, and know that I could visit her if I wanted." He turned to her and the grief on his face was like a hand grabbing her heart. "It is so strange that losing the freedom to do something I never did should take all meaning out of life."

She reached her hand a little and saw his own movements. Perhaps he reached back a little before he turned away. Watching him carefully for the tiny shift-of-weight that she knew would give her less than a heartbeat to grab him, she thought of the sword on her hip, then gently laid her hand on the hilt. "Foscúil," she thought, "You'd better be there."

* * *

Réalta let her horse follow Lady Cathúa's horse out of the pine woods. The sun was shining and the birds were calling, much more now they had reached the pasture. The black Forest around here was dangerous, between Aclaí's Forest People in all their forms, occasional monsters, and bears and wolves. But Réalta was following an Immortal – one of the oldest and most experienced in walking the Forest. She kept reminding herself how ridiculous it was to feel fear.

Cathúa guided her horse down into the valley, towards a village by the river, and one of their warriors came out to meet them. The people here were north-men: Lord Liús' people. It was something he had said that had first attracted Cathúa's interest to this area.

"My ladies," called the warrior in his accented speech. "What do you want?"

"Lord Liús told me about the Graveyard and I wanted to see it for myself."

The warrior's pale skin became a little paler, Réalta thought.

"It is bad luck," he replied. "Unquiet spirits dwell there. They are not our ancestors."

"I am Sea People," Cathúa replied. "I am not affected by 'bad luck'."

"What about me?" the warrior grumbled.

"I will keep you safe."

Reluctantly he led them across the countryside and to the hollow. Cathúa got down and rummaged around in the dirt. Her pendant swung loose on the thong and the emerald eyes glittered as if it was searching too. Réalta got down beside her mistress but she was not intending to rummage in anything. Cathúa stopped and looked at Réalta. She held something brown between her fingers.

"See?" she asked.

Réalta saw a piece of pottery.

"How do we know what it means?" Réalta asked.

"The Words of Identification will tell us what we need to know," Cathúa replied. "But, if you look carefully, you can tell a lot just by examining it." She turned to the warrior and showed him the potsherd. "What do you see?" she asked him.

"It's a broken piece of pot, my lady," he replied.

"Do your people make pots like this?"

He looked at it more carefully. It looked like it was made of cords of pottery pressed together to make the shape.

"Nobody makes pots like this around here," he told her.

"And they haven't, not for centuries," Cathúa replied. She said her Words of Identification, then added, "This piece of pot is as old as the City. It was made before the City was founded but broken a few years after." She bent down again and rummaged in the dirt.

"What are we looking for, my lady?" asked Réalta.

"Either a weapon or a piece of bone," Cathúa replied.

Now that she tried Réalta found that searching the ground was not enough. She needed to mentally step back from the detail and see what the ground had to offer. She glimpsed a small yellow-white object and picked it up.

"Will a tooth do, my lady?" she asked.

As she spoke she looked around at Cathúa. Cathúa had the gauntlets of her armour on and was digging something out of the dirt with the blades on the fingertips. She turned her head without moving her hands from the work.

"A tooth will be perfect, Réalta," she answered.

Réalta went over to her and saw she was digging up a roughly shaped piece of Metal. It was the sort of thing that Forest monsters might use as a weapon. Cathúa shed her gauntlets, stood up, and took the tooth from Réalta. She spoke her Words of Identification.

"It's a tooth," she agreed. "The woman whose tooth it was lost it in a fight, just four years after the City was founded."

Réalta looked at the weapon Cathúa had half-uncovered in the dirt. "So they were wiped out by Forest monsters?"

"They were."

"Just after the City was founded?"

"It appears so."

"So what does..?" and Réalta stopped as she realised what that meant. "My lady?" she asked.

"What is it?"

"Is this when the war against the Forest started?"

"I think it is," Cathúa replied. "The settlements close to the woods are fortified after this but before they didn't bother to build walls. They built walls after the monsters attacked."

"My lady, we are taught that the City was built to protect us against the Forest. But you are saying that the City came before the Forest monsters were a threat. Does that mean we started the feud with the Forest?"

"I think that is the simplest explanation, Réalta."

"So the history we are taught is a lie, Lady Cathúa? You give lectures to us on history. Do you teach the lie?"

"I don't discuss the relationship between humanity and the Forest before the formation of the Key of Creation."

"What does the Key of Creation have to do with this, my lady?"

"Do you know what the Key of Creation is, Réalta?"

"It's something to do with Manifestations of Creation, my lady. But I don't really understand what a Manifestation of Creation is. I understand what a Manifestation of Fire or a Manifestation of Forest might be like. I can sort of get how a Manifestation of Evil might behave. But I can't imagine what a Manifestation of Creation is like."

"Well, Réalta, the first thing to understand is that the Manifestations are related directly to the letter-sound-ideas that make up the Language of Power. Each of them represents a part or a facet of reality, just as you were taught in your Great Principles lectures, but the forms they take vary. Each form is related to the facet of reality they represent but our senses are not good at sensing all of reality. So a Manifestation of Light is easy to see but a Manifestation of Good is much harder. A Manifestation of Fire directly affects its surroundings in a way we can perceive but a Manifestation of Fear does not."

"I think I see. So all the Manifestations are equally real but some of them are invisible?"

"Well, they are not equally real. There are hierarchies among them. The Manifestations of Creation represent the process by which things that are probable turn into things that are certain. They create reality – which makes them quite important in that hierarchy."

"Is that why we use them for the House of Power?"

"They have a strong Breath, which makes it easy to use them to power the things that make our lives easy. And it is easy to give them orders to take forms which, although they have Breath, do not have Will. But they also have the ability to alter reality. The Mentor grants Mastery of Creation to us at Sixteenth Rank, allowing us to give direct orders to the Great Principle of Creation and hence to alter reality directly. He limits our access to it but it provides us with a power which is without intrinsic limit."

"The Great Principle of Creation... is the Key of Creation linked to the Great Principle of Creation?"

"The Key of Creation is the Great Principle of Creation. The Mentor persuaded it to take an inanimate form: that of a jewel on a chain. Since it has an inanimate form it cannot think or reason so it cannot oppose humanity. The Mentor gives it orders and allows us to give it orders but all it can do is obey. It is programmed to obey the one that holds it."

"Isn't that dangerous?"

"That is what the Battle of the Blue Peaks was about, Réalta. The Mentor took the Key of Creation out of the City and the Forest counter-attacked to try and get it back. I would think the Forest creatures, which are tied to Manifestations themselves, would want to allow it to return to its natural form."

"Would it be angry?"

"It's a Manifestation of Creation. You know how hostile they are to human life."

"Is that why? Because the Mentor has their king imprisoned?"

"I wouldn't have expressed it in such anthropomorphic language, Réalta." Cathúa sighed. "But I think you are correct."

"So if it is allowed to return to its true form the whole of Creation would turn on humanity?"

"I think it would."

"Aren't you scared, Lady Cathúa?"

"I am terrified," Cathúa admitted. "But there is nothing we can do about it. What will happen will happen. Immortality doesn't mean living forever."

"What do you mean, my lady?"

But Cathúa turned away and crouched down in the dirt. She rummaged around where Réalta had found the tooth and, with a little scrabbling, she managed to uncover a whole skull. A deep gouge started at the eye socket and slashed down to the upper jaw. One tooth was missing and the next one broken. Cathúa fitted the tooth into the empty socket.

"Look at her," Cathúa said. "Look at this skull, Réalta: once she was a young woman like you, with loves and ambitions, hopes and dreams. We don't know her face or her name. Words of Identification would tell us both but they would tell us nothing about her. Her voice is silenced forever. She was a girl loved by her mother and perhaps a boy or two. Perhaps she was loved by the whole village. But one day monsters came out of the Forest and they cut her down. She fell to the ground and lay there dying. Do you think she wondered what the point of her life was as her blood spilt on the ground?

Cathúa looked at the skull in her hand then turned it so she could stare into those empty eye sockets. "Sweet child," she said, "I am sure when you were a young girl your heart was full of emotions, that every look you got from a boy was more important than the Sun and Moon and the stars in the sky. But all that is forgotten, overtaken by your death.

She looked over at her companion. "Réalta, little star, everything we do is trapped in fate. When a thousand years have gone by our civilisation will be gone like hers. If we are remembered at all it will just be as legends and folk-tales. Our names and faces will be forgotten and we will be as silent as her. Look at her, Réalta. This is the true meaning of life."

Réalta looked in fear from her mistress to the bone in Cathúa's hand. "I don't understand, Lady Cathúa."

"You have heard me teach that time is like a trail that we walk from our starting point to our destination? Well, this was her destination. What I haven't told you is that the trail is fixed. Time travel only makes sense if events are pre-destined. If our trail ends in a cliff and a long drop into the sea we can wish that there was a bridge or something to carry us on and make the journey longer. But none of our wishing will change things. Our future is fixed, Réalta: fixed in the fate of the City. The trails we walk have a fixed length. And, however you measure it, the length is always 'too short'."

It only took Foscúil a few Breaths to get the Flyer into the air. He guided it carefully along the paths of the palace gardens, out of sight, until he was due north of the tower. Then he skimmed the ground to the base of the tower and rose up next to it before circling around just below the rail. He stopped when he saw Aclaí's leg hanging down. He whispered Words of Strength as he stood up then reached up and grabbed Aclaí's ankle. One hard tug and Aclaí was sprawling in the Flyer. A heartbeat later he was struggling to his feet, with fury in his face and his sword in his hand. Foscúil turned his back and guided the Flyer back to the gardens.

"What game are you playing?" Aclaí roared.

"I thought Eala taught you, my lord," Foscúil replied mildly. A part of his mind wondered if Aclaí was crazy enough to strike him as he piloted the Flyer but most of him ignored the possibility. They landed by the fountain behind the palace.

"What are you doing?" Aclaí demanded again. "I go up to my tower for a few quiet breaths alone, but ye won't leave me alone, will ye? First Damhánalla comes up to pester me, then you come and play some practical joke! I won't have it! Ye all know what we are doing here: surely ye must understand that this is serious. I need to be able to rely on ye more than I ever have, but ye've lost yere minds, all of ye."

"My lord," Foscúil replied, "I've been reading Eala's book. In her chapter on social interactions she talks about things that make whole groups of _"

"I am not going to be distracted, Foscúil. I want to know what is happening here."

Foscúil reached for the book on his Silver Cord and opened it. "She writes about crowd thinking, but she finishes 'Of course an alternative explanation for everyone suddenly behaving differently is that the common factor is you.' I have wondered if it is a joke, my lord, or if she was being serious."

"You are saying that this is me?"

"I'm asking you a question about Eala's teaching, my lord. You studied under her. I never took the opportunity."

"And yet your implication is as insolent as ever."

Foscúil laughed a moment. "I am a Sea Hound, my lord."

"Would you repeat your question with a sword in your hand?"

"I won't, my lord. If you want to strike off my head then do so. It turns out that I only care about one thing – and that one thing only makes sense if you can pull yourself together and start leading us."

Foscúil heard the sound of a sword being sheathed, then Aclaí sat beside him in the Flyer. "What is that one thing, Foscúil?"

"It turns out that I want to avenge Abhainne's death, my lord."

"By destroying the City?"

"By deposing the Mentor. If the City falls, so be it – but I don't think that the City has to fall."

"Oh, the City will fall, Foscúil."

"Even so, I don't believe our Order needs to end. You teach Words of Power, I will teach sword and, between us –"

"Let it die, Foscúil. It is time."

"Why must it die?"

"Have you been reading Eala's books?"

"I have read one of them. As I said, I never studied under her."

"What about her last book?"

"I haven't read it yet, but I heard that it describes the culture of the north-eastern Archipelago, my lord. They are not like us. Us Sea Hounds enjoy life for as long as life goes on. We take big bites even if that means the meal does not last as long. But up that way they are crazy. They fear death and yet they invite it into their houses."

"I don't doubt it. But the City's culture has inherited everything that is bad about the culture of those islands, twisted around to maximise the pain and misery it creates. The Mentor loved Éirime but he killed her. If someone in the normal world does that we talk about how out-of-character it is. But that sort of thing happens in the City all the time." Aclaí turned to Foscúil, close enough for him to see the tears. "Maybe we will re-build our Order one day. But the City needs to fall. That evil needs to die."

"As you wish, my lord. But to get there we need you to lead us."

"And I will. But leadership is done from in front. It's lonely at the front and I need to be comfortable in my isolation."

"Damhánalla told me that she thought you were going to jump."

"A couple of years ago, the month after we put her on the pyre, I might have. But those days have passed. My heart was dying and that hurt. Now it is dead and I don't care."

"You frightened... them in those months, Aclaí. We have served you for centuries but suddenly we don't know you anymore. I watch your face and hear your voice but I don't recognise who you are."

"I don't recognise me anymore, either, Foscúil. I told you: my heart died. But what is left is my intelligence and my anger to guide it. We will depose the Mentor. Don't remember me as I was. Just trust me as I am. I will see this thing to the end."

When Evening Meal was over Réalta watched the Mentor shuffle out of the hall. Lady Cathúa supported him on one side and Lord Liús supported his other arm. She got up and followed the crowd out into the Court of the Novices. Her bed was the only one in the dormitory that was made up: she had slept alone since the night Osna and the others had died.

The servant was waiting for her. "I brought your new dress, my lady."

"Show me."

The servant lifted the dress where Réalta could see it. It was yellow silk with many vertical folds between waist and hem. "It's a little short," Réalta commented. "Why do you always bring me such short dresses?"

"Lord Liús suggested that it would be the sort of thing that the Mentor might like, my lady."

"Very well, I'll try it on." She walked up to the servant and raised her arms. The servant undressed her quickly and lifted the new dress. Réalta shrugged it on and it settled over her hips. Then she said the Words of Fitting and it slid over her skin and pulled a little closer around her waist. She looked at the mirror. The servant stood beside her, ready. The servant's tunic was at least two fingers' width shorter than her dress. She turned and looked at the way the silk sat over the shape of her buttocks. "It will do," she said. "He probably won't notice me anyway." She wondered who would notice. Lord Liús shared Lady Cathúa's bed. Would she ever be invited to join them? Was that why he chose these things for her?

Réalta sat down and the servant helped her with oil of jasmine and her jewellery. The butterfly with its gold and turquoise wings gathered her hair at the back of her head, while the pendant of three rubies hung down between her breasts. The servant fixed smaller rubies through the holes in her earlobes and wrapped tinkling gold chains around her wrists and ankles. She kicked off her sandals and said her Words of Freshness before the servant put the rings on her toes to match the ones on her fingers. A little bit of berry-juice to redden her lips and a thin line of greased soot along the edge of each eyelid and she was done.

She sat on the bed and found her sword on her Silver Cord. She thought of Cathúa.

what is it réalta

"Do you want help with the library tonight, my lady?" Réalta whispered.

if you wish

"I will come right up, my lady."

Réalta stood. "Wish me luck," she said to the servant.

"Good luck, my lady," the servant replied.

The night air was cool around her legs as she walked up the steps to the top of the Hill. The chains around her ankles tinkled tunelessly with every step. She knew the guards at each gate admired her as she went by every evening. At the Court of the Veterans the boy watching smiled at her and, as she walked away, she heard the girl rebuke him for his inattention. Réalta slightly exaggerated her movements, feeling the hem of the dress brush the backs of her legs.

The watcher at the gate of the Court of the Favourites stood in her way. "Good evening, Réalta," he said. "Has Lady Cathúa invited you?"

"She has," Réalta smiled.

"Good. Then you can pass." He stood aside.

"Thank you, Lord Póg."

Liús watched her from the Chamberlain's room. As she walked past the fountain he spoke. "You're very pretty tonight, child," he said. "That dress really suits you."

He saw the blood in her cheeks colour the brown of her skin. "The servant said you chose it for me, my lord," she replied.

"I did. He needs beauty and youth around him, child."

Réalta hardly felt beautiful. She felt lumpy and wobbly, unlike the unselfconscious grace of Lady Cathúa. But the Mentor was nowhere to be seen and the only person to appreciate her was Lord Liús. She imagined his eyes watching her as she crossed the courtyard. She found her mistress in the library, huddled over a book. Cathúa didn't look around and Réalta quietly closed the door behind her. She saw the way Cathúa's shoulders shook and she realised. She sat beside her mistress and put her arm on her shoulder. "What is it, my lady?"

"It's all so futile," Cathúa replied.

"What is?" Réalta looked at the book that was open on Cathúa's desk. She saw mathematics but she didn't understand it.

Cathúa sat up straight. Her hands strayed up to the thong around her neck. "Look at this thing," she said, pulling her gold pendant up. "See the eyes?"

"I see it," Réalta replied.

"See how they glitter?"

Réalta saw them. "Occasionally they catch the light, my lady. Do you clean them?"

"I use Words of Freshness, of course. We all do. But there are Words of Power carved into the gold."

"So the glitter is deliberate? What does it mean?"

"It means that the world around me is real. When did you last see them glitter?"

Réalta frowned as she tried to remember. "I only noticed it a few times, my lady. Once was when we visited the... that old battlefield near the Black Forest. But you bent down and it came out of your dress, my lady. So the sunlight would have caught it."

"I made it forty-six years ago. This is the thirty-eighth time it has glittered. It glitters on average less than once a year. Less even than that since the events occur in clusters. Most years it doesn't glitter at all. And yet it has glittered seventeen times since they killed Eala and twelve times since the Day of Autumn."

"So it is getting more frequent?"

"It is."

"Why does it glitter?"

"Réalta, do you remember that, when we observe the tiniest parts of reality, most of it is only real when observed?"

"I remember that. It is confusing."

"It is confusing if you try and understand it in human terms. In mathematics it makes sense but human brains are only equipped to understand a narrow slice of reality."

"My mathematics is not nearly as good as yours, my lady."

"But you can follow it. Réalta, the problem is that sometimes the tiny changes become real because they are directly observed. More often their consequences are observed in the human scale. The motions of individual particles in our brains are amplified and become our thoughts."

"Like prophecy, my lady?"

"I made this when investigating prophecy. The eyes glitter when some aspect of my immediate surroundings is made real by observation."

"Some aspect?"

"Most of what we call reality is not real at all. Perhaps our words are real, but other things around us are not. For example, the order of the books on the third shelf from the bottom in that bookcase over there – chances are that is not real at all."

"But I am looking at it, my lady."

"That doesn't help. Most of ourselves is not real. A few things we do, a few things we say, they are real. Nothing much else."

"I don't understand, my lady. My brain is not equipped, I suppose."

Cathúa sighed. "Have you still got your stories on your Silver Cord?"

"I have, my lady."

"Find your favourite story and read it to me, then."

"As you wish, my lady." Réalta reached for her favourite book and it was there in her hand. She opened it and found the story. "I hope you won't be offended –"

"Don't worry about that, Réalta. Just begin."

"Very well, my lady. 'Once upon a time in a certain city there was a poor boy and girl. Their parents were good friends and they played together in their father's fields as they grew up. They didn't notice it, of course, but he grew up handsome and she grew up beautiful, with deep eyes and soft –'"

"Réalta?" Cathúa interrupted.

"What is it, my lady?"

"What colour were the girl's eyes?"

"I don't know. Brown, I suppose."

Réalta looked up and saw Cathúa's blue eyes. "Does it say in the text?"

"It doesn't, my lady."

"We imagine that the story is a description of a reality, don't we?"

"I suppose we do."

"So what about the girl's eyes? You imagine them as brown but I imagine them as green, like the Mentor's eyes. Someone else might imagine them blue or gold. They are undefined because the writer never observes them."

Réalta wondered why her mistress was belabouring the point. Then she realised. "So our reality is like a story? The storyteller hasn't told his audience what books are on the shelf so they aren't really there?"

"Well, they are there but the the details of them – their titles, order, contents – are not decided yet."

Réalta smiled. "So maybe the human brain is able to understand your mathematics, my lady. I can see the idea of our world as like a story. But that is just a model. You warned me about the difference between a model and reality."

"I did. But I also taught you that we can refine our model by using it to make predictions about reality. If your model doesn't allow you to make predictions about reality then it is not a good model."

"What do you mean?"

"Well, for example a story has a storyteller. What predictions can you test about your model that proves a storyteller is necessary?"

"Necessary, my lady?"

"Remember, we choose the simplest explanation that fits the observations. Unless there is a need for something as complex as a storyteller, telling your story in a shady side of the market square, then your storyteller has to be left out."

"Because she makes the model more complicated? Reality has to come from somewhere, my lady."

"But there are simpler explanatios. For example, what if every decision is taken randomly?"

"You would still need a mechanism for the dice to be rolled."

"But the mechanism would be simpler than your storyteller. Your storyteller needs a whole universe to exist in. And anyway, Réalta, that doesn't even explain anything. If your storyteller is the cause of our universe you have just moved the problem up one level. What is the cause of the storyteller's universe?"

"Oh." Réalta frowned. "And who is her storyteller, and so on? So the storyteller cannot exist because that would be illogical?"

"The storyteller might exist," shrugged Cathúa. "But because we cannot test the existence of a storyteller, and because we have simpler explanations that don't require a storyteller, logically we assume that the storyteller doesn't exist. And," she added, "mostly when we do more experiments the simplest explanation turns out to be the right one. Chances are there is not a storyteller. Our universe is just a bunch of random events that happened."

"Are you sure we cannot test the difference between a random fate and an intelligent storyteller?"

"Here is an obvious difference: stories have happy endings. If we are in a story that has a happy ending then we are not the heroes of the story."

"Not all stories have happy endings, my lady. Sometimes audiences can let a story release all their bad emotions. They feel better when the bad feelings are released."

Cathúa laughed a bitter laugh. "If what you were saying is true we might just be there to make the audience feel sad?"

"Or we might be the villains of the piece, my lady."

"Then Lord Aclaí is the hero?" Cathúa laughed. "It is a seductive idea, but I don't believe it. We are not the main players in a story. This thing has told me I am in a decided reality just twelve times this year." Réalta saw Cathúa's chin tremble and she wanted to embrace her again, but didn't dare. "Life isn't a story, Réalta. It is meaningless coincidence – a game of chance. I am one of the losers." She glanced down at the little gold cat with its glittering green eyes. "There are a lot of losers in this game of chance."

"Are you sure, my lady? Surely the increase since –"

"The hypothesis is untestable, Réalta," Cathúa snapped. "That means there is not any point in wasting more time on it."

Réalta watched as she turned away. Her voice sounded irritated but her body-language spoke of something far worse. Réalta put a hand on Cathúa's shoulder.

Cathúa looked around at her. Anger – or whatever she was feeling – had brought tears to her eyes. "I don't care anyway," she explained. "Why would I want to believe in a storyteller who hates me so much?"

Réalta thought of answers as Cathúa turned away again. But there was nothing that she could say. If half the things Cathúa had told her were true then, it seemed, the storyteller really must hate her. And, if the storyteller of their lives hated Cathúa so much, what words of comfort could Réalta offer? "My lady," she finally asked, "Why remind yourself of this?"

"I have to be strong. I have to do my best."

"You know you will fail."

"I do. But the only way I have found to comfort myself after past failures is by knowing that I have done my best. I will regret this more than I regretted anything in my eight-and-a-half centuries of life. I need to convince myself that I am doing absolutely everything I can to stop Aclaí."

Then Réalta remembered the forbidden book she had read and she knew what she had to do. She reached up to her mistress and touched the back of her neck. Cathúa misinterpreted the gesture and wrapped her arms around Réalta. Réalta held her as she sobbed but her fingers found the thong beneath Cathúa's soft curls. She picked the knot open with her fingernails and the thong came loose.

"My lady?" she whispered.

"What is it?"

"I want to take this."

"I was using it to collect data."

"I know. But you have a good sample size now, my lady. The experiment is weakening your resolve by reminding you."

"I know. I cannot forget."

"But you don't think of it all the time. The feel of this on your skin reminds you that things aren't real. You should not wear it anymore."

Cathúa sighed. "You are right, Réalta." She sat up a little more straight and let Réalta take it off her. Réalta glanced down at the little gold cat in the palm of her hand. She saw the glittering emerald eyes still accusing her. "I wish you'd met Eala," Cathúa whispered. "You have her kindness."

"I wish I'd met her too. But I feel I know her anyway."

"You must keep that a secret, Réalta. Her books are Forbidden Art."

"I know, my lady. I will."

The door to Cathúa's library opened. The old man sitting by the fountain looked up. He saw a young brown girl in a yellow dress rubbing her eye with one hand. Rubies sparkled on her breasts and, slightly above them, a little cat pendant stared at him with glittering emerald eyes. As she came out he saw that she was holding the hand of a slender, pale girl in leather tunic, leggings and boots.

"Cathúa," he called. "And... Réalta, is it?"

"I am Réalta, Mentor," the girl agreed, stifling a yawn.

He peered up at them as they came over. "Cathúa, are you giving this Novice girl gifts?"

"Gifts?" asked Cathúa, frowning.

"I think the Mentor means this, Lady Cathúa," Réalta explained, holding up the cat pendant.

"I... it is a gift, Mentor," said Cathúa. "I told Réalta that I had grown tired of it. She took it."

"And how did she pay you back?" he asked.

"Pay me back?" Cathúa asked, even more confused. She looked up at Réalta and wondered that she should be so shy and bashful around the Mentor.

"We are friends, Mentor," said Réalta. "Nothing more."

"You must be sure not to presume too much," Méar told her. "Cathúa is the oldest and highest-Ranked Adept on the Hill. You are a purple Novice."

"We share an interest in books, Mentor," Cathúa interrupted. She looked down at the Mentor. Then she added, "You told me that I should make new friends, Mentor."

"When was that?" he asked.

"It was on your Nativity Day, Mentor, forty-six years ago."

They watched the puzzlement cross his face as he tried to remember what he had done forty-six years ago. Then the wrinkles deepened. "You would be well advised not to make friends with people who learn Forbidden Arts."

"As you wish, Mentor," Cathúa said.

"You remember what happened last time?"

"We both remember, Mentor."

"Good," he said. He got up. "Do try and remember." He walked towards his own door. Cathúa came over and took his arm as he shuffled along. Then, hesitatingly, Réalta took the other arm. The three of them walked from the fountain to his door. He looked from one to the other. Then he smiled. "Come in," he said. Cathúa came in with him while Réalta hovered at the threshold. "Come on," he repeated.

Réalta came in as Cathúa helped him to sit on the bed. "Come closer," he said to Réalta.

She came close to him and felt his hand on her leg. She looked down at him and the feelings overwhelmed her as quickly as that. She felt him pulling her underclothes down and then she felt his hands return. She reached out and stroked his cheek, watching carefully to see if he minded. He didn't seem to mind so she ran her hands on his neck and shoulder, watching the effect.

"Did you ever learn the Mind Craft?" he asked her.

"I am a purple Novice, Mentor," she whispered. "Who would have taught me?"

"I don't know," he said, looking at Cathúa.

"Nobody taught me, Mentor," Réalta said.

"Good." He looked at Cathúa. "She's still wearing clothes," he said to Réalta.

"I think..." Réalta looked down at him. "Do you want me to undress her, Mentor?"

"I think that would be interesting to watch," he said.

Réalta undid the toggles at the top of Cathúa's tunic and then lifted it over her body. Cathúa held up her arms to make it easier. She put the tunic down and looked at the Mentor. "Go on," he said. "Everything. I want to see your hands on her body."

Réalta's face reddened as she looked at Cathúa and saw the way the tips of her breasts crinkled. It wasn't that cold. She knelt before Cathúa and undid the thong that held the leggings around Cathúa's hips. She pulled everything down in one movement. As she undid each boot and lifted Cathúa's feet she felt her hand on her head, steadying herself. She suddenly realised she was surrounded by Cathúa's scent.

She stood up, feeling the heat on her own face, and looked down at the Mentor. "Kiss her," he said. "I said I want to see your hands on her body."

Réalta looked at Cathúa, hoping not to see revulsion or embarrassment, but all she saw was curiosity. Réalta reached up to Cathúa and they were hugging for the second time that evening. He watched as they kissed and saw how Cathúa's hands slid under the hem of Réalta's dress and how Réalta lifted one foot and leaned in to Cathúa's embrace. He slid a hand up the back of the nearest leg on each of them and found the places he wanted. Then he whispered the Words.

He heard them both gasp and saw how they held each other more closely. But he also saw how both of them turned to look at him as the Words took effect. He let them hug each other while he grasped them both. Then, at last, he let go.

"Mentor," Réalta gasped. "I love you."

Cathúa stepped back then moved a little into the space between them. "I am sure she didn't mean it, Mentor," she said.

"You think she doesn't love me?"

"I mean... I mean that I am sure she didn't mean to say it. She is only a purple Novice."

"I know what you mean, Cathúa."

"Please, Mentor, be kind."

"I will be kind," he promised. "*She* would have wanted me to be kind."

"I am sure she would have," Cathúa agreed.

"I am sorry, Mentor," said Réalta. "I didn't think that... I was speaking out of turn. I am sorry."

"It's all right. You haven't been trained very well, have you?"

"Trained, Mentor?"

"That is what I mean. Come over here and lie on the bed beside me."

"Should I take off the dress, Mentor?" she smiled.

"I think that would be best."

Réalta took the dress off and placed it over Cathúa's tunic. Then she lay down on the bed beside him. Cathúa came and sat the other side of him. He turned to Réalta. "Last time you were in here you told me that you had not had a man."

"I hadn't, Mentor."

"And what about now?"

"I still haven't, Mentor."

"Why not? Doesn't any man please you?"

"I haven't met anyone who I would want to, Mentor."

He turned to Cathúa. "Train her," he said.

"Should I show her?" Cathúa asked.

"I think so," he said. He lay back and let Cathúa put her hands on him. He felt the way her hands moved and looked over at the girl beside him. She was lying on her side, with her head on the pillow, watching. Then Cathúa lifted her leg over and sat down on his lap. He turned back to her. "Liús really has been teaching you well," he said. "It is a long time since I let anybody do that."

"I know, Mentor," she said. "Liús instructs me for you."

"Of course he does. He is nearly as good a Chamberlain as Rónmór was."

"He is different."

Méar lay there as Cathúa sat in his lap and caressed him with her hands. She shifted her weight enough to make sure that she retained his interest but she never hurried. He looked up at her. "*She* wasn't very skilled," he said. "She had good empathy but she hadn't enough experience."

"I am sure she did her best," Cathúa whispered. "And I cannot offer the same embrace that she gave you."

"What do you mean?" he whispered back. Then he looked into her eyes. "Oh," he said, "Please don't cry. It's all right. I don't want to hurt you."

"You are not hurting me, Mentor," she said. "I am sorry but my emotions are getting the better of me."

He looked up at her as the first tear ran over her cheek. Then suddenly it spilled over and he grasped her waist and held her hips to him.

Afterwards she looked over then got off him very carefully.

"I'm not that fragile," he told her as she lay down beside him.

"She has fallen asleep," Cathúa whispered. "We have been out all day and she is still very young. Please forgive her. I will take her out if you wish."

He looked back at the desk. "*She* would want me to forgive, Cathúa. Let the poor child sleep. Have you been taking her patrolling?"

"I took her up to the land of the Kurghans, Mentor."

"Why?"

"We were looking at what was left of the old people from before the City."

"Why?"

Cathúa propped herself on one elbow. She looked down at the jewel on a chain around his neck. "Mentor, how did you win the Key of Creation?"

"I sent a party of Novices out to find it. I told them to force it to take this form and then to bring it back. I gave them Words to make it take a form."

"Words that Bind Manifestations," Cathúa said.

"Of course," he answered.

"How did Novices bind one of the Great Principles?"

"A Novice can use those Words, Cathúa."

"How did they find the Breath to overcome it?"

"By trickery." Méar looked at Cathúa's expression. "Why all the questions?"

"Mentor, when you founded the City, before you bound the Key of Creation, was the Forest hostile?"

"Of course it was," he replied. "You should know that of all people. You are City Archivist."

"I am City Archivist, Mentor," she agreed.

9

City of the Lost

Éise thought of herself as patient but, by the time it was getting dark, she had waited long enough. "Come on, Tintreacha," she called. "We are going to Aunt Úlla's house."

Tintreacha came running. She lifted her in her arm and wrapped her cloak around them both. They all knew in Acra and, even if Liús wanted to pretend they were peasants, Éise thought that there was not any point in being cold for nothing. Besides, Tintreacha had liked the comfort of the cloak since she was a baby.

She whispered Words of Seeing Heat and walked through the monochrome landscape to Úlla's house. "Úlla," she called, "are you in?"

"I am, my lady," Úlla replied. "What do you want?"

"Will you mind Tintreacha for me? I am going to look for that husband of mine."

"I will, my lady. When will you be back?"

"Before midnight, I should think."

"As you wish, my lady," Úlla agreed.

Éise took her daughter and placed her on her feet, over the threshold. "Come along," said Úlla. Tintreacha followed her into the house.

"Be good," Éise called after them. But her daughter was not listening.

Éise walked back to her own house. She found herself a bright yellow silk dress and a red jacket. She put sandals on her feet to replace the muddy boots she wore in cold Acra. Then she said her Words of Freshness and dabbled perfume here and there. Then she drew aside the curtain and stepped through the gateway that Liús had made.

"So remember to practice what I showed ye," Cathúa concluded. "Don't worry about enunciation. Ye're all high enough Rank to not worry about enunciation. Stand tall, breathe from down in your belly, relax, and project your voice."

They filed out of the lecture room and she gathered up the hangings and books she had been using. She realised someone was watching her and she looked around. The Mentor was in the doorway, leaning on his stick. She dropped everything back on the desk and went over to him. "Mentor," she said as she took his arm, "Come and sit down."

He let her lead him to the end of one of the benches and she knelt beside him as he sat down.

"You are good at lecturing," he told her. "They learn well from you."

"I only do it because you don't, Mentor."

"And, seeing how well you do it, I don't feel so bad."

Cathúa looked up at him but her face was a mask. "Well, you should, Mentor," she chided. "These Veteran lectures are not just there to teach Words of Power. These senior Veterans are trying to achieve Immortal Breath."

"Which is why your advice is as much about improving their Breath as it is about the Words."

"I cannot teach the way you can teach, Mentor. They will not learn Immortal Breath from me."

"They won't learn it from me, either, Cathúa. My Immortal Breath has failed."

"You should still try, Mentor."

"Cathúa, you defeat him. When he is defeated I will get my Immortal Breath back. There is a way I can do it but not until he is defeated."

"I can't," she replied. "I'm sorry. I will try my best, my very best, right until the very last day, but the City will fall."

"You know something. Tell me."

Cathúa leaned forward until her hair brushed his knee. "Mentor, I –"

"I know what you are doing there, too." Then he spoke the Words of Truthful Aura.

"Please, Mentor," she said as the silvery light gathered around her head. "I don't want to –"

"I know you don't," he replied, the light around his head remaining as clear as hers. "But you know, don't you?"

"I don't want to say."

"Tell me, Cathúa."

He saw the tears in her eyes. "I know, Mentor."

"So why do you lead the defence?"

"Because I am the oldest left in the City, Mentor. Because I promised I would. And because Immortality doesn't mean living forever."

He sighed and put one hand on her shoulder. "Do you think I can do anything to stop it?"

"I don't know, Mentor. I don't believe you can oppose Aclaí. I am not sure how these things work but the only solution I can imagine is one where you survive Aclaí defeating you." She bent her head until her black curls fell forward over her face.

"You think I should surrender to him?"

"I think you will die if you don't."

"And that is the only thing that can save the City?"

"Mentor, I'm sorry."

"Is it?" he demanded. "Tell me!"

"Mentor, surrendering to Aclaí might save your life. I don't believe it will save the City. I can't think of anything that could do that. The City will be destroyed, Mentor. He has promised to do it and it will be done."

"If I surrender to him I will lose my last chance to recover my Immortality, Cathúa."

"Perhaps there is another way. How will you recover your Immortality?"

"It is a secret," he said. "None of ye should know. Ye will learn when the time comes."

She buried her face in his lap and he stroked her hair. But he seemed to be listening to something else. Then, suddenly, he spoke Words of Power. She pitched forward a little as he vanished but she put her hand down rather than bang her head on the bench.

She stood up, said her Words of Freshness and went back to gathering her books and hangings. She could only think of one way the Mentor could recover his Immortality but she could not imagine who he thought would help. She was the City's archivist: she knew that Foscúil was the only one left. All the other Immortals who had The Gift were dead. Who was left to help him?

Éirime stood outside the houses and looked up. She was in the lee of the Furnace House, keeping warm, but around her the wind was carrying snow along the valley. Directly above her the sky was alive with coloured fire as the Sun's Wind was bent and twisted by the field that emerged from the Earth's pole. She knew that if she read one of Cathúa's books she would find an explanation for it. But she did not want explanations. She was watching the unearthly flickering light illuminate the landscape of snow and ice as part of her mind sought music that could convey that beauty.

She was also thinking of Geana and wondering that life seemed to continue even when everything that gave it meaning was gone.

Very faintly in the wind she heard a woman's voice singing. Perhaps not quite everything was gone. She ran across to the nearest of the circle of houses and went down the steps to the underground passages that linked them. In those stone tunnels it was impossible to hear what direction Blátha's voice was coming from. She sang Words of Light and found her way through the gloom.

The singing stopped. Then she heard Blátha's voice and the voice of another. Éirime found her sword and armour on her Silver Cord but she didn't find her metal boots. As she ran through the darkness she softly sang Words that End and then Words of Seeing Heat.

"Where is she?" the Mentor demanded.

"Who?" asked Blátha.

"Éirime."

She took his arm and led him to a seat. "Mentor, sit down. Do you want me to take you back to the City? You know you are in danger here."

"Trees don't grow on this barren land. I am safe enough." But he allowed her to support his weight as he shuffled over and sat down.

When he had sat down she sat beside him. She took his hands the way Geana used to take Caora's hands when she wanted to comfort them. Éirime blinked as she watched it. "Mentor," Blátha said, "you have forgotten."

"Forgotten what?" he asked.

"Éirime was killed. Aclaí found her dead in Áthaiteorainn."

"How do you know about Áthaiteorainn, Blátha?"

"I lived there for forty years, Mentor."

"You were my Favourite once, Blátha. Do you remember?"

She breathed Immortal Breath. "I remember, Mentor."

"Why did you betray me?"

"I was young and in love, Mentor."

"With Éirime?"

"With Croí, my lord. But he is long dead. That was three hundred years ago."

"So who do you betray me for now?"

"I don't, Mentor. I only want what is best for you."

"So would you lie to me?"

"Only if I thought it was best for you."

"Who dares to decide what is *best for me*, Blátha?"

"The Elder Immortals do, Mentor. Surely you know that."

"I only granted that Rank once, Blátha."

"If someone's Breath becomes strong enough for the Rank, do they change when you grant it?"

"Ye need my permission to believe ye can do it. Someone with Immortal Breath will not attempt Immortal Rank Words until I give them Rank."

"But not Elder Immortals, Mentor. You give them Rank because you know they will take it anyway."

"Sometimes they do take it anyway, Blátha. I never gave the stronger Eibheara Rank." He leaned closer to her, looking right into her eyes. "You serve her, don't you, Blátha?"

"I had to choose, Mentor. She loves you. They both do but the other one is crazy."

"Did she tell you to lie about Éirime?"

"She didn't, Mentor. She told me to look after her. That is all."

"Did she know that I would kill you for it?"

Blátha smiled a crooked smile. "I think she must have, Mentor."

"Did you?"

"I'm not surprised, Mentor. But Immortality does not mean living forever." Blátha leaned forwards until her mouth brushed against his. "Do you want one last time before you do?"

"You are not afraid of me, are you?" Méar asked, surprised.

"I am not. I understand now. I trust in my mistress and the future. I don't see any reason to be afraid."

"I could hurt you very badly, Blátha."

"I don't think you could, Mentor. I am stronger than you, I still have Immortal Breath and, if you take me back to the City, you might reveal Éirime's existence to –"

He looked past her. "Éirime," he called, "come in here."

Blátha looked around as she came in. She came over to the other side of the bench and sat behind Blátha. "I won't let you hurt her, Mentor," she said.

"Oh, she's right," Ceann answered. "This body is too weak anyway."

Blátha turned to Éirime. "I'm not going to fight him, love. He can kill me if he needs to."

"You might not fight him but I will," she replied. She looked him in the eye. "Why do you want to do this? You told me to hide myself and I have hidden myself. Why do you mind if I have a companion?"

"Very well," Ceann said. "I concede. Why don't we three sit down and have a drink together? We could pretend we are the Mentor and two of his Favourites."

"I will get wine," agreed Blátha. She got up. Éirime saw that she was not walking in the direction of the kitchens but retracing Éirime's steps back outside.

Ceann looked across the arms-length of bench to where Éirime sat in her armour. "Won't you dress for company?"

Éirime lifted off her helm then unclipped the armour piece by piece, taking her time. First she removed the arm sections then the leg sections. Blátha returned with mugs and a stone jug. She sat between them and then she filled the mugs. As she poured Éirime removed the chestplate and backplate. Beneath it she was wearing white linen and she pulled the material down to cover her thighs. Blátha set the jug down on the stone floor with a clink. The stone jug was still filled with wine.

"Interesting," Ceann said, looking down at the jug. "Can it be emptied?"

"I don't know," Blátha replied. "There are a number of food containers in the kitchens which are always full of fresh food."

"I see. Does the fuel for the fire come from the same place?"

"The heat comes from a furnace in the middle of the village, Mentor. The furnace is powered by some process that I don't understand but I certainly know is dangerous."

"How often does it need to be fuelled?"

"I am not aware of it needing fuel, Mentor. It has never been fuelled. We are forbidden from entering the building that contains the furnace. It is that building where Eala got the poison that nearly killed her when she was a Novice."

"I see." Ceann raised the mug to his lips. "What should we wish for as we drink?" he asked.

"Long life," suggested Blátha. Her eyes smiled at him over the rim of her mug as she drank deep.

Cathúa looked up from her reading. Réalta was at the door with the darkness of night behind her. "What kept you?" Cathúa asked.

"I'm sorry, my lady," Réalta replied.

Cathúa looked at her face more closely. "I didn't mean that. I wanted information. Are you all right?"

"I am fine, my lady. I was cut at sword practice and I was looking for someone to heal it. Míol the healer was out in Lorgcoiseaigéan and I had to get a lift in the Patrol Flyer to find him."

"Are we so short of Flyers now?"

"For Novices we are, my lady."

"You could have asked me."

"I didn't want to bother you, my lady."

Cathúa got up. "Look, Réalta, I'm not very good at communicating my emotions. But that doesn't mean you should avoid me. I told you: I don't want to be 'my lady'. I want to be your friend."

"As you wish, my lady."

Cathúa checked Réalta's eyes for irony. She thought she saw enough and she smiled. "How did you get cut?"

"I was at sword practice, my lady. I was receiving the attack and the sword was knocked out of my hand. It struck me here..." she indicated her upper arm and shoulder, "... and also here." She moved her hand to point at her cheek. "I know enough Words to stop the bleeding but not enough to heal deep cuts."

"Of course you don't, not yet."

"I wish I didn't have to practice sword. I don't go on Patrols anymore – I am not sure I see the point in it."

"There is a point to it, Réalta. In the last year more Adepts have been killed by humans and near-humans than by Forest monsters. The City is full of humans and most of them are armed with swords."

"Even so they fight outside the City's walls."

"Lord Aclaí's forces are closing around us, Réalta. They are like a noose around the neck of the City. One day we will fight them here in the Court of the Favourites. On that day there will be nowhere to run to."

"Will it be soon?"

"A few months at the most. Besides, even if you do survive, your best chance at learning Immortality is through the sword."

"You said that you learned Immortality through Words of Power, my lady."

"I did. But by the time you need it that path will be lost, Réalta. If you have any chance of learning Immortality after the City falls it will be through sword craft."

"But I can't even hold the sword."

"Show me," Cathúa said.

Réalta found the sword on her Silver Cord. She held it in front of her, stiffly. Cathúa walked around and stood to one side of her. "You need to relax," she said. "You must feel your Breath, like water, flowing down your arms." Cathúa touched Réalta's arm and ran her fingertip along the underside of it. "The Breath flows down, under here, and all the way to the fingers. These two fingers, the little fingers, they are the most important.

If they are holding your sword-hilt right the others are not important at all."

Réalta tried to understand what Cathúa was telling her and tried to relax and feel her breath in her arms. But it did not make much sense.

Liús was sitting in Rónmór's room among the scattered books and abandoned notes. Somebody else would be Chamberlain that evening – if any Chamberlain was needed. The Mentor was not in his room anyway. Alone in Rónmór's room Liús surveyed the jumble and looked back over his lost life.

Ever since his first death he had felt cold. He had tried not to let anyone know, and he knew his body still seemed as fresh and vital as ever, but deep inside he knew. He thought of how the fear of death used to excite him before the reality of death had destroyed his illusions.

He could not call the Manifestation his friend but he knew that it wanted him to. Instead, aware of what he was dealing with, he invoked it carefully. He drew the circle on the ground with chalk then spoke the Words. The air seemed to acquire the heavy, greasy feeling that he had grown used to.

Liús, it said, *I am here.*

Only then he wondered what he wanted to say. "Where is the Mentor?" he asked.

Keeping secrets from you, the Manifestation replied.

"And what secrets are you keeping from me?" snapped Liús.

I keep your secrets very well, my friend, it replied. *If they knew on the Hill that you have a daughter, what would they do? If they knew you are a dead thing –*

"You know that Rónmór found Words to destroy your kind? Not just to banish you back to where you belong but to destroy you utterly as if you never existed?"

But I am your friend, Liús. I keep your secrets because I am your friend.

"Be silent."

But, although the Manifestation confined within the circle kept silent, the accusing thoughts inside Liús' head screamed on. He remembered how Toirneach had threatened him with death – how Toirneach had promised him death. He knew he had deserved it and he wondered, using Eala's arithmetic, if that was why he had sought it. And, he wondered, how much of his feeling of coldness was guilt at pretending to be alive when secretly he knew he was dead.

You love death, Liús. You have always been in love with death.

"I told you to be silent," he muttered. But he remembered the things he had shared with Toirneach. And, before then, the Mentor's hand on his throat as his heart had been forced open with Words of Power. He had never known before then but afterwards it was something he could never forget.

Toirneach had known somehow. They had found tribes that celebrated the Days with human sacrifice and, with Words of Misdirection or the authority of their blue cloaks, they had witnessed so many give their lives in pointless rituals. And eventually, under Toirneach's prompting, he had returned to his own people to show his lover how they dealt with moral failings where he came from. Seeing it through his lover's eyes he had realised how –

"Liús?" He heard Éise's voice outside.

"Éise! You're back!" replied Cathúa's voice. It sounded like she was further away, probably in her library. Liús spoke the Words of Banishment to send the thing in the circle away. He looked at the scattered notes. Now he knew that Rónmór had left one vital piece of information out of his writing. Rónmór had described that two types of Manifestation were interested in communicating but he had not offered any reason to choose one over the other. But he could not make both choices and Liús had made the other choice to Rónmór. He now knew that he had chosen poorly.

"Liús?" Éise's voice took him by surprise. She came in and sat beside him. He felt her hand on his shoulder. "What is it, my love?" she whispered.

"I have... I am dead, my love. You are a widow."

"Not so loud," she chided. Then she whispered, "What are you talking about? Is this because Eibheara thinks she killed you? You don't feel dead to me."

"She did kill me. She strangled me. She started raving about me being a traitor and she strangled me. Before I lost consciousness I felt her stab me with a blade, too. I know she killed me except that I can't die. But I can't live either. I feel dead inside, all the time."

"That is guilt, my love, nothing more. You need to tackle this guilt of yours."

"I can't, dear heart. It won't let me forget. I must converse with it to be an effective Chamberlain."

"Like Rónmór?"

"Rónmór chose the other Manifestation."

"How do you know? Have you found something among all this?"

"I haven't, my love. We have gone through this lot many times and removed everything of value. But I compare how I feel with how Rónmór was. This thing is corroding me from inside. The hurts I carry in my heart from my childhood are like a wound and this thing picks at it, infects it, and won't let it heal. My heart is dying inside me and it is the fault of the Manifestation."

"Rónmór wasn't so different, you know? He was aloof and strange. He didn't really have friends. Maybe that is the effect of communicating with Manifestations."

"Eala was Rónmór's friend. So was that Immortal girl. His mind was sort of alien but he wasn't like me."

"How can you tell what he was like inside?"

"My heart is dying, my love. I don't think I am going to be able to function for much longer. The wound on my heart has turned bad."

"Because of your childhood?"

"Because that thing won't let me heal from my childhood."

"And you can't dismiss this thing because you are afraid you will fall from your position?"

"The City is dying too, my love. Cathúa is the only other Immortal left. She has resolved to see this through to the end. The end won't be long but we need a Chamberlain to help him remain strong."

"Then we need to find a way to heal your wound." Éise turned towards her husband and watched his face. "You never told me about that part of your childhood, my lion. What did they do to you?"

"They killed my mammy," Liús wept.

Éise wrapped her arms around her husband and held him close to her. She felt his sobs. When he breathed again she whispered, "You told me that she died in childbirth."

"I did not. I told you that I was her only child and that her next pregnancy killed her. It did. My father was an old man, a chieftain. After he died she was supposed to be a good widow. But she wasn't. I didn't understand why they turned on her."

"How old were you?"

"I had six summers." Liús looked up at his wife. "They dragged her out to the bog, they stripped her and cut her hair. They beat her, they put the rope around her neck. Then they... afterwards they choked her and pressed her down into the mud. Then they walked away and... and I never saw her again."

"Hush," she said as she stroked his head.

"I can't forget, Éise. I hear the men telling everyone how wanton she was – cursing her as they killed her. I hear the villagers shouting encouragement. And... I hear my mother's voice crying out. I didn't understand then but I understand now."

"What do you understand, my lion?"

"That I can be like my mother or like the men that killed her."

"How could you be like them? I can't even get you to spank me properly."

"It was my father's other sons who did it. He would have done it without hesitation. I am my father's son, dear heart. I would not have a blue robe otherwise."

"You said they brought you to Selection to get rid of you."

"They did. But the Mentor chose me. He chooses killers."

"He chose Eala, my lion."

"Eala was a killer, Éise. She tried not to be but she was. And so am I. That *thing* reminds me that I am a killer. It wants me to be my brothers, not my mother."

"What if he hadn't chosen you?"

"Then I would have returned to the village. I would have been caught, Éise. I am as wanton as my mother was. Without a blue cloak I would be sleeping in the cold bog beside her."

Then Éise understood. "Your wife is wanton too," she whispered. "What will you do with her?"

Liús exploded in her arms. He pushed her away and she fell backwards onto the bed. He was over her and he had his hand pressing on her chest. "*Cac*, Éise," he growled, "Do you think this is a game? The things I could do to you..."

"Whatever you need, my lion," she told him. She opened her arms and ran her hand over his body. "You see how wanton I am?"

He tore her dress and he pulled her hair. But she arched her back and cried out and, when he had poured out his anger and grief into her, her loving embrace reminded him of how much healing she had to give.

The three riders emerged from the dense woodland onto the road. Trees lined either side of the way and they turned towards the rising ground. The stone walls varied in age: some were older, covered with lichens and moss, but others were young, pointed and laid within the last couple of centuries.

Aclaí looked over at the rock that stood away to one side. It was as large as a cottage and the top looked as if it had been carved. The stone was shaped with two legs, roughly cut off, as if there had once been a statue. He smiled, remembering.

"This will really make a difference," Foscúil said.

"Providing they accept these gifts," suggested Miotal. "I am not sure I would like a House of Power wrapped around my finger. Not even a small one."

"You think that they will be afraid?" Aclaí asked.

"I still remember trying to hold the line at Ceatha," Miotal replied.

"That's where Damhánalla found them," Aclaí said. "Each is just one of the Manifestations of Creation that broke loose at Ceatha. You can see that is not such a large threat."

Foscúil grinned. "It is fitting," he laughed.

"What dark irony is amusing you this time?" asked Miotal.

"We are giving these things to the Forest Houses to help them counter the City's command of Words of Power. With one of these an ordinary warrior is the match of an Immortal."

"So?" asked Miotal.

"So these things will help bring about the destruction of the City. But these things are only in our hands because the City tried to destroy us."

"All right," Miotal smiled, "That is funny."

They rode right up to the front gate of the fortress. They had been watched for some time, of course, but the guard at the gate stood forward to challenge them. Four young Forest People stood on the bridge over the dyke, with swords drawn.

"Who goes there?" the leader demanded.

"My name is Aclaí and I have come to bring gifts."

Foscúil smiled as the leader's face acquired an expression of shock and fear. "My lord," she said, "I didn't recognise you."

"It is hard to recognise a man in armour," Aclaí replied.

"But it seems unlikely that anyone from the City would make it as far as the House of Andánacht," added Miotal.

"If they did, my lord, they would be of very high Rank. We couldn't hope to oppose an Immortal."

"Well," Foscúil said, "Let us see what can be done about that. Is the Andánacht able to receive us?"

"I would think so, my lords," she answered. "Come this way."

Servants took their horses and they were led through passages of vaulted stone and into the great hall. "Lord Aclaí is here," their guide announced.

The leader of the fortress came over to greet them. "Lord Aclaí, you are welcome," he said. "Ye will have to excuse our guards. There are rumours that an Immortal from the City patrols deep into the Forest, still. They may only be rumours, my lords, but we would find it very hard if an Immortal came here from the City."

"They are not just rumours, Andánacht Scamall," answered Foscúil. "I know that one of them Patrols the Forest. She is Eighteenth Rank and her knowledge of Words of Power is second only to the Mentor himself."

Miotal looked at Foscúil. "You never mentioned this."

"I made sure the commander of Aclaí's forces knew. He took the necessary steps."

"And what necessary steps did you take?" laughed Aclaí.

"I made sure that we had a way to counter this threat. In the short term I advised our own Patrols to not engage, to track her, and to inform one of us. In the long term... well, that is why we are here today."

Aclaí turned to Scamall. "Damhánalla has been working on the problem of how to oppose an Immortal Rank Adept. Here is her solution." Aclaí opened a small leather bag and took out a dull black ring. He handed it to Scamall. Scamall saw that it was adorned with a bright spot of red. He lifted it to see the decoration more clearly and realised it was a pair of tiny red sparks. The red sparks watched him like a pair of eyes.

"It is a strange thing," Scamall said.

"It is a Manifestation of Creation, forced to take the shape of a ring," Miotal explained.

"It is as if you could wear a House of Power," added Foscúil. "It confers upon the wearer a limited Mastery of Creation."

Scamall smiled. "Well, my lords, that will make a big difference. Is this thing hard to use? Will we require a lot of training?"

"Damhánalla has worked hard to make sure it is easy and safe for anyone to use," Aclaí replied. "I think you will find that, within a ten-day, you won't have any reason to worry about the three Immortals left in the City."

It was Ceann that refilled the mugs. When Blátha had emptied hers again Ceann sat close to her on the other side from Éirime. He put his arm around her shoulder and she turned her head towards him. She was hesitant but it was her who started the kiss.

Éirime shook her head and reached for the jug. She suspected that when he was done with Blátha the Mentor would put it in her but she didn't have to be awake when he did. She found her harp on her Silver Cord and began to play. Her song was a lament. She was not interested in setting the mood for the other two.

Blátha lifted her dress for her Mentor and Ceann put Méar's hands on her body. He was rough enough to make her flinch but also to make her body rise in response. Then he broke off and refilled Éirime's mug.

When he turned back to her Blátha took his tunic off. She took that little part of Méar's body in her hands and saw that it could stiffen in spite of the signs of age in his face. She bent down to kiss him. Éirime shook her head and drained her mug again. This time she reached for the jug herself. Then she began to play a dance on her harp: a fast tempo out of step with the slow rhythm Blátha was keeping.

"I'm going to kill you," Ceann whispered to her.

"Afterwards?" she whispered back.

"I might let you have one or two first," he replied. "If you are a good girl."

She glanced over to where Éirime was engrossed in her playing. "What about her?"

"I won't kill her, Blátha," Ceann replied.

"Do you promise?"

"Do you know she can breathe Immortality into others, Blátha?"

"Is that so?" she asked.

"It is."

"Then you think she can restore your youth?"

"She can."

"Then why don't you ask her?"

"Because if I do Aclaí will know she is still alive. As soon as my battle with Aclaí is over I can tell her to breathe my Immortal Breath. Then I will be young again."

"How do you know that, if you don't treat her well, she will still do it?"

"She is Initiated, Blátha."

As he whispered Éirime picked up the jug again. She looked down at the level and frowned. She shrugged and she lifted the jug.

"Éirime, love –" Blátha began.

Ceann got up and hooked a hand under one of Blátha's knees. As Éirime looked around she saw the Mentor force it into Blátha's body. Blátha cried out and Éirime saw the face her lover made. She raised the jug to her lips and began to drink.

By the time she had realised what was wrong with the jug her companions were deeply involved in each other. She saw how it went in and out of her lover's body and how her lover's flesh quivered and trembled. She knew it would be her turn next and, knowing how drunk she was, she wondered if she would even notice. Her fingers tingled and trembled as she carefully put the jug down. She knew she couldn't play anymore so she closed her eyes to listen to the music in her head more clearly. She held the mug she had been using tightly in her hand to keep from dropping it.

Blátha was gasping when she heard the mug smash on the floor. She held the Mentor's body and saw how his face reddened. She felt it inside her and she stroked his face.

Afterwards he caressed her chin and her throat. "Thank you, Mentor," she whispered.

"You could have still been a favourite," he whispered back.

"I don't think so," she replied. "But be kind to her. She is close to Elder Immortal Rank, isn't she?"

"Of course she is," Ceann whispered back.

"When she is an Elder Immortal she could oppose you."

"But she won't progress while her belly and head are full of wine," Ceann sneered. "She doesn't care now. I can preserve her in alcohol until the battle with Aclaí is over."

"You could still make peace with her, Mentor," Blátha replied. "She could hold Aclaí back for you."

"I can never make peace with her or Aclaí," Ceann replied. "You don't know what I am." Then Ceann whispered Words of Strength.

"Oh," said Blátha. She felt the tears in her eyes. "Will you put it in me again first?" she asked.

"If you wish."

"Thank you." She opened her body for him again.

Ceann did as she asked, then put his hand on Blátha's throat. He didn't squeeze all the arteries but he made sure that she could not speak Words of Power. "I am not the Mentor," he whispered, bearing down on her with his enhanced strength. "The Mentor has given up on you and your precious City. He is going to let me and Aclaí fight over it." Then, as Blátha struggled beneath him, he tightened his grip. "I am not even human: I am a Manifestation that happens to have control of the City. And the thing I enjoy most is watching ye die," he whispered. "The City will fall. Everyone will die. I am going to enjoy that so much."

When he had finished Ceann got up and went over to Éirime. Behind him Blátha's body slumped sideways onto the floor. He found a pendant on Méar's Silver Cord and put it around Éirime's neck. The Words of Strength that had allowed him to crush Blátha's throat also allowed him to lift Éirime's sleeping form. Then he spoke the Words of Folding Space and was gone.

The Keepers of the Furnace had been told that heat was not required any more. So, as Blátha's body cooled to room temperature, the room temperature kept on falling. She lay there beside the couch, frozen for thousands of years, waiting for the only mother she had ever known to find her and carry her to the heat of the pyre.

10

Preparations

After the Evening Meal Liús, Cathúa and Eibheara followed the Mentor up the Hill. Liús had been watching him all evening. Tonight he was the sociable, amusing one who would kill without emotion. For most of the last ten-day he had been the quiet one who grieved. Liús resolved to talk about it with Éise. He still had not made up his mind which one to encourage. He wasn't sure which of them had the better Immortal Breath – or which one had the better chance of recovering Immortal Breath.

When they got to the Court of the Favourites the Mentor waited until the guard closed the gate of the Court. He turned to them. "Liús, Cathúa, would ye come to my room?"

"As you wish, Mentor," Cathúa replied. She took Liús' hand and they followed him in. He sat on his bed and they sat either side of him. Cathúa leaned forward a little to let her breasts show through the silk of her shirt.

He glanced down at her. "Cathúa, if you want that sort of thing take Liús to bed later," he said. He looked around at Liús. "Don't look so surprised, ye two," he added. "I see everything. I know what ye get up to while Éise is otherwise occupied."

"Éise doesn't mind, Mentor," Liús answered.

"I'm sure she doesn't," the Mentor agreed. "Anyway, that's not why I called ye in here. Cathúa, where is Féileacána?"

"I don't know, Mentor."

"Is she still alive?"

"I don't think we have had news of her death. We could see if the sword-hilt will communicate with her."

"I think that would be a good way to alert her to our intentions. I would rather discover without drawing attention to her."

"What do you want with her?" Cathúa asked. "Is this part of the general purge on the Mind Craft?"

"It is not, Cathúa."

"Do you want her to be alive?" asked Liús.

193

"I want her to be dead," replied the Mentor. "Do ye think ye can arrange that?"

"As you wish," agreed Cathúa.

"I will," added Liús.

"Then off ye go," said the Mentor. "Go and organise it and don't tell anyone. Don't discuss it with anyone off the Hill – not even her."

They got up. Then, hand in hand, they went.

The sword class stood in neat rows: more than a hundred warriors waiting. Foscúil always let them wait a little. It got them nervous, those who were still prone to nerves. Then he signalled to his assistants and together they walked into the sword hall. He stood before them, drew his sword and saluted. They all returned his salute.

He chose Damhánalla to demonstrate on. She stood beside him. "Attack!" he said.

In a fraction of a heartbeat her sword was in her hand and she was turning to him. Her attack was a simple overhand swing, but he also saw what her right hand was doing. He raised his own blade to deflect hers but he saw the other hand thrust forwards. A quick tug of the Silver Cord and the thrust of her right hand was extended by the blade. He let the sword-point come within a fingers-width of his belly before he bent a little to let it pass. He moved his own sword-blade forward enough to catch the wrist of her left hand, the one that had originally held the sword.

A heartbeat later she was raising the sword-point in surrender. She dropped the sword and her gauntlets. Blood squirted from her left wrist. Two of her fingers would not bend. She squeezed the cut closed with her right hand and said the Words that Heal Sinew.

"That was a clever attack," acknowledged Foscúil, "but there were two problems. You over-extended the feint with your left hand, which is why I cut your wrist. But the main problem is that you held back your attacks. I could feel that the feint wasn't properly committed."

"Teacher," she acknowledged, flexing her healed hand.

He turned to the rest of them. "It is normal to hold back. Something always holds us back: fear, anger, grief, or even some distraction, some remembered thought. Ye must put them aside. When ye attack just be the attack. Nothing else." He looked at them. "Form into groups of equal Rank and try it. Use something simple: let us say the first single-hand form. This is not about technique. This is about the attack. Be nothing but the attack! Begin!"

They formed into groups and saluted to one another. He walked through the sword-hall, keeping aware of the deadly practice going on all around and watching how they performed their attacks. He watched each group for a few breaths. Sometimes he offered some comment or guidance and sometimes he moved on without saying a word. Eventually, as he wandered through the crowd of greens and browns, he came to the corner of bright blue-green.

He watched Miotal attack Aclaí but he did not comment. Miotal's commitment was good although it needed perfecting just as he had seen everywhere else in the hall. Then it was Miotal's turn to receive the attack.

Damhánalla waited a moment, her sword in her hand, breathing Immortal Breath. Then, like the moment when a trap is sprung, she uncoiled in a simple savage movement. Miotal deflected the movement with a calm movement of his own. Foscúil smiled and Miotal's stance relaxed. Then Foscúil saw him tense and lean backwards a fraction. Aclaí stood ready and Foscúil turned to watch him. There was little point in watching Miotal: he had already been defeated.

Aclaí's movement was fast and precise and Miotal was not quite quick enough. The sword point skidded over his armour as he stepped back. "Stop," said Foscúil.

They stopped.

"I am sorry, teacher," said Miotal. "I cannot oppose him. He has Elder Immortal Breath."

"I wasn't talking to you," Foscúil replied. "Lord Aclaí, do you remember the point of the exercise?"

"You said to 'be the attack', teacher," Aclaí replied.

"So what did I want you to have in your brain when you attacked?"

"The attack, I suppose."

"And what was in your brain when you attacked?"

Aclaí raised his visor and smiled back at Foscúil. "Part of me is thinking that I don't want to kill my friend."

Foscúil was sure there was more. But he wasn't going to argue. That wasn't his way. Instead he said, "Then you are not doing the exercise, are you?"

"Our efforts would be severely hampered if I were to kill Miotal," Aclaí replied. "You know that, *teacher.*"

"It doesn't matter what I know, *Lord* Aclaí. You know how I conduct my lessons."

"But you also told me to choose someone of equal Rank for the exercise."

"So I did," Foscúil conceded. He lowered his visor. "All right then, *Lord* Aclaí, show me you can follow the exercise."

Foscúil was expecting Aclaí's Breath and he didn't think he had reacted the way Miotal had. He let his Breath extend aware of what he was facing. He knew Aclaí would delay the physical attack to allow his stronger Breath to prevail. He knew the lesson had stopped as everyone watched their duel. If Foscúil could keep extending long enough for –

Aclaí's sword was halfway to Foscúil's belly. His full weight and strength were piled behind it. Foscúil knew his defence was far too late even as his own blade cut down. Aclaí's Breath came out in a shout of rage that jolted every onlooker.

Foscúil made a full cut. He tied the sword-blade to his own centre in the hope that his Breath would be strong enough to deflect Aclaí. It was not a technique he had ever taught: he was improvising. The deflection was only partial and the blade-tip scraped across his belly-plate and into the gap between belly and thigh.

His own blade crossed in front of Aclaí's moving knee and he leaped aside. Aclaí's strength through his own sword-blade twisted in the gap in Foscúil's armour, catching his leg-section and knocking his feet out from under him. Foscúil felt the blood squirt out inside his armour. He twisted his body and put an arm down to catch his weight. As he lowered himself to the floor he became aware the sword in his leg was gone again. He rolled over and raised his sword-point to concede. As he did so he felt another wave of blood filling his armour.

Aclaí stood before him. He sat up and looked down at his own leg. The leg was not working at all. It was just lying at an unnatural angle in the armour. The blood was pouring out through the joints. He knew he had cut the main artery and that, without Words, he would be dead in five breaths. But to heal it he needed to touch the wound and that meant getting the armour off. He removed his gauntlets and popped the inside catches. The leg was twisted under the other one and he couldn't get at the outside catches. As he struggled to shift his weight he felt the blood still pumping out. His vision was starting to go grey around the edges. He smiled in spite of himself. How amusing that this might be how he ended his last sword lesson after the way he had begun his first.

Two lovers lay beside each other in a cluttered room and took comfort in the nearness of each other. One of them sat up and whispered Words of Light.

"Are you ready?" asked Cathúa.

"I am. How are we going to find her, then?" said Liús.

"I have listed all the Adept's homes," answered Cathúa. "I think that is the best place to start."

"Does that work?"

"It normally does. A lot of Eala's Adepts just went home to be with their own families when they abandoned the City." Cathúa found her golden tablet and asked it for the register of novices. She flicked through them until she found Féileacána. "She was born on Midwinter's Day 1072, in the southern half of the Westland, in a tributary of the Great River. There's a map but it's a big country."

Liús took the golden tablet in his hand and squinted at the glowing writing. Cathúa stood up, whispered her Words of Freshness and found a tunic, boots and leggings on her Silver Cord. Liús looked up. "So she is three hundred years old," he said.

"Two hundred and ninety-seven years," Cathúa corrected. "But she has only been at the City two hundred and eighty years." She looked at him with a sideways smile. "You should put some clothes on."

"I've only been at the City for two hundred and forty years," Liús said. "She is older than me."

"But you have been taught by Foscúil in the Court of the Favourites for most of that time. We are both two Ranks above her."

"Perhaps," Liús agreed, "But I am quite a new Eighteenth Rank even if you have been an Eighteenth Rank for a long time. And it is a long time since she last came to Evening Meal. She might be better than the Rank she is given."

"You will be fine," Cathúa told him. "We will take a Flyer out there and see how it is. If she fights we will defeat her but I suspect we can ask her to come with us. If we use Innealta's Net on her when we find her we can either bring her to the City or we can kill her on the way and dump her in the sea."

"Why would we not bring her to the City?"

"Because Aclaí's people still claim the right to pursue the Mind Craft faction. If they decide that the Mentor has ordered her death because of the Mind Craft they might try and seize her."

"Perhaps we should just take her head, then."

"Probably we should. But only if she doesn't fight."

"That is what Innealta's Net can do for us."

They went out into the Court of the Favourites. Eibheara was sitting on the edge of the fountain waiting for them. "Are ye looking for Féileacána?" she asked.

"We are," agreed Cathúa, unaware of Liús' suspicious look. "I was going to start at her home village."

"Don't start there," said Eibheara. "Start up the river. There's a village on a lake, on stilts. She is married to the headman of that village."

"How do you know?" asked Cathúa.

"I know an old friend of hers," Eibheara said.

"Do you know what the Mentor ordered?" asked Liús.

"Of course," she smiled.

"Doesn't that matter to you?" asked Liús.

"Why would it?" asked Eibheara.

"If she is a friend of your old friend, I thought that might mean something to you. Old loyalties?"

"Old something, Liús," Eibheara laughed. "But not loyalties."

"Do something!" Damhánalla screamed, "He's dying!"

Aclaí seemed to remember who and where he was. He dropped his own sword and knelt by Foscúil's side. He tugged hard at the leg to free it and, as the armour opened, the whole leg came away. Aclaí said the Words that Staunch Blood. Then he unlatched the armour on the severed leg and on Foscúil's body. He picked up the leg and pressed it back in place as he said the Words that Make a Body Whole. The most powerful of the Words of Healing weren't any real effort for him but he heard the reaction of their audience.

Foscúil's eyes opened. He smiled and propped himself up on one elbow. He looked around him at the blood pooled on the floor. "Painting the sword-hall red," he laughed, "Just like old times, my lord." He got to his feet, found his missing armour on his Silver Cord, and smiled at the shocked faces around them. "Carry on!" he shouted. "I never told ye to stop!"

They returned to the exercise. But Aclaí stood. "Foscúil," he said, "I have to hold back my anger. I need it to destroy the City but, if I don't control it, it will destroy everything close to me and the City will survive unharmed. I cannot do your exercise."

"I am sorry, my lord," said Foscúil.

"And so am I, Teacher," Aclaí replied. He raised his sword in salute. Then he turned and walked out of the sword hall.

Although it had been before midnight that they set out it was dawn by the time Cathúa guided the Flyer down to the village on stilts.

"Are you sure this is the right place?" asked Liús.

"I don't think they have good records. They said that nobody called Féileacána lived in the last village. But either my records are wrong or they don't know her. On the other hand they said that there was a woman called Féileacána in this lake village." She pointed down. "That is probably the closest you will get to 'on the lake'."

"It does fit the description," Liús agreed. "Looks like Eibheara was right."

"Why wouldn't she be?"

"Eibheara's body language is not so hard to read. She was settling old scores."

"I see," said Cathúa. "Against Féileacána?"

"Well, it appears so. But, with Eibheara, it is always hard to tell who is the intended victim of her schemes. We should be careful."

Cathúa thought about it a moment then dismissed it. The politics of the Court of the Favourites had never made sense to her. She looked down at the village in the lake. "How do we land there? I think you could take charge of the Flyer and I could jump down."

"It's an obvious approach," he agreed as he took control. "But I suppose she won't easily make a run for it." Liús guided the Flyer close to the largest of the huts.

As Cathúa jumped down her blue cloak swirled around her. An old man looked up at her. "Hello, my lady," he said.

"I'm looking for a woman called Féileacána," she replied. "Where does she live?"

"That house over there," he answered. "Her husband is headman."

"Thank you," Cathúa replied. She climbed back onto the Flyer and Liús guided it over to the other house. He brought the Flyer right down until it was as low as a boat. A young man was working on the bindings of a flint spear. He stood up when Cathúa stepped onto the platform. He still had hold of his spear.

"Can I help you, my lady?" he asked. The point of the spear was a little lower than Cathúa would have liked when she was not wearing any armour.

"I am looking for Féileacána," Cathúa said.

"Mammy!" the young man called. "There's blue-robes here to see you."

Cathúa counted ten breaths before the front of the house opened. Féileacána stood there. An old man stood beside her with one hand on her shoulder. Two small naked children stood behind her, looking around her legs at the strangers. She looked at Liús and Cathúa. "What do ye want?" she asked.

"We've come to take you back to the City," Cathúa replied, using all the skill she knew to sound sincere.

Féileacána's face fell. She turned to the people beside her and spoke in a peasant tongue. Cathúa whispered Words of Comprehension.

"*– knew you would go one day,*" the old man said.

"*I might be back again, like last time,*" Féileacána said. Then she turned to Cathúa and spoke the tongue of the Sea People. "Will I be coming back?"

"I'm sorry," replied Cathúa.

She watched as Féileacána said her goodbyes to her husband and children. Then she stepped onto the Flyer and sat beside Liús. He breathed a sigh of relief as they climbed up into the sky.

"So, which side are ye on?" Féileacána asked.

"It's complicated," replied Liús. Féileacána turned to him and Cathúa dropped the Net on her head. It settled on her scalp and she stopped speaking. "*Cac,*" Liús breathed, "That was a whole lot easier than I expected."

He took the Flyer out across the vast forest that filled the basin of the Great River. Then, when they were over the sea, Cathúa found her sword on her Silver Cord. Féileacána turned to follow the bright movement but her face did not register any interest. One blow of the sword and Cathúa put the head in a bag. She heaved the body out into the ocean, then said Words of Freshness. She saw the splashes of blood on Liús' cheek disappear as the Words took effect. The Net came away cleanly in her hand.

Liús landed near the Flyer House and left it with the Veteran on duty there. He walked with Cathúa up the steps. The sun was shining as they walked through the abandoned Court of the Immortals. Nobody was in the Court of the Favourites except a couple of servants tidying the gardens. Liús went back into his own rooms and Cathúa sat by the fountain and watched the servants work. She knew she should get them to cut down the big rhododendron before the Day of Harvest.

The warmth of the Sun soaked through her skin and collected as drowsiness in her head. She had not had enough time to sleep even for an Immortal of her age. She used the last of her wakefulness to get up, pick up her bag and go to her own bed.

Aclaí climbed out of the bed. Innealta was still asleep and he replaced the covers so the cold air would not wake her. He whispered his Words of Freshness as he walked out into the courtyard of the Midsummer Palace.

"Lord Aclaí?" Foscúil whispered.

He turned around. Foscúil was sitting on a bench looking up at him. He stood up and took Aclaí's hand. Aclaí allowed himself to be led to Foscúil's quarters. The room was still warm and Aclaí knew Foscúil had not been awake long. Aclaí sat on the bed and Foscúil sat beside him.

"Freckles, my lord," Foscúil said.

"I never –"

"That wasn't why I wanted you here," Foscúil explained. "I have been reading."

"How many times did you scorn Cathúa, Foscúil? How many times have you said 'Books? I am a swordsman'?"

"I think I have said things like that in the past. But, my lord, even Immortals can learn."

"Some of us, anyway," Aclaí laughed back. "So did you find a book about the sword?"

Foscúil leaned over to the table beside his bed. He found three books and passed them to Aclaí.

"These are Eala's books," Aclaí said.

"Well, two of them are Abhainne's books. But Eala wrote them. Abhainne taught me Eala's Art. Her method of commanding an army is rooted in Eala's Art."

"The first book is all you need. The second is concerned with how to govern peasants in peacetime and the third is about the traditions of an island in the north of the Archipelago."

"I've read them all, my lord."

"Did you find them interesting?"

"The first one I already knew because of what Eala and Abhainne had taught me. The second one was slow going."

"It is all about ways for people to get along without fighting, Foscúil."

"I found it interesting that she should expect blue-robes to be subject to her laws. Why did she think there was any need for that?"

"It makes things easier. That seems counter-intuitive but it is true."

"Because people follow leaders who seem to be better than they are. The judges of Eala's code have much stronger authority if they abide by their own moral code. I understand why it makes it easier but Eala didn't write that it was easier. She wrote that it was *necessary*."

"In Eala's way of looking at things, it is."

"Will you do that?"

"I would if I replaced the Mentor. You know that I won't do that."

"I don't understand why you keep saying that you won't."

"It is because of the Key of Creation. Until I can find a way to safely unbind it I will need to stay away from the City. There are too many people with ambition who would want to take it from me. I won't be able to Initiate them."

"Will you keep your most loyal followers by your side, my lord? You know that I would never take it from you. You must know that Damhánalla would never take it from you either."

"I do. But we will have to see how things are when the City is defeated. I might need ye to keep the City for me while I try and unbind it. Or the City itself might fall."

"Perhaps, my lord. Plans never survive the reality of the battle. A commander must improvise." Foscúil turned to Aclaí. "My lord, it was the third book I found most interesting."

"I would have expected you to find that the least interesting. What did you find in it?"

"I found the Mentor, Aclaí. I was from the Sea Hounds. We took slaves from among the other islands of the Archipelago. I am descended from Sea Hounds but I am also descended from slaves taken from the islands of the Archipelago. I recognised a lot of the observations Eala made in her book."

"Nostalgia?"

"Not just nostalgia," Foscúil replied, scornfully. "I'm a swordsman not a bard. I don't care for tales. But the culture that Eala studied is clearly the Mentor's culture."

Aclaí looked at Foscúil with admiration. "You are a lot more than a swordsman, Foscúil. You have learned something important by reading a book. That is the sort of thing Cathúa does."

"So it is. But it is not so hard. I think we could use Eala's Art and, in particular, his cultural values to predict how he will react to the attack. It wouldn't be as good as having his Motivational Chart, but–"

"I have his Motivational Chart," replied Aclaí. "He believes he has an ancestor that tells him how to run the City."

Foscúil stopped smiling. "How long have you kept that from us, Lord Aclaí?"

"Probably too long. I keep too many secrets."

"Did you tell Eala?"

"I did in the end. There is a part of it I don't understand. She didn't understand it either. His Motivational Chart suggests that the ancestor is real. But we know that ancestors cannot be real."

"Is he as deluded as Eibheara?"

"That is my assumption. But she has changed. My spy tells me that she doesn't switch personalities anymore. She has not changed since she has returned to the Hill."

"You have a spy who can watch what happens on the top of the Hill?"

"Of course. But we knew Eibheara was convinced that her own enemy was real."

"Aclaí, if there is only one Eibheara that could put us in a lot of danger. One of the Eibhearas has stronger Breath than you, my lord."

"It is the other one," Aclaí grinned. "If it was the more powerful one she would be by my side."

"How can you be sure?"

"She lived with me like a wife for forty years, Foscúil. I know the difference. The less powerful one fought with me, struggled against all of ye and picked fights with Damhánalla. It was the less powerful one that forced things with Eala. But the more powerful one tried to help me as best she could."

"Why didn't you try and sort her out?"

"The more powerful one told me that it was pointless. She told me that there was not any way she could exert control over the less powerful one. She told me to get rid of her because of the less powerful one. But I knew she wanted to stay with me so I kept the less powerful one for the sake of the other. I hoped she could be victorious. I should have listened to her but I am too sentimental. One of my biggest weaknesses is people who love me – and the Elder Immortal Eibheara loves me more than anyone else ever has. So because of that I didn't do what she asked me to. If I had done as she told me I think we would still have Eala."

"If you had followed my cousin's advice, or even left Eala and the others in Áthaiteorainn, Éirime would still be with us."

It was a long time before Aclaí finally replied. "Anyway, Eibheara said that she would not change until she could explain why she was two people. She also said that I should not forget that the Mentor might change. So I have been watching him to see if he does."

"What are you watching for?"

"There is a physical manifestation to his ancestor worship. He keeps his brother's skull in a bag."

"How do you know?"

"When Eala persuaded him to run away, back when she was a purple Novice, I searched his room for the Key of Creation. I didn't find it but I did find his brother's head in a bag. He was a twin and he keeps his twin brother's skull in a bag in his room."

"That leather bag that he always has on his desk? So *that* is what that bag contains?"

"It is – and until he disposes of it we cannot help him."

"Besides, my lord, you don't want to help him. You want revenge."

"That is what the strong Eibheara was trying to tell me. He could make it better, Foscúil. It is not him that Forbids us from recovering Éirime. It is the memory, the insanity that he thinks is his brother. That is the real target of my revenge."

"What about Abhainne, my lord?"

"Who do you think ordered Abhainne's death?"

"Then... you will defeat the Mentor to take revenge on what? A piece of dead bone in a leather bag?"

"That piece of dead bone in a leather bag is believed by humanity's apparent ruler to be the true ruler of humanity."

"But you know that –"

"I know that he believes it and, because of who and what he is, his belief makes it true. If he turns his back on his imaginary friend I might be able to forgive him. I will do my best to forgive him for the Elder Immortal Eibheara. But not before."

"I won't forgive him, my lord. I don't see why we should forgive him for being so stupid."

"You read Eala's book, Foscúil. He is not Sea People, not like us. We were trained to be rational. He was brought up in that savage culture until one day someone put a blue robe on him. But that doesn't make him one of us. If he lets go of that superstition we should forgive him. That is what Eibheara was telling me: we should take him in hand and teach him to be civilised. Initiation is the only thing that could bind the City together. If he dies the City will fall."

"And to end this all he needs to do is throw away the head in the bag?"

"That is right, Foscúil."

"What about Abhainne, my lord?"

"If the Mentor obeys me then he will permit me to Restore her. If she is Restored then she can take her own revenge."

"She wouldn't, Aclaí. You know that."

"And neither would Éirime. I know." Aclaí saw Foscúil's face. "Look, my friend, Eala would have said that avoiding the fight was necessary. But you have read her book now: can't you see that this is a better way than destroying the City?"

"I can, my lord, if her way works. It still seems like a tiny weak thing compared to a sword."

"It is. But it can be strong too. We will try it and if it doesn't work then we will use a sword. We will use ten thousand swords – or we will use Eala's method."

"But for that he needs to throw away his head in a bag?"

"That is all."

The great doors opened and Cathúa led the Mentor to his place in the Evening Meal. Liús and Éise were the other side of him and Eibheara was behind her. She remembered how she had sat at his right hand many years ago when she had first been called to the top of the Hill – when she had been Favourite. Once she had sat there so he could put his hand on her easily. And, foolish thing that she had been, she had never understood. Now she was there to put her hand on him to steady and help him when his hand shook too much.

They all looked at him as he drew breath. "Tonight I will announce Rank," he said. "To Cathúa, Nineteenth Rank."

"Thank you, Mentor," she whispered.

"You have earned it," he whispered back. "You are the most loyal Adept I ever made a favourite."

"Thank you, Mentor," she repeated. She looked around at the faces that were watching.

"Carry on," he said. She listened as the buzz of conversation rose and saw as they looked back at her. She realised that hers was the first Immortal Rank to be announced since Aclaí's. Was it simply to boost their morale? Was it just to give them hope when there was nothing to hope for?

After the Evening Meal the Mentor led all four of his Favourites back up the Hill but he shook them off and would not let them take his arm. He managed to escape them all and get back into his own room before the grief could overwhelm him.

As soon as the door closed Eibheara touched Cathúa's arm. Cathúa turned. "What is it?" she asked.

"Did you find her?" Eibheara whispered. "Is that why he gave you Rank?"

"We did," Cathúa answered. "But he doesn't know. I should probably tell the Mentor about that."

"Did she suffer?"

"She never saw it coming," Cathúa replied. She turned away from Eibheara's disappointment.

Méar was sitting down in the darkness when he heard Cathúa's voice at the door.

"Mentor, may I speak with you?" she called.

He sighed and slipped Eala back into her bag. She never spoke anyway.

"I got what you wanted," Cathúa continued.

He tried to remember what he had told her to fetch. But he couldn't. He knew his brain was playing tricks on him. "Come in, then," he called back, hoping he would remember more when she showed him.

She came in. She was wearing some sort of little black silk dress which would have been much more pretty if it had not looked like she had slept in it. She was also carrying a bag: evidently the thing she had promised to bring. He motioned for her to sit on the bed beside him. The closeness of her and the scent of her hair reminded him of how things had been when he could still breathe Immortal Breath. He needed to breathe again.

But she was un-lacing the bag. He leaned closer to catch a glimpse of what was inside but also to be closer to her. In the darkness he saw what looked like black sheeps-wool that was matted and tangled. Then she reached in and the thing turned.

He recoiled from her. "Cathúa!" he said, shocked. "Why do you think I want a head in a bag?"

"I'm sorry, Mentor," she replied. "I thought you would want to see for yourself."

"Get rid of that," he said.

She drew the bag closed again and got up. A moment later he was alone again. He remembered the scent of her. He needed to get Immortal Breath back. But of course he could not do that until he had dealt with the problem of Aclaí.

Méar fretted a while thinking about it. Then he sighed and got up. He spoke Words and, with a soft pop, he was gone.

The old man walked across the room. It was late and a woman was sweeping the straw off the floor and humming a tune while her husband cleaned the pots. She looked up. "It's you," she said.

"And a good evening to you too, Scéala," he replied.

She was short with curly silver-grey hair framing a face that had once been beautiful. "She is in the back, asleep," Scéala said.

The old man walked towards the back door. As he passed Scéala's husband he found a small leather bag and put on the table before him.

The bag clinked with gold. "Keep on taking care of her, Abhras," he said. As he closed the back door behind him Abhras opened the bag.

Scéala came over to her husband. "What has he left this time?"

Abhras poured the bag out onto the wood. There was a bracelet in the form of a coiled snake, with emerald eyes. A leaping tiger on a thong made a pendant. Gold earrings in the form of sprays of flowers, each petal beaten out and joined together, had diamonds as their hearts and a little bee carved of amber.

"Who do you think he is?" Abhras asked.

"I don't care," Scéala replied. "We find her a corner to sleep in, we keep her topped up with wine, and we don't ask questions. Her singing brings crowds which keeps us busy and, if that wasn't enough, the old man comes and gives us treasure for the effort of taking care of her."

"How do we know that he is not being cruel to her?"

Scéala turned one of the flower earrings over in her hand. "Why do we care?" she asked.

Cathúa closed the door behind her and stood a moment in the darkness. She had used the Words of Seeing Heat and she could clearly see the outline of him partially obscured by a blanket. She was surprised to see that he was the only one in the bed. She stretched her fingertips in front of her as she remembered the feeling of the sword-hilt in her hands. Her Silver Cord could bring it in an instant. She weighed the temptation in her mind and wondered what the outcome would be if she was to cut his head from his shoulders. Would she save the City?

But that wouldn't be enough, she knew. She could remove the external threat to the City but Aclaí's death wouldn't persuade Foscúil to help the Mentor. And nothing else would do, not now. Without the Mentor the City would be gone. She suddenly realised what would happen if the Mentor was to die naturally. Her hands shook as she imagined it.

"Eala?" he asked.

"Eala is dead, remember?" she replied. "You killed her."

He sat up quickly and, in one fluid movement, he was kneeling on the bed with his sword in his hand. He whispered the Words of Light. "Cathúa?" he asked. "What are you doing here?"

"We should talk."

"All right," he sighed. He put the sword down and sat. "Sit down and talk."

Cathúa thought of all the skills that Liús had taught her and of how he spoke of Aclaí's knowledge of the same arts. Then she remembered the forbidden art that had been used on Eibheara. She backed away towards his desk then sat on the edge of that.

He looked at her sat there above him and smiled a momentary smile. "How long have you been in my room?"

"Ten breaths?"

"You could have killed me," he said.

"I could have," she agreed. "What do you think would happen if you were to die?"

"The Mentor would live a little longer," he replied.

"What would your followers do?"

"I think... some of them might Retire. Some might March."

"Would any of them come to the City?"

"I don't think so."

"Neither do I. And the Mentor would die anyway."

"So you don't even think what I am doing is relevant?"

"Not really. Either you come to the City and kill him or he dies anyway. He has lost his Immortal Breath and –" Cathúa saw him move through her blurred vision and her sword was in her hand. She blinked and felt a tear run over her cheek. He stood by the bed with his bare chest a hands-width from the point of her blade. His hands were open as he drew them back.

"I'm not going to hurt you, Cathúa."

"I'm leading the City's defence, Lord Aclaí. It is my role to stand in your way. I told you that I would oppose you."

He sat down on the edge of the bed again. "But you let me live? Why are you here then, if not to kill me?"

"I think we... I wanted to know what we would... what will you do when the City has fallen?"

"I don't know."

"You should know. When you have killed us all and destroyed the City you will still have the Key of Creation."

"What if I don't take it?"

"Come on, Lord Aclaí. You remember the Battle of the Blue Peaks? Do you really think it can be discarded?"

"Do you want it?"

"If I wanted it you would be dead."

"Why?"

"I am the only Favourite who stays on the Hill. If he dies a natural death someone will have to take it from him. The only alternative is for someone to kill him and take it from him."

"And you think that will be me?" Aclaí frowned. "So you would prefer it was me than you? So why are you opposing me?"

"I promised that I would."

"Do you believe I will kill you?"

"At the Fall of the City? I think that is the most likely outcome."

"Cathúa, does the City have to fall?"

She knew enough not to allow herself to be seduced by hope. "It will fall," she told him.

He could see she would not help. "What about before?" he asked.

"You won't kill me before that day. Neither will anyone else."

"You sound confident."

"It's logic, Lord Aclaí. Nothing more than that."

"So what do you think should be done with the Key of Creation?"

"It needs to be defended. The powers in the Forest will destroy humanity unless they are opposed."

"Do you think we could stop them from coming to Earth?"

"They could be hampered if the physical laws of Earth were changed. We know that the parts of the Forest where Words of Power don't work tend to be empty of monsters. But there would be nothing more than swords to oppose them if they did break through."

"Cathúa, you haven't seen how many Forest People I have."

"I know you have a world like a great wheel, that –"

"How do you know about that?" Aclaí demanded.

"Patrols have reported from the place. They didn't understand what they were seeing but it is not hard to work out." She smiled a little but the sword-point did not waver. "So, Lord Aclaí, will your armies in the Forest defend Earth after the City falls?"

"Of course they will. But my Immortal Breath won't last forever either. You are curator of the City's knowledge. What can we do about the Key of Creation?"

"I don't know."

"What do you know, then? What can you tell me about it? How did we get it in the first place?"

"It isn't in a natural form. It has been compelled to take the form it has. The form it has doesn't possesses any intelligence so it lacks the willpower to turn itself back."

"What natural form would it take?"

"I would assume it would take the form of a Manifestation of Creation."

"They can be compelled to take inanimate forms. Provided they are not interfered with the inanimate forms are stable. If they are interfered with the effect is rather like a House of Power coming unbound."

"That is correct. It cannot be unbound unless something is done to prevent that."

"I don't even understand how it was bound in the first place. How did a bunch of Novices – and that is all there was in the early days of the City – ever go out deep into the Forest and get a prize like that?"

"The Forest didn't used to be hostile to humanity, Lord Aclaí. My theory is that the Forest became hostile after the Key of Creation was captured."

"Why do you say that? I mean, what is your evidence?"

"There are traces of the old civilisations from thirteen centuries ago still to be found. They were all attacked at about the same time. From then on people lived in fortified places. I believe the Forest counter-attacked – but it was us who started it."

"How do we end it?"

"I don't know. I can't see how we can. As soon as the Key of Creation is unbound the Forest will destroy humanity."

"So what do you want from me?"

"I want you to take it. When you've killed him, when you've killed us all, you need to take it. If you can understand how to un-bind it safely then you should do so. If not you still must take it anyway. It cannot be allowed to fall into their hands."

"You are right, Cathúa. I will take it. After all this is over will you help me to find how to un-bind it? Please?"

"Lord Aclaí, I promised to oppose you."

"I wish you wouldn't make those sort of promises. You take them so literally."

"You have to believe that I will do what I said I will do. I cannot allow you to change my mind."

"This might be more important than that."

"Lord Aclaí, I don't expect to survive the Fall of the City. If, by some mischance, I do, I will leave all of ye. I don't want to be part of this anymore."

He reached out a hand to her, using all Geana's skill to convey gentleness. "Cathúa," he said, "The City doesn't have to –"

But, as his hand was about to touch her arm, she said the Words of Folding Space and was gone.

The old man knelt stiffly down in the straw beside her. He wrinkled his nose at the smell of vomit and whispered Words of Freshness as he touched her hair. She stirred and started to snore.

It took him a few heartbeats to get to his feet and then to start to shuffle back towards the door. Behind him the snoring stopped.

"Mentor," she said. "What do you want?" Her voice was slurred by the wine.

He turned back and he sat beside her again. "Are you well, Éirime?" he asked.

She sat up and looked at him. "You killed my Geana," she accused.

"Are they taking care of you?"

"They take better care of me than you did on the Hill," she replied. "But Geana took better care than this. Blátha took better care of me than this as well. Did you kill her too, Mentor?"

"Éirime, I explained to you. Aclaí is trying to kill us all. If he finds you he will kill you. Their lives were a threat to your own because he could have used them to find you."

"So many lies, Mentor. Don't you ever get sick of the lies?"

He knew that he had aged: even fifty years ago he would not have tolerated any Adept talking to him like that, not even Eala. But he could smell the wine on her breath and knew that he could not have disciplined her anyway. He could strike her but she would not feel it anymore than her servant girl, Eala's sister, had felt it. She was too drunk to feel pain. To discipline her he needed to use words.

"Éirime, when I have defeated Aclaí I will Restore them all: Eala and her sister, even Blátha if you want her."

"Look at you," she whispered. "You are dying."

"I know you can Breathe Immortal Breath into another."

"But you don't know that I will, do you?"

"I know that you taught Eala how to do it. I will Restore her body and she will take away my age. They will serve me on the Hill and, if you wish to be with them, you will have to return to the Hill and serve me too."

She turned to look at him and he was startled by the look in her eyes. "It will never happen, Mentor," she whispered.

"Don't you believe that I would...?"

"You will never defeat Aclaí, Mentor," she told him. "He will kill you instead. It is him I will serve on the Hill, not you."

11

Fate

Cathúa remembered to say Words of Freshness and to put on some suitable clothes before she went down. She chose herself a tunic of leather and a silk shirt in bright red to go under it. Over it all went her blue cloak. She walked all the way down the Hill and across the bridge. As she crossed the bridge she looked at the boats on the waterfront, trying to pick out the largest and strongest. In the end she chose none of them: instead she picked out a sea-stained raft that was arriving. The raft was packed with sheep and jars and being poled through the mouth of the haven and under the raised bridge. She walked down to the waterfront to wait for it to put in.

Then she saw the lost-looking girl standing on the quay and looking over at the City Hill. She was wearing a blue cloak and her curly black hair tangled in the wind. *It's today!* Cathúa thought. She wanted to run but she knew she should not. Knew she had not. *What did I say?* she thought. But her brain raced in panic and she couldn't remember at all. Her feet carried her over to the other girl.

"Cathúa?" she called.

She thought that the other girl must run but of course she stayed. *Do I really look as nervous and confused as that?* she wondered. *And do I really look so scruffy?* The other Cathúa shrugged and came over. "What is..?" she began. Then she said, "Oh, this is silly. You know what I need to know."

"Tomorrow is the Day of Harvest 1370."

"Of course." Cathúa smiled, shyly. "I hope we live through tomorrow."

"So do I," Cathúa laughed.

"Will it be long?"

"Not long." She put her hand on Cathúa's wrist, remembering as she did so how strange it had been to be touched by herself but how it had been the first time anyone had touched her for so many days and nights. "Treasure these days," she said. "We're going to miss them when they're gone." She felt the tears in her eyes and then the other Cathúa embraced her. She remembered how she had welcomed a hug from herself and she remembered how it had been to see herself so scared. "While we remember Eala she is not completely gone," she whispered to her other self.

Other Cathúa looked startled a moment then smiled. "Then we should try and remember her for as long as we can."

"If I live through this I will. I will run far away from blue-robes. I will Retire forever and keep my memories alive as long as I can."

Other Cathúa kissed her cheek then turned and ran away into the town, towards the Gate. Cathúa looked after her and wondered if she would ever get a chance to follow her.

Instead she waited for the boat to put in.

Servants brought out the midday meal in the Hall of Maoineas. Aclaí gathered food and walked to a table. Foscúil sat beside him. "We are ready for tomorrow," Foscúil said.

"I don't think I am," Aclaí whispered. "Do you think you could do it without my orders?"

Foscúil looked around. Aclaí saw the muscles around his jaw tighten. "I don't know, my lord," he admitted. "Are you going to lose your nerve?"

"I hope I will find it."

"What happens if you don't?"

"I don't know."

A shadow fell over them. They looked up. Innealta and Damhánalla were standing holding food. Aclaí gestured for them to sit down. He looked back at Foscúil. "I will find it," he said. "Everything will be ready for the morning."

"Will you stay here?" Foscúil asked.

"I won't," Aclaí answered. "I will return to the Midsummer Palace. I will be back before dawn."

"You better be," Foscúil growled. "We're hardly going to start without you and we have to be there for the changing of the Patrol Watch."

Aclaí glared at Foscúil's insubordination but realised as he saw Foscúil's face move under his freckled skin that it was just nerves. They really were going to do it. He looked down at the food in front of him and he stood up. "Damhánalla," he said, "would you take me back to the Midsummer Palace?"

"Of course, my lord," she said. She put her own food down then followed him.

Innealta put her hand on Foscúil's wrist. "He'll do it," she said as they watched Aclaí and Damhánalla leave the hall.

"The Mentor does deserve it, doesn't he?" Foscúil asked.

"Oh, he deserves it all right," Innealta replied. "Not just for what happened to Abhainne. I saw so many cruelties at the top of the Hill. Geana taught me... she taught me to see all the injustices of the City. The City was fashioned just the way he wanted it, Foscúil, and it is fashioned to be minutely cruel. It is cruel in large matters but it is also cruel in small ones. He did that, Foscúil. He deserves what Aclaí will do to him tomorrow. He deserves every bit of it and more besides."

When Cathúa had given her orders to the boat's crew she returned to the City and went up to where she knew the Mentor's lecture was scheduled. She whispered Words of Concealment so as not to disturb them then opened the door at the back. The Veterans were studying Words of Power, learning enunciation and projection exercises. But it was Eibheara leading them not the Mentor. *He must be in his room,* she thought.

It did not take long to get back up to the Court of the Favourites. She called softly at his door, afraid to disturb him, but she did not hear an answer. She opened it but he ignored her. He was sitting at his desk and, before him, were two skulls. She heard him whispering and she came a little closer to listen.

"I've lost her," he whispered. "I told her to hide herself better, just as you suggested, but now I can't find her. That innkeeper and his wife do not know where she is, and –" He stopped and she waited for him to turn around and address her.

But then he started speaking again. "I know we don't want Aclaí to find her but, if she is hiding from me –"

Then she waited again. But he just whispered more nonsense. "There is the sword but, if she refuses to answer –"

Suddenly she realised why he was not taking any notice of her: she had used the Words of Concealment so as not to interrupt the Veterans lecture. She went out again and whispered Words that End. Then she called at the door again.

"Come in, Cathúa," he replied. She went in. The skulls were gone and he was sitting facing away from the desk. "What do you want?" he asked.

"I looked for you at the Veterans lecture on Words, Mentor."

"Eibheara took it."

"She can't give them what they need, Mentor. It has to be you."

"Are you nagging me, Cathúa?" he asked.

"Oh, it's too late anyway," she answered. "Aclaí attacks tomorrow."

"Is it as soon as that?" he asked. He smiled a grim smile. "He's going to kill me, isn't he?"

"I don't know, Mentor."

"But you know the future."

"I have some clues. Tomorrow is the day that Aclaí attacks."

"How long have you known?"

"Since the day Eala was caught, Mentor."

"You never told anyone?"

"For the last three years I have been building the City's defences. Everyone is prepared for tomorrow's attack. Everyone is on Patrol tomorrow. Everything that could be done to resist Aclaí, I have done it."

"Do you think it will be enough?"

"I... I don't know, Mentor."

"Eala told me that learning her Art would make it harder for people to lie to me, Cathúa."

"I am sure she was right."

"I am sure too. So, Cathúa, why are you here?"

"I have done everything I can. There are still things you could do."

Cathúa saw his jawline tense and the way the wrinkles of skin seemed to hang from his chin. "Like what?" he asked.

"If you addressed tonight's Evening Meal you could improve morale. Morale makes people fight more effectively."

"Would it make the difference we need?"

"Probably not."

"Then I cannot do any more, can I?"

"There are other things you could do, Mentor."

"Like what?"

"It is not too late to negotiate with Aclaí."

"What could I offer him?"

"Whatever he wants. Mentor, he will kill you if you don't."

"Maybe killing me is what he wants."

"Maybe, Mentor. But... do you want to take the whole of humanity with you?"

"What do you mean, Cathúa?"

"If Aclaí destroys the City tomorrow then who will protect humanity from the Forest?"

"I don't know. If I am dead why will I care?"

"Is that the legacy you want to leave humanity, Mentor? You could have saved them but you didn't?"

"Why should I care about saving peasants, Cathúa?"

"Eala would have cared."

"Get out," he shouted at her. "Get *out!*"

She noticed that his sword was in his hand. She got out.

In a little stone house in Acra two Delving People sat by the fire. The smoke rose cleanly from the hearth and straight out of the hole in the roof. It was a gift from the village blue-robes. They heard one of those blue-robes call at the door and one of them got up.

"What is it, my lady?" Úlla asked.

Éise stood at the doorway and from within her robe little Tintreacha peeked. When she saw the door open she ran forward into the warmth of Úlla's house. Úlla turned to catch her but Éise caught her wrist.

"Let her go," she said. "I need to talk to you."

"What is it, my lady? Do you need to leave her here again?"

"I do, Úlla. You are her midwife."

"I never delivered her, my lady. You didn't need me. You are Sea People."

"Well, Úlla, even if I am my daughter is not."

"Some day she will be old enough for Selection, my lady."

"Some day she will. But by then the City will be gone. Lord Aclaí will destroy the City tomorrow."

"I thought Lord Aclaí was your friend, my lady."

"He is my friend and my lover. But my husband is Chamberlain too. I have to be in the City tonight."

"Will ye return tomorrow evening?"

"I don't know. By tomorrow evening I may be dead. Tintreacha may be an orphan."

"Ye are Immortal, my lady."

"*Immortality doesn't mean living forever,* Úlla. If my little girl is an orphan tomorrow night will ye take care of her?"

"Of course, my lady."

"Thank you. That is all I need to know." She came in to the house and scooped up her daughter. "Will you be good for Aunt Úlla?"

"I will, Mammy," Tintreacha agreed. "Will you back in the morning?"

"Not as soon as that, dear heart."

"Then when?"

"We will have to wait and see," she said.

Once she had put her daughter down Éise left them alone. "Why was Mammy crying?" Tintreacha asked.

"Sometimes mammies cry," Úlla told her. "Don't worry yourself. Come and have some honeycomb."

"I love honeycomb!" Tintreacha answered.

The servant girl bumped the door open with her hip and wiggled into the kitchen. She had a tray in each hand and, with the practice of years, she placed both trays on the table without tipping any of the mugs. Her friend was scouring and rinsing things. He looked up as she entered the kitchen.

"Fionna, how were they today?"

"Subdued," Fionna replied. "There is something wrong on the Hill. Lady Cathúa ordered hardly any Patrols today and she is ordering everyone out tomorrow morning. The gatehouses are unguarded tonight and hardly guarded tomorrow. They have one Novice appointed to guard the gate at the Court of the Favourites in the morning."

"I suppose that means you could get down here without too many hands under your tunic."

"Nobody touched me, Donn." Fionna started un-stacking the trays for Donn to wash. "I never thought I would say this but I would rather they had. There is something really wrong in the City."

"What do you mean?"

"Donn, tomorrow is a Celebration Day. What preparations have we made?"

"Lady Cathúa said that we shouldn't prepare," Donn replied.

"That has never happened before. Celebration Days are always occasions in the City. What happened to make Lady Cathúa cancel the Day of Harvest?"

"I don't know and I don't care," Donn replied. He put down the mug he had finished scouring and turned to her. "I'm glad," he said. "Remember Midsummer's Day?"

Fionna flinched and then the expression left her eyes. "Lady Éise healed me," she replied.

"You still have nightmares about it."

"Donn, we've talked about this before. My mother sold me because she couldn't afford to feed me. I have never been hungry again. You were sent to Selection. You don't know how grateful we should be to have full bellies: you've never been hungry for more than a ten-day." Fionna started to stack the scoured mugs on the drying rack. They rattled together as she put them up.

Donn put the scourer down and shook the water off his hands. He wiped them and stood behind Fionna, putting his hands on her shoulders. "Please don't be angry with me, love," he said.

"I'm sorry," she said. "I'm just scared." She turned in his arms and they hugged each other.

Méar's mind paced back and forward, like an animal in a cage, looking for a way out. He felt that he was missing something – that there was some tiny detail that he had missed. He was sure that he could make some simple decision, give some inconsequential order, and everything would go back to how it was. But, however hard he puzzled, he could not imagine what it might be.

He looked around the room and his eyes fell on his desk. The two bags were there and he looked at the one on the left: Ceann's bag. Ceann used to help him, it seemed, but now all he wanted to do was rebuke Méar. How did our relationship turn so sour, he wondered. But of course he knew the answer. It was only a couple of hand-widths to the right. Eala would have known that straight away. Family was often jealous of a new wife.

So who could help him? There must be someone. Then he heard feet outside his door. "Who is it?" he called.

"It's me, Mentor," Eibheara replied.

Méar remembered the things they had said about the Battle of the Blue Peaks and that strange winter when Eibheara had first admitted that there were two of her. His breath came quickly for a moment. Was Eibheara here to rescue them? "Come in," he called, gratefully.

She came in and he looked around, half expecting to see someone else. But he did not see one of her illusions. It was Eibheara.

"Come and sit by me," he said.

She came and sat. "Mentor," she began.

"Which one are you?" he asked.

"I am the younger one," she admitted.

"Can you call the older one?" he asked.

"I can't, Mentor. I... well, I can, but I... but she won't listen. She will remember today and, even though she knows we want her here, she is not coming. I guess she thinks it is futile."

"How does she know?"

"Because I won't forget tonight. So she will know but she still won't come – or she would be here now. She knows that I hate her but she doesn't hate me. She just has my sense of humour."

"What does that mean, Eibheara?" He sighed. "I don't understand you most of the time. I don't understand Cathúa either. Am I getting senile?"

"I don't think so, Mentor. I don't understand me either."

"But you won't help me?"

"I will help you in any way I can. But I cannot... I can only think of one way I can help you."

"How? Some way to kill Aclaí? Some way to improve our defences?"

"I couldn't kill Aclaí, Mentor, any more than I could kill you."

"She is Elder Immortal, Eibheara. Elder Immortals can defy Initiation."

"But I am not, Mentor. I cannot oppose him."

"Then what can you do to help?"

"I could go to him and try and make peace."

"What would you offer him?"

"What would you like me to offer him, Mentor?"

"I don't know. What do you think he would like? My head in a bag, perhaps?"

"I think he might settle for your surrender, Mentor."

"Is that all? Nothing too much, then?"

"Mentor, I will offer him anything you permit me to offer. Or I will go and simply ask him."

"Depriving me of one of my last four Immortals?"

"I won't be much use anyway."

"None of you will, though, will you? He is going to come here and kill us all."

"I... I am sorry, Mentor."

"So what did you want?"

"I came here to offer company, Mentor. I thought I might be able to offer distraction, or comfort –"

"Do you think I am a child, Eibheara?"

"Of course not. I think you are Mentor."

"But you think I need distraction or comfort?"

"I... I came to offer," she said. She stood up. "I can see you don't want my company tonight. And, since we both know you won't get another opportunity, I can see you don't want my company ever again."

She walked to the door without waiting for a reply.

He waited until she was gone and then he reached for the bags on his desk.

* * *

Aclaí returned to his room. He wanted to sleep, if only for a few hours, to be fresh for what he was sure would be the longest day of his life. But, when he got to his room, Lá was waiting. She was sitting on his bed in a white linen dress. "My lord?" she whispered.

He sat beside her. "Do you remember when you tried to persuade me to stop sulking and start acting?"

"I remember, my lord," she told him. "It didn't work."

"Not that night," he said.

"That's not something I can do at any time, either," she told him. "It has to be Spring and this is Autumn. Our next child won't be born for months."

"I won't see it, Lá. Tomorrow I march on the City."

"Aren't you coming back?"

"I cannot. There is a thing called the Key of Creation and, even if I survive the attack and gain it, I can't bring it back to Anleacán." He put his hand on hers. "I am sorry, Lá, but you will have to bring your next baby up without me."

"I think we always knew," she answered.

"We? How many of ye are in the room?"

Lá shrugged and her wings made the gesture more expressive. "How would I know?" she asked. "I know that Bánúa is here but I don't know about any others."

"I think we are all," said Bánúa. "I asked the others to stay away."

"Why?"

"Because you need us," Bánúa said, "But I don't want to show everyone your vulnerability."

"Vulnerability?"

"My lord," said Lá, "We used to speak to Mistress Geana."

"She taught us a lot," Bánúa smiled.

Aclaí saw that Bánúa had chosen a servant's tunic but he could not meet her green gaze. "*Cac*," he whispered.

"She told us that one day you would need to release your feelings. She told us what we needed to do to help you do that."

"She meant for you to marry Lady Éirime, my lord, not to avenge her."

"But you can't marry her now," said Bánúa. "Avenging her is all that is left."

"I am still subject to their manipulations after all this time," laughed Aclaí. "They taught ye how to manipulate me?"

"Mistress Geana instructed us," Bánúa replied. "Lady Eala never told us anything."

"I couldn't tell them apart, my lord," said Lá, "But the lady in the blue robe never instructed us."

"It was all Mistress Geana," agreed Bánúa.

"But Lady Eala didn't need to instruct me, my lord," said Lá. "I saw what she did to you the night before you killed her."

"You watched?"

"I always watch," Lá whispered. "You don't touch me, my lord, and –"

"I'm sorry," he told her. He put his hand on her neck, just below her pointed little ear. She tilted her head until her cheek brushed his thumb.

"It's not too late," she said.

"It soon will be," he answered.

"You could still give her what she wants," Bánúa objected.

Aclaí's face tightened into a smile. "Was that what Geana suggested?"

"It is the right thing to do," replied Bánúa. "Give her what she wants and help build your own emotions. It will help you remember the woman you are going to avenge."

"I never could argue with Geana's logic," laughed Aclaí. "Not even when she is dead." He turned back to Lá. "So, what do you want?" He looked at her face rather than her body, wondering if he could do it without Words.

"I just want to sing to you, my lord," she said.

"If you wish," he agreed. "But you will seem less like Éirime if you sing."

"I know," she whispered. "But remember, my lord, I was there when you were with Lady Eala."

"Mistress Geana taught us the song, Lord Aclaí," said Bánúa.

"The Sea People do not marry," he told them.

"Then you don't have to accept our offer," Bánúa said. "That choice is yours."

"But we would like to make it," said Lá.

"Very well," he agreed. He wondered if he would maintain any kind of control of his heart. But he needed to send himself mad.

"When Lady Eala sang she had already let you put –" began Lá.

"I remember," Aclaí replied. He reached out his arms to her and she came to him.

* * *

A shadow passed over the doorway of Cathúa's library. Her breath caught a moment and she looked up.

It was Eibheara. Cathúa could see the anger on Eibheara's face.

"Come in," Cathúa said.

Eibheara came in and sat down. She was shaking with rage. Cathúa tried to remember what Eala might have done and she put her hand gently on Eibheara's shoulder.

Eibheara looked around. "He is in there but he won't see anyone. I wanted to tell him but he won't listen."

"What did you want to tell him?"

"Aclaí is coming. I think tomorrow we will all be fighting against Aclaí and Foscúil. I know he's not listening, I know we're all waiting for it to happen, but... *cac*, Cathúa, I hoped he would at least let me be with him one last night." Cathúa sat beside her. Eibheara looked around. "You are logical, Cathúa. Tell me that I am worrying about nothing."

"I cannot prove beyond doubt that it is tomorrow, Eibheara..." Cathúa began.

Eibheara waited for her to continue. But Cathúa did not. Eibheara glanced at her face then looked back and stared. She saw that her eyes – logical Cathúa's eyes – were filled with tears. She reached up and touched Cathúa's cheek just in time to stop the first tear as it fell. She reached out and, as she took Cathúa in her arms, she felt Cathúa's body shake with sobs.

"Cathúa, my friend, I have never seen you like this," Eibheara whispered. "You know something, don't you?"

"I don't have proof."

"Cathúa, you don't need proof to have feelings. Carrying a burden is much harder alone."

"But it is even harder to fight when you know you are going to lose."

"Then you *do* have proof." Cathúa looked up and Eibheara saw the answer in her eyes. "You may as well tell me," she said. "I am compromised anyway."

"I have seen the future," Cathúa whispered. "The City is gone in the future."

"Prophecy?"

"This is far more certain than prophecy."

"Tell me."

"After we met... the future you I wanted to prove time travel was possible. There was always the possibility that the Words of Folding Space or the Words of the Gateway could be used to travel through time. So when I got back to the City after we met... her, I tried it."

"And?"

"I sent a servant back one day and she didn't return."

"How would she return without Words of Power?"

"The same way that people normally get from today to tomorrow. She was supposed to go into the village to take lodging and meet me in the morning."

"And?"

"And, when she didn't return, I set off to rescue her. I had sent her back to Gainmheach on the Archipelago. It was her home and somewhere I was sure that nobody was going to notice. Nobody in the village would admit to seeing her so I used the same Words on myself. I went back one day then walked to the village and asked the date. Then I knew that the calibration was worse than I thought."

"When did you get to?"

"It was the Twelfth Day of Flowers, 425. But when I found my servant it was about five centuries earlier: I had sent her more than a hundred years before the Mentor was born. She was married with grandchildren. I never did calibrate it: there is too much uncertainty. Time travel is possible with Words of Power. *Accurate* time travel is not, it seems."

"That makes sense. Once you stepped outside the present instant you would be faced with the interchangeability of time and space units. A heartbeat is equivalent to three hundred million paces. Space and time are distorted by gravity. Bridging over those distances –"

"I thought it was a calibration problem at first. I already knew it could work so I was surprised when it went wrong. I didn't use the Words of Folding Space again. I used the Words of the Gateway after that."

"So you could get back?"

"Certainly. But calibration wasn't the problem. At first I made the choice every day: go through the Gateway and return if I was further from my home time. After a while I gave up and just made my home in the woods. I lived in 777 for... many ten-days, anyway. A whole summer. Every morning I would make the Gateway then walk into town and ask someone the date. Then I'd go back, close the Gateway and rest so I could use the Words again next day. I stopped hoping to return to the instant I left. I told myself that if I got within the month, I'd stay. Then I told myself that if I got within the year I'd stay."

"How far in the future did you go?"

"I don't know. One time I stepped through the Gate I fell into the sea. I am not a strong swimmer, Eibheara, and the edge of a Gate is dangerous.

I had to hook my sword-hilt over the edge and haul myself carefully up. One slip and I could have lost a hand – and then drowned. When I got back through I had to use the Words of Restoration. I lost a day."

"Couldn't you have Levitated? Or used Words of Strength? Or something?"

"Words of Power didn't work anymore. Neither did Mastery of Creation. By the time I realised that I had been blown so far from the Gate I nearly didn't get back. I couldn't lift myself properly into the Gate and of course it didn't have a frame. I left my legs behind, here, above the knees. I couldn't avoid it because I didn't have any way to climb up that high. I stopped the bleeding and then I slept all night like that, trying to rest my Breath enough for a Restoration."

"Then sometime in the future the whole of the City is gone?"

"The whole of the Land of Immortals is gone, Eibheara. The Land of the Immortals is tectonically unstable. It is only Words of Power that hold it above the ocean. This is all sea-bed. When Words of Power stop working it will return to the bottom of the sea."

"What about the Coral Mountain?"

"The Coral Mountain was an island when the Mentor made the Land so it will be an island when the Land returns to the bottom of the sea. I made myself a personal Flyer and went up to the Coral Mountain to make the Gateway. Eventually I found myself on an island and I spoke to survivors. They told me that the day the City falls is the Day of Harvest 1370."

"That's tomorrow, Cathúa." Eibheara's eyes were wide with horror. "How... you have been preparing for Aclaí to arrive? How long have you known that?"

"Three years. More, if you count all the time I spent trying to get back to three years ago."

"Then you are a stronger person than me, Cathúa." Eibheara hugged her and felt her body shake. "I would have run."

"I couldn't run, however much I wanted to. I'm the favourite who stays with him when the rest of ye go. I have been alone with him on the Hill for months at a time."

Eibheara tried to think of a distraction. "Remember there was talk of using Words of Transmutation to make a proper continental foundation for the Land? We should have seen that one through."

"We were worried about earthquakes. If we started over that's what we should have done."

"Should we try and do it tonight?"

"The earthquakes might level the City and destroy our defences. And, by this time tomorrow, Words of Power would still be gone."

"Then what is your plan?"

"Try and stop Aclaí. If that fails, try and stop... anything from blocking Words of Power. I don't know. See it through, I suppose. I don't have a plan, really." Cathúa wiped her eyes. "Maybe the future can be changed, Eibheara. We just don't know. I hope it can but it is not a great hope. Logic inclines me to believe the future is fixed. But I don't know."

"What is your logic? Perhaps it is flawed."

"The servant I sent back came from the Mentor's home village. The Mentor took her to bed because he noticed her accent but he dismissed her as soon as he heard her name. He told her that he had the same name as his great grandmother."

"So?"

"So she was the one I sent back when I first experimented with time. She didn't share the name of his ancestor. She was his ancestor. She was his great grandmother: his ancestor at least three ways. You know what small villages are like today. This was a century before the City was founded. I asked him about his family tree and compared her family to his ancestors. His parents were cousins because they both had a parent who was one of her children. He –"

"I don't see the logic yet."

"Without his ancestors he wouldn't have been born. He was born because I sent her back with Words of Power."

"Agreed."

"But her great grandson taught me Words of Power so I could send her back. One cause of my experiment was also one effect of my experiment."

Eibheara was about to speak but then she stopped. Her jaw slackened and her lips parted.

"You see?" Cathúa continued. "I *could* send her back only because I *had* sent her back. I had to send her back because I had sent her back. Either we get tied in loops of causality without a beginning or an end or causality is an illusion. Logic suggests that causality is an illusion. If you imagine that our lives are a story the storyteller has already decided how the story ends. Our hypothetical storyteller has all the loose ends of the plot tied up even before she says 'long, long ago'."

"Could the Mentor still have been himself without her for an ancestor?"

"She had genes that, back then, were unique in the world. He inherited them from her."

"But do those genes make a difference?"

"Without them he would not be the Mentor. The City's existence depends on her being his ancestor. I allowed the City to come into being by sending her back."

Eibheara frowned. "All right, I can't fault your logic. For some events involving time travel causality is an illusion."

"The simplest explanation –"

"... means nothing, Cathúa. You don't know if the time-travel itself is what forces causality to be an illusion."

"All our lives are touched by time travel, Eibheara."

"Your life and mine are touched by it."

"The Infiltrators have been here among us, in the City, for centuries."

"Perhaps so. But that doesn't mean that the City is going to vanish just because Aclaí arrives tomorrow. Even if the battle goes ahead the City would survive."

"The buildings might survive but the City is not buildings. Words of Power didn't work, Eibheara. Mastery of Creation was blocked. Can you imagine what life will be like without Words of Power or Mastery of Creation? There is nothing for us in the future except the things our own muscles will do. There will be not be any difference between Adepts and peasants."

"What about the Forest, Cathúa?"

"I don't know. The day after tomorrow the deadliest weapon we will have against the monsters of the Forest will be a sword. I cannot imagine how we will survive. Humanity wouldn't survive even if we were seven million Foscúils. There aren't many trees on the Coral Mountain. It may be that the survivors I spoke to were... will be the last humans alive on Earth."

"Were there any of us among them?"

"None."

"How did you get... wait. Did you get back onto your own time-line?"

"I did."

"You got lucky?"

"You took me back. Or you will take me back. Or something. I met you on the day before the Mentor's birthday in 1317. You were checking it was safe to drop Yanti off – and trying to prevent the necessity of doing so."

"The day before Eala left? Then my enemy self was supporting Eala?"

"Your enemy self was trying to stop the City from falling apart, Eibheara. She was trying to prevent the City from ending up where we are now – from where we'll be after tomorrow."

Eibheara drew back. "So I'm the bad one and she's the good one? How long have you thought that, Cathúa?"

"I've suspected it since... Eibheara, the Mentor showed me a Vision a long time ago: a Vision from his own youth. You were in it with an Elder Immortal sword. Everything I've seen since has added to that evidence."

Cathúa saw the anger gathering in Eibheara's face. "So when you've been pretending to be my friend..?"

"Eibheara, I am not good at this sort of thing. I have experienced time travel and you haven't, not yet. Time travel is a terrible thing. We do what we have to do but we know we are doomed to fail. Even if my mind can stand it my heart cannot. One day you will be someone who comes back and endures that horror and grief to try and save us all. It might be that one day you will be the greatest hero in history. I don't hate you, Eibheara: not you who was her or you who will be her. I admire you for the courage and strength you will one day show."

Eibheara did not answer for a while but Cathúa watched as her breathing calmed and the tension left her body. Then she turned and spoke. "Cathúa, isn't that evidence that the City will survive?"

"It might be evidence that new civilisations will one day rise to replace it. As you told us – will tell us – one day it may not be Forbidden to raise the dead. You told us that you had died – will die – before you meet yourself back then. The other Adept I saw in that Vision is now dead. And I have seen your Flyer. You will have a Flyer that flies accurately through time. You took me back to find Gruaige my servant. Nothing on your Flyer made any sense to me. It was like a ship with a crew but it was full of mechanical and electrical contrivances that made it do things."

"Toys?"

"They were not toys. They were how it worked. She... you told me that you were from a long time in the future. The crew spoke the tongue of the Sea People but only one – two – of them spoke it like we do. They had learned it at the City but we grew up speaking it. Even if they wore blue they might not be Adepts as we know them."

"Yanti was an Adept. We both recognised her as such."

"But Yanti did not grow up in a world ruled by the Sea People. She grew up speaking a peasant tongue. Most of your crew was... will grow up speaking a peasant tongue. It must be far in the future and, even then, I think their Order will be much less influential than we... were."

"I Identified Yanti's Nativity. I know it will be thousands of years in the future. And we identified that other key date, too, even if we didn't identify what it means. All the prophecy that Yanti's presence spread among us centres around that date."

"The last day of Flowers in 7646? Sixty-two centuries in the future? How many of us will live to see that?"

"Immortality does not mean living forever, Eibheara. I think you may be the only one of us to survive. If you survive. Perhaps your future self is Mentor."

"He asked for her," Eibheara grumbled. "He wanted me to be her. Where is my enemy self now, Cathúa?"

"I don't know. Part of me hopes she will come and rescue us tomorrow like she did at the Battle of the Blue Peaks. The rest of me recognises that it is illogical to expect any such thing. But I just don't know."

"Of course not. We don't know how time works. The Fall of the City might destroy that future. We don't know anything about it. You travelled back in time and came back to the City – had anything changed?"

"I was careful. Remember that most of the Universe doesn't exist? I tried very hard not to interfere and I hoped that, if I didn't cross any of the important parts, I will not have had any effect. But I don't know for certain how time works. Meeting people from the future doesn't tell us that future still exists."

"Perhaps not. Or perhaps your burdens of proof are too heavy. But anyway, even if I am the only one to survive for thousands of years, the fact that I will survive tomorrow means that others may survive with me."

"You already said that you don't know if you can fight."

"I –"

"Eibheara, I am not calling your courage into question. But I do know that the person who leads the defence tomorrow is me. I have studied history, Eibheara. I know that, when a siege falls, the leader of the defenders is at the mercy of the victor. And Aclaí has very little mercy in him these days." She began to weep again. "I have lived through the golden age of humanity and, now I know that it will soon be over, I wish I had spent less time with books and more time with people. Tomorrow the world slides into savagery. Tomorrow might be the last day of humanity and I have spent far too little time with humans. I want to make up for it by marching into the Mentor's room and demanding he pay me attention."

"I'd take you with me, Cathúa. But I have already tried that. He doesn't want us anymore. If we all survive we will see if he wants us tomorrow."

"I almost hope I don't survive tomorrow. I am going to miss this place so much."

"He isn't the only person who can pay you attention, Cathúa."

"What do you..?" But her question was cut off as Eibheara kissed her. Cathúa's hands hovered a moment, unsure. Then she reached up and buried her fingers in Eibheara's curly hair.

* * *

They heard someone at the door and Lá and Bánúa were gone. He called out and the door opened.

It was Damhánalla. She was wearing black silk, embroidered and crocheted, with small holes all over that revealed her pale skin. The material was very like black spiderweb and it came down only to the tops of her thighs. Her hair was severely tied back. Her eyes were dry but reddened. He wondered if she had overheard Lá singing.

But he breathed his Immortal Breath and asked, "What is it?"

"You are going tomorrow," she answered.

"I've gone before, many times."

"This time you are not coming back," she told him.

There was not any point in denying it.

She continued, "I know you tired of me a long time ago but I hoped you might say goodbye at least."

"Whatever made you think I tired of you?" he asked.

"You haven't come to me in seventy years."

"You never asked me to."

"Since when have I had to ask?"

"Since about seventy years ago, Damhánalla."

"Was it Eala, Aclaí? What did she say about me?" Aclaí could hear resentment in her voice.

"She didn't say anything about you. She talked about relationships and she made me realise the importance of consent."

"Nobody told me that things had changed."

"Eala tried to tell you," Aclaí reminded her. "Remember how she wanted to talk to you when she visited here? You wouldn't let her."

"She wanted to push me out. Like Eibheara did. Like Miotal does."

"She wanted to be your friend, Damhánalla."

"I should not have come," she said. She turned to go.

Aclaí got up and went over to her. She began to open the door but he held it shut. She turned on him. "Don't you tell me that she wanted to be my friend, Aclaí. She didn't. Nobody does. I thought you did but you want to leave me without even saying goodbye. I've been useful to you but you don't have a use for me anymore. So you're leaving without a word."

"I've used you, Damhánalla. That is what Eala showed me seventy years ago. And you're right: I'm going tomorrow and I doubt I will ever come back. Even if I am still alive when the sun goes down again I won't be free. I mean to take the Key of Creation from the Mentor. If I get my hand on it I won't be able to let go of it again. He could only use it in the City and I mean to destroy the City. I will have to make it safe and then guard it somewhere away from everything I hold dear. I need to understand it and probably to unbind it but I don't know how to do that. I don't even know that it is possible without destroying humanity. So I doubt I will ever see you again."

"Let me go," she said, and pushed him.

"Damhánalla, stop fighting me," he told her, putting the Breath of an Elder Immortal into the words. She jumped and then she stopped fighting. "Go and sit on the bed," he told her.

She went over and sat down. Her blue eyes glared and her breath heaved in her chest. She sat with her knees parted enough to make her dress too short. He remembered how they had been in bed in the past and he felt the old desire. He had told her what he wanted and she had given it. But instead he walked past her to his writing desk. He picked up a note and took it over to her.

"What is this?" she asked.

"Read it."

She read.

> *My friend Damhánalla,*
>
> *You know that I am unlikely to survive today's fighting and, even if I do, you probably realise that I am unlikely to return.*
>
> *There are many things we should have said to one another while you have been in my service. For that I am to blame. I wish I had the time to say them to you and to win the trust I know I would have needed from you to make you believe them.*
>
> *More than anything else, though, I wish I could have given you what you want from me. But my heart is not mine to give: it was lost to me centuries before you were born. Instead, though, I want to give you the closest thing I have to my heart, the thing I care about most.*
>
> *I have given instructions to the Maoineas. When I am gone they will acknowledge that you are Lady of Anleacán. Anleacán is yours. I ask only that you keep it always a place of safety for the Midsummer People, for it is their birthplace. They did not ask for what Eibheara did. She gave one of them your face because she saw how much I love you.*

> *Anleacán is all I have to give you, Damhánalla. I feel that after your years of loyalty and love I should have more to give you.*
>
> *I hope you will love Anleacán as I have loved it and that this parting gift will help you remember me with happiness.*
>
> *Aclaí*

She looked up at him and he finally saw the tears. "I don't need this, Lord Aclaí. I came looking for a much smaller favour than that."

"I know," he told her. "Will you accept my gift and I'll give you what you came for too?"

"I can't change your mind and persuade you not to go, can I?"

"You can't."

"And you won't take me with you, will you?"

"I won't."

"Then I will be the Lady of Anleacán and I will remember you with happiness." She stretched out her hand to his.

He took it and he sat down beside her. "You can't stay all night," he told her. "In the morning I need to work on my anger. But you can stay a while."

"Work on your anger?"

"Tomorrow I may have to kill the Mentor."

"Aclaí, I was born on the Day of Death. I cannot tell you the sort of superstitions I suffered when I was a young girl. Sometimes I told myself that I only came to Selection to get away from the boys calling me 'bride of death'. And tomorrow you and your army will kill more than anyone has in history. You are death, Aclaí. You are the destroyer. If you spend your last night with me then it will be funny in a sort of dark way."

"Is that what you want, Damhánalla?"

"Nobody has ever asked me what I want, Aclaí."

"I know. That's what Eala taught me."

"Is that all you were waiting for, then? For me to ask?"

"That is all." He looked at her with tenderness in his face. "I should have told you earlier."

"I should have guessed," she said. "All that wasted time and now so little time left." She smiled at him. "I'm glad I came and asked – that I got this from your hand. I'm glad we still have one night left." She lifted the hem of her dress. "Come on then, Lord Aclaí."

* * *

In one of the dormitories in the Court of the Novices a girl sat on a bed. The other beds in the room were all empty now: she was sole survivor of her Patrol. She looked around the room at the other beds and, as she saw, she remembered each occupant. Beside her Osna had enlivened her world with her poorly-translated jokes. But at the other end, beside the door, Coinín had held court on his bed and the others had watched. She had sat with Osna on her bed and...

"*Cac*," she whispered to herself. She got up and sat on the empty bed where they had watched together and wished she could put her arms around her friend. She had assumed that Osna had held back from Coinín's bed out of the same disdain she had felt. Then she had learned what Osna was like and she knew that Osna had chosen to stay with her. She remembered how she had hugged Osna's back and shoulders as they had watched. She realised that Osna had never been afraid of Coinín. She had been protecting her.

Réalta felt her own breath catch and break up into sobs. I can't do this, she thought. My breath has to be calm to say Words of Power. I need to fight before I die, like Lady Cathúa, but I can't do this. She wanted to run home to her mammy. Mammy had talked about how life at the City would help her grow up. But she didn't feel grown up at all. She didn't want it to be Coinín but she had wanted it to be *somebody*. She had imagined herself beside Lady Cathúa when she entertained Lord Liús. That would have been good. But she had waited for them to invite her and, of course, they never had.

Should she have asked? She was just a Novice and they were highest Ranked in the City. How could she have asked? But then she realised. What was the worst they could have done, she wondered. They could have killed her for her impertinence. She could have died – just like she would die tomorrow anyway.

I've wasted my life by being too timid, she thought. I've daydreamed my life away when I should have taken what I wanted. Mammy was right about me and I never listened.

"Too late now," she whispered in the darkness. But nobody answered her.

* * *

They were in the courtyard and he was already on the Flyer. "I'm sorry about Éirime," she said. "I know you always loved her and I hoped that one day she would have come from the next village. I wanted you to be happy with her."

"You were always jealous, Damhánalla," he reminded her.

"I was, Aclaí, but not of her. She was there before me, you see."

"Did that make a difference?"

"It did."

"When did you know?"

"Not long after I came into your service. Miotal told me. He was jealous of her because she commanded your heart but I never was. I always knew how she made you unhappy."

"What could any of us do?"

"Nothing," she replied. "The Mentor forbade me from interfering and now it is too late."

"She doesn't command my heart now, Damhánalla. I know she is gone. But my heart is gone with her. Before I met her I didn't care about anyone but Aclaí and his ambitions. She didn't teach me but having her there taught me to feel differently. Eala saw this in her studies. Many men's hearts can only nurture when they are joined to the hearts of women. Those men can love one another but it's a different sort of love: a love of blood, a love of battle, a love of strength. At Éirime's funeral I found out that I am one of those men. There is not any nurturing in my heart anymore, Damhánalla. I used to think I was nurturing you but I know now that all I do is use people to achieve my goal. I can't make love anymore. All I can do is make war."

"Neither you nor Éirime chose what happened to ye both." She laughed at it. "I'm not the only one who was never given a choice." She stepped back off the Flyer. "Goodbye, Lord Aclaí. However small the chances are I hope I will see you again."

"I hope I will see you again too, Damhánalla."

He leaned off the Flyer and kissed the top of her head. He held her with his eyes closed and breathed in the scent of her hair, wanting to stay close to her, not wanting to release her feminine softness. But he knew it was too late for that now. He had to go to the world of war and the company of men. He let go of her.

"Goodbye, my lord. I will remember you with happiness," she told him. He gestured the Flyer into motion and she watched him fall into the sky.

As he shrank to a dot away to the south she watched, straining her eyes until he was lost in the sky.

She whispered after him, "Remember me when you kill him, Aclaí my love."

12

Mars and the Sea People

Foscúil strode across the great courtyard where his warriors stood assembled in rows. He knew they were all watching him although not one of them moved. He entered the palace where his officers lived and found the room where Aclaí slept when he visited. He could hear a girl singing. Who was going to sing songs on a day like today? He went into the chamber.

Aclaí was there, sat on his bed, watching a Vision on the wall. The Vision was of a room with stone walls and wooden rafters supporting thatch. The viewpoint was shaky and far from ideal: occasionally a head would get in the way. A fire burned on an open hearth in the centre of the room and filled the space under the rafters with smoke. Men and women in simple clothes watched as a young girl played the harp and sang. The child was wearing a woollen dress and an arm-less sheepskin jacket. Foscúil didn't know much about women's clothes, nor about who was a popular singer, but the girl reminded him of Éirime.

"It is time, my lord," he said.

"And about time," said Aclaí. Foscúil could see the anger in Aclaí's face, the anger that they had seen that terrible, beautiful day in Áthaiteorainn. But then the anger had been raw and intermingled with grief. Now, Foscúil could see, it was pure and focused.

"Is that Éirime?" he asked.

"It was. They sent an Adept to make Visions on the day that the City first came to Anleacán. That Vision persuaded Saileacha to choose her as entertainment for the Selection Day. That was the year that the Mentor chose only one." With a gesture, he cut off the Vision. "Now she is dead and I only care about one thing." As he stood up his cloak appeared on his shoulder with armour underneath and his sword at his hip. "So let's go do that thing, shall we?"

Miotal fell behind them as they went back out to meet the troops. Foscúil wondered what it was that drove Miotal. It couldn't be revenge: Miotal swore to avoid anything as irrational as revenge. Innealta waited for them out beside the troops with a hundred Flyers around her. Foscúil recognised the crews and he took his Flyer while Miotal clambered up onto his. Foscúil raised his sword in salute and they all responded.

Aclaí rode a horse down to the woods to meet Andánacht Scamall and the cavalry of Maoineas. He returned their salute and then, with a kick of his heels, led his company of cavalry among the trees and out of sight.

Foscúil's sword hilt tingled. It was Aclaí. *take them to the gate in idireatarthu and wait for my order*

"I will, my lord," he replied. He felt Aclaí release the sword-hilt and, with a gesture, he led the Flyers into the sky. As they swept over Anleacán they accelerated and the countryside blurred past. It was not long before they were descending beyond the mountains towards the gateway on the coast.

As he descended his sword hilt tingled again.

"Lord Aclaí?" he asked. "Are we ready?"

not quite ready Aclaí's words replied. *i think we have a problem*

"What sort of problem?"

just give me a few breaths and i will resolve it

Réalta could not sleep and she gave it up before the dawn. She put on her armour and went out. The Patrol Leaders were assembling in the Court of the Novices. "Watch Leader," she called, "Should I go to my assigned post?"

"Of course," the watch leader replied. "But you won't be able to leave until the day is over."

Which meant never. "I understand," Réalta said. She walked up through the Court of the Veterans, through the Court of the Immortals and to the gateway that led to the Court of the Favourites. She took up her position: on the right side of the gateway since she was left-handed. Her mind strayed – slipping away from the terror like the seed of an orange that flies away from finger and thumb rather than allow itself to be crushed.

Above her the sky was brightening away to the East, over the sea, and a single bright star stood heralding the dawn. The star scowled down with an orange glare: the Red World, the location of the City's House of Power.

Two servants came up carrying breakfast on trays. Réalta could see the fear in their faces. It seemed that everyone knew. Cancelling the celebrations for the Day of Harvest was all the confirmation anyone needed. Most of the City did not know why Cathúa had selected that day to prepare for Aclaí's attack but the most popular theories were that she had a spy among

Aclaí's forces, that she was using a prophecy or that she was planning to initiate matters by leading the attack herself.

Réalta knew that Cathúa was using prophecy but it did not matter. She was simply glad that she had been assigned the role of guarding the Court of the Favourites. If the battle came that far up the Hill then it would surely be over for the City.

The servants returned, their errand complete. As they walked away from her down the Hill Réalta saw the way their steps were synchronised. The hand of the brown servant found the hand of the pale servant, like a son taking his mother's hand. Watching them, seeing their bodies beneath their open tunics, Réalta knew how they would comfort each other in their fear. She wished she had found someone who could comfort her but she had never known love. I can't die today, she told herself. I can't die having never known love.

But as the two servants went out of sight she knew it was too late for that kind of regret.

Aclaí had not led them far through the Forest before the scout came out of the trees. "My lord," he shouted, "the way ahead is blocked!"

Aclaí turned to Andánacht Scamall. "I know they have been preparing but I wouldn't have expected them out this far. The City must be undefended."

"It is not the City," the scout said. "Come and see, my lord."

Aclaí followed the scout. As he did he saw smoke drift through the trees and smelled a familiar smell. He put his hand on the hilt of his sword.

The sheer size of the thing fooled him for a moment. The head was larger than a horse and he could not stop his own horse from panicking. He jumped down as it turned and ran. His sword was in his hand. This monster was as big as the one Eala had found in the cave in Clochán Ard. Green and brown dapples rippled over the scales as it moved among the trees. Why today of all days? he thought. Then it occurred to him: Cathúa must have arranged this. Well, either he needed to defeat it or they needed to call off the attack for another day. Looking up at that great maw he wondered not just if he could defeat it but if he could survive to attack another day.

He was just considering calling for reinforcements when he heard a strange noise: a deep booming sound that formed words. It was inviting Aclaí to talk.

Suddenly Aclaí remembered going and asking Cathúa to help him with the dragon at Clochán Ard. Eala had recommended talking to it. Of course they had laughed – she was just a Novice – but, remembering it and hearing that terrible voice, Aclaí had a lot more respect for what Eala had suggested. His hand found his sword hilt and in a moment he warned Foscúil that there might be some delay. Then he thought very carefully about how to arrange the words to avoid accidentally stumbling upon a Formula.

"*Then talk,*" he called back. "*I will to you listen.*"

First it asked him about heads and bags and who his real enemy was.

"*If he the head discards,*" enunciated Aclaí, "*Then him forgive.*"

It seemed to approve. But then it was asking him about the Key of Creation.

"*Must take,*" he replied. "*in his hands cannot after all leave.*"

But it did not seem to understand: it was telling him that everything could be undone with the power of the Key of Creation. And that the things he thought he had lost were not lost but merely hidden from his sight. He wondered that a Greater Manifestation could equate death with things merely being hidden. But of course nobody really understood the Great Principles.

"*Creation undo,*" he replied, knowing it might not make sense. He frowned but he could not think of any way to say *Key of Creation* in the Power Language. "*Creation free,*" he added.

But it was telling him that humans worked together to solve problems.

"*Nobody to trust,*" he explained.

Then it asked him about the girl who was a swan and the girl who was a nose. And, just for a moment, he looked back and saw the road he had walked that led him to this clearing at the head of this army.

"*I swan girl killed,*" he told the monster, his Breath choking in his throat.

He heard the deep voice express regret and sorrow for all his grief and loneliness yet to come. And the dragon turned away from him. Great wings filled the sky and, when the shadow passed, Aclaí was alone with his men.

Perhaps he could still have turned back on his path if a gentle hand had taken his hand to lead him. But all the gentle hands in his life had gone: embittered, driven away, or murdered.

So he resolved only to look forward. He called to his men and they fell in behind him.

* * *

Fionna led Donn down into the Court of the Novices. But, instead of leading him back to the kitchens, she led him to the servants' dormitories.

"Where are we going?" he asked.

"I need this," she told him.

He saw the tears in her eyes. "We will be needed to set out breakfast in the Great Hall," he told her. "Cnámh will beat us."

"We will still have time," she said. "Do you really think anyone will want breakfast this morning? They all know. The Adepts are all out on Patrol anyway. This is supposed to be a Celebration Day but nobody is celebrating. It's today, Donn. Today Lord Aclaí and his men kill us all."

Donn put his arms around her. "They won't kill us, love. We are not blue-robes. If they take the City we will serve them. If they destroy the City they will take us home with them. We are not enemies. We are booty."

"What if they take us to separate places?"

"We should stay together and make sure that we are both taken by the same person."

She led him into the dormitory. With the shutters closed it was dark and they could hear the breathing of the servants who were still asleep. She gently pushed him back onto her bed.

As he felt her wriggle and grind against him he knew she was also weeping. He knew that she had not believed his reassurances. But then he had not believed them either. He thought she was disturbing the others but she would not stop.

Andánacht Scamall rode through the trees. Beside him Aclaí walked. He felt uncomfortable to be riding when his lord was walking but Lord Aclaí was a better Forest walker than he was. Without him they could never have hoped to get onto the Land of Immortals – let alone onto the City. Scamall knew that Lord Aclaí could have led them straight onto the Hill and into the Mentor's back garden.

Aclaí looked up at him. "We are close now, Andánacht. Ready them."

Scamall let his hand fall to the sword and thought of his chieftains. As his mind formed the orders he looked up at the cold light before dawn. He heard the horses behind and around them and saw that they were arranging themselves into battle formation among the trees.

Scamall turned to his trumpeter. "Sound the charge." As the trumpets sounded the horsemen urged their horses to a trot. Lord Aclaí ran with them into the river and behind a willow. Ahead of them were fields and, in the distance, they could see the City and the Hill. The Gate was to their left and the road ran by the river. Travelling merchants with trains of pack animals looked around as the first of them emerged. When they saw Aclaí's blue cloak most of them looked away. Then more and more of the horsemen emerged in a stream from beneath the hanging leaves of the willows.

Scamall raised his sword and brandished it so the ranks could see him. Then he let his sword fall and urged the horse on with his heels and his Breath. He felt the cold darkness spread out from the ring on his hand to envelop his whole form, protecting him. Around and behind him the hooves of five thousand horses pounded the fields and road.

Aclaí turned towards the Gateway as the cavalry rode ahead. He grasped the sword-hilt as he saw the Flyers emerge. "Flyers," he told them, "go and stir up some mischief on the Hill. Stay together, don't get yourself killed, don't draw attention to the Gate. You are a distraction, understand?"

He watched the guard at the north of the City as his Flyers streaked overhead. He could see two blue-robed figures just getting up from their chairs. From the way they fumbled about and from how slowly they became armoured he could see that they were nothing more than Novices. Three Flyers landed around them and swords flashed as his own people cut them down. Then they were lost to sight. Aclaí unfolded his own Flyer and sat on it. Quickly he was in the air and looking at the battlefield.

Looking back at the City and the Hill he could see the tiny specks that were his the Flyer Company diving on the City like wasps attacking. He saw a ball of fire roll up from the harbour and saw that a number of the boats were burning. He saw fog roll down the Hill from the Court of the Immortals and knew that his people were spreading confusion. As he swept down again towards the City he saw the two Novices were down and his own people were in control. The Forest Warriors of Andánacht were riding hard down the road: mostly towards the City but a few back towards the Gate.

As he descended towards the City he saw two figures in blue cloaks standing at the edge of a plantation of trees. They were both in full armour but he recognised them from the way they stood. He landed beside them. "Foscúil," he said, "what are you doing here? I thought you were going with Innealta."

"You are going to walk the Forest right into the Court, my lord."

"How do you know?"

"It's what I would do. You will have to face all of them."

"I don't care if I live or die, Foscúil. Ye both know that."

"But we care," Miotal answered.

"I've been preparing for this for centuries," Foscúil added. "I'm not going to let you throw it all away. We're coming with you."

Aclaí shrugged and drew his own sword. Miotal drew at the same moment as he did and fell in behind him.

Foscúil hesitated a moment then drew his own blade and raised it in salute just as he would at the start of one of his lessons. He glanced up at the brightness and, beyond it, at the Red World rising before the dawn. "Abhainne," he said to himself, "today you will be avenged."

Foscúil and Miotal had left Innealta in charge of the lead Flyer. She knew they would be looking to her so this was not the time to panic like a purple Novice. "Lord Aclaí says we should go stir up some mischief at the City," her right-hand man said.

She placed her hand on her sword-hilt. "Right flight go around the dunes," she told them. "Left flight go around the Low City and come in over the harbour."

Innealta gestured the Flyer for speed at first and accelerated across the fields. She turned her head around even though she knew situational awareness was the responsibility of her crew. She looked along the echelon to her right: seven Flyers in a neat row and the others behind her – thirty-five of them relying on her to guide them. She looked back ahead and wondered if she could do it. "Tell them to break left and right as we go over the harbour. Keep the City busy but watch out for the other two flights. I'll pick the targets."

She eased down until she could feel the buffeting of the ground-effect under the Flyer, as if they were skimming on water rather than air. A few peasants were out working the fields. They and their animals scattered as the Flyers passed. Innealta saw the City Hill grow ahead of her. She lifted the Flyer a little as she went over the houses of the Low City. In the last instant she thought she might have left it a fraction of a heartbeat too late. But the thatch blurred beneath them. She smelt the smoke of their houses and wondered if she wanted to die before she got to the City.

Now, she thought. She stood up on the Flyer and said Words of Illusion. With her sword she designated the targets: the Flyer House and the stables, the veteran dormitories and – her heart felt it – and the House of Power in the Court of the Favourites. She sat down hard and lifted the Flyer over the masts of the boats in the harbour. She gestured right and left with her arms and her flight broke away from her.

Ahead of them, on the City walls, fire gushed out towards them. From higher up the Hill a thin ray of light stabbed down and the Flyer to the left of her was gone. She leaned right and left, steering the Flyer in a snakelike movement to try and avoid the attacks. Another ray came by her. She saw the Flyer on her right spin out of control and glimpsed the crew falling away from it: small beasts that had been men a moment before. The Flyer crashed into the walls of the Court of the Novices.

But Innealta's Flyer came through the heat and flames. She just had time to pick out the Flyer House and her left-hand man poured fire down. It blurred beneath her as she saw the fountain and dodged around the big cypress. Then she slammed forward to dive down the other side of the Hill. A heartbeat later she was leaning hard left to curve out over the sea and come back. She looked left. The City was burning and she could see the rest of her flight circling and diving around the Hill like bees attacking a bear.

Nobody had scored any hits in the Court of the Favourites though. She knew why: she felt the same reluctance. Nobody was willing to be the first. It would have to be her. She eased the Flyer back down onto the ground effect over the sea and Breathed calmness. "I want to drop one right in the fountain on the top of the Hill," she told them. "Hold fire until we are right at the top."

"My lady," they replied in acknowledgement. She concentrated, watching the cliff ahead as it grew, leaving it until the last minute. She saw a blue robe flutter on the Mentor's balcony. She saw Éise's wicked grin and realised with a flash of anger that she had misjudged. They should have put fire right in his window, right into the room where he first made her –

There was a hard impact. Innealta looked down and saw the City falling away. But where was her Flyer? Had she hit the cliff? She jerked her armour on her Silver Cord in case any of it had come loose. She saw her twisted and broken Flyer tumbling away beyond the Hill. The fountain came up to meet her. It was not myself I was planning to drop into the fountain, she thought. Let's see if I can do more damage than Words of Power. Then there was another impact. She slid down. The entire Court of the Favourites was protected by a Crystal Sphere. She saw one of them standing guard outside the House of Power. It was Cathúa.

Innealta landed on her feet in the Court of the Immortals. The stone roof of the palace she landed on collapsed as she broke through it. She found herself engulfed in darkness. The armour had held but she was completely trapped. She whispered Words of Strength and began to wriggle up out of the wreckage. That was slow work as, even with Words of Strength, moving the heavy stone slabs of the roof meant finding the right way to push or pull.

It was safest to stay buried until the battle was over but her flight would not be able to attack the top of the Hill. Someone needed to break through the Crystal Sphere. She was in the Court of the Immortals, where the most dangerous people in the City lived, but she was Immortal herself. She would get out and go to the gate that led to the Court of the Favourites. How many times had she imagined returning to the Court of the Favourites?

And, if she didn't make it, Immortality didn't mean living forever.

The Mentor heard the sounds and he knew what it meant. Aclaí's forces were here at last. He reached for the bag. "Ceann," he asked, "what do we do?"

We show them, replied Ceann. *Come to the House of Power.*

Ceann strode through the morning sunlight, ignoring the pain in Méar's joints and the fire and light in the sky as the City Adepts fought Aclaí's Adepts. The entrance to the House of Power was dark and, as his eyes adjusted to the darkness, he found that the thickness of masonry muffled the sounds of fury outside. He came before the Wall and the sparks appeared, tracking him. He knew he was looking through a Gate and that what he could see was the Red World. But the distance didn't reduce the menace he felt from the attention of so many Elementals.

"Now what?" Méar asked Ceann.

Now we show them. You have the Key of Creation?

"I have it," Méar answered, holding it in his other hand.

Throw it in. It will destroy Aclaí and all his followers.

"It will destroy me too, Ceann. It will destroy the City, all of humanity. Nobody will survive when it un-binds."

He will kill you too when he gets here. He is going to destroy the City today. Do you want to feel him rape you before he kills you?

Méar looked at the bone in his hand. "Ceann," he told it, "When we were boys together you used to be full of life. I used to want to take revenge and it was you who persuaded me to enjoy life instead."

Don't you want revenge?

"I've always wanted revenge. But why do you want revenge?" He looked at the empty eye-sockets, feeling stupid. "What are you? You are not my brother."

Your brother is dead. You will be dead soon, too.

"What do you mean?" Méar whispered.

Your brother is dead. The dead know nothing, you know that. But instead you have followed me for thirteen centuries. The problem is, Méar, you didn't follow me well enough. You let the rest of the City get out of control. You let that Eala take the City away from me. Now it is time to bring it all to an end. This is the end. When we convinced Aclaí that Éirime was murdered he lost his mind. Now he will destroy everything.

"You told me to do that. I obeyed you –"

So you did.

"You said we needed to hide her –"

And you believed me, Méar. You actually believed me. Now it is too late. Aclaí will not stop until you are dead. Éirime could have stopped him with just one word but you have lost her. You lost her when I raped and killed Blátha. Perhaps Eala could have stopped him but she is dead too. So now he will rape you and then he will kill you just like I raped and killed her. Do you want that to happen? The only way you can stop it is to unbind the House of Power. Otherwise you are doomed.

"Not as doomed as you are," Méar answered. "I have followed your advice and you have taken away from me everything I cared about."

He thrust the skull back into the bag. Then, before he could change his mind, he lobbed the bag into the darkness. The spark-eyes watched it come as if they were anticipating their prey. The bag disappeared into the black.

"Everything except my revenge," Méar whispered to the darkness.

Fionna was in the kitchen when they had first attacked. She had heard the sound around her like thunder but too close and too heavy. She ran out to see.

She saw a Flyer skim across the Court of the Novices a man-height above the cobbles and moving as swift as an arrow. She screamed and threw herself down. The stones beneath her shook and then she was pelted with more stones on top of her.

When the movement stopped she lifted her head. There were rocks scattered across the ground and other things, some burning. She realised that the thing in front of her was a large piece of a pot, blackened and broken. Cnámh will be furious when he hears that someone has broken the cooking pot, she thought. Then she sat up. The kitchen was shattered, the roof collapsed and burning. She felt on her shoulder and her leg where larger stones had hit her. She was bleeding. Her hands were cut where she had landed and her hip was scraped too, but mostly she was covered in dust. She stood and looked up.

Another Flyer was turning high above her, ready to come back. She felt like a mouse caught in the open when an eagle starts to dive. Donn had been serving in the Hall. She ran that way and around to the servant's door.

The Hall of the Novices was full of dust, drifting down from the stone slabs of the roof. Three blue-robes brandished swords at her, making her jump. But, as they recognised she was a servant and relaxed, she saw that they were as scared as her. She didn't think any of them were much more than half her age.

Beyond them the hall seemed empty. Then she realised that the hall had plenty of people in it but they were hiding under tables. She ran between the tables and spotted Donn. He reached his hand out to her then made room for her. She crawled under the table with him. There were three servants and two Novices hiding there.

As she shuffled in beside him they heard the sound of rushing wind as a Flyer roared overhead. Then there was a bang and a shower of stone chips falling from the roof. Donn's arms wrapped around her and she held him tight.

Réalta stood at the gate of the Court of the Favourites. She was standing guard but Lady Cathúa had made a Crystal Sphere, so she was not really in danger. She saw something fall out of the sky and demolish one of the palaces in the Court of the Immortals. Part of the wall collapsed and the roof fell in after it. Flyers flashed by overhead and she saw fire leap up from the Court of the Veterans.

There was so much to see but she found her eyes drawn back to the collapsed palace. It was called Míne's House but she did not know who Míne was. Certainly it had not been lived in for decades. She kept seeing movement among the stones. She thought it must be settling after collapse.

Then a large stone moved and a Metal-armoured hand appeared. Réalta saw it fumble around then grab a piece of a lintel and pick it up by the end. The lintel was tossed aside and the hand felt around for another rock to move. She realised the person must be using the Words of Strength – and realised that they must have Immortal Breath to be so strong.

The Flyers passed overhead again, sowing fire among the ruins. Réalta could not help flinching. When they had passed over she looked back at

Míne's House. The hand turned around and she saw the arm beyond the elbow. Then a head appeared and, a moment later, she saw the whole body wriggle out of the rubble. She drew her sword as the dusty figure walked over to the gateway towards her. The figure had their own sword out and Réalta could see how the light of the flames around them flickered off the jewel in the other's sword-hilt.

Réalta hoped Lady Cathúa's Words of the Crystal Sphere held. She could not expect to duel with an Immortal and survive.

Andánacht Scamall led his men across the fields. He grasped his sword-hilt and gave orders to his ten companies. He sent nine to the City but kept the last to secure the Gate, the only way home if it all went wrong. He saw the nine companies ride away as he led the tenth to the Gate.

The Adepts stationed at the Gate had plenty of time to see them coming. Andánacht Scamall raised his hand high and the black ring on his finger spilled Words of Power. He saw a couple of the Adepts point swords at them and he saw the green flash, but the malevolent power bounced off the protection accorded by his ring and flashed harmlessly into the sky. Then he gestured with the other hand and red liquid fire fountained out and splashed among them.

The fireball engulfed the Gate and the defences before his cavalry even got there. The blue-robes were running around, on fire, and his men dove on them with swords and spears. It was only the work of ten breaths before they had defeated their enemy.

Andánacht Scamall put his hand on the sword hilt. "Lord Aclaí," he thought, "The Gate is secure."

In the distance he saw his nine companies in the low City and riding over the bridge into the Court of the Novices. Above them the Flyers of Maoineas dipped and dived and, beneath them, the City erupted flame.

Innealta strode up to the gateway of the Court of the Immortals. Her sword-hilt was in her hand and she thought of Foscúil. She noticed that behind the Crystal Sphere was a single guard, some Novice Rank.

innealta

"I am at the gateway to the Court of the Immortals," she told him. "There is a Crystal Sphere and I am about to break through. There is just one Novice Rank guard."

break through and take the gatehouse his words replied *but do not advance into the court*

Innealta walked up to the Crystal Sphere. Here and there dust had gathered on the surface making it quite visible. The Novice guard shadowed her on the other side of the wall of force. The guard's intent was easy to read: as soon as the Crystal Sphere was dispelled the guard would try and attack, using the advantage that Innealta had to concentrate on Words of Power to break through rather than defend herself.

Well, it could not be helped. Innealta took comfort in remembering that she had been trained by Foscúil through most of her Immortal life but this Novice had probably only trained a couple of years and certainly had never met Foscúil.

An old man sat in the darkness. To one side of him was the only source of illumination: the glittering red sparks of the eyes of thousands of Manifestations of Creation, held back by Words of Power. In his hand was a skull. He often talked to skulls but this time it was the skull of a woman, not a boy. He searched her bleached face, hoping for some shadow in the eye sockets, but all he saw was dead bone.

"Oh my love," he whispered, "I have been so stupid. I need you back. Won't you talk to me and tell me what to do?"

But the bone in his hand did not answer.

"I can't do this, Eala. I know we both grew up in the shadow of our twin. You worked out how to come out of that shadow and into the light but I do not know how to do that." He moved the skull in his hands and imagined how she had moved when she had lived. What would she have advised? "You wouldn't want me to simply use Mastery of Creation to remove Aclaí and his followers from reality, would you? You would... you would want me to talk to them. You would want me to try and find a peace."

He started to get to his feet. "And you tried to tell me about Forbidden Art, didn't you? He is gone now, nothing is forbidden me anymore. We will be together as soon as I have made my peace with Aclaí. Will you be shamed by my surrender, Eala my love? Or will you kneel beside me at his feet? Will you save me the way you saved your sister, the first day I met you?"

He put Eala's skull back in her bag and hung it from his belt. He would speak to Aclaí off the Hill where nobody could see his defeat. He hoped he would be able to bear his humiliation if nobody saw it.

"It won't be long now, love," he told her. "I just need to deal with Aclaí. Then we will be together and I will want to live again."

Innealta needed plenty of Breath to break the Crystal Sphere with her Words that End. She touched the Crystal Sphere with the point of her sword, making sure the blade was pointed straight at her Novice opponent. She felt a soft pop as the bubble burst and saw the dusty surface break up like smoke. The Novice's attack was clumsy: sword raised high to bring it down on Innealta's head. She jabbed up along one forearm and her sword-point slid under the cuff of the gauntlet and into the Novice's wrist and hand. She pulled back and stepped aside as the Novice sword clattered to the ground. She stepped around the folding-up form and into the gatehouse. Beyond she could see Foscúil and Cathúa staring into the sky. Aclaí and the Mentor were nowhere to be seen.

She turned back to the Novice. "Get up," she commanded. "Surrender the gatehouse to me and you will live." The Novice raised arms in surrender then opened her helm. Innealta frowned, trying to remember that round brown face. Her hand was dripping blood through the gauntlet. "Heal yourself," Innealta advised, "before you bleed to death."

The Novice opened her gauntlet. Half her hand was missing, presumably still inside the armour's fingers. She said the Words that Heal Skin: probably all she knew. Innealta knew she needed more but, until she knew why the fighting had stopped, she wasn't going to exhaust her Breath healing enemies. The girl would live. Now, where did she know her from?

Then she remembered. "You were Selected last Autumn," she said. "I remember you from the Visions. You were first Initiated."

"You are correct," the guard agreed.

"How can you defend him after that?" Innealta asked.

"How can you betray him after your Initiation, my lady?" the purple Novice replied.

Innealta laughed. "Do you still believe he loves you, then?"

"I don't, my lady," the girl replied. "I never believed it. I am not a Favourite. But you see, my lady, the wisest Immortal who ever spoke to me told me this: the only way to curb regrets is to make sure we have done the best we can. Even when we are doomed to fail we must still do our best."

"Who advised you of that?" Innealta scorned. "That doesn't sound like anyone left alive on the Hill."

"It was Lady Cathúa, my lady."

"Then she spent too long listening to Eala."

"I don't believe she has. But Lady Cathúa is Librarian. She knows how to read."

"Well," Aclaí muttered as he splashed up the stream, "Let's see if they thought to cut down the cypress."

"They didn't, my lord," answered Foscúil. "I checked before I got off the Flyer."

"Stupid," said Aclaí.

"We will teach them," Miotal giggled.

"May I lead?" Foscúil asked. "I know their sword techniques well and —"

Aclaí pushed into the hedge, remembering to listen to the sound of the water. The sound was behind and then ahead: they had not drained the fountain either. He shouldered out of the big rhododendron just as a sword-blade poked at his helm. He felt the attackers Breath an instant before he noticed the blade tip, giving him a fraction of a heartbeat to turn his head. His sword-arm was trapped. He let go the hilt and surged forwards into the attacker. As he did he stretched his fingers and his Silver Cord to regain his sword.

The attacker gave ground and he stood up facing them. Eibheara stood there with her sword in her hand. Behind her Liús and Éise were ready. Two Adepts were fighting at the gate to the Court. Cathúa was standing beside the House of Power, watching them. Aclaí thought a moment: what would he do if he was alone? He circled around them, around the fountain, cutting off Cathúa. He expected her to double back to meet him before he got to the Mentor's House but she stayed by the Library and the House of Power. Surely her books couldn't be more important than protecting the Mentor?

He waited a heartbeat for Foscúil to break through. Foscúil called out. As they turned Aclaí ran forwards and attacked Cathúa. But Liús was too quick. Aclaí just had time to notice Liús had stepped in the way before Liús crouched down and set his sword-hilt in the stones. Aclaí jumped to avoid being impaled and crashed into the fountain. Liús leaped in after him.

The Mentor came out of the House of Power. Cathúa looked around just for a fraction of a heartbeat. Foscúil ran lightly and swiftly towards him. Eibheara stepped in front of Miotal. Éise started to move to anticipate

Foscúil but Cathúa pointed with her sword. Orange light shot out of the tip and Foscúil was instantly enveloped in flame.

"Cathúa," the Mentor called, "Are there Flyers?"

Cathúa dropped her sword and tore off her gauntlet. Éise struck and stabbed at the burning Foscúil again and again but, even if he were blinded, he dodged out of the way. Eibheara stood over Miotal and stabbed her sword down. It scraped as the Metal cut the stone beneath him. Then Foscúil shouted Words and the fire vanished. He pointed at Éise and Éise crumpled.

Cathúa pulled a silk scarf from her neck and shook it. As she did it stiffened and she skimmed it at the Mentor. As he caught it he realised it was a Flyer. His face contorted in pain as he flopped onto it and, with a sound of wind rushing away, he was gone into the sky. Water splashed over them all as Aclaí found his own Flyer on his Silver Cord.

Cathúa raised her visor. "Foscúil," she called, "they've gone. This is not our fight anymore. Whichever one of them wins, the City will belong to them. And, whichever it is, they will not want to return to see the City shattered."

Foscúil raised his visor. "Very well," he replied, "I will give the orders if you will." He stepped over Éise's body and walked towards her.

Cathúa saw through her own blurred vision that Foscúil was still laughing.

13

The Day of Harvest

Cathúa glanced over at the fountain as she went to check on Éise. He was face-down and the water was tinged with red: Liús was dead. As she crouched by Éise Foscúil called to a servant. "You there! Do you have a gaming table?"

"I... I will see if I can find one, my lord." The servant ran.

"Do you think this is time for games?" Cathúa asked. Éise was breathing but she was still unconscious. Cathúa could not see any injury on her.

"What do you think we are doing here?" Foscúil replied. He gestured around the sky, where the City's Flyers hovered above the Hill and Foscúil's Flyers circled, just out of range. "Your stones are here in the City and mine surround them. When the circle closes I will take your stones off the board, Cathúa."

Two servants came out with a table and chairs and set them out in the courtyard. Cathúa breathed Immortal Breath then sat with her back to the House of Power. She was facing towards the fountain. Foscúil sat facing her. She hoped Liús would recover without Foscúil noticing. "What forfeits should we play for, Cathúa?" Foscúil asked.

"It is a hard day for forfeits, Foscúil," she replied. "But, if you insist, how about the thing we talked about last time we met?"

"I have orders," he replied.

"Your orders are to defeat not to destroy."

"That is true." Cathúa saw Foscúil's wariness. "Did you ever apprentice to Eala, Cathúa?"

"I did not," she replied.

"But you read her book?"

"I am the librarian."

"You can learn a lot of an Art from reading a book, Librarian."

"How would you know, Swordsman?"

Foscúil laughed. "So, if I win, what will your forfeit be?"

Cathúa leaned forward over the gaming table and Foscúil imagined how her body pressed against the inside of her armour. "Whatever you want," she told him.

"I will hold you to that," Foscúil replied. He reached into the pot and placed a stone on the board.

Méar was scared. He had just started to realise he didn't have his... he didn't have the thing that had called itself Ceann to help him anymore. He strained to make Cathúa's Flyer go as fast as he could. It was a fast Flyer, especially for a bit of embroidered silk scarf, but behind him Aclaí still gained. He put his hand on the bag that held Eala. "Please," he whispered, "I need your advice more than I have ever needed it. I need your help."

They skimmed low over the sea, much faster than sound, the shockwave of their passage smashing waves flat in a cone behind them. Aclaí was left to struggle with the turbulence but still he gained.

He saw a line of blue-grey on the horizon like a cloud. Then, as it grew, he realised it was land. He dived towards the shoreline hoping to lose Aclaí in the detail of the land. Sand flashed past and he was just above the treetops. But glancing behind he saw that Aclaí was still catching him up. He zig-zagged across the forest, tipping the Flyer sideways to stay on as the force of each turn pressed his aching bones into the supporting silk. He wriggled until he was on his belly but the effort of holding his head up through each turn was agony in his neck. He wondered how it would feel when Aclaí cut his head off. It would be soon now, he knew.

He saw a clearing flash by with water glittering at the bottom of the shadow. It was as good a place as any, he thought. He leaned the Flyer over and turned a wide loop as the trees flashed by his left elbow. As he did so he thought of leaning back and the Flyer slowed. He brought it to a rough landing among the trees.

The clearing was caused by a hole in the ground. Some underground cave had collapsed in and ancient trees leaned drunkenly towards the edge. He found a spot where he could hide and gathered the bright silk around him – where it would not give him away.

With shaking hands he fumbled with the bag. He tried to remember the Words of Restoration. "I'm sorry," he whispered. "I hope you will be able to save me from Aclaí. If you can't, he will rape us and kill us both."

"Put that down!" ordered Aclaí. Méar turned and saw that Aclaí was in his armour with the sword in his hand. His visor was open and his face filled Méar with fear. Aclaí looked down at the bag in Méar's hand.

Méar stood up carefully, avoiding sudden gestures that could be mistaken for directing Words of Power or using the Silver Cord. "What do you want?" he asked. "Have you come to kill me?"

"I want the Key of Creation."

Méar replied, "Step back, put up your sword, and you shall have it."

Aclaí stepped back. Méar put the bag back on his belt then reached up to his own neck. He saw disgust on Aclaí's face but it seemed his neck would remain undamaged, somehow. Perhaps Initiation really worked even for Elder Immortals. He lifted the chain over his head. "Here it is and you are welcome to it," Méar said. "It is too heavy for me. I've grown to hate it over the years. It has kept me from everything I've cared about." He glanced at Aclaí's face. "But first will you answer me honestly?"

"Put it down and I will take it. Then ask your questions. When I have it in my hand I will not lie to you."

The Mentor half-bent, dropped it to the ground and stepped back: three blind steps along the edge of the abyss. He realised, looking down at it among the fallen leaves, that the only thing he cared about was in the bag at his hip.

Aclaí stooped and had the thing in his fingers. A heavy gold chain supported a single jewel. The pale green of the Crystal had a shadow in it. He glanced in at the shadow long enough to see that it was an elemental of creation but not long enough to catch its gaze. He did not trust that he could match minds with a First Elemental – not even one trapped in Crystal. Most especially not this First Elemental. He plaited it onto his Silver Cord with whispered Words and a few deft movements. There was not any resistance or obstruction: the Mentor really had released it. But, to be sure, he felt into it. Was it real?

He felt the coldness of the Power of Creation flooding into his awareness. The thing was there and ready to do his bidding. He framed his orders simply: the matter of this world to not respond to the Words of Power and the Key of Creation to not respond to the bidding of any other but the one holding it. With the City destroyed, nobody would care: that afternoon did not require any further disaster to complete the destruction.

As an afterthought he spoke Words of Concealment over the thing. A concealment affected only the mind: he was pleased to see that his rules worked correctly. He looked up at the Mentor.

The Mentor looked back at him. The tears on his face burned Aclaí's heart and he struggled to remember long-dead Geana's arithmetic.

"You have thrown away the thing that separates men from animals," the Mentor whispered. "You have thrown away every hope and dream the City ever had. Do you really mean to do that?"

"Men have been living like animals for all my life, Mentor," he replied. "The peasants live like animals anyway and the City is filled with worse animals. That is the way your rules have made us live."

The Mentor seemed about to say something but instead he asked, "So why?"

"Something changed, Mentor. I stopped wanting to be one of the Sea People."

The Mentor's gaze, once so unrelenting, looked down. "When?" he asked.

"It was when I stopped being Favourite," Aclaí replied.

"Aclaí," he replied, "You never stopped being my favourite." Aclaí watched as his voice stumbled. The Mentor carried on, "You bring all this destruction because you felt rejected?"

"It was not the rejection, Mentor. I didn't do all this because I couldn't cope with rejection."

"Then what, Aclaí? I don't understand."

"I felt it when you took Éirime away from me, Mentor. I didn't understand it at the time but that was what changed me. That is when I didn't want to be one of the Sea People anymore." The Mentor seemed to be about to speak, but Aclaí continued. "I did what you told me: I never spoke to her about it. I did what you taught and kept it controlled. Then Eala taught me what was wrong."

"Eala taught you?"

"She did, Mentor." He didn't mention Eala's sister even now. To name her was to think of her lover.

"You were the one who killed her."

"I did, Mentor. Did you think I would deliver another friend of mine to you after what you did to Abhainne?"

"You learned the Mind Craft under her and then you killed her? You hunted down the mind craft Adepts when you were leading them?"

"I did, Mentor."

"I don't understand. I don't understand you at all."

"Mentor, you don't. But I think I understand you."

"And now what?"

"Now I take the Key of Creation somewhere safe – away from monsters and most especially away from Sea People. If I can un-bind it safely then I will. If I can't then I'll have to keep it until I think of something else."

Méar hesitated. "Take me with you."

Aclaí stared. "What?"

"I am sorry, Aclaí" he said. "I haven't led the Sea People: I have allowed something else to lead them and it has destroyed everything I care about. Everything we care about. And, now it's gone, I'm alone. Please don't leave me." He struggled to breathe Immortal Breath, then added, "Please, Aclaí."

"I have to leave you, Mentor."

"I can change. I promise I can change."

Aclaí looked down at the bag at Méar's hip and revulsion crossed his face. Then he reached up to touch the Key of Creation. "I have to take this away from all the Sea People. Even you."

"You can lead me. You can be Mentor."

"I cannot. I saw that a long time ago. It is you we love. Even if I used the Words of Initiation on every one of us they would not forget you. It would make things worse."

"Like Eibheara?"

"I had to be sure, Mentor."

"Aclaí?"

Aclaí looked around. "I have to go."

"I will forbid nothing to you. Éirime..." he offered. Again he saw Aclaí look down at the bag at his hip. "You can even have Eala," he offered, "If you still want her."

Perhaps the muscles in Aclaí's face tightened but his voice was still mild.

"I am sorry, Mentor. They were Sea People, too." He turned back towards the Forest. "Goodbye, Mentor," he said.

Cathúa and Foscúil were both experienced players and the first handful of stones went down quickly as they set the battlefield up for their conflict. Cathúa concentrated on distracting him from looking at the fountain.

"I will be in yere power anyway," she said.

"But if I defeat you then you will—"

"I awoke this morning not expecting to see the day end. But I find that I am willing to risk everything to try and help him even if I do not expect to succeed." She took another stone from the pot and put it down on the board.

He could see that she was trying to lengthen her placement and command a large section of the battlefield. He put a stone down near the middle of her formation. She could remove it by surrounding it but that would take several placements which would prevent her from expanding. And, if he could get a few more down, he would force her to choose between losing her whole flank or allowing him to divide her forces completely.

The battle to break her formation spread over the centre of the board. Several times he tried to lure her into a trap but she anticipated it. He looked up into her eyes and was distracted a moment. "You are different, Cathúa. You are utterly changed."

"So are you. Perhaps, if–"

Then the pots on the table rattled and she looked at Foscúil, accusing.

"It's not my people," he said. Then he added, over the growing rumble, "That's an earthquake!" He looked up and Cathúa saw three or four Flyers falling towards the Earth. Some of their pilots were struggling to regain control while others were flailing through the air.

Cathúa quickly formed the Words of Falling and the Words of a Crowd as she gestured up at them with her sword. But nothing happened. "Words have failed," breathed Cathúa, as she watched them fall into the sea or onto the City. Then she felt in her mind for the Mastery of Creation. There was nothing there. "The Key of Creation has failed, too. Foscúil, this island is geologically unstable!" she shouted over the rising sound, "we have to get to the harbour!"

"You go to the harbour," Foscúil replied. "I will go to the Gate."

"The Gate will work," agreed Cathúa. "It's driven from the other side. Take your forces back to Anleacán. Take everybody and wait for our call."

"Come with us," he said.

"I need to get a ship," she replied. "Someone will need to rescue the Mentor."

Foscúil hurried towards the gateway. The ground was shaking and, as he approached, the gateway collapsed. Cathúa didn't see the lintels fall: she was distracted by checking Éise again. But Éise was still sleeping.

Foscúil climbed over the stones even as they collapsed but Cathúa held back and waited for things to settle. She had seen others standing near the gateway and she wanted to see if she could help. Réalta stood beyond, in the Court of the Immortals, hugging one hand with the other. As Cathúa clambered over the stones she saw Metal glint beneath her.

"Is anyone under there?" Cathúa called.

"I'm here," a woman's voice replied.

Cathúa picked her way through the dust as it cleared. The woman's head and shoulder stuck out of the fallen stones. Cathúa could see from the way her body lay that the weight of the lintel was on top of her. As Cathúa reached Réalta the woman opened her visor with her free hand.

"Are either of ye hurt?" Cathúa asked.

"I used the Words that Heal Skin, my lady," Réalta answered. "But she caught my wrist. My right hand is severed inside the gauntlet."

Cathúa was about to say The Words that Heal Bone but realised that they would not work. She looked back at Innealta. "What about you?" she asked.

"My armour has held," Innealta answered. "But I can't move." She tried to wipe the dust out of her eyes and then she said the Words of Freshness. Cathúa saw her eyes grow round. "Words of Power have failed," she said. "It's like we're in some abandoned part of the Forest."

"Mastery of Creation has failed too," Cathúa added.

"How am I going to get out?" Innealta asked. "It's going to take a lot of people to clear this."

Cathúa looked down the Hill. The sea-wall was half submerged and some of the boats were starting to drift up among the houses. The evacuation needed to get going before the ships were damaged. "I'll see if I can find help," Cathúa said.

"Geana taught me the Mind Craft, Cathúa. I know you won't."

"Oh," Cathúa replied. "We haven't time. The island is sinking."

"Then I'll drown."

"I'm sorry," Cathúa replied. "Do you want me to end it for you?"

"Don't," Innealta replied. "I'm back in the Court of the Favourites. You go and help save people." She stretched out her free hand and her sword was in it. "I'm not in any hurry. I'll sit here a while and watch the sea. Watching the sea has always given me calmness, Cathúa."

Cathúa turned away. She couldn't run down the Hill. The steps were uneven, shifted by the earthquake, and there were stones scattered across the path by the buildings that had fallen. Réalta followed after her. The palaces of the Court of the Immortals had fared particularly badly. She looked up at the crooked lintels over her head as they ran through the gateway into the Court of the Veterans. A squad of Foscúil's warriors looked around as they appeared. They lowered their spears.

"Don't be stupid," she told them. "The City is doomed. Go back to the Gateway and save yerselves."

"We don't have any orders, my lady," one of them said.

"Then ye have to think for yerselves. Think or swim."

She didn't wait to see what they would do. The gate that led down to the Court of the Novices had held. The servant's quarters had fallen but the dining hall seemed to have survived. A crowd was gathered around the doors. One of them was poking the point of his sword into the gap between them, trying to pry them apart.

She ran over. "Stop that!" she told him.

"Lady Cathúa," he said, "there are people trapped inside. The doors are jammed."

She pointed up. "Of course they are jammed. The lintel has sagged. The whole weight of the roof is resting on the doors."

His face paled and he pulled his sword out carefully. He held the Hilt. "What do I tell them, my lady?"

"There is a servant's doorway around the side. Even if that has jammed it will be small enough that it won't weaken the wall as much. We might be able to break through without bringing the whole lot down."

She walked around the outside of the Hall. The Chief of Servants was directing them as they cleared rubble from the door. "Don't spend too long on that," said Cathúa. "The sea will be here in a thousand breaths."

"My lady, there are Adepts trapped inside."

"I know. But don't throw away yer own lives. If ye don't have time to get down to the Gateway then leave them."

"But they –"

"Immortality doesn't mean living forever," Cathúa replied. "They know that. Can you spare me fifty of ye?"

Cathúa saw the conflict on his face. "Of course, my lady," he replied.

"Get everything ye can find that will carry fresh water and fill it. Then take it down to the harbour. There is a big boat down there from Lorgcoiseaigéan. Put the water on that."

"As you wish," he said. He turned to the servants and began to give orders.

Cathúa hurried back to the stables. She picked out a pony and Breathed on its head until it was calm enough to take her. From the horse's back she could see further and people could see her. She put Breath behind her voice. "To me," she called. "Veterans follow me down to the harbour. Novices and servants go up to the Grey Gate. If ye're coming down to the harbour bring as much water as ye can carry."

"I don't want to leave you, my lady," said Réalta.

"Go with the others down to the boat. I will see you there."

"As you wish, my lady," Réalta reluctantly agreed. She led the Veterans away leaving Cathúa behind.

Cathúa put her hand on the Hilt of her sword and thought of Éise. She had just realised why that might not work when she felt the sword-hilt tingle.

what

"Éise, we need to get everyone off the island. It is sinking."

i was asleep she replied. *what is wrong with words of power*

"I don't know. But Words and Mastery have both failed. The island will sink. I need you down in the harbour."

where is liús

Oh *cac*, thought Cathúa. She is going to turn all emotional and be useless. We do not have time for that. But Éise had already let go of the sword-hilt.

Cathúa scrambled onto the pony and rode it up the Hill. The pony stumbled on the steps but she kept it under her Breath. Innealta would not look at her as she rode past the fallen gateway.

After the sounds of the battle stopped there was the silence. Donn and Fionna waited a long time before they poked their heads out from under the table. They stood up together, holding hands, amazed to be alive. A few blue-robes had gathered around the main door of the hall but they were unable to open them.

They waited patiently for a while then a rumbling sound began. The rumbling grew louder until it shook the whole hall. Dust and stone chips started to fall and Fionna looked up to see the stones in the walls shifting. She saw a few of the crowd, servants and blue-robes among them, suddenly dive under the tables again. Over the roar, she heard a new word: *earthquake.*

Éise was sitting on the edge of the fountain with her sword beside her. Liús lay beside her with his head in her arm. We don't have time for this, Cathúa thought. How would Eala have handled this?

"They killed him," Éise screamed at Cathúa. "I have to take him back to Anleacán."

Then she knows, Cathúa realised. "I need you, Éise," she replied. "These people will take him."

"How can I trust them?"

"I will ask Foscúil to give the orders," Cathúa replied. She found her own Hilt with her hand. "Foscúil," she thought.

what is it cathúa

"There is a unit of your people up in the Court of the Favourites. I want them to take Liús' body back to Anleacán."

we have more important things to transport than bodies

"Foscúil, I need Éise to help me rescue the Mentor. I need to convince her that he will be taken back to Anleacán."

why do you think i would care

"Because you were Initiated, Foscúil. You follow Aclaí but Aclaí is gone."

aclaí came here to kill the mentor

"But he didn't do it, did he? You are Immortal: you know that Aclaí has taken the Key of Creation. But perhaps he has spared the Mentor's life. The Mentor needs his favourites."

i am not a favourite

"But Éise is."

Cathúa waited for a reply and wondered what had distracted Foscúil. But then his words came. *i will give the orders*

"Thank you," Cathúa told him. Then she let go of the Hilt just as one of the Forest warriors stiffened and reached for his sword. She knelt by Éise.

"Foscúil has agreed to take him back to Anleacán."

"I'll never see him again," she replied.

"You don't know that. But first we need to rescue the Mentor."

"We will be trapped here, though."

"If the Grey Gate still works the Sky Gate will still work too. We can take him with us to a place where we can use Words of Power. The City can be re-built in a shadow world."

"How will we meet up?"

"The sword-hilts still work. Once through the Sky Gate we can walk the Forest."

The Forest warrior let go of his sword. "Lady Éise," he said, "Lord Foscúil has given orders that we are to take Lord Liús back to Anleacán with us."

"Do you trust them?" Éise asked her.

"I don't think we have a choice." She leaned closer. "Words of Power work on the Grey Paths," she whispered. "Even if they just dump him as soon as they are through then things will be all right."

"You are right," Éise agreed. She stood up. "I will watch from afar as you take him up the road," she told them.

"As you wish, my lady," they said.

Cathúa climbed back onto the horse. "We need to warn the townsfolk."

"Why?" Éise asked.

"Because it is the right thing to do," Cathúa snapped back. "If you don't see that get to that big boat. Get water and food on board. Water is the most important thing."

"Why?"

"Because we can't drink seawater without Words of Power, of course!"

"Oh," Éise answered. "Words of Weather Mastery won't work either, will they?"

"They won't."

"This might be the most stupid thing I have done in my whole life."

"He needs us, Éise. If that doesn't mean anything to you then go follow your husband's body."

"The Sea People do not marry," Éise muttered.

When the ground first moved Eibheara was walking along the waterfront away from the bridge. She wanted to get to the sea-wall and so back into the City via the Sea Gate. The ground rolled beneath her as if she was on one of the boats rather than on the shore. Then she watched one the big Flyers of Maoineas splash into the harbour and the flailing bodies making their own splashes. She realised Words of Power had failed. She felt for the Key of Creation but a Will stood in her way: Aclaí's will.

"*Cac,*" she said to herself. She considered her options for a moment as the sea slopped around in the harbour and the boats bumped into each other. Aclaí would return to Anleacán: she would not be welcome beyond the Grey Gate. Which left the Sky Gate. She picked the largest boat and walked up to it.

"What cargo is on this boat?" she asked.

"Oranges, olives, wine and sheep from Lorgcoiseaigéan," the master told her.

"Good," she answered. "How much has been unloaded?"

"Not a tenth part, my lady," he replied. "We only arrived yesterday and an Adept lady told us to stop unloading and load water last night."

"How much did you load?"

He pointed at some jars. They were secured with rope through the handles and each was as tall as a man.

"Are your crew to hand?"

"They are nearby, my lady. The lady who gave us the orders insisted that they must be close by."

"Gather them. We sail immediately."

She sat on the raft while the crew were mustered and watched the bridge. She thought about Liús in the fountain and Éise beside him. This time he would stay dead, she thought to herself. She watched as an Adept rode along the bridge and got down in the midst of the crowd. She saw others, Adepts and servants, wandering out of the City and across the bridge, burdened with their belongings. Then she saw the Adept with the horse leave again, into the City, and she saw another follow. A moment later she heard their voices.

"Get this ship moving," she said.

"Where are we going?" the master asked.

"Up to the bridge," she answered, pointing.

They had to paddle the raft out to the bridge as the wind was blowing from the West. As they approached some of the Adepts collected at the waterfront beside the bridge and waited for them. She recognised a few faces. Most of them were Veterans although the girl that Cathúa had for a favourite was among them. Eibheara tried to remember her name.

They bumped into the stone of the waterfront and the crew tried to secure the raft as the Adepts swarmed aboard. They were carrying pots, jars, wine-skins, buckets, anything that would hold water. Eibheara found the girl among them.

"Réalta," she asked, "Where is Cathúa?"

"I don't know, my lady. She told us to bring water and come to the boat. She didn't say why."

"The sea is coming," Eibheara explained. "The Land of the Immortals is kept above sea level by Words of Power."

"I understand, my lady. I think she means to join us here."

"I think she does. I hope she won't be long."

Éise rode her horse right up to the boat and jumped down. "Eibheara," she called, "Cathúa said to load water."

"She told them to load water last night," replied Eibheara, indicating the jars. "Where is she?"

"We have been warning the townsfolk to get to the Grey Gate. I am sure she is just a few breaths behind me."

"There she is now!" shouted Réalta.

Cathúa rode up beside Éise's horse. A moment later she had climbed on board. "We have to go," she told the master.

"At once, my lady," he said. He gave the orders to the crew and they began to paddle the boat out into the harbour. "The water is loaded, my lady," he added.

"Good." Cathúa sat by the mast where she would be able to see everyone and Réalta sat beside her.

As they paddled across the water a rumbling began. It felt like they were falling a moment and the raft bobbed up and down. The sea poured over the harbour walls and the boat was caught on the waves and bumping against the harbour wall. "Hold on!" shouted Cathúa. "If you fall you will be lost!"

The master shouted at the crew as they poled the boat along the harbour wall towards the break. The wooden bridge had fallen off the wall and was being carried in an eddy just inside the harbour. As they approached the water changed direction, like a fantastically speeded-up tide, and carried the bridge through the gap and out to sea.

"Come on, lads," shouted the ship's master. "One big heave should do it." He waited a breath as they approached the gap. "Now!" he screamed. They heaved and the boat bumped into the harbour wall again. Then, spinning around, it was thrust out by the flowing water. The current carried them rapidly out to sea. "Get the sail up," he shouted. Then he came beside Cathúa. "Would you make a little wind for us, my lady?" he asked.

"I can't," Cathúa replied. "Ye will have to manage with the natural wind."

"Surely you are Eighteenth Rank, my lady? We need wind if we are to make progress. If we don't get away when the land sinks we will be sucked down."

"Ye will have to use what is there. Words of Power have failed."

"Oh," he said. He turned away. Above them the sail filled and the raft started to make progress. Fortunately the wind was from the west and it carried them away to sea.

"My lady?" Réalta asked.

"What is it?"

"I know you have been researching prophecy, my lady."

"What of it?"

"It was you who ordered them to take on water, wasn't it?"

"It was."

"Did you know?"

"That the City was going to sink? I did."

"How long have you known?"

"Since... three years, Réalta."

"So you knew before I came to Selection?"

"I did."

If Réalta made any kind of reply it was lost. They felt another lurch and, as they watched, the whole City shook. A few breaths later the sound hit them: a rumble of falling things punctuated with louder bangs. Cathúa shouted to the master. "Ye will need the sail down. The wind is about to change."

As they hastened to comply Réalta spoke. "Why will the wind change, my lady?"

"The whole City just fell several man-heights." Around them they felt the wind start to blow from in front of them.

"It has not sunk into the sea."

"That is because the sea sits on the world beneath it. If you fill a bowl with water and lower the bowl, the water lowers too. The surrounding sea needs to fill in the gap."

The rising wind whipped Réalta's hair. "Where is the wind coming from?" she shouted.

"It is being pushed by the sea."

"Pushed by the sea?"

Cathúa pointed. "Hold on," she shouted. Ahead of them the sea was a wall of water, coming straight towards them.

"I can't, my lady," Réalta protested. "My hand is damaged and I don't know great enough Words of Healing."

"I'm sorry," Cathúa said. "Nobody has great enough Words of Healing anymore."

"Do we survive this, my lady?" Réalta shouted over the howling wind.

"My prophecy doesn't say, Réalta," Cathúa replied. She looked up at the mountain of seawater before them. "Let's find out, shall we?" She put her arm around Réalta and dug the fingertips of her other gauntlet into the mast.

She glanced back at the City for the last time. Goodbye home, she thought. I will miss you when you are gone.

When the *earthquake* stopped Fionna stood up again. Now the crowd were more anxious to open the jammed doors. Fionna saw them try to shoulder the door and then she heard them shouting to people outside. They stood back and a sword-blade forced through between the doors. Donn and Fionna listened to the wood creak and groan as the sword-blade twisted.

Then it stopped and was pulled out again. A Veteran woman started and put her hand on the hilt of her sword.

When she let go she spoke to all of them. "Lady Cathúa has given us orders. The Land of the Immortals is sinking. Veterans are to go down to the harbour. We are to take as much fresh water as we can carry. Novices and commoners are to go to the Gateway."

"What about the City?" one voice asked. "What about the Mentor?"

"The Mentor is gone. The City is lost. Words of Power have failed and this will be sea-bed before nightfall."

The crowd by the doors surged forward. "Stop!" the blue-robe woman shouted. "The lintel is resting on the door. Go out of the servant's door."

Donn and Fionna let the crowd surge by them then they walked out together. There were two Flyers parked in the Court of the Novices, abandoned. Everyone walked by them: they were nothing more than elaborate Metal boxes, useless without Words of Power. As the crowd crossed the bridge to the Low City Fionna and Donn saw another Flyer crashed into the ruins of a cottage. There was crimson splashed among the tumbled stones and they smelled the blood as they hurried by.

Looking around the crowd with them Fionna realised that they were not just Adepts and their servants. Among them were Forest people in green clothes – armed but not enemies any more. Everyone was pressing forward to the Gate and the hope of safety.

"What is through the Gate?" Fionna asked Donn.

"I've never been through this one, love," he told her. "But the Sky Gate leads to a sort of grey place. Beyond that are other Gates. They lead to other worlds."

"Will we find someone to take us in, do you think?"

"My parents were farmers, Fionna. If I can find land, maybe a few animals, I can take care of us."

The *earthquake* started again and the crowd broke into a run. She held his hand tighter as they ran along with the crowd, stumbling over the moving ground, out of the City and towards the Gate.

Innealta lay under the fallen lintel. At least she wasn't directly in the sunlight, she thought. Her armour protected her from the weight of the stone that held her trapped but she had to keep breathing and extending her Breath into her legs to stop them from going to sleep.

There was another earthquake. The ground beneath them just wouldn't sit still. She thought her helmet onto her head and looked around. If the stones slipped again she might get her face covered. She didn't think she could bear it if she was trapped in the dark waiting for the sea. There was a rumble and a big section of the facing stone on the House of Power slipped down. The stones splintered in the courtyard. One bounced into the fountain, spraying water into the air, and another rolled across and overturned the gaming table where Cathúa and Foscúil had been playing. Innealta saw the stones scatter across the ground.

The vibration subsided. That was a big one, she thought. She tried her strength again but the stones that trapped her had not moved enough. She looked down at the waves in the harbour bobbing debris around. Many of the warehouses and taverns along the waterfront were now inundated – even the ones that were still standing. The big raft was caught against the harbour wall as the water spilled in and waves slopped over the stones and down onto the deck. She heard a woman's voice calling orders clear across the water and up the Hill. It would be Cathúa, she realised. Innealta could not remember the Librarian ever raising her voice yet she was leading them all.

Turning the other way Innealta saw that the Grey Gate still stood. Most of them had gone that way: the City's whole population jammed in the streets and surging up the cobbled road towards safety. Vaguely she wished she could go with them but she knew that was not going to happen. Immortality doesn't mean living forever, she reminded herself.

Much more urgent was her wish to scratch. Trapped by her armour and unable to reach her own legs the itch behind her left knee had the potential to send her insane. I will not give in, she told herself. I will think of something else until it passes.

Down in the sea she saw they had pulled the big raft out of the harbour somehow. The sail was up and a wind from the West blew them out to sea. She waved although she knew nobody could see her. Go on, she thought. Safe journey, all of ye. Give my love to the Eastern Lands.

She turned back towards the Court of the Favourites where she had so many memories. The houses were empty now: the doors open and the spaces within abandoned. Her own home had crumbled: the back wall collapsed and the roof fallen in. Water spread among the rubble strewn by the House of Power. The big stone must have cracked the fountain. How many times had she sat on the edge of it? If she could just walk among those houses one more time, sit by the water and remember, but –

She felt the earth shake again before she heard it. This time there was a big drop that she felt in the pit of her stomach. The ground lurched and dust enveloped her. Above the deep sounds from the tortured earth she heard the screams and shouts of the few that were not yet through the Gate. With the grinding of the rocks she also heard a pattering noise. As the dust cleared she realised what it was. It was spray from the sea. The harbour was gone and the current along the bay was dragging the raft out to sea, making it pitch and toss like a stick in a white water stream.

But where was the water going?

The low grey shape along the horizon did not make any sense to her eyes for a heartbeat. Then she realised what it was. It was a wave. She saw the little raft, one of the largest in the City fleet, ride up the mountain range of water as it swept in. The raft was many man-heights above her: higher than the island that used to be a Hill that she lay upon. Then the raft disappeared over the crest of the wave.

I hope you make it, she thought.

She saw the water smash into the lower part of the Hill where she had stood for Selection centuries before. She lifted herself up on one elbow to stare down her attacker. She was still Sea People and she would not show fear. The wind pushed by the wave tore at her skin and the salt spray was in her eyes and mouth.

She had her sword in her hand and she gripped it tight as she drew breath for one last scream of defiance.

Epilogue

The queen opened her eyes and focused on the timbers of the ceiling. In the bright day the nightmare receded into the shadows of her mind. She turned and saw her king regarding her with sorrowful brown eyes.

"The City has fallen," he said.

She reached out to brush a tear from his cheek. "For you, Rónmór, the City fell years ago."

"I thought so too," he replied. "But my heart tells me otherwise. It still hurts."

"What about your Manifestation?"

She saw his expression change and she felt the familiar lightness in the air. After a long while he spoke. "It's over," he said.

"Forever?" she asked.

"I don't know," he replied. "But I think it might be over for us. We have your kingdom to rule. Our job isn't to mourn the fallen City. Our job is to build a better one."

"Without the Sea People?"

"I am Sea People," he told her. "You know what that means better than anyone else in the kingdom. But the city we will build will not be like the City of the Sea People. The Manifestations that guide our rule will be the very opposite of the ones that ruled the old City."

"Together we will do it, dear heart," the queen told him. Then she took him in her arms.

Cathúa was resting in the ship when her sword hilt tingled. For some reason the Silver Cord still worked although she knew she could not take things off it or add new ones. The sword was in her hand and she was ready to tell the caller to leave her to sleep. It had been a hard struggle getting people onto the boats – saving everything that could be saved.

271

Then she looked at the illusion of light on the hilt and touched it. There was not any Rank shown by that illusion.

"Mentor," she vocalised.

cathúa where are you

"We got people on a ship and most of the rest in the City fled through the Grey Gate. Foscúil took those. We're in the Central Ocean. The wind is taking us East. With luck we will make the land near the entrance of the Inland Sea in about two ten-days. We might not have enough water."

can you come to me

"Where are you?"

in the neck of the westland

"We don't have Words of Weather Mastery, Mentor. We are just drifting. If the wind changes or if we don't have rain we will all die of thirst. What happened to our power?"

aclaí did it he has the key of creation

"How far does the effect extend?"

the loss of the creation power is universal but i think the words of power have failed only in this world there was a pause *or in this universe perhaps*

"Because of the Forest?"

because the forest people need words to protect us

"Can we Forest Walk out to somewhere we can re-group?"

we cannot cathúa i tried

"The Grey Gates still work although the one in the City is now beneath the ocean. Lots of people escaped that way. We could meet at the Sky Gate."

who is there with you

"Many of us, Mentor."

who among the favourites

"Eibheara and Éise," she answered.

there may be others came his words. *you should search as you go and you should make for the two rivers region* Then he added, *go to the sky gate and regroup in another world* he told her *without words of power we are nothing more than animals anyway*

"But what about your Immortal Breath, Mentor? Do you have time to rebuild the City?"

There was a long pause. *i have a way to solve that too*

Cathúa breathed her joy, knowing he could not tell. "Forbidden Art, Mentor?" she asked.

what forbidden art are you considering when words of power dont work

She thought about it. "I forgot, Mentor," she replied

aclaí made the universe ignore our words of power

Cathúa knew his Immortal Breath was gone. If he couldn't heal his own old age, he would die. As it concealed joy, the sword-hilt concealed disappointment.

Then more words came. *everything is going to be all right i have prepared for this possibility* he told her *i just need to make one more journey to secure my immortality*

"Where to?"

i dont know yet i am about to find out where to meet her

"Her?"

i can call someone and she will save me from aclaí There was a pause. *she will save me from old age*

Cathúa did not know what he was talking about. Then she realised. "I will call and arrange to meet you," she replied, knowing there must be another Adept with the Gift of Anleacán somewhere. But who? She thought of the sword hilt in her hand. "Or I could fetch... this someone... for you. We might need to wait for the right season if there are oceans to be crossed."

cathúa

"Mentor?"

im sorry came the reply *i love you*

She blinked the tears from her eyes and wondered how to reply. But he was gone.

Who can help him, she wondered. Who is it that has the Gift and Immortal Breath?

The river flowed by the inn at the Sign of the Ram and Pot and the patrons were dancing to the music of a harpist, a piper and a drummer. But the harpist suddenly stopped singing. She got up and stumbled out of the room, out to the waterside.

"*Hey, Ashee, come back*," they called after her in the slurred peasant tongue of the Two Rivers region.

The other two musicians picked up the song, somehow, and the dance recovered. Outside the harpist who called herself Aisce sat down behind some piled animal pelts. On the other side were logs, brought up the river. Nobody took any notice of her, even when there was a sword in her hand.

She looked at the sword-hilt and saw by the light on it, by the lack of Rank, who was calling. She stared at it and struggled with her heart.

Then she got up again and threw sword and scabbard into the river. The muddy water engulfed the light around the hilt and it was gone.

Éirime watched the river swirl past the dock. Then she turned and went back into the inn, where she had friends who would get her another drink.

Glossary

The Sea People spoke the language which was the ancestor of the gaelic family and I have rendered the spelling of their names using Irish: the gaelic language that is closest to that ancestor. However, I have borrowed a gender-convention for names from the romance languages: names ending in an A or an E are feminine and names ending in other letters are masculine.

The language of the Sea People, like most gaelic languages, has a distinction between second person singular and plural, and this has carried over into Hibernian english. I have used these second person plural forms, ye for (all) you, yere for (all) your, to communicate this distinction.

In the pronunciation guides, any single vowel is short. They should be pronounced as p*a*t, p*e*t, p*i*t, p*o*t, p*u*tt. Long vowels are represented as vowels in combination with other letters: aw, ay, ee, oh and uu, prounounced approximately s*aw*, s*ay*, s*ee*, s*ew* and s*ue* respectively. Where a syllable has a single vowel I have sometimes put an H on the end to remind English speakers to pronounce it short.

The sound represented by TCH is a blend of the T and the CH; the sound represented by KH varies from the hard sound of the German *ich* and the softer sound of the Scottish *loch*, depending on the nearest vowel: the softer sound is next to an A, an O or a U; the harder sound is next to an I or an E.

The pronunciations offered are only very approximate. Irish is a very rich language phonetically, and those of us who have grown up speaking English struggle to distinguish all the sounds. Even among the Sea People, there would have been different accents and, certainly in modern Ireland and Scotland there are several pronunications. These are outside the scope of this appendix, but there are some excellent sources available.

Names which have no meaning in the language of the Sea People have been omitted from this glossary.

Abhainne (*AH-wan-eh*; in the old City accent, *AWN-eh*) abhainn is a river.

Aclaí (*AK-lee*), means agility.

Acra; (*AK-ra*), means a tool.

Ainnire: (*AN-near-eh*), *ainnir* is a maiden.

Aisce: (*ASH-keh*), means free

Andánacht (*AN DAWN-akht*) dánacht means boldness.

Anleacán (*un-LEKH-awn*), means The Slab.

Arrachtumair (*AR-akt-oo-mar*) is a monster from a tank: an artificial lifeform or genetically engineered organism.

Áthaimín (*aw-ha-MIN*) the ford over the Minn, a river to the north of the Teorainn. The atha- prefix on a place-name is equivalent to the English suffix -ford, and means a river crossing.

Áthaiteorainn (*aw-ha-TCHOR-an*): ford over the Teorainn.

Báisteacha (*BAWSH-tee-kha*): báisteach is rain.

Bánúe (BAWN-oo-eh) means dusk

Beatha (*BA-hah*) means life.

Blátha (*BLAW-ha*) bláth means a flower.

Bodach (*BOD-akh*), big lout, is a rather disparaging term for an important person

Broc (*BROK*) means a badger

Cabairí (*QAB-ah-ree*) cabaire means talkative.

Caora (*QIR-ah*) is a sheep

Cathúa (*QA-huu-ah*): cathú is guilt.

Ceann (*KEE-an*) is a head.

Cearca (*KAR-ka*) cearc is a hen.

Ceatha (*KI-ha*) ceath means a rainstorm.

Ceathrúa (*kah-HROO-ah*) from ceathru, fourth.

Cloch (*KLOKH*) is a stone.

Coille (*QILL-eh*) means forest.

Colm (*QOL-um*) means a dove or a pigeon.

Cora (*KOR-ah*) means a weir.

Cnámh (*KRAWV*) means a nut

Croí (*KREE*) means heart

Cuspa (KUS-pah) means a model

Damhánalla (*DAUWN-alah*): damhán alla is a spider.

Diase (*DI-ass-eh*): dias is the ear of a grass or grain.

Dóchas (*DOH-khas*) means hope

Donn (*DUN*) means brown

Dubh (*DOOV*) means black.

Duille (*DWOO-leh*) means a leaf.

Eala (*AY-lah*), means a swan.

Eibheara (*ee-VAR-ah*) from eibhear, granite.

Éirime (*ay-RIM-eh*) from éirim, a talent.

Eilite (*AY-lit-eh*): eilit is a deer.

Éise (*AYSH-eh*): éis means after, or following.

Féileacána (*FEEL-ah-qawn-ah*) féileacán is a butterfly or moth.

Fia (*FEE-ah*) means a deer.

Fionna (*FEE-on-ah*) *fionn* means blonde

Flannbhuía (*FLANN-wee-ah*): flannbhuí literally means a fiery yellow – orange was not a distinct colour in the language of the Sea People.

Fómhara (*fo-WAHR-ah*) an Fómhar is the autumn.

Foscúil (*FOS-kuul*) closed, hidden.

Gainmheach (*GAN-vakh*) means sandy.

Gallán (*GAL-awn*) means a standing stone.

Gamhain (*GAW-an*) means a calf.

Geal (*GUAL*) means bright

Geana (*GUENN-ah*): gean means affection.

Geanúile (*GUEN-uul-eh*) means affectionate.

Gruaige (*GRU-geh*) Gruaig is hair.

Idireatarthu (*id-IR-ay-thar-hoo*) means a connection between things. Idireatarthu is the town that has the Grey Gate in Anleacán.

Innealta (*INN-iltch-ah*) neat and tidy.

Iolar, (*UL-ar*) means an eagle.

Lá (*LAW*) means the day.

Láidir (*LAW-dir*) means strength.

Linn (*LIN*) means a pool; and also a period of time.

Liús (*luus*) means the fish called a pike.

Lorgcoiseaigéan (*lorg-COSH-ah-gaynn*) means the footprint of the ocean, and refers to a big natural harbour over the ocean, East of the City.

Luaith (*LU-ah*) means quick, fickle.

Luchóg (*LUKH-ohg*) means a mouse.

Maoineas (*MO-nas*) means an endowment.

Méar (*MAYR*) is a finger.

Míne (*MEEN-eh*) mín means soft, smooth, courteous.

Miotal (*MITTH-al*), means metal. The Sea People knew gold, copper and another metal that is not known to us, but is simply referred to in the text as Metal. It is a synonym for hardness, and is the material out of which they forged their weapons and armour.

Nóiníne (*NO-neen-eh*) nóinín is a daisy.

Oíche (*EEKH-eh*) means night.

Ordaigh (*ORD-ayh*) means to prescribe
Ordóg (*ORD-ohg*) means a thumb.
Póg (*POWG*) means a kiss
Portán (*PORTH-awn*) means a crab
Préachán (*PREE-khawn*) means a crow.
Réalta (*RAYL-tcha*) *réalt* means a star
Rian (*REE-an*) mark, trace, track.
Rónmór (*ROHN-mohr*), literally big-seal, is a sea-lion.
Scamall (*SKAM-all*) means cloud.
Soilbhir (*SOL-vir*) means cheerful.
Spéire (*SHPAY-reh*), sky.
Spideog (*SHPID-ogg*) means a robin.
Srutha (*SRU-ha*): sruth means a stream.
Teorainn (*TCHOR-ahn*) means border.
Tintreacha (*TCHIN-tchre-kha*): tintreach means lightning.
Tírcapall (*TCHEER-qap-al*) horse-land.
Tírcúpla, (*tcheer-QOOP-lah*), double-land, twin-land. Tírcupla is a pair of islands separated by a narrow strait.

Tír Mór Deisceart (*TCHEER-more-desh-kart*) big southern land. Tír Mór Deisceart is an island continent in the Southern Ocean.

Toirneach (*THOR-nekh*) thunder.
Tonn (*THUN*) is a wave, as in the sea.
Úll Oileán (*ool-OH-lawn*) isle of apples.

www.ingramcontent.com/pod-product-compliance
Lightning Source LLC
Chambersburg PA
CBHW060902250626
47159CB00008B/2845